FOOLS *in* LOVE

FOOLS IN LOVE

FRESH TWISTS *on* ROMANTIC TALES

Edited by

ASHLEY HERRING BLAKE

& REBECCA PODOS

RP | TEENS
PHILADELPHIA

Running Press Teens
Hachette Book Group
1290 Avenue of the Americas, New York, NY 10104
www.runningpress.com/rpkids
@RP_Kids

Printed in the United States of America

First Edition: December 2021

Published by Running Press Teens, an imprint of Perseus Books, LLC,
a subsidiary of Hachette Book Group, Inc. The Running Press Teens name
and logo is a trademark of the Hachette Book Group.

The Hachette Speakers Bureau provides a wide range of authors for speaking events.
To find out more, go to www.hachettespeakersbureau.com or call (866) 376-6591.

The publisher is not responsible for websites (or their content) that are not owned by the publisher.

Print book cover and interior design by Marissa Raybuck

Library of Congress Cataloging-in-Publication Data

Names: Blake, Ashley Herring, editor. | Podos, Rebecca, editor.
Title: Fools in love: fresh twists on romantic tales / edited by Ashley Herring Blake and Rebecca Podos.
Description: First edition. | Philadelphia: Running Press Teens, 2021. |
Identifiers: LCCN 2020056409 | ISBN 9780762472345 (hardcover) | ISBN 9780762472352 (ebook)
Subjects: LCSH: Short stories, American. | Romance fiction. | CYAC: Short stories. | Love—Fiction.
Classification: LCC PZ5 .F7393 2021 | DDC [Fic]—dc23
LC record available at https://lccn.loc.gov/2020056409

ISBNs: 9780762472345 (hardcover), 9780762472352 (ebook)

LSC-C

Printing 1, 2021

FOR BRITNY AND ERIC,

WHO BELIEVED IN THIS BOOK

FROM THE FIRST TWEET.

AND FOR ALL THE FOOLS LIKE US.

CONTENTS

FROM THE EDITORS

Dear Readers,

When we sold this anthology and recruited our contributors, it was January 2020. None of us could've guessed how the world would change in the months to come, or how our relationships would change—with our families and friends, with partners and potential partners. Some grew stronger under the pressure, or more intimate despite the distance. Some did not. It's no surprise that romance stories set before or beyond the pandemic (or in a different world altogether) have been a welcome escape. Romance tropes are familiar and beloved blueprints for relationships that take on lives of their own, and we've loved disappearing into these characters' lives for a while. There's struggle and sadness, sure, but the Happily Ever After on the horizon always keeps us going and gives us hope.

As the months passed and the world seemed to fall to pieces, reading these stories and writing our own was a balm. With every word penned by the amazing contributors we're lucky to feature—whether they're about finding your soul mate across time and space, rival superheroes realizing they don't hate each other at all, or two teens at a Passover Seder faking and then falling in love—we found a respite. Not only was it entertaining and just damn fun, it was sustaining. Love, as it turns out, still conquered all.

By the time this anthology is published, we have every hope that the world will be a brighter and healthier place. We hope we'll get to see our readers in bookstores and gush over our contributors in person. And, in the meantime, we hope you'll enjoy escaping into these stories, losing yourself in your all-time favorite trope, and rooting for the happy ending we all deserve.

♥

The Editors

FOOLS *in* LOVE

SILVER AND GOLD

"Snowed In Together"

Natasha Ngan

THIS WAS THE HARDEST PART OF THE RACE.

This, of a race so deadly it claimed on average one of its competitors' lives each year—and that was not including the wolves. Over nine days and almost one thousand miles, the contenders had braved the dead-tree forests of the Bone Maze; made it through the blizzards of the Shali Mountains' highest peaks; navigated the Ghost Plains, whose ceaseless fog-sea caused many riders to lose their way such that they were never seen again. Then, after all that: Devil's Pass. A barely there sliver of a path that hugged the teetering cliff edge like a dancer's silks, with its ice-slicked floor and hairpin turns that, with just one tiny miscalculation, would lead to a drop onto the sharpened rocks of the sea below.

And still, the most dangerous stretch was to come.

It was also the last. The final twenty-one miles of the Kiroki Trail that would decide everything. No more checkpoints. No more stops for food, sleep, or warmth. Nothing but the competitors and their wolves, and the driving push to the finish.

Mila Solis was one of just twelve challengers left.

They'd begun as thirty.

Even Mila's older brother, Bastian Solis, as bold and strong as his name sounded, and in second place—*second place*—had been forced to admit defeat at the last checkpoint. Mila had arrived at the mountaintop camp of Amber Head Cap to find Bastian in the trail doctor's tent, her brother sweating under layers of bear furs in what the doctor diagnosed as the mid-stages of hypothermia. One hour more exposed to the elements and he'd have been dead.

"I'll stay with you," Mila had said, Bastian gazing up at her with the clear grey eyes they shared, both of them knowing she didn't completely mean it.

"You're fifth," he replied, before amending without bitterness, "fourth, now I'm out. The timings are tight. Tio will fall behind before he's even reached Chulao Lake, you know that. His handling of descents is terrible. You'll overtake Verggia on the lake—your cubs are faster than hers on flat land. Then there's . . ."

He didn't need to say her name.

Something sharp twinged Mila's chest. The name, *her* name, was coiled under Mila's ribs like a sleeping serpent that had just tightened a little around the soft flesh of her heart. But she kept her face calm. She'd never told anyone what happened at last year's race, and if Bastian ever suspected, ever caught the look on his sister's face as she watched the dark-eyed, wild-haired girl while she climbed the ice-sculpted throne to claim yet another win, he never said anything.

"Second place, Mi." Bastian's voice was quiet, yet full of pride.

Mila was grateful he didn't attempt a lie. Everyone knew only one girl was taking first.

The corner of his cracked lips quirked. "And your best time yet. This is it."

Mila brushed a swift kiss to her brother's forehead. Then she stood. "This is it," she repeated, feeling something reverent in the words, less a hope and more a statement.

A statement, five hours and thirty minutes later, she was seriously reconsidering.

Eyes scrunched against winds so ferocious it was akin to battling a stampede of bison, Mila charged her wolves across the frozen lake. There must have been rain recently; it was the most slippery she'd ever felt it. Her gloved hands shook on the helm of the sled. It was taking all her strength to remain upright, the winds were so strong and bone-deadening cold, and her pack sprinted fast, excited to be let loose after those slow, winding routes along Devil's Pass. Now the mountain was behind them. All that lay ahead was flat ice and victory.

A shiver ran through Mia that had nothing to do with the cold. She knew her wolves could feel it, too—the win, so close.

Her brother had been right. She'd overtaken Tio five hours ago on the descent, then Verggia just half an hour later, at the very edge of the lake. The old veteran and her pack had seemed tired. Mila had felt a twinge of guilt—Verggia was a legend in the community—before an overwhelming sense of triumph swept it away.

Only one competitor was ahead of her now. All she had to do was cross the lake safely, and the silver medal was hers.

Mila had always preferred silver to gold, anyway.

"Hap!" she shouted, urging her wolves on. Her voice was barely audible above the pound of seven pairs of powerful paws. The wind roared in her ears, itself an animal, wild and untamable.

At the head of the pack ran a small, tight-limbed wolf, all grey with black-tipped ears—Evie, Mila's lead. She howled, and the others howled in response. They moved so fast the sled was practically flying. Ice flakes churned up from beneath their paws.

At a distance, it might be hard for noncompetitors to understand why Chulao Lake was the most perilous stretch of the race. Framed by the cloud-tipped peaks of the Shali Mountains on all sides, the lake was expansive, yes: its frozen surface glittered under the low afternoon sun, stretching on to the amber horizon. But what was so hard about traversing a frozen lake when there'd been towering cliffs, disorienting cloud plains, forests with trees clustered so close together they snagged the wolves' fur as they slalomed through them?

Chulao Lake's dangers were worse, however, because, like the most dangerous things in the world, they were not immediately apparent. They hid. They lied. They were secret.

Until they were not.

When Mila first arrived at the lake, conditions had been near-perfect. Good visibility. The wind strong and steady at her back—what riders called the High Woman's Hand because of the way it felt as though the spirits themselves were helping them along. Only the ice-slip posed a problem, but Mila knew her pack could handle it.

Now, though, as they approached the midsection of the lake, everything changed.

It had taken mere minutes. The wind was first. The High Woman's Hand fell abruptly away and gales blew in from all sides, treacherous crosswinds that sliced at her and her wolves, making them skid even more on the ice. Worst of all, the crosswinds had brought in dense clouds. Fog swirled fast and low across the great width of the lake. Overhead, the sky closed over, steel grey. Mila had just enough time to pray the fog would pass when she felt the first flakes hit her face and she was enveloped in clouds in an instant.

A whiteout.

Mila's heart hammered. She shouted a warning to her pack. They slowed a little, but on smooth ice at such high speeds the momentum was too much. They raced on. Snow pelted down, blurring everything. Mila could barely see her own gloved fingers. She hunkered low behind the helm, aching thighs screaming in protest, and swallowed a lump of fear.

Not now. Not *here*—

A scream flew from her mouth as the sled careened to one side. A mass of black rock loomed from the white, disappearing almost as soon as they'd passed it, missing it by inches. Mila had barely caught her breath when her wolves veered again.

They weren't quick enough this time. Mila cried out as the left side of the sled whacked into an enormous spur of rock. The impact jerked her sideways; she only just managed to cling on. Pain whipped through her as her head smacked against the metal of the helm. Her vision turned black. Then it was back to white as she licked her lips, tasting blood—and had one split second to brace herself before the next stomach-lurching swerve.

Chulao's Teeth. That's what the riders called the midsection of the lake, after the rocks that jutted up through its ice-capped surface. On a day with good visibility, they were tough to handle.

During a blizzard, they were near impossible.

Panic drummed a sickening beat in her chest. But Mila spat away the blood dripping from her forehead and refocused, shifting with the sway of the sled, calling out to her pack and trusting in their movements. She'd raised all seven of them from cubs. She knew everything about them, and they knew her, and together, they could do this.

For a moment, her thoughts went to the rest of the remaining competitors. They'd have seen the blizzard sweeping in. They'd have had time to stop, set up camp to wait it out. No rider in their right mind would chance a crossing during a whiteout.

Ru.

Mila's gut twisted. Rushanka was ahead of her. Mila had no idea how far; Ru hadn't even waited for sunrise before setting off from Amber Head Cap. She could be a mile ahead, or ten. Had she made it far enough to beat the storm? A vision came of Ru battling the winds and snow, warrior-like in the face of the blizzard, her thick hair a mess of ice flakes, a determined smirk tugging her lips.

Ru was incredible. The best rider anyone had ever seen—even old Verggia admitted as much. Still, Chulao Lake in a snowstorm . . .

The world tilted once more, all thoughts of Ru flying from Mila's mind as they narrowly missed another hulking stone spear. Then a few things happened at once.

The clouds dispersed.

The storm quietened.

The shape of something enormous loomed ahead.

Blood dripped into Mila's eyes, blinding her before she could process what she was seeing, just as Evie let out a howl Mila hadn't heard from any of her wolves in a long, long time.

Mila couldn't hold it back anymore. Panic lanced through her as she scrubbed the back of one glove across her eyes to clear her vision. Blinking away the red, she saw what Evie's wail had already warned her of.

They'd entered one of the strange pockets of clear air found sometimes in blizzards. All around, thick clouds circled, a roiling wall of white. They were still in Chulao's Teeth—here and there, massive rocks burst through the ice, ragged and menacing— yet they were nothing compared to the monster that had erupted from the black depths below.

The monster they were heading straight for.

It reared high out of the lake, broken slabs of ice scattered around it, some seesawing in the water that was splashing up all around it. The creature's bulbous body glistened in the eerie storm-light. Eight tentacles, each as thick as five tree trunks put together, lashed through the air as it raised itself higher, and, like something out of a fever dream, eight more limbs emerged—lanky, hair-covered legs this time, tipped in pincers.

A wave of nausea flooded Mila at the sound of the scythe-like pincers scraping ice as the thing clambered out onto the frozen lake.

An even bigger one hit as she looked up and saw twelve horrible pairs of eyes blinking down at her.

The giant spider-squid was one of the Kiroki Trail's many myths. Scary stories to tell on deep winter nights to make excitable children giggle or set a flame in the hearts of adventurous riders who, with a heady mixture of wonder and fear, imagined one day facing it for themselves. It was part of the reason Chulao Lake was the trail's most deadly stretch. Yet no challenger had ever come across it in Mila's lifetime—at least none that lived to tell the tale. And though she'd heard the story of Verggia's famed escape from its pincered, tentacled clutches twenty years ago enough times now to know it by heart, Mila had never quite believed it to be true.

She was an idiot.

Evie's frantic howl snapped Mila alert.

Her wolves were still speeding straight for the terrifying creature, and she could hear the distress in their yowls. Even worse, behind the spider-squid lay a line of jagged rocks she hadn't noticed before. They stretched on past the clearing, a wall of imposing black.

The monster had picked its ambush spot well.

Mila didn't take long to make the decision. Though she loathed to reenter the white-out whilst still in the midst of Chulao's Teeth, she preferred her odds with the rocks than the awful thing rearing ahead of her.

She yelled a set of orders. Gripped the helm hard as the pack veered—then yelled again, this time in shock, as the sled hit a patch of water spewed up from the monster's thrashing and tipped up on one side. Mila threw her weight to stop it from completely turning over. High-pitched yelps came from some of her wolves. They were slipping, too. Then Mila felt great fat drops of water hit her—rain, in a snowstorm?—and she looked up.

Her stomach plummeted at the sight of one of the spider-squid's giant tentacles flailing overhead.

"HAW!" she screamed, her wolves skittering sideways just in time.

There was a *whoosh*.

A thunderous crash rent the air as the tentacle smashed into the ice.

The ground tipped.

Wind blasted Mila's cheeks as the sled lifted. For a second, she really *was* flying. And then her bones juddered as the sled came crashing back down. Her shoulders almost popped from their sockets at the impact, yet somehow she kept herself upright. More blood filled her mouth; she'd bitten her tongue.

All around, the clouds seemed to be closing in, swirling in tighter circles. It felt as though they were herding Mila right toward the spider-squid's eager maw.

Something fierce charged down her veins. She glanced around at the clearing, the storm beyond, the slabs of broken ice and the awful monster—and in a moment of either insanity or clarity, changed her mind.

Mila spat out a bloody wad. Shook the wet hair from her eyes. Glared at the giant spider-squid as it waved its tentacles from where it crouched in the water, blinking eyes still fixed on her.

My wolves are the herders, Mila thought, staring it down. *And I am not your prey.*

You are mine.

She called out a string of commands. The pack changed course, diverting from where they'd been aiming to leave the clearing and instead heading directly towards the monster. Clinging to the helm with one hand, Mila reached with her other for the spear strapped to her back. It slid from its sheath with a metallic *shing*. As Evie led them closer to the broken gaps in the lake, Mila steadied herself, shifting into position.

The spider-squid opened its horrid mouth to reveal rows upon rows of razor-like teeth. An alien screech split the air. Gooseflesh pricked along every inch of Mila's skin. One of the creature's tentacles slapped out; she ducked just in time to miss it. Two of its pincered legs lashed towards her, but neither Mila nor her wolves backed down. She called out to them and they circled closer, yipping and growling with the same heady adrenaline charging her veins.

Mila stared up at the spider-squid and its hideous gleaming eyes, readying her throwing arm. She was almost within striking distance, *almost—*

The very moment she was about to release her spear, a new sound split through the clearing. Not the creature's high awful screech, but a bellowing battle cry. Powerful. Determined.

Human.

The twelve sets of eyes that had been blinking down at Mila flicked away.

The spider-squid shrieked again. It reared, this time away from Mila and her wolves, and towards something—*someone*—else.

Mila had just enough time to see a whirr of speeding wolves and a mass of dark hair blowing in the wind before a rush of ice-cold water surged towards her as the spider-squid shifted.

Her wolves yelped.

The sled skidded, tipped, then flipped onto its side.

Mila was thrown from its back. She slid across the flooded ice. Water rushed over her, *into* her, down her open, silently screaming mouth, filling her lungs. She thought, *This is it.* Not like before, when her brother had said it, that it was time for the win, but that it was time instead for the ultimate loss. She choked and spun a bit more. Then, like the perfect opposite of a whiteout, everything went black.

Mila was dreaming.

She had to be. It was a dream she'd had often, both during sleep and waking hours, half memory, half hope, entirely useless, she knew, yet she kept dreaming it anyway because it felt so nice. Ru's strong arms strapped round her. The thud of the girl's steady heartbeat. Her scent—pine and wolf fur, and something else, something she'd never been able to name—mingling with the smoke of a lit brazier. The warmth of blankets. Wind snapping the tent.

The details were spot-on. Mila had to congratulate her dream-mind. It could have been a year ago, that night during the party. Except . . .

Except Mila's body *hurt*. Not the usual type of pain after the trail, but a hard, bruised, wounded kind of pain, burrowing deep into her bones. And she could taste blood.

Blood wasn't usually involved in her dreams about the night Rushanka Laikho, golden girl of the Kiroki Trail, entered her tent without so much as an invitation and, wearing that infuriating grin of hers, took Mila's face in her hands and started kissing her.

Mila's eyes cracked open to find Ru grinning down at her.

"Hello, gorgeous," the girl said. "Welcome back."

It took a few moments for Mila's brain to fight between shoving Ru away, kissing her, crying, crying *and* shoving her—oh, or crying *and* kissing *and* shoving her. Or simply just passing back out to avoid having to deal with any of it. After the adrenaline of facing the spider-squid, going back to sleep seemed a good option. Yet maybe some of that adrenaline still buzzed in her veins, because Mila surprised herself by trying to sit up. She stopped with a wince. Too painful. Instead, she settled for glaring up at the beautiful girl who had once kissed her—more than kissed her—before never so much as looking in her direction again, and snarled, "What in the spirits, Ru! You nearly killed me!"

Ru's grin barely faded. Mila didn't think it ever fully went away. She even smiled in her sleep.

Mila hated that she knew that.

Ru started to say something when Mila's eyes widened. This time she did find the energy to push herself up from where she was lying against Ru's chest, crying, "My wolves!—"

"All fine," Ru said, coming around to crouch in front of her. She kept an arm laced round Mila's shoulders. "Except this one, of course, but I've patched her up. She'll be back to normal in no time."

Mila's eyes fell on a bundle of fur at her feet. Grey with black-tipped ears. "Evie!"

She lurched forwards, then doubled over as fresh pain lashed through her. After panting for a moment on hands and knees, she shuffled forwards, curling herself over Evie. She ran her hands through the wolf's thick fur. In more than one place, her fingertips passed over bandages. Mila's stomach contracted.

Evie was breathing heavily—but it was steady, and her heartbeat strong. One eye opened to reveal a flash of honeyed brown.

Relief flooded Mila. She felt the heat of tears. "Hey, little cub," she cooed, nuzzling her face down to Evie's. There was a scrape of rough canine tongue. Mila laughed, crying a little, then pulled back, shushing her, smoothing her hands down the wolf's warm, firm body. "Get some rest, you. I'll be here, and your sisters and brothers are right outside. We're all here. We're all here."

She spoke softly. The brazier crackled, its light a golden underwater glow. Wind and snow beat upon the tent. The blizzard hadn't let up yet, then. Mila heard the wail and snickering sounds of wolves outside, recognizing Luka's and Amhr's and Fell's voices amongst less familiar ones. Ru must have tied their packs together. Mila resisted the temptation to run out and check on them. Her wolves could handle the snow and the cold.

The question was, could *she* handle Rushanka Laikho?

After a little while, Evie fell back to sleep. Mila sat up with a grimace—her chest felt battered from all the choking. She cricked her head round. "Thank you," she said, not quite meeting Ru's smiling eyes.

"For looking after your pack?" Ru asked. "Or—how did you so sweetly put it— *nearly killing you?*"

"Well, you did!" Mila winced, bringing a hand to her ribs. "I had the shot. The spider-squid was mine. And then *you* came out of nowhere and distracted it, and I was thrown from my sled and almost drowned in ice-water, and Evie was hurt and now I'm here, stuck in a tent with you! Again!"

Mila wasn't fully looking at her, but even from her sideways view she could tell Ru was practically beaming.

"Why were you even there in the first place?" Mila growled, the same fiery thing that had reared up within her to challenge the spider-squid rekindling now. Lifting her chin, she turned to properly face Ru, who was indeed grinning broadly, her whole face shining.

Mila narrowed her eyes, as if looking into the sun. That was what it felt like sometimes, looking at Ru.

"You left Amber Head Cap before sunrise," she pressed. "You should have been well clear of Chulao's Teeth by then. You shouldn't have been caught up in all of this"—

Mila waved a hand, indicating the storm roaring and whipping the tent walls —"at all."

Ru shrugged, flicking a tangle of windswept curls over her shoulder. "I ran into some trouble," she replied simply. Her grin sharpened into a smirk. "Anyway, isn't it better this way? I seem to remember we had a lot fun the last time we were alone in a tent, Mila Solis . . ."

Mila's cheeks reddened. She forced herself not to look away from Ru—startling, statuesque Rushanka Laikho, with her laughing eyes and wild beauty, a girl who seemed every bit as powerful and predatory as the seven wolves who'd carried her to victory each year since Mila had known her.

It had been both their first times on the Kiroki Trail when they'd met. It was the day before the race. Mila was in line for the riders' pre-race examinations and Ru was ahead, being checked, her back to the queue. The two trail doctors were laughing. Ru was joking with them as if one of the biggest days of her life wasn't just around the corner, while Mila's own stomach was tying itself in knots. Mila knew she'd never get the image out of her head: that big, broad-shouldered silhouette, head tipped back in a laugh, or arrogance—or, knowing Ru as Mila did now, probably both. A bushy mass of black curls glinted in the winter sunlight. Her coat was speckled with frost.

Then Ru had turned, as if sensing Mila watching. She'd looked straight past the rest of the waiting challengers to meet Mila's eyes, and flashed a grin so fierce it had literally stolen the breath from Mila's lungs.

Now, in the firelit tent with the blizzard pounding outside and Evie's rumbling snores at her feet, and Ru close, *so* close, Mila felt breathless all over again.

"Here." Ru shifted, grabbing some things. She held out a leather flask and a palmful of dried herbs. "For the pain."

Mila took the herbs—a brush of skin—and chewed on them, instantly scowling. They tasted about as good as most herbal remedies. With a laugh, Ru passed her the flask. Expecting water, Mila took a great gulp, then almost coughed it all up.

"Ru," she spluttered, "this is alcohol!"

"An expensive one too, so don't waste it."

Mila glowered, debating throwing the flask at Ru's gorgeous head. In the end, she drank a bit more, enjoying the warmth the alcohol spread through her and the way it quickly masked the bitterness of the herbs. Within seconds, she felt the pain in her chest subside. Ru had given her good stuff.

She returned the flask and Ru took a deep swig. Then the girl leaned back on her hands, looking at Mila in a way that made her feel like her four layers of clothing were a few layers too few.

Dark eyes sparkling, Ru said, "So. Second place, and your best time yet. How does it feel?"

Mila knew it was every rider's duty to know where the other challengers stood. Yet she felt a pleased glow all the same. "It'd feel better had I not almost been drowned due to another competitor's interference," she grumbled.

Ru only grinned more broadly at this.

Mila couldn't help a tiny smile quirk her own lips. "And now said competitor is trying to get me drunk. I should report them to the trail runners for subterfuge."

"Subterfuge!" Ru looked gleeful. "What a delightful word!"

Mila rolled her eyes. "What would *you* call it, then?"

"Seduction."

Ru's voice was practically a purr.

Knowing her cheeks had turned an indecent shade of purple, Mila busied herself with checking back on Evie. All the while she felt Ru's gaze on her, as direct as fingertips to the nape of her neck. Mila had only been touched like that once, but the memory was strong enough to seem as though it had happened hundreds of times, imprinted upon her skin like a tattoo. Then she stiffened as suddenly Ru's fingers *were* there, not a memory this time but actually there, on the exact same spot at the back of her neck, sweeping aside her short hair, Ru's skin as rough as Mila remembered, like the pads of wolf feet.

Mila swirled round. "What in the spirits are you doing!"

"I was about to kiss you," Ru said. "I thought that was obvious."

"Nothing about you is obvious."

It was out of Mila's mouth before she'd even thought it. She froze. Ru's face grew about as serious as it was capable of—which is to say, she was still smiling, though not quite as broadly anymore, the edges of her eyes unwrinkled.

They stared, barely a foot apart on the heavy fur rug. Evie's snores rumbled around them. The brazier's flames danced shadows across Ru's face. Mila wished the girl would say something, but for once Ru was quiet. The air felt thick. Mila fiddled with the hem of her shirt, heartbeat racing, until she couldn't bear it anymore.

"We spent a night together, Ru."

The words came out in a whisper. She'd never spoken them aloud. They sounded ridiculous, too short and straightforward to convey all the things that night meant to her. The precious hours on which Mila had spent the last year feeding, taking moments out one at a time and turning them over and over in her mind, in her soft, secret, velvet desires, until their edges were as smooth as lakeshore pebbles.

Ru watched. Waited some more.

"And then you never spoke to me again." Mila's voice was tiny. She twisted away, looking through blurred vision at the tent wall. "Two months later at the Marura Trail you were kissing that—that guy, the one with the big blond moustache—"

"Gregorio Suh."

"*Gregorio Suh*, and then three months after *that* it was—"

"Hela Greenfield."

Mila's shoulders crunched with anger. "Yes, *her*, and then it was time to come back here, and I thought . . . I thought maybe you were just waiting. Waiting for the Kiroki because it was *our* trail—" Her voice caught. She swallowed. "I mean, it was the place we first met. Shared a night. And I don't know, maybe you just like to kiss the same person at the same trail. But then eleven days ago at camp you just walked right past me as though you didn't even see me, didn't even wish me and my pack good luck, and—*don't laugh at me!*"

Mila whirled. Her shout cut off Evie's rumbling snores and Ru's laughter. For a moment even the storm seemed to pause, shocked into silence by her outburst.

Then Evie made some snuffling noises and fell back asleep, and the world slowly spun back into rhythm. Only now, Ru wasn't laughing. Her lips were flat. Her eyes were soft. She looked so different without her eternal grin that Mila almost wanted to crack a joke to bring it back.

With a sigh, Ru unfurled her legs out from under her and cupped her socked feet in her palms. She smiled, but it was small. Sad. "I wasn't laughing *at* you, Solis. I was just . . . laughing."

Mila said stiffly, "I am aware what laughing is."

Ru snorted, then fell serious once more. "I don't—I didn't mean . . ." She sighed again. "I laugh. It's what I do. And . . . I do see you." Her voice dropped. "Of course, I see you, Solis. How could anyone *not*?"

Something tightened in Mila's belly. She smoothed her hands out from the fists they'd curled into. "You make it look easy enough."

Ru turned her neck sharply. Her dark curls bunched around her shoulders like a mass of storm clouds. "It's been *anything* but easy."

Mila blinked. She wasn't sure she'd heard Ru right. She started to ask why when a howl rose up outside, then another. Mila moved automatically towards the pinned entrance of the tent when a firm hand gripped her shoulder.

Ru drew her back, dragging on her coat at the same time. "Let me."

She disappeared outside before Mila could argue. Mila hunched back, one hand absentmindedly roaming through Evie's thick coat, her pulse running fast to keep up with her thoughts.

Ru had liked—no, *still* liked her?

But she'd kissed all those pretty boys and girls at other trails. Had ignored her . . . but it had been hard? Why? Why make it hard? Why hadn't she just grabbed and kissed her like she'd done that night one year ago? She'd made it seem so easy, after all. And what did she mean about laughing being *what she did*?

Mila had still not made sense of any of it when the tent flapped open, letting in a rush of icy air. Flakes fell from Ru's coat as she shook it off and knelt by the brazier to warm her hands. Her hair was white with snow.

"They're fine," she said. She set down a knife Mila hadn't even noticed her pick up before she'd left. Its blade was clean. "A bear came down from the mountains, but I scared it off. I've never camped on the lake before. I took us east towards the Shali foothills to get away from the spider-squid, but maybe I went a bit too far."

"Did you kill it?" Mila asked, quiet. "The spider-squid?"

"Spirits, no." Ru looked round, and she was grinning again, chin tilted, dark eyes twinkling. "That would have made the mother *really* mad."

"The—" Mila's eyes went wide. "No."

Ru's grin broadened. "Yup."

Mila stared, and then a laugh bubbled up from nowhere—and didn't stop. She buckled at the waist, gales of laughter streaming from her now, waking Evie, who snuffled at her inquisitively. When Mila looked up, wiping the tears from her eyes, Ru was smiling at her in a soft, strange way that made Mila's heart flutter.

"So that was the trouble you ran into," Mila stated. When Ru didn't contradict her, she went on. "I still don't get it. You were so far ahead. The spider-squid . . ." Her stomach contracted at the thought of the adult version of the monstrous thing she'd encountered. "If it was a cub, then its mother wouldn't have been far."

Ru nodded. "It wasn't."

"So you were at Chulao's Teeth around the same time as me."

After a beat, Ru nodded again.

Evie was licking Mila's hand, but she didn't look down. She couldn't drag her eyes from Ru, who seemed to be glowing with something more than just flame light and the snowflakes caught in her hair.

"You were waiting for me."

Ru didn't reply, but Mila saw the confirmation in her eyes. She was about to say something more—though she didn't know quite what—when Ru moved forward. She crouched before Mila, so close Mila could see the tiny freckles painting a constellation across the bridge of her nose. A constellation she'd once stared at during a long, clear-skied night, committing it to memory.

Ru's breath warmed Mila's face. She smelt of pine and wolf fur and that other indescribable thing. A thing that made Mila want to cry and laugh at the same time. That both warmed and hurt her heart.

Silence stretched between them.

Ru broke it. "I was two-thirds of the way across the lake when I sensed the weather change. I knew a storm was coming, and I knew it would take you unprepared. It was building to the northeast, and back at the other end of the lake you wouldn't have the right vantage point to notice. Still, I probably wouldn't have turned back were it not for the spider-squid. I'd crossed it—the mother—hours earlier when I passed through Chulao's Teeth, and I knew from your time that it would put you exactly within its nesting area when the blizzard hit—"

This time, it was Mila who, with a wild grin, took Ru's face in her hands and kissed her.

Ru kissed her back.

A lot.

Finally, laughing, Ru pulled away with a smirk. "You didn't let me finish. I was about to say I've won enough times, anyway. It's getting a bit boring, Solis. This way, we can have a *real* race to the finish."

Mila matched the girl's challenging smile. "Oh, don't worry," she murmured, bringing her lips close to Ru's. "You're getting disqualified, remember, Rushanka Laikho?"

Ru's eyes glinted. One of her hands was wound around Mila's waist. The other was tangled in her hair. "Oh, yes. What was it again? Something about . . . subterfuge?"

"Seduction," Mila corrected her, and Ru's laugh was so loud Mila had to quieten her with her mouth.

Later. Limbs tangled on top of thick furs. Ru's sweet breath. The flickering brazier painting their bodies in orange and gold.

Mila's lips felt mussed and sweet from all that kissing.

Her whole *body* felt mussed and sweet.

Evie snored at their feet. Outside, the blizzard was finally calming, snowflakes still pattering but with less force now, the wind a moan, not a howl. The wolves were quiet. Mila wondered faintly if the other challengers had safely waited out the storm. Perhaps now it was calming they were ready to get moving again.

Perhaps *she* should be getting ready to move again.

As if reading her mind, Ru said, "They won't set off for at least another hour. We've got time."

Smiling, Mila kissed the sweat-licked curve of Ru's shoulder where her face was resting. "How did you know what I was thinking?"

"You're a Kiroki Trail competitor, Solis. One of the best riders there are. It's exactly what you should be thinking."

"Is it what you're thinking?"

Ru laughed, squeezing Mila closer. "Of course not. I *am* the best rider. I don't need to worry about anyone else but myself."

Mila felt herself blush. "And me."

There was a pause. "And you," Ru echoed, quiet, lovely words that made Mila bury her face into the girl's warm neck and breathe her fragrance in until she was giddy on it.

But after a few blissful moments, Ru's words took on a barbed edge. Mila drew back, eyes scanning Ru's face. The girl was staring up at the ceiling. A smile danced on her lips—lips Mila wanted so badly to keep kissing. If she never stopped, maybe *this* would never stop, like it had one year ago, after a night almost exactly like this one. Questions stuck in her throat.

Ru cocked her head. Raised a brow. "Go on," she prompted.

Mila took a breath. Even though it made her face hot, she muttered, "You ignored me. Why?"

Ru's smile flickered. Something darkened her already ink-dark eyes. "I didn't *want* to see you," she admitted. "I've always been focused on this. The race. The win. It's how I was brought up. My parents both died on the trail when I was too young to remember them. I grew up with my uncle, and he was . . ." She stiffened, then pushed out a slow breath. "He wasn't a nice man. But it taught me how to be strong. How to laugh when all you wanted to do was—" She cut off abruptly and turned back to the ceiling.

"I think something's broken inside me. I think I got too hard, and now I don't know how to be soft. Take my wolves." Her smile returned, warm and genuine. "I've seen the way you are with yours. You and your pack are more than a team, Solis—you're family. As much as Bastian is your brother, these wolves mean much more to you than just a route to the gold. I like my wolves, yes, and I take good care of them. But they are not my family. They are replaceable."

The words stung, even though Mila had no real reason to feel hurt by them. She focused on Evie's soft grating snore. Thought of the rest of her cubs outside, curled into one another in the snow. Of how they'd looked as newborns, hairless and so impossibly tiny she could hold two at a time in each hand.

Not one of them was replaceable.

Then she pictured young Ru. Parentless and with an uncle who taught her hardness and how to laugh so as not to cry. The thought of it made her own eyes sting, and she realized what a wonderful thing it really was, to be able to cry and not be ashamed for it.

To not be afraid to drown in your tears.

"So, you saw me," Mila said slowly, "but you didn't want to. And the others— the other ones you were with—they helped you *not* see me."

Ru gave a small nod. Then she shook her head. "That's not fair to them. I liked them too—at the time, at least. In the moment. But that's always been enough for me. You . . . you lingered."

Mila's lashes flicked down. One of her arms was draped across Ru's bare belly, and she drew it back now, smoothing it slowly over her skin until it came to rest over the girl's chest. She could feel her heartbeat, strong and steady.

Tears wet Mila's cheeks. She understood, now. Rushanka Laikho, star of the Kiroki Trail, always moving, always racing, always chasing that which was within her reach and speeding away, away from anything that was not. Away from anything—and anyone—that might become irreplaceable, because irreplaceable things, once lost, could never be recovered. Like parents, and true family.

And love.

The thought made Mila's heart ache.

They were silent for a long time. Mila curled closer to Ru, and together they listened to the patter of the flakes. Just a thin tent wall away, yet it all seemed so distant, another world. A world that, in just a few hours, they would be reentering.

Mila wasn't sure she was ready.

Gently, she kissed Ru's lovely shoulder and asked one final question, although she suspected she knew the answer. She could see it already, even though it felt so far away. The two of them emerging into the new dawn, squinting in the dazzling light. Boot-crunch on freshly laid snow. The lake a sweeping sea of white before them. Both packs of wolves would be yowling and yipping in excitement. The wind on Mila's bare face would feel so cold after the warmth of Ru's kisses. They'd pack the tent together in silence—it'd only be fair, after all. Ru *had* come back for her. She had probably saved her life. Mila imagined Ru mounting her sled, her mass of hair flying wildly about her face, and turning to her with that wild, winning smile.

She wondered who would leave first.

She wondered whose wolves would be faster.

She wondered how gold would look on her instead of silver.

Perhaps more than anything, Mila wondered what would happen *after* the finish line. Whether later that night she'd once again be visited by a dark-eyed, grinning girl whom she knew now had another girl within her, small and scared, forever running because it was too painful to stop.

What happens when the storm goes away?

Mila's question hung between them for a long time. Then Ru, with a deep-bellied laugh that once again startled poor Evie awake, rolled on top of Mila, took her face in one hand, and, beaming so brightly it really *was* like looking at the sun, kissed her. And this time, those kisses felt somehow to Mila like a reply all of their own.

FIVE STARS

"Mistaken Identity"

Amy Spalding

THE DOOR TO MY PRIUS FLIES OPEN. TECHNICALLY, IT'S DAD'S PRIUS; we just moved to Los Angeles three weeks ago, but he almost immediately traded in his giant pickup truck for this shiny hatchback. A scream would have flown out of me, but my heart pounds so intensely I can't make noise. My former classmates warned me that L.A. was dangerous and that I was too soft for it, but I blew them off. I was from the kind of small town where the biggest news of the year was that the Gas U Go started carrying Coke products instead of Pepsi. ("More like Pepsi U Go!" we shouted when we found out.) I'd visited my aunt so many times in L.A. that I laughed behind their backs at their tales of urban violence, knowing that while the city might be big and busy, it was one of those things that had never been scary.

And yet, here I am, on my nineteenth day in Los Angeles, trying to leave school after showing up for a talent show that is being put on by the show choir that I'm not even interested in joining just so I could, I don't know, meet people and pretend I had a social life here. And my reward—apparently being carjacked. Carjacked!

Okay, think, Krista, what do you do if you're being carjacked? Call 911? Okay, actually, that's probably what you're supposed to do. That is something even a soft person from the Midwest can handle.

I reach out to my phone, resting safely and legally in its dashboard mount. Hopefully my shaking hand can connect with the right numbers. After all, there are only three. Two, really, one's a repeat. Oh my gosh, I'm melting down, I can feel it, maybe—hopefully this is the kind of carjacker who's just going to throw me (and my phone) out, and even though Dad will probably be upset that the car's gone, I'll be safe and, well, I don't know how insurance works but hopefully it'll all work out on the money side.

"I'm here, I'm here, I'm here."

I flick my gaze into the rearview mirror, even though I don't think you're supposed to make eye contact with people in the process of stealing you and/or your car. But I also am pretty sure carjackers don't normally announce their arrival with a triple "I'm here" either so all rules are out the window.

Oh my—holy—

It isn't a carjacker. It's Audrey Kim.

Audrey Kim is in my backseat. Again, technically, Dad's backseat, but he isn't here, I am and I'm in the Prius alone with the hottest girl I've ever seen in person.

"Sorry," she says.

Audrey Kim, what could you be sorry for? Audrey Kim, your face is perfect and your hair is perfect and you're now breathing the same air as me. You owe me no apologies.

"I think everyone's getting a Rydr," she continues, tossing her phone into her bag without looking at it, "so there are, ya know, twenty-seven black Priuses out there. It took me some time to find yours."

"Oh, sure," I stammer, instead of *I am not your Rydr driver, I am not a Rydr driver at all! I too was just trying to get out of this weird surge of post–talent show traffic!*

"Sorry too about the destination," Audrey says, so breezily. How does anyone talk to a stranger like that, just a casual sentence cast out there without any anxiety about how it could come back to you? Even in my group of friends, it was never a true fearlessness. If I said everything that I thought, maybe I would have ended up saying *everything*. And I prided myself on just how much I kept to myself.

"Oh?" I try to sound like I'm not too interested. Rydr drivers are never very interested, and that's on top of the fact that *I'm not actually a Rydr driver and I have no idea what Audrey Kim's destination is.*

It's already, as we all know, past the point in time when I should have said something, obviously. *Hi, Audrey Kim, you obviously don't recognize me, but I'm in your chemistry class and your American lit class, and before I moved here, I guess I didn't really think there were girls like you in high school, but here you are, existing.*

Oh! But not just that, obviously. *Also, Audrey Kim, while this is a black Prius adorned with a Rydr sticker, it is not on duty, as my dad is the Rydr driver (Rydr drivr?) in the family, not me. This is an off-duty Rydr car. You should go catch your real ride now.*

But, as we've already covered, I am not someone who just says things. So, I drive away from South Valley Academy, one of many shiny black hatchbacks in a line at the light at Coldwater Canyon Avenue like little beetles being let out into the world.

"The Grove at rush hour is a real masochistic move on my part," Audrey continues, thank god, because even though I've only lived here for three-plus weeks, even I know what The Grove is. It's an outdoor mall with a weird trolley and a movie theater, and I've already gone there with Aunt Margo for dinner the week we moved here and again last week. So instead of fessing up to Audrey—it's already too late to tell her she got into the wrong car, isn't it?—I tap *the grove* into Waze and watch as the directions display before me.

"It's fine," I say, trying to sound nonchalant but kind, as Dad says the best Rydr drivers are. You don't want to talk too much and annoy someone, but you should be friendly, too. He and Mom moved here to work with Aunt Margo, whose artisanal mustard business has taken off in a huge way, but L.A.'s a lot more expensive than the-middle-of-nowhere Missouri, and so Dad's driving for Rydr in his nonmustard time. Even though it's a part-time gig, he's dedicated himself to learning the ways of Rydr.

"No, The Grove at any time is like one of the seven circles of Hell," Audrey says, and despite my knowledge of good Rydr driver behavior, I laugh. I laugh like it's the funniest thing I've heard in my entire life.

"Normally it's one of the outer rings, but at rush hour? It's second or third from the center."

I continue laughing like someone the camera zooms in on during a recorded stand-up comedy special. *Get a grip, Krista.* I mean, it's not *not* funny, but Audrey Kim is not exactly reinventing comedy in here.

"Anyway, I know it's your job, but it's still a terrible drive, so, I'm sorry," Audrey says. "Normally I take the bus, but I'm running late, so we're here instead while I come up with an excuse when Mom sees this on her credit card statement."

I glance in the rearview mirror, and accidentally make eye contact with her. Unless eye contact is okay? Dad didn't cover this in any of his Ryder ramblings in the last nine-teen days. I look back to the road, which is safest no matter the proper eye etiquette.

"Dude, I'm sorry," she says. "I have no idea why I'm saying so much. Well, I do, it's because I'm nervous as hell about—anyway, *sorry*. About the ride, about my mouth."

"Nothing's wrong," I say. "With the ride or your mouth."

Oh, god, *ew*, why did I say that? I chance another look back, but Audrey just smiles.

"Thanks," she says. "Five stars!"

I realize she's talking about Rydr's driver rating system, and I wonder what she'll think when it's time to actually give the tip and review at the end of the ride. It certainly won't say Krista P. and won't feature my photo in a little bubble. But that'll be later, after I drop her off, when I'm on my way back to my new house that doesn't feel anything like home yet.

When Mom and Dad announced we were moving to California, I didn't know what to feel. My old classmates were right; I *am* soft. I cry a lot and I'm scared of horror movies and I wore half of a cheap BFF necklace for six months, because I didn't want to say anything negative, before Emily noticed it was turning my skin green. (We pivoted to bracelets woven out of embroidery floss after that.) Moving, much less to a big city, didn't seem like it was for me.

But a small town—my small town, at least—wasn't for me either. I always felt different, somehow, somewhere buried beneath my skin. For a long time, I attributed it to the things I could tick off a list, like all the ways I was too soft, or how during the last presidential election we were the only house with a Democratic yard sign on our whole street. (Not our whole block. The whole goshdarn street.) But it was more than that, and all those things added up sounded better suited for Los Angeles. It was my way out. Here I'd see yard signs that matched ours, here my softness would be enhanced by the scent of orange blossoms at dusk, and here I'd kiss a girl and not wonder what anyone thought about it.

But, so far, none of that has happened. There are no elections going on right now, my selfies look the same even with orange blossoms in the air, and my first kiss has still not happened. My first girl kiss, that is, because I don't count anything that happened before I knew I was queer—oh, gosh, I'm queer, that's a thing I am that I think about myself now. A real thing I have a word for, not just some vague differentness about me.

But, still, California is different than the Midwest, or at least the specific place I landed is different than the specific place I left. There I'd been, whispering words into my mirror, alone, and now here I am, where a girl like Audrey Kim just *existed*.

The car feels silent—too silent—and I try to remember everything Dad's told me about being a great Rydr driver. "Can I put some music on for you?" I ask, in a voice that comes out more squeakily than intended. For a moment I worry that my five stars are in jeopardy and then remember *I am not her actual driver, this whole thing is a weird accidental sham!*

"That'd be great," Audrey says. "Whatever's good for me."

I realize then that I have to turn on the car stereo, which is connected to my iPhone, and which I only paused leaving school because I wasn't used to driving this car out here at all, so I needed a few moments of silence. When my phone reconnects to the stereo, there's nothing to be done. The cast recording of *Be More Chill* is going to blare out into the car directly into Audrey Kim's ears.

Obviously, of course none of this matters because Audrey Kim looks like a Wildfang model and I look like a librarian who graduated a decade early but still readily embraces lumpy cardigans and sensible shoes. And Audrey doesn't recognize me from American lit or chemistry. I'm no one, so my penchant for musical theater won't change her opinion of me *as she has no opinion of me*. My five stars aren't in jeopardy. This embarrassment will be extremely short-lived while I search for anything that would be even slightly cooler.

So, I hit the power button. I try not to watch Audrey's face in the rearview mirror; I should be focusing on driving and also: What's the coolest album I could switch to? I don't even know what's cool! Maybe my attempt would be even nerdier than extremely earnest musical theater.

Audrey's eyes light up though. She leans forward a little.

"I *love* this show," she says, and I almost do the very clichéd thing of pinching myself to see if I'm dreaming because, oh, let's see, the girl of my dreams is in my car and it turns out she likes musicals too? Or at least she likes *a* musical. In fact, she *loves* a musical, the musical I just happen to have on.

"Me too," I say. "Though I haven't seen it live or anything."

"I got to go the other year," she says, brushing her black hair out of her face. Her hair is short all over except the top, which falls into her eyes constantly. Why is watching someone push their hair back so dreamy? "My mom had a business trip to New York and she brought me. It was pretty amazing."

"I bet." I try to go back into professional driving mode, even though I wish we were still talking about the show, about other shows, about anything on Audrey's mind at all. Instead I'm quiet while "Michael in the Bathroom" plays, though I glance back to see if Audrey smiles at the same lines I would, if I weren't trying to be extremely professional.

"How long until we're there?" she asks.

"Um, thirty minutes, is that okay?"

She laughs. "What are you going to do if it's not okay? Call me a Rydr helicopter?"

"Yep, that's our next service we're unveiling," I say. "Sorry, I'm just new to L.A., and I feel like I should apologize that it's going to take thirty minutes to drive ten miles."

"I wish it was three hours," she says quickly, but then I see her waving her hand. "No, thirty minutes is fine. Sorry. I just have to see my ex-girlfriend tonight and I wish I—" She laughs a little. "I mean, I wish I didn't have to. That'd be perfect."

"Oh," I say, because for some reason even though Audrey's gorgeous and wears great clothes and is always surrounded by people at school, I haven't thought of her having a girlfriend. Sure, an ex-girlfriend, but still. In an ideal world, whoever came before was so far in the past she wouldn't warrant a mention.

"Sorry, this is annoying of me, I know, I just have this bad habit of verbally vomiting on people when I'm nervous and since you're the only one around, lucky you."

"I guess it's good you couldn't take the bus then," I say, and she cracks up. I can't believe I'm making a hot girl laugh, this kind of thing would never have happened in Missouri.

To be fair, back home, I just didn't know anyone like Audrey. I'm not sure if I was the only queer person back at my old school, because no one said. And how could I complain, because I didn't say either! I kept hoping it would just happen, somehow, a new girl would roll into town and she'd be visibly queer and I wouldn't have to wonder if the eye contact we were making was just nice or if it was *significant* in some way and she'd be experienced enough to make the first move.

But instead of that happening, the mustard business exploded, and I left without a word to anyone about who I really was. Am. And then I sat down in my first-period chemistry class on my first day at my new school and watched as this girl walked into the room. Jeans, a printed button-down, perfectly worn Dr. Martens, and that haircut. But I knew anyway, there was something about how she walked, moved, sat. I realized why I hadn't had any crushes on girls before, and it's because where I was from, girls didn't look like this.

I wanted to text heart-eye emojis *to myself*. But instead I buried my flushed face into my chemistry textbook and tried not to stare. Later, when Emily and I were texting about how my day went, I typed out what felt like a thousand different ways to say it . . . *I have a crush on someone and her name is Audrey Kim* or *I saw the hottest girl today and she's levels beyond me but now I completely understand when you were obsessed with Paul Leavitt freshman year* or even just *hey, I'm queer, I should have told you sooner, but now that I have can I tell you about my first irl crush?*

I didn't though. And obviously I didn't get up the nerve to talk to Audrey either. Until today, and I'm still not even sure this counts.

"It was all over months ago," Audrey says. "I'm fine now, and anyway, I'm the one who broke up with her. But she has a new girlfriend, and even though I've moved on emotionally, I really hoped I would have moved on first, you know, in that way.

"But instead she's posting kissing selfies every night and I'm—oh, god, seriously, I'm sorry! I warned you but, come on. It's getting worse, isn't it?"

I shake my head. "It's fine. I hate being nervous on my way anywhere. I was nervous the entire drive to California, and that took three days. I stress-ate five bags of Gummi Twin Snakes and—well, it didn't work out great for my stomach, I'll say."

Audrey laughs again. "No, dude, why would it? So why did you move here?"

"My aunt opened this fancy mustard store, and it's gotten really popular, and I guess my parents were looking to change things up, so they're working for her now and here I am."

"Oh, shit, are you talking about Colonel Mustard?" Audrey leans forward again, so that her extremely cute face is practically in the front seat next to me. "My mom is *obsessed* with that store. She puts mustard on everything."

"Yeah, that's it. I guess it would be weird if there were two hipster mustard stores."

"In L.A.? It wouldn't be *that* weird. Do you like it so far?" she asks. "L.A., that is, not the mustard store."

"It seems fake sometimes," I say. "The palm trees, how is this real? It looks like we're in a postcard. But the weather is nice and people seem . . . I don't know. Cooler about stuff."

"It's the only place I've ever lived," she says, "but I like it. I bet you'll like it when you've been here longer, too. More, I mean, besides the weather and the palm trees."

"I hope so," I say.

We're quiet for a while, as "The Smartphone Hour" plays out of my speakers, filling all the silence. I haven't driven this far across L.A. before, but despite the practically unbelievable number of cars on the road, it's not actually that scary. It's a lot, but it's just driving, and I know if I miss anything that Waze will tell me.

"It's bad that I wish she was still alone, isn't it?" Audrey asks, and then shakes her head a whole bunch. "No, sorry, why am I being so inappropriate? Don't answer that. Unless you want to. My Rydr ranking is going to plummet after this ride, though it wasn't great before."

"Why?" I ask, regardless of whether or not it's my business. I guess it feels like we're already past concerns like that.

"My friend KJ dropped an entire Frappuccino in a backseat, just a real sticky mess. We tried to pay the guy to get it cleaned but my Rydr reputation was done for. No matter what, I'll never be five stars."

"You're five stars in my book." I hear how the words come out of my mouth, and it's not the way I talk to anyone. Like something extra soft is wrapped around each word. I'm *flirting*.

Audrey's smile in my rearview mirror confirms that maybe I was right to do so.

"Are you in college?" she asks. "Is it bad to say I think you're the youngest Rydr driver I've ever had?"

"High school," I say, even though it's dangerously close to the truth. I mean, it is the truth! It's dangerously close to the bigger truth, which is that I'm not at all what she thinks I am, and we might not be sort of flirting over show tunes if I were to admit that. No, there was no *might* about it. We wouldn't be at all.

"Oh," she says, and "good," and then "oh, god, never mind!"

It feels like it means something, even something that would never actually come to be, and my whole face feels warm and tingly.

"Also," I say, probably treading into more dangerous waters, "I don't think it's bad you wish she was still alone. I'd probably wish that too. Not that I've been in the situation. But I can tell what I'd feel, if I were."

Yep, that was probably a heck of a lot beyond proper Rydr protocol, but we connect our gazes in the rearview mirror, because I'm at a stoplight. I can't believe how safe literally all of this feels: the traffic, me driving in it, and Audrey Kim in my backseat. Earlier today she was a crush, just someone to look at, really. She was more like a metaphor than a real girl, if I was honest with myself. She was freedom and confidence and being out in a way I still couldn't completely imagine. But now, in a matter of minutes, she's transformed into something way more and less than that all at once. Just a girl I feel like I could understand and who maybe could understand me.

It's way, way too late to say anything, though, isn't it? I try out more versions in my head. *I should have said something sooner, but you got into the wrong car and I didn't know how to tell you. I was so happy to see you in my backseat and also so happy you weren't a carjacker so I just kept driving. If you wish you'd met someone new before your ex-girlfriend did, what about meeting someone new right now, also what if the someone new is me? Oh and by the way I am not actually your Rydr driver.*

No. It's too late. We're going to have this perfect drive and then it will be over. And then the very best thing I can wish for is that she continues never noticing me at school.

"Can I ask you a weird question?" Audrey asks, and then I realize she's covering her face like she's embarrassed. Like I, of all people, am making her nervous. "What're the rules for communication with Rydr drivers after a ride? Would it be weird if I—sorry, no. My therapist always says my anxiety makes me talk without thinking, and she is absolutely right."

"No," I say, because I think Audrey Kim is about to ask for my number. This is like a wild fantasy for me, even though I know for most people wild fantasies involve actual sex. Mine so far kind of stop at the getting someone's number stage, considering how far-fetched even that seemed before. But here I am. "Ask the weird question."

"Okay, Archie, would it be okay if I contacted you after the ride? After your five stars and your tip, of course."

Why is she calling me Archie? Oh my *gosh*, that must be the actual Rydr driver's name. Who probably canceled out on Audrey long ago and is carting someone else around now, legally. Not that what I'm doing is illegal, just . . . unethical. Maybe.

"Yeah," I say, and I wish I could enjoy it more, but is there a way to say *please call me by my full name, Krista* and get away with it? That would just make the situation worse, won't it?

Audrey gets out her phone. "I assume I should get your number directly and not just go through the app, right?"

"Definitely," I say with perhaps too much force, but I'm back to feeling this, wanting this. A girl is asking for my number! I never dreamed this would be happening to me, not now, not before I went off to college and had some more freedom or whatever this situation required.

I pull to a stop, even though we're nowhere near a light, as traffic slows even more than the crawl it's been at for most of the drive. Waze tacks another minute onto our arrival time. Audrey's quiet, so I assume she's tapping through to her contacts to get ready to add me.

But then I glance into the mirror and see her expression.

"Uhhhhh . . ." Audrey stares at me. "What's going on?"

My inability to talk to strangers or people who intimidate me, which had miraculously disappeared this afternoon, has returned. I open my mouth, but nothing comes out.

"I just saw I had a notification from Archie J. that my ride was canceled because I never showed up," Audrey says, her tone colder and sharper. Like an icicle.

"I'm—I'm sorry, I—I should have—"

"What the fuck is even happening?" She's no longer leaning forward, and the backseat of this tiny car has never felt so far away. "Who are you? Why am I in your car?"

"Do you want to get out?" I ask. "I can, like, pull over and let you out. If you don't feel safe or—"

"No, I want you to tell me what's going on," she says. "Then maybe I'll have you let me out. But also I have to get to the fucking Coffee Bean & Tea Leaf at The Grove before Jenn's shift ends at 5:30 or she'll kill me. So, I guess I'm stuck, which means you're talking."

"I'm not a Rydr," I say. "I mean, this car is, sometimes. My dad's a driver. I was just leaving school, same as you. I'm new and . . . it sounds dumb but since I love musicals I thought maybe if I went to the show choir talent show today I might . . . meet people to be friends with or something.

"I've never had to make friends before, and it's really hard. And of course I didn't talk to anyone because talking to new people scares me—usually. Anyway, I was just trying to leave, and then you got in and—"

"And you didn't say *hey, this isn't a Rydr, get out of my car?*"

I don't know what to say.

"Shit," she mutters.

Normally, I'm too soft for cursing, but *shit*.

Traffic keeps crawling. I try to keep my eyes on the road, but it's hard not to keep glancing back at Audrey. Her expression stays unreadable, and I wish it was okay for me to cry. In general, crying should be more socially acceptable. I know at this point that good Rydr driver protocol is out the window, so to speak, but even decent human protocol says that openly sobbing is generally frowned upon.

I should have known that it all felt too perfect. By the time I was considering pinching myself, I should have taken a big step back. Of course, I was destined to mess it up. Then the album ends and automatically cycles back to the first track. I'm aware that it's just my Spotify settings, but as the show starts again, I wonder if I can start again too.

"Audrey, I know it sounds so stupid, and I should have told you, but like . . . I just couldn't find the right moment?"

Audrey's face stays blank, but then—to my surprise—she starts laughing. "You don't have to find the right moment! Why were you being polite to me? I was the asshole who just leapt into your car like a carjacker!"

"Seriously, at first, that's what I thought was happening to me. I was just so relieved it wasn't, and that it was you—"

She's leaning forward again. "That it was *me*?"

My face is all hot and tingly again. *Oops.* "I . . . I had a really big crush on you."

"Oh," she says. And she doesn't move away.

"I didn't mean to kidnap you."

Audrey laughs again. I've never, ever been so relieved to hear Audrey's laugh. "You didn't kidnap me. As far as I know, you're taking me to my destination. *For free!*"

"I totally am. We're five minutes away."

She sighs. "I have to give Jenn this stupid bracelet back. Her mom loaned it to me for homecoming and then we broke up afterward and . . . I guess it's expensive or a family heirloom or something, and she's right to want it back but . . ."

"You can't give it to her at school?"

"Jenn goes to Marlborough, over on this side of the hill," she says. "We met in the lottery line for *Hamilton* the other year."

"You've seen everything!" I say, which I know isn't the right response. Luckily Audrey laughs. "Sorry, it sucks about your ex and about the bracelet and about . . . now."

"Now's okay," she says.

We both smile.

"I'm kind of glad you got into my car," I say.

"Just *kind of*?"

We both laugh, and I see up ahead that we're nearly to The Grove. This weird little miracle has almost ended, and then I'll have to drive back to my new house and explain to Mom and Dad why I was gone so long without saying anything about the truth at the core of it.

"What's your actual name?" Audrey asks.

"Krista. Krista Parker."

"It's good to officially meet you, Krista Parker. I'm Audrey Kim."

I pull the car into the left turn lane, so I'm not looking into the rearview mirror for a bit. When I do, I see that Audrey's tapping something into her phone.

"Can I still get your number?"

I practically shout it at her I'm so relieved. Maybe the miracle doesn't have to end. My phone beeps with a message from an 818 number. It's a single car emoji.

"Just so you know it's me," she says.

"I wouldn't forget you." I look around as I drive toward the shopping center. "Where's the coffee place and tea thing? Is there a good place to let you out?"

"There's no good place, you can just pull over."

I do my best, only getting honked at twice, and turn back to say goodbye to Audrey. But maybe . . .

"Audrey," I say, "since we go to the same school, we probably live near each other. And I have to drive back anyway so . . . do you want me to wait for you and give you a ride home?"

Thankfully I don't have even a moment to worry if that's a creepy thing to ask, because I see Audrey's face light up. I can't believe the girl I thought was cool and untouchable is a smiley musical theater nerd. I thought she was one kind of dreamboat, but it turns out she's another kind that's a better fit for me anyway. What on earth would I do with cool and untouchable?

"I'll hurry," she says.

"Don't. I'm fine. Take as long as you need."

She gets out of the car, and I grab my phone to safely store her number before I somehow accidentally delete the first cute message a girl has sent to me. I jot off a quick text to my group chat with Mom and Dad that I'm running late and will explain later, and then I realize that there's no reason why I can't actually fully explain later. It'll be awkward but my parents have only said supportive things about the LGBTQ+ community. I don't think that'll change now that they know I'm one of its members.

And then—I can't completely explain it, maybe it was the text from Audrey or the warm tingles that have not left me alone—I scroll to my chain with Emily and tell her every detail of this afternoon before she can get a word in. It's the kind of story I know Emily will love; she practically collects awkward anecdotes. I try to pretend I haven't revealed vital information about myself within the story, especially once I see the dots that she's typing.

OMG KRISTA YOU KIDNAPPED YOUR FIRST IRL CRUSH BUT STILL MANAGED TO GET HER NUMBER?

You are a hero for awkward girls everywhere. They'll put up
a statue of you, but in some awkward place like next to a
public restroom. I MISS YOU CALL ME LATER OK TELL
ME ABOUT THE RIDE HOME

My car door opens, and—oh my god. Audrey's sitting down in the front seat.
This close she smells like jasmine and fancy hair product. I thought she was close
before, but before was nothing.

"I figured I'd earned front-seat privileges," she says, and her eyes widen. "Oh, shit,
you're the new girl!"

"Wait, you did notice me from school?"

"Not the back of your head and your eyes only, but we have classes together. You
wear all those soft sweaters, you're always kind of . . ." She leans in and rubs her thumb
on my forearm. I practically gasp. "Fuzzy."

I had no idea that *fuzzy* could sound sexy. I had no idea I even knew I could tell
what things were sexy, with zero experience, but here I am with a girl mere inches away.
I don't know what I'm doing but it's not as if that stopped what's already happened
today. I want to kiss Audrey Kim, and she's close enough that I don't really have to try
hard to make it happen. I turn my head just a little and feel her breath against my face.

She moves as I do, and our lips touch gently. It's more electric, though, than her
thumb on my arm through my sweater, a billion jolts of energy between us. Her fingers
clasp my face, pull me closer, and I try running my fingers through her tousled hair as
our faces tilt to find new angles. Our lips brush, over and over, until they slowly part
and we're breathing each other as air.

We kiss until we're out of breath and what seem like a million cars have angrily
beeped their horns at us. We don't care about them; we laugh and kiss once more with
ragged breath and swollen lips.

"We probably should get back to the Valley," Audrey says, though she keeps her
fingertips on my face. "My parents lose their shit if I'm not home for dinner."

I let her tap her address into Waze while I catch my breath and then lose it all
over again.

"Five stars," she says again, and I grin. "Friendly driver, good music, great kissing."

"Even if you spilled a Frappuccino, five stars for you, too."

UNFORTUNATELY, BLOBS DO NOT EAT SNACKS

"Kissing Under the Influence"

Rebecca Kim Wells

THERE WAS NO TRAIN TO LEESIDE.

Tess stared up at the boards, watching them flip back and forth to announce platforms and times. She watched for two cycles, almost unblinking, but the information did not change.

She looked down at the printed schedule in her hand. She'd underlined it three days ago, as they were preparing to leave the academy. *Tuesday, Leeside, 4:00 sharp.*

And yet there was no train on the board.

There had to be a mistake.

Davina, who was flopped on an uncomfortable-looking bench eating a scone, looked up at her. "What's the trouble?"

"Nothing!" Tess replied with false cheer. The last thing she wanted was to let on to Davina Winters, of all people, that there was a problem.

She looked around for a conductor. Not seeing one, she parked her trolley next to Davina's and announced that she would return shortly. Davina's reply was muffled by the scone, rendering it unintelligible.

Tess pretended she hadn't heard anything, which was for the best, because if Davina had said anything particularly Davina-y, Tess would've had to scream. She took a deep breath, straightened her coat, and marched over to the ticket master's window.

"Hello," she said brightly.

The woman behind the glass looked even older than Tess's grandmother, who was ninety-seven. "Yes?" Her voice was as creaky as an uneven staircase.

"I don't wish to trouble you, but I need to know when the next train to Leeside departs."

The woman blinked very slowly. "Leeside?"

"Yes," said Tess, feeling impatience creep up her neck. "Leeside. I have transfer tickets and my schedule says 4:00, but there is no train listed on the board."

"Leeside," the woman repeated, almost incredulously.

"Yes," said Tess. She put her schedule on the counter and turned it around to face the ticket master. "Just here, see? There should be a train at 4:00 today."

The ticket master adjusted her glasses and peered down at the schedule. Tess resisted the urge to tap her foot. "Your schedule is out of date," the ticket master said eventually.

"Out of date?" Now it was Tess's turn to be incredulous. "I bought it five days ago. How could it be out of date?"

"Because," the ticket master said, as though explaining something to a very small child, "there are no trains to Leeside."

Tess opened her mouth to say something—she had no idea what—when an arm fell over her shoulder.

"Thank you *very* much," Davina said, smiling brightly at the ticket master. "Now, come along, my darling—"

"*Don't call me that*," Tess hissed, throwing off Davina's arm as she led her away. "What did you do that for?"

"Because I know you would have gone through three or four more rounds. I know you, Tess Griffin. You're extremely persistent. But we're burning time. There are no trains to Leeside. We're going to have to figure out another way to get there."

"But it says *right here*—"

"I'm aware of what the schedule says," Davina said in that infuriating tone of hers. "Are *you* aware that this is an exam?"

"Of *course* I know that, what does that have to do with—" Tess stopped speaking. Her cheeks flushed as she realized what Davina meant. Of course. Of *course*. She cleared her throat. "Very well, then," she said. "We'd better see about alternate arrangements."

The envelope had been slipped under Tess's door six days ago, just after midnight. Tess had grabbed it immediately—she'd been staying up so she could do just that.

This academy exam was the last thing standing between her and graduation, followed by a position as a full-fledged junior investigator of magical malfeasance. As such, it was *extremely* important, and she would take any advantage she could get. Her fingers vibrated with excitement as she slit open the envelope and pulled out the piece of paper. Then she felt her stomach drop through the floor—because she had studied for every eventuality. Every eventuality, that is, except the one where Davina Winters was assigned as her examination partner.

She'd barely skimmed the rest of the letter—*magical activity in Leeside unaccounted for in last week's projections . . . identify cause of activity (neutralize if applicable)*. That part was of little consequence—it was standard exam fare: create a small magical anomaly in an out-of-the-way town (which was generously compensated for their troubles, of course), then send in students to deal with it. Evaluate.

Of course, what she'd failed to realize at that time was that the exam didn't start when she and Davina reached Leeside. It had started the moment they had gotten their assignment. Which meant that someone had been observing her as she chose and packed her instruments. And someone had stopped the trains to Leeside *on purpose* just to see what she and Davina would do.

Tess pressed her lips together. Well. She'd been caught off her guard once. It wasn't going to happen again.

The other problem was that there were no coaches to Leeside, either. Nor were there wagons for hire, nor convenient riverboats, nor even bicycles with cargo compartments large enough for her instruments.

By this time it was after 5:30 and Tess was beginning to get just a little bit desperate. It didn't help that the weather was much warmer here than back at the academy. Tess pinned up her braid, which had little effect. What she really needed was to change out of these long skirts, but there was no time. She had to find *some* way to get to Leeside, some way to carry all of her things, some way to ensure a reasonable night's sleep once they arrived—

"Tess."

"*What?*" She whirled around to see Davina snacking on a pear. *How* had she managed to pick one of those up?

"Let's go," Davina said, seemingly unconcerned by the mountainous obstacle that had just been set in their path.

"Go . . . go where?" Tess replied.

Davina finished chewing. "We're not going to get to Leeside tonight. So let's go. I've booked two rooms for us. We'll figure out what to do next."

"You booked rooms?" Tess said. "Without asking?"

Davina raised an eyebrow at her. "You booked train tickets without asking, didn't you?"

"Well—yes," Tess admitted. "But I know what I'm doing! We can't afford to lose the time!"

Davina made a noncommittal *hmm* sound and Tess wanted to strangle her. "Well," Davina said, "you're welcome to stand around with your bags all night if you like. *I'm* getting some sleep."

She turned and walked away, and for a moment Tess was certain, absolutely certain, that she would have to stand on the street until the morning just to avoid admitting that Davina was right. Then her better judgment got hold of her. This was an exam. She had to succeed no matter what. And after this was over, she never had to see Davina again. If only she could survive the next few days . . .

Gritting her teeth, Tess turned her trolley around and followed Davina away from the train station.

To her credit, Davina refrained from commenting when Tess pulled up next to her outside the inn. She just handed Tess a key, and stood aside as she manhandled her bags inside. The inn itself was surprisingly adequate, considering that Davina had found it. After twenty minutes of dragging bags upstairs, Tess had no complaints, although her stomach was beginning to growl. She checked her watch: 6:23.

She'd been too nervous to eat this morning, and the first train had given her motion sickness. Then there had been the transfer debacle, and . . . well, she was hungry now. She changed her blouse, took a moment to wash her face and tuck any flyaways behind her ears. Then she went downstairs in search of supper.

It was easy to spot Davina—her purple hair caught the warm lamplight as she joked with some travelers at a booth in the corner of the dining room. She looked quite at home. But then again, Davina always looked at home, no matter the situation. She had the uncanny ability to appear as though whatever she was doing, she was doing it on purpose and with great confidence. Tess straightened her blouse and walked over.

"So," she said, sliding into the booth. "We should talk."

Davina slung one arm over the back of the booth, lounging across the seat. "Oh?"

"Yes," Tess continued. "We need to regroup. Restrategize."

"I see. So now that you've run out of ideas, you're willing to listen to mine."

Tess recoiled. "That's not what I meant."

"Isn't it?"

A waiter bustled up to the table and set down an assortment of small plates before them, then melted away into the crowd. Davina reached for a winter plum and picked up a knife. She began to cut the plum into methodical slices, all in uncharacteristic silence. She was clearly waiting for *something* from Tess.

Tess looked away. It wasn't that Davina was incompetent. It was just that—that—well, it was just that the very first time they'd met, Davina had barreled into her in the dormitory hallway and instead of apologizing, had just grinned and winked at her and kept barreling on. *Winked!* And she carried that same lackadaisical attitude throughout all her classes, leading to a number of memorable mishaps including setting a rare spindlebush specimen on fire, botching a growth potion that enlarged a cat to the size of a horse, and (most infamously) filling the breakfast hall from floor to ceiling with unpoppable soap bubbles—and yet *somehow* she managed to come in as a close second at the end of the term, all with that infuriating grin on her face. It simply wasn't *fair*. Tess had studied harder than she'd ever studied in her life for her marks, but Davina got everything she had without even trying.

Tess dipped a piece of bread into the tureen in front of her and ate it slowly. She took a deep breath. "Perhaps I was a bit hasty earlier," she mumbled.

"What was that?" Davina asked.

Tess's lips thinned. "You heard me," she said.

Davina arched an eyebrow. "What I thought I heard was the sorriest excuse for an apology I've ever had the pleasure of receiving. But then I thought, that can't be right, because Tess Griffin *never* apologizes."

"That is untrue!" Tess said, scandalized.

"Which part—that it was an apology, or that you never make them?" Davina softened her retort with a wink, and bit into another slice of plum.

Tess opened her mouth, then closed it once more. Davina was right. Much as she hated to admit it, she *had* done everything without asking. Under the guise of efficiency, certainly—but this was Davina's exam too. She deserved to be involved in the process.

"I apologize," she said stiffly. "You're right. I shouldn't have booked tickets without consulting you."

Davina's eyebrows shot nearly into her purple hair. "I accept your apology," she said. "Now—I think we need to talk about the walk to Leeside."

Tess stared at her. "But that would take over a day! And what about our equipment?"

"Well," said Davina, "it's mostly *your* equipment. And I suspect you'll have to leave most of it behind."

For a moment Tess's mind went completely blank. "Leave it behind? But— I need it."

"And I imagine that's why there are no trains, and no coaches, and no carts," Davina said. "To force us to go on without it."

"That doesn't make any sense," Tess said, trying to ward off her growing panic. "Detecting the general parameters of destabilization, identifying schools of enchantment—how can they ask us to do any of it without the proper instruments?"

"'A student of magic must learn the art of the ineffable, for the greatest mysteries may not unravel without a touch of impossibility.'"

"Poppycock," Tess muttered. She'd always hated Professor Willow's opaque lectures on the incomprehensible roots of magic. She much preferred things that could be measured, studied, replicated. She preferred *answers*. And—and what if she couldn't do it?

The specter of failure ghosted through her mind, followed by a steadily increasing ringing in her ears. She'd done everything right, everything the academy had asked her. It wasn't fair that the exam was breaking the rules—no, not just breaking the rules—that they were throwing out the rulebook entirely. This felt uncomfortably like the essence of magic class that she'd had to take as a third year, and barely passed. Davina, of course, had finished with top marks, and a commendation from the professor.

A gentle hand covered hers and Tess jumped at the unexpected touch.

"Hey," Davina said. "Look at me."

Tess looked up into Davina's surprisingly dark eyes.

"We can do this. They wouldn't have given us anything we couldn't handle."

Davina's sudden compassion was surprising and a little unnerving, but in this moment Tess clung to it like a lifeline.

"Thank you," she said quietly. The ringing in her ears quieted. The sounds of the inn slowly returned. She was suddenly aware that Davina's hand had been touching hers for the better part of five minutes—that their hands were still touching, in fact. Oh, she must look a complete wreck for Davina to have been driven to comfort her. To be undone by the academy exam—her, the top-ranked student? Her cheeks flushed with embarrassment.

She cleared her throat awkwardly, and the spell was broken. She shifted one finger and Davina pulled back her hand as if burned.

"So we're walking, then," Tess said.

Davina blinked, as if she'd completely forgotten the topic at hand. "Right. And we'd better get an early start. Be ready to leave by eight?"

Eight in the morning, and she could only bring what she could carry. Tess took a deliberate breath, trying to stay calm.

By the time Davina knocked on the door, Tess had slept less than five hours, packed and unpacked no fewer than six times, and was still second-guessing every decision she'd made.

"It's open!" she called frantically.

Davina came in, carrying a small knapsack and a breakfast tray. "Wow," she said.

Tess paused in her rush around the room, and for the first time took in the chaos around her. There were books everywhere and boxes upon boxes of different equipment stacked in various corners. At one point Tess had attempted to sort them in order of importance, but had gotten stuck comparing a brooch that detected abnormal levels of ambient magic in liquids and a ball of yarn that would lead its bearer to their desired destination, and had given up on the endeavor entirely.

"I didn't realize you could even fit that much into your luggage," Davina said.

"It's called being prepared," Tess said. "Are those cinnamon rolls?"

"Not so fast," Davina replied, holding the tray up and out of reach. "Are you ready to go?"

"Almost. I just have to—"

"Nope. No breakfast until we're on the other side of this door, and it's locked. So whatever decisions you need to make, make them now."

"You can't possibly expect me to—"

"Let me remind you that according to Professor Willow, mages of yore tamed the earth with nothing but twigs and bottles of water drawn from the springs of the eastern mountains," Davina said, adopting their professor's lofty tone. "Surely you, Tess Griffin, holder of the first marks in *every* subject, can do with what's in that bag. I trust you've made good decisions in the last ten hours."

Tess glared at her. "You're insufferable."

"I just paid you a compliment, and that's your response? How about this— for every minute you waste, I'm going to eat another roll." Davina stuffed an entire cinnamon roll into her mouth, chewing loudly.

Tess rolled her eyes. "But you see, that plan is going to backfire, because if you eat all the breakfast, we're going to have to stop to get more, and besides, I don't even think you can eat—"

"Not listening!" Davina said around a mouthful of pastry. She backed out of the room, leaving Tess alone with her equipment . . . and the tantalizing smell of warm cinnamon.

Tess ran her fingers along the seam of her bag. She *had* chosen well. There was nothing to be worried about. She could do this. Couldn't she?

Two hours later, having made reasonable progress down a road that was getting ever narrower as it traversed fallow fields, Tess was certain she could not. The problem wasn't the road, which, though narrow, was clearly marked. It wasn't the weather, which had settled into the perfect combination of gray and slightly breezy. It wasn't even her bag—somehow, Tess's overnight panic had not led to overpacking, so she was quite comfortable for someone who had not known until yesterday that she would be walking all day. No, the problem was Davina.

She was enthusiastic about *everything*. The trees, the rocks, the animals, even the different sets of footprints on the ground. Everything merited a grin or an exclamation, and sometimes a momentary detour as she stepped off the road to investigate a particularly alluring flower.

Tess tried to tune her out. It wasn't Davina's fault that they'd been assigned to this exam together, or that the exam was very quickly sliding toward Tess's nightmare scenario—confronting whatever it was without any of the equipment she'd trained for years to master. But why, oh why, did Davina have to be so preposterously cheerful about the entire affair?

So it was that the fifth time Davina paused next to a particularly violet cornflower that Tess couldn't take it any longer.

"Must you be so—so—enthusiastic all the time?" she burst out.

Davina looked up from her cornflower, eyebrows raised. "Enthusiastic?" she said.

"*Yes*. The sky, the grass, the flowers, the squirrels—not everything is cause for comment! And in case you'd forgotten, we *are* on a timeline." Tess fought the urge to squirm under Davina's amused gaze.

"We're making good time," Davina responded, a grin breaking across her lips. "And as far as enthusiasm goes—it makes me happy to know there's a beautiful field of cornflowers here, just minding their own business. That it seems to wind *you* up is just a bonus."

Davina winked at Tess, put her hands in her pockets, and started off down the road once more, whistling a cheerful tune.

Insufferable. Absolutely, positively insufferable.

And yet Tess could do nothing but stomp after her, determined not to appreciate a single cornflower from here to Leeside.

They stopped to make camp as the sun began to sink below the horizon. According to Tess's map they had covered reasonable ground. Leeside was only about an hour away. After a good night's sleep, the distance would seem like nothing. And then . . . the exam.

Tess spread a few blankets on the ground, then sat down and reached into the basket she had purchased from the innkeeper that morning. She pulled out a jam sandwich, then handed the basket over to Davina. The night was cool, but Tess didn't want to draw any attention with a fire. Instead she pulled a blanket around her shoulders and huddled into it.

"Do you think the academy paired us together on purpose?" Davina said after a while.

Tess looked over at her, surprised. "Well—we are top of class," she said.

Davina flopped on her back and laced her fingers behind her head, staring up at the sky. "True. But I don't think anyone would have expected us to work well together. You're neat as a pin, for one."

Where Davina had a tendency to get as messy as possible, Tess thought to herself as she felt a flush rise on her cheeks. "Order is—"

"An essential part of wizardry, of course," Davina said, rolling her eyes at Tess's invocation of one of the core tenets of spell casting.

But something about Davina noticing that was unsettling to Tess. At the academy, she'd thought herself almost invisible. She was there only to achieve what needed achieving. It was just a stepping stone to the next thing she would accomplish. So she kept her head down and stayed out of trouble. However, she hadn't realized that other people were watching her. And it was discomfiting to realize that she had been seen—not only that, but that *Davina* had seen her.

"Well," Tess began, somewhat frostily.

"I like it," Davina said quickly. "That you always have your ducks in a row—I like that about you. Always have."

Well. For perhaps the first time today, Tess didn't know what to say.

"What are you planning on doing after the academy?" Davina asked, changing the subject. "I'm sure with your standing, you have your pick of offers."

"Investigator," Tess said automatically. It had been the goal since the academy acceptance letter had arrived.

Davina made an unsurprised sound. "Of course."

Because that was the position that any academy graduate worth their salt aimed for. A position at the Department of Magical Investigations guaranteed a stable income *and* the visibility necessary to move on to other, more prestigious departments. Tess's mother had dreamed about having a council member as a daughter for years. *Everything* about Tess's trajectory was unsurprising—except for the seed of ambivalence that squirmed inside her every time she thought about leaving the academy, of putting on the investigator's uniform . . .

"Well, at least it's a job," she said. "And you?"

"I don't know. I've had a few offers, but I've been thinking of taking a break after the exam. Spending some time in a place where you can see the *stars*."

The stars. Tess had never much enjoyed being out of doors. Out of doors was hot and sticky and buggy and inconvenient—all the things she hated most. She would take a cozy parlor with a stack of books and a good cup of tea any day over all of that. But there was something to what Davina was saying—something about the wildness of the sky, and the stars so much brighter and closer than they appeared from the academy's observational gardens. Looking at them made her chest hurt in a strange, not unpleasant way.

"You're not concerned?" Tess asked.

"Concerned about what?"

Everything, Tess wanted to say. Making the right decision, choosing the right job, selecting the right dress, the right meal, the right person . . . "About—doing the wrong thing. Or missing something important," she said.

Davina smiled, though in the night Tess could barely see it. "That's why I'm doing it. To make sure I don't."

And once again, Tess was rendered speechless. So instead of scrambling for the right words, instead of going over her notes as she had planned, she took off her jacket and spread it out on the ground to catch the dust, and lay carefully back so that she too could tip her head back and look up at the stars.

But before she did, she turned her head and watched Davina, whose face was soft and eyes were half shut already, and Tess realized—she realized that perhaps she had gotten Davina wrong. Perhaps she was right about there being more to life than toeing the lines laid out for you. Perhaps . . .

The thought drifted away from her as she drifted to sleep.

In the morning, Tess and Davina discovered that the town of Leeside had disappeared.

There was a signpost hammered into the ground that clearly stated *Welcome to Leeside*, but beyond that, there were only the same rolling hills and fields with which they'd become intimately acquainted.

Davina studied the post. "We're definitely in the right place. The town should be here."

And yet there was nothing. Tess felt faint. *This* was the exam? She'd studied years of academy exams. They were usually in the vein of an escaped vine-strangler or a vanishing shadow. Not . . . a *disappearing town?*

"We're going to fail," she murmured. It was her worst nightmare come to life. She'd never studied something like this—had never even *heard* of it, beyond vague mentions of higher magics. This was it. Years of study down the drain. She'd have to start over completely in another field, but who would have her? She would be a washout, completely pitiful, absolutely unemployable—

"Let's not be hasty," Davina said.

"*Hasty?*" Tess nearly shrieked. "Tell me, do *you* know what's going on here?"

"No," Davina admitted. "But the assignment didn't say we had to *fix* whatever is going on here. Just identify it."

Precise identification might be possible with a few days of study, Tess realized. Except that said study required most of the instruments that she had left behind at the inn. She moaned in dismay. "And how do you propose we do that?"

Davina's lips twitched in what Tess was *certain* was an ill-disguised smirk. "Well. Not sure yet." She stared at the space where Leeside was meant to be, then pulled an apple out of her pocket and took a large bite. *How* did she always have a snack with her?

Tess sank to the ground. This was worse than the inn. Two nights ago her fear had grown out of all the ways she could imagine the exam going wrong, but she had never imagined *this*. And Davina was treating it like it was just another day!

Davina. Tess closed her eyes, remembering Davina in the inn, the way their hands had touched. Davina had believed in her ability to handle whatever the academy threw their way. Davina still believed in her.

For precisely eighty-three seconds, Tess allowed herself to panic. Then she pulled herself together and opened her bag, sorting through its contents. The divining rod would be useless, unless the city had somehow been sucked underground without disturbing a single blade of grass. And her modified radial detector—*why* had she packed it? It barely worked, and only by practically jumping out of her hands every time it sensed a natural laws violation. The laboratory had been a veritable wreck after the last time she'd tested it, to her eternal mortification. Perhaps the thaumaturgy meter? She pulled out the box and fiddled with a few of the knobs. It wasn't her first choice—the sensors weren't up to current standards—but she'd brought it because it was capable of measuring along more than twenty vectors. Most of the state-of-the-art tools only did three or four.

"Well," she said a few moments later. "We can rule out anything having to do with electricity. And it does seem unlikely that this is the work of a *single* mage. Perhaps a group?"

"But for what purpose?" Davina asked. There was usually a narrative behind whatever magical malfeasance the academy had devised. Two or more mages conspiring to disappear a town because . . .

"Ascendance of a great evil?" Tess said.

Davina laughed. That was what Professor Territ said every time there was no immediate explanation for an instance of magic, no matter how small. True ascendance of evil hadn't been catalogued in decades.

Tess frowned as a dial on the meter twitched. "Wait. There is something. The ambient levels are shifting. Just barely."

"Ambient levels of magic?" Davina asked, her eyebrows creasing together.

Tess nodded. The two looked around at the open field. Once a magical casting was complete, ambient levels were stable. They should only be changing if a casting were still in progress. Which meant . . .

"Is it possible that Leeside is still here?" Davina said. "It seems unlikely that they could have *moved* it, given the exam budget."

"You mean—"

"What if the spell is still in progress? What if they turned it invisible? Or somehow camouflaged it?" Davina got up and put her hands in her pockets, then started down the road that should have led to the town.

Just then a very loud *meow* came out of nowhere. Tess clutched at her heart as there came another *meow*—and then, a small black cat stepped out of thin air onto the road, completely unconcerned about the chaos it had just caused.

Davina knelt down and offered a hand to the cat. The cat butted its head up against Davina's palm. She laughed. "I guess that settles it. Because this cat clearly just came from somewhere."

Tess's heart sank. "So we're going to have to go in."

Davina nodded. "I'm afraid so."

Tess stared into the empty space in front of them. What if they'd gotten this wrong and they were about to be yanked into a vortex curse? What if everyone in the town was dead? What if . . . There were too many bad possibilities.

She was tempted to simply turn around and go back to the academy.

But if she did, she would fail. And the academy wouldn't have created a problem that caused *lasting* harm . . .

"Fine," she said, straightening her blouse. "Well, there's no time like the present."

"All right," said Davina. She gave the cat one more scratch behind the ears and stood up. "I'll cast a warding charm."

Tess nodded sharply and stood still while Davina raised a hand and muttered under her breath. Once Davina was through, Tess rifled through her knapsack in search of anything that could be used as a weapon. The best she could come up with was freezing powder, which, if used in high enough quantities, could turn someone into a statue for a few minutes—or rather, just long enough to run away. She tucked the sachet of powder into her pocket.

"What do you think is in there?" she said.

Davina shrugged. "Nothing good."

Right. Tess was about to walk into the unknown with only freezing powder at her disposal. Wonderful.

She held out a hand to Davina. Davina raised an eyebrow.

"Just in case," she said.

Davina shrugged and took her hand. Tess swallowed around the sudden lump in her throat.

They stepped forward, the cat prancing in front of them.

It was a strange thing, vanishing.

Tess had no idea what to expect as the air shimmered around them and *here* became abruptly *not here*. Her fingers tightened instinctively. Davina squeezed her hand back.

The sensation was similar to that of squelching through mud, if the mud was higher than their heads. It was difficult for Tess to keep her eyes open. If it weren't for Davina's warding charm, it seemed possible they might become trapped, for this *was* some sort of magic, though what sort, she truly couldn't say.

And then they were through. Tess blinked hard into the sudden light. When her vision settled, she stood, gaping at what she saw.

They were standing in the center of a small town square. For the most part, everything looked as it should. There were trees and animals and colorful streamers hung between holdings. But one thing was very wrong. The people crowding the square stood still as statues.

"This is not right," Davina said slowly.

"Agreed," Tess said. Were all of the townsfolk playing along with the academy? This was on a scale so large, it didn't seem possible.

Davina carefully approached a plump woman with an open and friendly face. She was standing by a young ash tree, hands on her hips. She didn't move as Davina greeted her. Nor was there any response as Davina wrapped a scarf around her hand and tentatively touched the woman's shoulder. After a moment, Davina pushed slightly harder. The woman's body swayed at the impact—and then she fell backward onto the ground.

Davina flinched backward.

A cry of dismay escaped Tess's lips. The woman hadn't moved to catch herself. She lay prone, her smile fixed, her eyes vacant.

Tess stared at Davina. "Is she dead?"

Davina looked as though she was about to throw up. "She felt warm—alive. Just . . . not moving."

"And *this* is the exam?"

Davina shook her head. "I don't know."

Tess scanned the town square. Motion caught her eye—the black cat darted around a corner. But every person in the square remained utterly still.

A shiver ran down her spine. "There's something really wrong here. This is too much for the academy."

"Agreed."

However the people had been frozen, it must have been during a celebration. In addition to the streamers, there was a seated band frozen in mid-song, and everywhere there were baskets filled to the brim with golden pastries bearing the painted likeness of a dark-haired woman holding a thistle.

"Agathe's day," Davina said softly.

"That was a week ago!" Tess said. The cat appeared again, twining its tail around Tess's leg. "Not now," she muttered.

The cat let out an affronted *meow.*

"We should get out of here," Davina said. "Forget the exam, it's compromised anyway. And the academy needs to know about this."

Tess looked around. Davina was right. This was far beyond anything they'd encountered, but she wasn't sure how she felt about leaving all these people in this state. How could they have been trapped like this? Most of the square looked as though it had been frozen in place just as everyone was going about their day. Over in one corner, however, was a group that looked different, clustered in a way that seemed off, though Tess couldn't have described exactly how.

Tess walked toward the cluster.

"Where are you going?"

"I just want to see something." The more information they could bring back to the academy, the better. At least, that was what she told herself as she made her way across the square, giving the frozen people a wide berth.

As she approached, it became clear that there *was* something different about this group. They were standing too close together, each looking in a different direction. A child who had been skipping rope now lay on the ground on their back. It was as though someone had come along and moved them from their original frozen positions—which, given the fact that everyone in this town seemed to be frozen, meant that someone *had* done so.

Which meant that someone else had been here. Or was still here.

Davina came up to Tess's side, biting her lip as she studied the cluster. "They must still be here. Otherwise the town wouldn't be frozen." Instead of sounding terrified, she sounded almost . . . intrigued?

Tess nodded, thinking hard. Getting back to the academy would take at least three days. By then, whatever was happening here would be finished. Whoever was *doing* these things would be long gone.

"We don't have to stay," Davina said. But Tess could tell that given the choice, Davina would.

Tess shook her head. "We can do this," she said. "We should." Not because it was an exam, but because it was the right thing to do. Because if this was an incident of ascendance of great evil, what they did right now *mattered*. And even if it weren't, these poor people still didn't deserve to be frozen by . . . by whatever was going on around here.

Davina looked around the town square. "Right. Then we should operate under the assumption that whoever is here might know that *we're* here too. We can't assume that we have the element of surprise."

Suddenly, despite the fact that it was the middle of the day, everything about Leeside seemed shadowy and sinister.

"Then we should probably get out of sight," Tess said.

Roads and alleys branched out from the square like spokes of a wheel. After some investigation, they decided on an alley with only one frozen person standing at the very end, mid-stride. It was small and defensible, and there was a view of the cluster.

"All right," Tess said once they were settled, trying to breathe through the tightness in her chest, the panic that threatened to overwhelm her. "What do we know? We know the town disappeared. There are no trains. These people have been frozen for about one week, but they aren't dead."

"And we know that there's someone in this town moving bodies around," Davina said. "So we should keep watch and see if they come back to move more."

Tess tried unsuccessfully to mask her squeak of alarm. "And then what?"

Davina grimaced. "We'll have to evaluate our options when the time comes."

What a typically Davina thing to say—but this time Tess couldn't argue. They had no way to plan because they had no idea what they were dealing with. Davina's was the only way forward.

The waiting was not particularly interesting. As the sun moved they shifted to stay in the light. After a while, Davina pulled yet another cinnamon roll wrapped in a cloth napkin out of her pocket. Tess reached into the nearly empty breakfast basket and pulled out a miniature peach pie.

"I hope this doesn't take too long—this is my last roll," Davina said mournfully.

Despite her similar worries, Tess snickered.

Davina grinned at her, and didn't look away even when Tess's laughter faded and they were quiet again. Tess suddenly realized that maybe she wasn't the only one feeling—whatever it was that this was.

She swallowed and looked away. The moment passed.

Of course that was ridiculous. Davina was popular, she flirted with everyone, she could *have* anyone she chose. There was no way she'd ever felt the strange fluttering feeling in her stomach that Tess had now.

No. That simply wasn't possible. She turned her head and stared determinedly out at the town square.

♡

They waited for a long time. After a while they decided to trade shifts, and Tess was beginning to nod off when Davina jabbed her in the ribs. "Look," she whispered.

There, on the other side of the square, something was moving.

Dusk had well fallen, but they could still see two people moving across the square. One was pushing a wheelbarrow. They walked over to the clustered group. There was a pause as they appeared to confer, and then the figures tipped two of the frozen people into the wheelbarrow. Tess winced as they landed.

The mysterious figures retreated the way they'd come.

Davina was already on her feet as they rounded a corner and disappeared from view. "Hurry up, or we'll lose them."

Tess tensed, but she grabbed her bag and followed.

As it turned out, it wasn't all that difficult to follow someone pushing a wheelbarrow that held two bodies. Tess and Davina trailed them to a large warehouse and waited as the newcomers opened the door and vanished inside. Davina picked up a stick, murmured an incantation, and tossed it toward the door as it began to close. The stick caught on the threshold, leaving the door cracked open.

Davina grabbed Tess's hand, and they made their way to the door.

"This is it," Davina said. "If you want to turn back, now's the time."

Tess shook her head, and pulled open the door.

It seemed they needn't have taken such care after all, for the noise in the warehouse was more than enough to mask their arrival. The sound was emanating from a strange machine at the end of the warehouse. It looked almost like a large tent placed over a moving conveyer belt. Atop the tent sat a translucent bubble that gave off a silvery, moonlit glow. They crept forward, watching as the people loaded one body onto the conveyer belt. Tess wanted to cover her eyes. She settled for covering her mouth as the person disappeared into the machine.

"Come on," whispered Davina. She led the way forward, creeping behind cargo crates as she made her way closer to the machine and the people.

Tess watched as the conveyer belt came out the other end of the machine. At least the frozen person looked untouched—but *something* must have happened.

The machine quieted, and the sound of voices clarified into words.

". . . should only be seven tonight."

"We only got four years out of that one," said the person putting the second body on the belt. They wore an unreasonably long black cloak. "If they're all like this, we might have to do another town."

Years . . . Time? These strange mages—they had to be mages, especially with the overly dramatic cloaks—had figured out a way to steal time?

Davina and Tess looked at each other, horrified. Time was one of the most potent magical ingredients, but its distribution and use were heavily restricted due to how ethically questionable it was to produce. Neither of them had ever worked with it, though Tess had once seen a demonstration.

The bubble on top of the machine swelled and glowed brighter. *Time.* That's what it held.

"We need to figure out how to break that machine," Davina said. "At least that way they'll have to stop what they're doing."

There was a lump in Tess's throat and an unexpected pit of rage in her stomach. These people couldn't be allowed to get away with this. She grabbed her bag and sorted through it, though honestly she didn't know what she thought she would find.

Something twitched against her fingers. The radial detector.

Of course, it was twitching—this was an exceptional violation of natural laws. It wanted to jump . . . which gave Tess a very Davina-y idea. The fabric of the machine couldn't be stronger than Professor Verene's triple-layered glass salamander cases. If she let it fly . . .

She only needed a clear shot.

"I have an idea," Tess whispered. "Cover me?"

She crept forward, the radial detector in one hand. Davina was right behind her.

The two mages were arguing now about whether to process an extra three people or an extra five. Tess crouched behind a crate and held her breath as they passed in front of her, cloaks flaring as they walked.

Leave, she thought. If they would just leave, she could take her time with the detector, and if *that* failed, then she could, oh, find a stick somewhere and smash the machine to bits.

Of course, it was at that exact moment that the cat decided to saunter into the light.

One of the mages sneezed. "How did a cat get in here—Hey!"

Tess looked up, into the mage's eyes. She smiled apologetically, then burst upright, toppling the crate forward and knocking the mages to the floor. She ran for the machine and lifted the radial detector. Then she whispered the incantation and threw the detector into the air.

The detector spun around, hesitated, and slammed sideways against the machine. It tore right through the bubble, releasing wisps of luminous smoke—time—into the air. Fierce triumph slammed through Tess's chest. For the first time, she was deeply satisfied at having wreaked havoc.

Davina's hand was on her shoulder as she whispered a warding spell. Tess reached into her pocket for the freezing powder and turned around, ready to face the mages.

They had managed to pull themselves out from under the crate, but as they stood and took in the damage to the machine, their eyes widened. They glanced at each other—then turned around and ran.

Tess didn't hesitate. She ran after them, and Davina ran after her.

The mages fled out of the warehouse and down the street. They were clearly familiar with these streets, but Tess was faster. And she was gaining.

She chased them around a turn, down an alley and through yet another small street—and then suddenly found herself in a series of carefully manicured gardens lit from above by floating lanterns. *Pretty,* Tess thought as she slowed to a stop, breathing hard.

They were here, hiding. She could feel it.

There was a rustle on the other side of the garden and Tess sprinted forward, freezing powder at the ready.

One mage sprang out of a bush just ahead of her, flinging something small to the ground. The world seemed to slow as Tess watched it fall. The object hit the earth, and where it landed, an enormous olive tree sprung into being right in the middle of the path. Tess swerved at the last moment but tripped nevertheless. She fell hard against the trunk. The tree branches shivered, and a strange, silvery powder shook off of its leaves and drifted down toward her.

Tess closed her eyes and put a hand over her mouth, but it was too late. She had already inhaled it.

"Tess! Tess!"

"No, don't come any closer!"

The world began to tilt. Tess turned, throwing out a hand to stop Davina's approach—and watched as the sachet of freezing powder flew through the air.

"No!"

The sachet fell to the ground several feet short of hitting Davina, and Tess began to giggle.

"Tess? Are you all right?"

Was she all right? *Was* she all right? She didn't know anymore. Why was she on the ground? And why was the ground moving?

"I think—something has got me. Magically speaking, I mean." Tess was vaguely aware that it had something to do with the mage. She patted the trunk of the olive tree. "This is a new tree. New to me."

She stood up. Rather, she *attempted* to stand up, but one of her legs did an odd little loop and she fell right back to the ground where she had begun. Which was really quite funny, actually.

But the ground had begun to roil, really move, and now it seemed that the appropriate course of action—the *only* course of action—was to hug the olive tree for dear life.

"Tess? Come on, then. We need to get moving."

Was there a cat talking to her? No—no, that was Davina. Tess squinted up at her, then fell back in horror. Davina had been turned inside out! She was nothing more than a purplish blob! A blob was speaking to her!

She gasped, aghast. "What have they done to you?" she whispered.

"Me?" the blob wobbled. "I'm perfectly fine. *You*, on the other hand, have been rightly discombobulated."

"Dis—discomboboo—" Tess started giggling again.

"It must be the tree," the blob said. It retreated momentarily. Then it reappeared. "All right, Tess. I need you to come over here, toward me."

"Noooooo," Tess said.

"Tess, I can't help you as long as you're hanging onto that tree. You have to come to me."

"So that I can turn into a blooob? No, thank you," Tess said.

"Tess," the blob said, sounding infinitely patient. "I'm not a blob."

"Davina, you have turned into a blob," Tess replied. This wasn't funny anymore. In fact, it was starting to feel . . . scary? Because Davina shouldn't be a blob. Davina was—she squinted up at the blob again. "Are you in there? If you are, you're going to have to come out of there."

"How about I make you a deal? How about you come out from under the tree, and then I'll come out of the blob?"

Tess shook her head emphatically. It seemed quite likely that the blob was going to swallow her too. Which meant—which meant that somehow, it was very important to say this in case she was about to die.

"I'm rather vexed with you, actually," she said.

"Really?" said the blob with Davina's voice.

She sniffled. It was sad—very sad. "How could you have let yourself be eaten by a blob? It doesn't make sense. Because . . . because you're so *enthusiastic* about everything. And *cheerful*, all the time! It's rather alarming. And your hair is purple— why would a blob want to eat someone with purple hair?" She could feel herself starting to drift, but if she did, the blob would certainly eat her. "You're too beautiful to be eaten, actually. But you're also very insufferable so perhaps it's a fitting end"— here she sobbed, just once, before pulling herself together again—"but the fact of the matter is . . . the fact of the matter is . . . I lied. You're not insufferable at all, I just never realized it because I was an utter buffoon—and now you're a *blob* and one cannot confess that they are rather infatuated with a *blob*, even one as dashing as you, so it's too late. For me. And for you. Which is rather unfortunate. Because—because I really would have liked to gather the courage to kiss you one day. And . . . because I know how much you love snacks. And blobs don't eat snacks."

And at that point she had to stop talking, because the ground had started shaking quite violently, and it was all she could do to hold on to the olive tree and keep herself from being shaken apart. And then, abruptly, there was blackness.

♡

Tess woke with a pounding headache. She blinked. At first there was only bright light. As she blinked again, the light began to resolve into a scene. She was in a room, on a bed. There was a nightstand next to the bed with a glass of water on it. Something leaped up onto the bed—the black cat.

"Hello," she whispered. Her tongue felt swollen and dry. She sat up slowly, reaching for the glass of water.

The door opened, and Davina walked into the room. She glanced at the bed, then smiled. "You're awake!" she said.

"You sound surprised," Tess croaked. "How long have I been out? Where are we?"

"Three days. And back at the inn."

Tess stared up at her. "Three . . . days? What happened?"

"You don't remember?" Davina frowned, a crease appearing between her eyebrows.

For a moment Tess didn't—and then it all came rushing back to her. Leeside, the machine, the mages, the tree—and those *mortifying* things she had said. She looked down, hoping that she wasn't blushing. "I remember Leeside. And there was a chase?"

"*You* were the chase," Davina said slowly. "You led the way after those mages. And then you got snared by some sort of befuddling spell."

"Right . . . ," Tess said, trying to sound agreeable yet confused.

"You really don't remember?"

She swallowed and shook her head slowly. "Most of it's a blur. Did you—did you turn into a blob?"

Davina stared at her. And then she laughed. "Tess Griffin, you're excellent at many things. But one thing you are not excellent at is lying."

Tess's cheeks flamed. "Oh no," she moaned, flinging herself back and covering her face with a pillow. "Don't judge me on that, I was befuddled. I hardly knew what I was saying!"

She was mortified. Utterly mortified. Confessing such things to *Davina Winter*, of all people—Davina, who had girls falling over her all the time. Davina, who had never taken her seriously at *anything*. Davina, who she'd spent *years* convincing herself of her utter indifference toward—

Davina's voice floated down at her from somewhere above the pillow. "Didn't you?"

Tess froze. "Didn't I . . . what?"

The pillow lifted off her face. "Didn't you know what you were saying?" Davina asked quietly. Their noses were almost touching. Tess had never realized quite how dark Davina's eyes were.

"I—"

"If you meant those things, Tess, you can't take them back. Because I've spent the last three days waiting for you to wake up so that I could say some *very similar* things back to you."

"You—you have?" Tess said. Something quite peculiar was happening. Her heart was threatening to beat right out of her chest. "But—you've always had so many other girls admiring you."

"Well, I've always rather liked *you*," Davina said. "Because you're an excellent scholar, and adorably precise, and you're funny when you don't mean to be, and *very* pretty.

"You just never took your nose out of a book long enough for me to get your attention. Don't you understand that I've been flirting with you this entire time?"

"But—but you flirt with everybody!" Tess cried.

"Maybe so. But not the same way I flirt with you."

And then she leaned down and kissed her.

Davina kissed her and it was like the answer to a question she'd only recently realized she'd wanted to ask. Like the world had paused, just for a moment, and Tess wanted it to never start again. There were only the two of them, Tess's hand curled around Davina's neck, Davina's fingers against Tess's cheek, lips against lips—

Meow! And a disgruntled cat, pushing between them to demand attention.

Davina laughed, and reached over to scratch the cat's ears. Tess could barely catch her breath. There was so much running through her mind, and strangely, the first thing that passed her lips was, "What happened to the mages?"

Davina waved a hand dismissively. "Ran out of town, the cowards. Clearly they were just lackeys, as they weren't particularly bright—once they crossed the town border, the freeze spell collapsed."

"So everyone's all right," Tess said, relieved.

"Pretty much," Davina said. "Of course, now there's the question of who ordered the whole operation, and why . . . Want to go poke around? I've already submitted our final exam report, of course." She winked. "Don't worry, they didn't *dare* fail us after all that."

So they'd passed the exam. Tess was surprised to feel only mild satisfaction at the news. A week ago this was all she had wanted—but the Tess of a week ago had cared only about the academy, the exam, the DMI, her *mother* . . .

Things had changed, Tess realized. She suspected they had changed very much for the better.

She placed a hand in Davina's and raised an eyebrow right back at her. "Why not? As long as it's with you."

EDGES

"The Grumpy One and the Soft One"

Ashley Herring Blake

CLOVER TRIPS AS SHE MAKES HER WAY ACROSS THE CAFETERIA TO her normal table. I watch it all happen. First her feet tangle and her tray tilts toward the floor. Then her body goes down. Soggy tater tots and, unfortunately, chocolate pudding smear all over her pretty little cardigan. She's splayed out on her belly, the bottoms of her heeled oxfords pointing toward the fluorescent-lit ceiling.

For a split second, the whole room holds its breath. Then she rolls over and starts laughing, plunging the entire senior class of Stoney River High School into convivial hysterics. She stands up, tortoise-shell glasses askew, wiping at her eyes and giggling while her friends cluck around her and dab at her sweater. Then she does this little curtsy that would be ridiculous if she wasn't so damn cute. The crowd goes wild, clapping and showering her with napkins. This absurd scene goes on for at least five minutes until Ms. Clearwater, one of the orchestra teachers, breaks it up.

I turn away, shaking my head as I poke at my rubbery cheeseburger. If that had happened to me, I doubt anyone would notice. The few who did certainly wouldn't be laughing *with* me.

I take one last stale bite of my lunch and then get up, eager to leave my solitary spot and retreat to the library. Usually, I eat outside, but it's freezing, the New Hampshire winter clouds aching with snow, and I was too hungry to skip lunch altogether. I don't mind eating alone. But eating alone while surrounded by a hundred other people who are decidedly *not* eating alone is not my favorite activity.

"Mac!"

Ever since my twin sister, Imogen, left for Huntley-Egars Academy, this performing arts boarding school in California, I'm not exactly flush with friends, so usually, when I hear anything that sounds remotely like *Mac*, short for Mackenzie, I barely even notice. But this time, it's the voice that stops me more than anything. I turn to see Clover heading right toward me, auburn hair falling in perfect shiny waves around her shoulders, despite her tumble. Her clothes are a different story. I doubt that sky blue cardigan will live to see another day.

"Hey," she says, still breathless from her little performance.

"Um . . . hi." I want to ask if she's okay. She did fall, after all. I really want to pluck the piece of lettuce out of her hair, feel the familiar silk between my fingers, but I can't do any of that. I won't.

Clover and I don't interact in public. I'm not really sure why. There's this unspoken rule and I can't decide if I'm okay with it or not. Her friends know that her parents are paying me to give her drawing lessons to amp up her college applications, but that's where our connection ends. At least, as far as everyone at school knows. It's like she's two different people. Or maybe I'm two different people. Maybe we both are, and all those little moments stolen in the quiet of my house are just that—*stolen* from our real lives.

If there's such a thing as a queer queen bee, Clover Hillock is it. She's on the competition cheerleading squad. She's second in our class and, by the time June rolls around, will probably have edged out Mateo Mendoza for valedictorian. She dresses like Audrey Hepburn and wears these glasses that make her look like a sexy librarian. She is my opposite, in almost every way, and I feel a familiar mask glossing over my features as she smiles at me.

"Did you see my epic fall?" she asks, laughing.

"Yeah, I caught that."

"I'm such a klutz."

"If you say so."

She frowns at my tone and wipes a hand down her stained sweater. She pulls her bottom lip between her teeth like she's nervous. But she can't possibly be nervous because I'm me and she's her.

"Well," she says, "I was just making sure we're still on for tonight. It's time to learn some shading, right?"

Her best friends, Sofía and Haley, hover behind her, running their eyes over my uniform of late—dark hair in a perpetually messy topknot, gray jeans, and a dark purple fleece hoodie, which technically belongs to Imogen. I was always stealing it from her, stuffing it in my backpack before she could grab it for herself or hiding it under my bed on laundry day. It became a game between us: who could get the hoodie first and who could steal it back the fastest. She even yanked it right off my waist in the hallway between classes one time, knowing I couldn't chase her down without getting detention for being late.

"I'll get a lighter one in California," she'd said back in June as I helped her pack. Her clothes were everywhere, veritable mountains of jeans and T-shirts on her bed and floor. She folded the hoodie and then tossed it into my lap. To anyone else, it would sound like she was rubbing her whole adventure in my face, but I know Imogen. She was just being my sister, trying to let me keep at least one thing that I loved.

I pull my hands inside the hoodie sleeves and stuff them into the pockets. "Yeah, of course we're still on," I tell Clover, making my voice softer. It perks her right up, which in turn, makes me frown. We're a see-saw of facial expressions.

"My self-portrait needs some serious help," she says.

"Can't deny that."

She smiles, revealing that little gap between her two front teeth that I love and hate the fact that I love it. "Hey, be nice."

"I'm being honest. When it comes to art, that's better than nice."

"So being honest means acting like a bitch?" Haley asks, folding her arms and glaring at me.

I lift a brow in her direction. "Sometimes."

"And you wonder why everyone misses Imogen and you have no friends."

"Haley, chill," Clover says.

"Who says I wonder?" I ask.

Sofía chokes a laugh and Haley rolls her eyes. Meanwhile, Clover just looks at me, that same kind of investigative glint in her eyes she gets whenever I show her my Frida Kahlo prints, like she's trying to dig under the layers of paint to get to the artist herself.

"Come on, Clo," Haley says, hooking her arm through Clover's.

"I guess I'll see you later," Clover finally says. She pauses, just enough for me to want her to pause a little longer, before she turns and disappears into her adoring throng.

"See you," I say to her back, almost wishing I'd told her I had other plans tonight.

Almost, but not quite.

♡

I lean closer to my sister's face on the computer screen, tapping the volume key until it's at full blast. Imogen's smile is wide and bright, practically neon, but I can still barely hear what she's saying over all the noise in the background. There are at least five girls behind her. Some of them are eating chips, some of them are tearing open packages of Oreos, all of them are laughing and loud. I catch the glint of a bottle of some brown liquid passed from mouth to mouth.

"We can do this tomorrow," I say.

"What? No, it's fine," Imogen says, waving off the chaos behind her.

A bright orange Cheeto flies across the room and lands in her messy bun. "You guys, stop!" she snaps, but she's grinning. Then she plucks the Cheeto from her hair and pops it into her mouth. Her friends erupt into more laughter.

"Sorry," she says, rolling her eyes at me while she crunches. "They just showed up in my room with all this stuff."

"Dorm life," I say.

"Right?" she chirps. "God, it's wild."

"How's the musical?"

"Ugh, so stressful." An Oreo plunks into her lap to more giggling. She simply picks up the cookie and starts munching on it.

"You love it," I say. Imogen is playing Little Red Riding Hood in *Into the Woods*, which is perfect for her rich mezzo voice.

She sighs and tucks a stray lock of dark brown hair behind her ear. "I do. Mac, it's so amazing here. The teachers actually *know* stuff and have stage experience and I feel like I'm already so much better."

"That's awesome." Except that I say it like it's the worst thing in the world, something that Imogen doesn't miss.

She clears her throat and dusts Oreo crumbs from her fingers. "Is it snowing there yet?"

"We got a few inches last week. It's just cold now."

"I miss it. It feels like spring here." As if for emphasis, she snaps the strap of her tank top against her shoulder.

"You hated the cold."

"Yeah, but sixty degrees in January is weird."

I nod and pick at my cuticles. Are we really talking about the weather?

"Hey, what's going on with Clover Hillock?" she asks.

My head snaps up. "What?"

"Grant told me you're giving her art lessons or something? Why didn't you tell me?"

Freaking Grant Silver. I should've known my sister's ex-boyfriend—who, for the record, is still totally in love with her and she's still totally in love with him but neither one will admit it because long distance sucks or something stupid like that—would report my every move.

"Because it's no big deal. I teach her how to draw a line. Then a circle. Sometimes we add a leaf to a tree or a nose to a face. Then I show her how to pick up a colored pencil and fill it all in. End of story."

She narrows her eyes at me and I press my lips together.

"She came out last spring, right?"

I huff an annoyed sigh. "You know she did. I'm amazed the *New York Times* didn't pick it up." If you're Clover Hillock, you don't announce that you're as gay as a glitter-covered rainbow without a lot of people taking notice. And by a lot, I mean our entire town of five thousand and something residents.

Imogen points a finger at me. "And you're bi," she says, like I don't know. Unfortunately, she pretty much yelled it to be heard over her friends' caterwauling, meaning all five of them have now clamped their mouths shut and are staring at me while my face pinkens on Imogen's tiny silver computer screen.

"Oops," she says, wincing.

"Whatever." I wave a hand.

It's not like I'm in the closet. I'm out everywhere and have been for a year. But Imogen was the first person I ever told and she knows how hard it was to tell anyone else. Our divorced parents. Our group of friends. Everyone was cool about it, even my stodgy Catholic grandmother who said, to Imogen's and my utter shock and delight, "I kissed my roommate in college. I kind of liked it." Still, all the acceptance didn't make the process any less nerve-wracking.

Then there was my boyfriend at the time, Danny, who I had been dating for a year and a half. I guess I didn't have to tell him. I wasn't planning on the fact that I was attracted to girls, attracted to *people*, affecting our relationship. But once I figured out this part of myself, I felt like I was lying by keeping it from him. Plus, I wanted him to know me and I thought he wanted to know me too. And maybe he did, but first, he panicked.

"Does this mean you want to, like, have a threesome?" he asked. "Because I don't know, Mac. That sort of freaks me out."

I remember gaping at him, totally clueless as to how he got from *Sometimes, I'm attracted to girls and nonbinary people* to *threesome*.

"Good riddance, asshole," Imogen had said when I broke up with him. I had nodded in agreement, but I had liked Danny. Maybe even loved. Imogen knew this and even while she rattled off all of his quasi-terrible qualities, she ran her fingers through my hair as I lay in her lap, tears soaking into her jeans.

And now she's just . . . telling people, like it's nothing, forgetting that it's not hers to tell, that it actually matters to me.

"I'm really sorry," Imogen says, her expression serious now.

Still, she doesn't move to go into the hall or anything. I'd prefer a phone conversation over this and I despise phone conversations. Behind her, her friends slowly come back to life, rattling chip bags and taking selfies.

"Okay," I say, picking at my cuticles.

"I'm just saying, Clover's pretty."

"She's also smart and not a complete bore. What's your point?"

Imogen smirks at me. "You just made it."

My heart flits toward my stomach. I think about Clover, about how after we finish her lesson—if that's even what you'd call my inept instructions on how to draw eyelashes and irises—we usually hang out for hours. We settle on the worn sofa in my living room and watch old episodes of *Buffy the Vampire Slayer*. My mom was borderline obsessed with the show in college and introduced Imogen and me to it when we were fourteen. Clover and I laugh at the campy special effects and stuff our faces with white cheddar popcorn. Sometimes, I don't even watch the show. I just watch Clover watching it. It's amazing, witnessing someone love something, even if it's a cheesy nineties vampire show.

Clover crowds my thoughts more and more lately, like a craving, and I don't think I like it. I *can't* like it.

"So, because she's gay and I'm bi and she's not hideous to be around, that automatically means we're going to hook up?" I ask Imogen. I don't know why this is what comes out of my mouth, but somehow, denying any connection to Clover feels super important right now.

Imogen frowns. "No, I just—"

"Because that's not how this works."

"I know that."

"Do you make out with every dude you find moderately attractive?"

"No. God, Mac."

"You're being an awful straight person right now."

Imogen's face turns red, her eyes darting to the girls behind her who are now crowded around one phone, eyes wide as some extremely loud video plays.

"I'm just trying to ask how you are," she says. "You know, things about your life. Like sisters do."

Sisters don't leave sisters to figure out crushes and kissing and secrets all alone is what I think.

"My life is peachy" is what I say.

"Mallory says you never hang out with them," Imogen says.

"Mallory is your best friend, not mine."

"She's still your friend. She says you stopped answering her texts."

"She was probably relieved."

"Do you even hear yourself?"

I shake my head and run my finger along the crease in my jeans. Truth is, I don't fit with Mallory anymore, if I ever really did. After Imogen left, she and Alice and Brianna invited me to stuff, but it always felt so forced, like they did it out of some loyalty to Imogen. Eventually, ignoring Mallory's texts was easier than trying to convince myself they wanted me with them. We all grew up together, but Imogen was my person, the glue that attached me to the world. And everyone seemed to know it but me. I went to a movie with Mom once, right after Imogen left, on a Friday night no less, and there Mallory and the others were, a happy little trio linked at the elbows.

"I need to go," I say now.

"Mac, come on, don't—"

But I snap my laptop closed before she can finish her patronizing sentence.

Mom texts to say she'll be late again. She's a real estate agent, one of the highest sellers in our town, and she's never home during what anyone would consider normal hours. Dad's been gone since we were six. Divorce lodged a bullet in the leg of our family, and then his decision to leave New Hampshire and move to Chicago with his high school sweetheart five years ago sent another straight to the heart.

All of this was fine before Imogen left. She was my partner in abandonment, the only one who understood what it was like to miss our mom even when she was sleeping down the hall. On Mom's late nights, we'd ignore her "There's a pizza in the freezer" instructions and make our own dinner, always trying to one-up the other on who could put together the weirdest—but still tasty—meal. Currently, Imogen has me beat with a legendary pasta-with-peanut-sauce-and-melted-cheddar-cheese concoction. It was horrifically delicious.

Lately, the quiet gets so thick that I sometimes flick on a random TV show just to feel like someone else is here.

I'm on the couch in the living room, glaring at my calculus textbook while a ridiculously attractive couple tells me how to flip a house, when the doorbell rings. One glance at the clock—seven thirty on the dot—tells me exactly who it is. Clover is absurdly punctual.

I dig myself out of the sofa, my half-eaten apple slices browning on the coffee table, and make my way to the door. Through the cut glass inlay, I can see her outline, and can tell she's standing with her hands folded in front of her, one hip popped out to the side. Her hair is up in a ponytail, exposing her graceful neck. My stomach fills with feathers. It's strange, how you can both hate and love something at the exact same time.

I open the door and Clover grins at me, dimples sinking into her cheeks.

"It's snowing!" she says, bringing in a rush of frigid air as she steps into the mudroom. Her Tiffany-blue peacoat is dusted with white.

"Ugh, again?" I ask, peering into the dark of the open door. Tiny silver specks fall from the sky, so slight I almost don't see them. Our house is surrounded by lavender fields that bloom purple in the summer, but in January, it's just dark, dark, and more dark as far as the eye can see. Plus, our driveway is about a mile long, cutting off the streetlight on the main road.

"You are such a winter wimp. Snow is *magical.*" She waves her hand toward the still-open front door before shrugging off her coat and hanging it on the brass hooks on the wall. Then she unzips her boots and tucks them into the cubby already overflowing with Mom's and my shoes. I watch her, mesmerized by how she knows where everything goes, by the graceful dance going on between her arms and legs and all the little things in my house.

"Magic. So, dry skin and numb toes are magical?"

She rolls her eyes, but she's smiling. "My little curmudgeon."

I stick my tongue out at her, but my breath hitches. *My.* It's the closest either one of us has come to acknowledging whatever it is we're doing together with actual words.

I grab a couple cans of soda and a bag of white cheddar popcorn from the kitchen, then we head upstairs to my room. Clover plops onto my bed and starts unpacking her bag, stacking her sketchbook and pack of cheap charcoals onto my navy comforter.

I set the food and drinks on my desk and sit on the edge of the bed, waiting as she organizes all of her stuff into neat little rows and columns. I know the drill by now, know exactly how she needs her surroundings before she can concentrate. Her gaze snags on mine and she smiles, a blush rising to her cheeks as she looks away and sharpens a pencil.

A knot tangles in my throat, sudden, ridiculous tears creeping into my eyes. I wipe them away before she can see, but I'm too late. When I glance back up, she's watching me, a concerned wrinkle between her brows.

"What's wrong?"

I shake my head. "Nothing. Something in my eye, that's all."

"I know when you're bullshitting, Mac."

I squeeze my eyes closed, but she's right. She does know. And I don't understand why. I don't understand what she's doing here, why she keeps coming back, why every time she leaves, I have to put my head between my knees until I can breathe the right way.

"Hey."

The mattress shakes with movement and when I open my eyes, she's right there, inches from my face.

"You can tell me," she says.

"I don't know what to tell. I'm just . . . I don't know."

Her hands drift up and she tucks my hair behind my ears, her fingers lingering on my neck. My blood runs hot, filling my stomach with heat. But it's more than that, more than just wanting to kiss or be touched. It's like a hunger, a bone-deep need for nourishment. I grip her wrists and pull her closer. Our foreheads bump, her glasses cool on my cheek, and I sigh out some relief.

"We should work on your facial shading," I say, but I don't really mean it.

"We are," she says. Her breath smells like winter, like warmth and mint. She traces a finger over the bridge of my nose and down my cheek, then around my ear and over my temple, sliding across my forehead to the other side until she's cupping my jaw. "See? I'm learning right now what a beautiful portrait looks like."

"Oh my god, that is such a line."

She laughs, her head arching back a little. I press my nose to her throat, then my lips, and her laugh vanishes.

She tugs on my hair a little, pulling my face up to hers until our mouths slide together. My tongue finds hers and her fist tightens in my hair, the best kind of ache radiating from my scalp all the way down my legs. I shift her back and she falls onto the bed, bouncing a little with me on top of her, my mouth never leaving hers. She laughs, wrapping one leg around me and I settle between her hips. We've never done this before, tangle like this, gliding between limbs, soft curling around soft. It makes me feel feral and starved.

"Is this okay?" I ask, sliding my hand under her fresh, pudding-free sweater and pausing.

"Yes." Her hips press against mine, and my teeth graze her lower lip before sliding down her neck to her collarbone to her stomach. I settle my mouth there, taste her, run my finger over the waistband of her jeans, but I don't go any lower. We haven't done any of this yet and I don't know how she feels about it all.

I let my hand drift up, passing clumsily over her bra, soft skin everywhere, before moving it back down to her waist again. Then her hip. Each spot feels like a destination, a new and beautiful city I've never been to before. I glide my thumb over the waist of her jeans again, freezing on the button.

"Do you want to?" I ask, my mouth muffled against her stomach.

"Do I . . ." Her heavy breathing stops and her whole body tenses under mine. "Wait, do I what?"

I quickly pull my hand away, sitting up while she scoots back and pulls her sweater down.

"What's wrong?" I ask. "Are you okay?"

She swallows, shaking her head and picking her pencil back up. She stares at a blank page in her sketchbook.

I blink at her, a horrible feeling like I've made a huge mistake washing over me. "I'm sorry. I didn't mean to pressure you. *Did* I pressure you?"

"No, you asked, so thanks for that, I guess." Her tone is flat. She drops the pencils again before pulling her legs up to her chest and resting her forehead on her knees.

"What just happened?" I ask.

She shakes her head, but doesn't lift it to look at me.

"Clover."

Finally, she meets my eyes. "Did . . . did you know you were my first kiss?"

"What?" I feel my eyes widen. "Like . . . ever?"

She nods.

"You never kissed a guy?"

She tucks her hair behind her ears, her throat bobbing in a hard swallow. "No. I had some chances, but something always stopped me. I think I've known I was gay for a long time. Like, maybe since I was ten or so."

I blink at her. "Okay. Well. You're the first girl I've kissed. I still don't understand why you're upset."

She sits back against my headboard and looks at me. Her eyes bore into me for way too long and I start to squirm, start to wonder what she sees, what flaws, what deficiencies.

"I want to know why you were about to cry earlier," she says, quiet as the snow outside.

"What?"

"I want you to tell me why you were about to cry, when we first got to your room and I was unpacking my stuff, and you—"

"I remember."

"Okay. So?"

"What does that have to do with anything?"

"Everything."

We stare at each other, my chest a grid of taut wires. Finally, she shakes her head and pushes herself off the bed. She starts packing her bag.

"Clover, wait—"

"Why do you think I asked you to teach me drawing?"

"Because you want to go to Yale or Harvard or . . ."

"Vanderbilt. It's always been Vanderbilt, which I told you when I asked you about some lessons three months ago after AP English."

"Okay. I'm sorry—"

"But it's not about Vanderbilt. It's not about college apps or my parents. They don't give two shits because I've already been accepted to Vanderbilt. Early decision."

I blink at her.

"I asked you because I like you. I think you're smart and talented and kind of weird, but in the best way. The portraits you draw are incredible. The ones you displayed at the art show last year? Of your sister and you separately and then how you blended them together, but you could still tell which part of the face was you and which part was her? I've never seen anything like that. The way you draw faces makes me feel more . . . I don't know. Just *more*. Like whole worlds live in our eyes and mouths. And then when we kissed that first time . . ."

I swallow hard, the memory sharp and lovely and awful. We were watching Buffy battle a truly terrifying demonic puppet, sitting on the couch in my living room, and I don't even know how it happened. We just kept drifting closer. My pinkie touched her pinkie, then our arms pressed together and somehow, my foot got wrapped around her ankle. Finally, miraculously, she shifted so her body was facing my body and I knew. I knew I was going to kiss her. I knew she wanted me to.

"We spilled the bowl of popcorn," I say.

She smiles. "I spilled it. My knee knocked it over when you put your hand on my face."

"I did?" I ask quietly, even though I remember it. I remember my hand shook with fear or happiness or something else I wasn't used to, how her mouth parted and her eyes went soft the second my fingers touched her cheek.

"I thought things would change," she says. "That you'd start talking to me at school or ask me out, but I—"

"Whoa, whoa, what do you mean start talking to you at school?"

"You ignore me, Mac. You walk right by me. You're rude when I ask you the simplest question. I don't even feel like I can tell my best friends about us. Unless we're at your house, you're totally closed off like you were earlier today."

"I didn't think you really wanted to talk to me."

Her face crumples a little, but she smoothes it out fast. "Can't you tell that I like you? Why wouldn't I want to talk to you?"

"Because you're—" *Clover Hillock* is what I think. *And I'm me.*

But right now, Clover Hillock isn't the one looking at me like I'm someone to be avoided, someone to be left, someone who's her dirty little secret.

That's how I'm looking at her.

She glances down, her lower lip pressing hard against her top. "Just forget it."

"Clover, hang on—"

"I said, forget it." She throws her bag over her shoulders. "I obviously had this all wrong."

Before I can think of how to respond to that, she's in the hallway. I hear her feet on the steps, feel the house shake as she slams the front door. I go to my window and watch her climb into her car and then she's gone, my little secret vanishing into the snowy night.

It's nearly ten o'clock by the time Mom gets home. I'm on the couch, an untouched bowl of white cheddar popcorn in my lap and *Buffy* muted on the TV while I roll over and over my conversation—fight?—with Clover. I can't get my mind around it, that Clover likes me, that I'm the one hiding her, that I pretty much asked her to have sex but didn't even realize that's what I was doing.

How did I not know?

How did I not know any of it?

I groan and sink lower into the couch cushions, wishing they'd swallow me whole.

"Oh, I love this episode," Mom says, plopping down next to me, her white blouse still fresh-looking and wrinkle-free. She kicks her feet up on the coffee table and we sit there in silence, our eyes glued to the show and a black-eyed Willow ready to destroy the world. Mom doesn't even ask me to turn on the sound. After about ten minutes, she sighs and gets up, stretching her arms above her head like a cat.

"I'm beat. Don't stay up too late," she says, bending down to drop a kiss on the top of my head. Then she drifts away and the only sound in the whole house is the soft click of her bedroom door snapping shut.

The tears come fast and hard and silent. Everything is so damn quiet, all the time. I pick up my phone to text Imogen, but then just stare at the screen, my fingers still. She's already texted me about a dozen apologies and a few cat GIFs, but none of it really helps. She can't fix the quiet, the lonely, her empty bedroom.

Since my sister left, only one person makes me feel like I'm not folding in on myself. Only one person has really been *my* person, but I didn't think—no, I couldn't believe—that I might be her person too.

The thought makes me cry harder, louder. It's a beautiful sound, really, because my tears, the way my breath hiccups, shatter the silence. I look at the bowl in my lap and knock it off, white puffs of popcorn skittering across the carpet.

♡

Everyone knows where Clover Hillock's house is. She hosts quarterly parties at her spacious modern Craftsman, including a huge pool party at the end of every summer since seventh grade. I'd even been to a few of her soirees, tagging along with Imogen and Mallory, ever the wallflower with the Solo cup of Coke without the Jack, watching my sister light every room.

I remember noticing Clover at those parties too. It was hard not to, the world seemed to curl around her, but it was more than just observing the popular girl. There was a tiny flare of want, even then, to know her.

I park the Civic I used to share with Imogen on the road and hurry up Clover's driveway. It's still snowing, but barely, tiny white flakes dancing down from the sky. It's nearly eleven o'clock and all but one of the front windows are dark. The last thing I need is her lawyer dad answering the door in his pj's, so I wade into the snow-dusted bushes and risk a peep through the window. I feel beyond creepy, but there's also something else going on in my chest, a spark of excitement.

The spark flares into a tiny flame when I see Clover sitting on the couch, her hair in a messy topknot. She's wearing yoga pants and a giant sweatshirt with the neck cut out, one slim shoulder bare and smooth. Her arms are wrapped around her knees and her face is tinted blue from the TV screen.

A full bowl of popcorn sits next to her.

A tiny smile tugs at the corners of my mouth.

Before I can change my mind, I pull off one glove and tap my nail against the glass. I can see Clover tense up at the noise, so I wave, trying to make sure she sees it's me and not some murderer.

It takes a few seconds for her to focus on me through the dark and snow, but when she does, her mouth drops open a little, a wrinkle between her brows. She sits up, but doesn't stand, and I wait there feeling small and stupid for what seems like years.

Finally, she pulls herself off the couch and points toward the hallway before leaving the room. I pick my way out of the bushes, snow and leaves clinging to my black peacoat, and reach the front door as it swings open.

Clover stands there, her brows still furrowed with questions or irritation or some other negative emotion that proves I shouldn't be here this late at night. I shouldn't be here at all. But I see her, and my muscles relax. I see her, and my lungs loosen up.

"Hey," I say.

She doesn't say anything, but her eyes narrow and soften at the same time, so I forge ahead.

"I'm sorry," I say. "I'm the one who had everything wrong. I did everything wrong, okay?"

My apology hangs between us, a flimsy white flag. She doesn't move, and I'm almost positive if she did, it would be to close the door in my face. I guess she'd be justified, but I've never wanted anything less.

"Please, Clover," I say as softly as I can. I sound desperate and I know she hears it because she sighs and rubs her forehead. Still, she opens the door wider and lets me inside.

I kick off my boots and shrug off my coat in the entryway before following her into the living room. *Buffy* flickers on the TV, the sound on mute.

"Are your parents asleep?" I ask.

"Yeah. Sound machine's whirring, ear plugs firmly in place. Don't worry, they won't wake up."

Clover curls back onto the couch and I sit next to her, but on the edge of the cushion. We stay like that for a few seconds, our eyes on the Vampire Slayer. I keep hoping she'll start us off, say something, anything, but I know she won't. I know this is up to me.

"Earlier, back in my room," I say, "I was about to cry because my house is always so quiet and I was glad you were there. I'd just had a fight with my sister and I was just . . . I was just lonely, I guess."

I feel her looking at me, but I can't seem to drag my eyes up to hers.

"Okay," she says. "Thanks for telling me."

"I'm sorry."

"You already said that."

"I know, but there's more than one thing I'm sorry for."

She turns so her back is against the armrest, her body facing me. "Such as?"

"Well, tonight, for one. I wasn't thinking clearly about what I was asking you to do. I wasn't thinking at all. About what it would actually be like between us."

"You mean if we had sex?"

I nod.

She huffs a single laugh. "I think about it all the time."

I risk a glance at her. "You do?"

"God, yes."

"I'm new at this being with a girl thing," I say.

"And no penis means no sex?"

"No. Of course not, but . . . yeah, I wasn't thinking. I've only been with Danny and with him, nothing we did seemed as big of a deal as when we actually . . . well . . ."

"Penis in vagina."

"Jeez, Clover."

She laughs at my blush. "What? It's just biology."

"I know, but . . ." I take a deep breath. "Yes. What you said."

"It's a big deal to me. Really, anything below the waist counts for me."

I nod. "I get that. You're right. I just wanted . . ." I trail off, a blush settling into my cheeks.

"You wanted what?" Clover asks. She sits up a little straighter, her eyes locked on mine.

"I just wanted to be with you," I say, shrugging.

"With me? Or with anybody?"

That makes me frown, but it's a fair question. I don't answer right away. I want to make sure I think this through, which is something I haven't let myself do since Clover and I started hanging out. Ever since Imogen left, the only thing I ever really feel is anger or loneliness. It's a speeding pendulum, never pausing for too long in the middle, always reaching for one extreme or the other. Both emotions are bone-deep and quietly violent, pushing me to everyone's edges.

But now, I wonder if I'm the one who's been pushing myself to everyone's edges.

"You," I say and I know without a doubt it's true.

It's always been true. Clover may have been the first person to come along in a long time to make me feel like I might be something human-shaped, something girl-shaped, something worth loving, but *first* doesn't make it any less real.

"You, Clover," I say again when she just stares at me.

She sucks in a breath, but doesn't break eye contact. "Then why?"

"Why what?"

"Why have you ignored me, been kind of a jerk, acted like who we are at your house doesn't mean anything?"

I scoot closer to her, the bowl of popcorn tipping between us. "Because I'm a complete and total idiot."

I'd hoped that would make her smile, but her frown deepens instead. "No, you're not."

"Okay, then." I take a deep breath. "Maybe I was scared."

That one sticks, an arrow hitting the bull's-eye. Clover nods and unfolds her legs, inching closer. "Of what?"

I swallow hard, my throat growing thick with the truth of it, the confession that makes me feel like the outer layer of skin around my heart has been sloughed away. "Being left. Being alone again after . . ."

Her leg presses against mine.

"After really being with you," I say.

She doesn't say anything for a few seconds. Long seconds that make me want to slide my palm over hers, squeeze her fingers tight.

"And now?" she finally says, a tiny smile on her lips.

"And now, I want to knock over this bowl of popcorn."

She laughs and leans toward me, the space between us shrinking more and more. "So do it."

I grin and reach for her immediately. No hesitation, no wondering. I slide my hands up her thighs to her hips, tugging on her and moving toward her all at once until we collide. Our mouths touch, but I make sure it's soft. I make sure it feels as deliberate as I mean it. I make sure she knows I'm kissing *her*. I move my hands to her face, swiping my thumbs over her cheekbones and she smiles against my lips. Her hands fist around my shirt, fingers brushing the skin at my waist. My whole body erupts into goose bumps and I kiss her neck, her collarbone, her shoulder. She pulls at me, tugs and gropes, but in the best way, until I'm over the dividing line and the popcorn bowl finally thunks onto the carpeted floor.

We laugh into each other's skin and I lie down next to her, our bodies aligning, soft for soft. I kiss her again and her fingertips trace the sensitive skin near my belly button.

"I do want to," she whispers.

"Want to . . . ?"

"Have sex with you."

I lean back so I can see her. "For real?"

She nods. "I mean, not tonight. I don't think I'm ready yet, but . . . maybe someday?"

I smile. Because I can see a lot of somedays with Clover, hours stretching into days into months, actual dates and campy nineties shows and more bowls of popcorn until we're both ready for that.

"Yeah," I say, letting my mouth drift over her shoulder. "Definitely someday."

♡

It's snowing again. I wait on the school steps before the first bell and watch the delicate flakes drift from the sky and blanket the ground, changing the world quietly. Students swarm around me, hurrying in from the cold, but I'm in no rush. No one says hi to me. I don't say hi to anyone either, but when Mallory passes me, I make myself look at her.

She's staring right at me. Over the past few months, I've caught her doing this before and I always yank my eyes away before she can say anything. Or *not* say anything. I always assumed she was smirking at me, looking at my dark hair and freckles and missing Imogen.

Today, she seems different. Or maybe I'm the different one. Her eyes are wide, a little sad, and I wonder if that's how she's looked at me this whole time. I wonder if maybe I'm the one who gave up on her instead of the other way around.

I don't pull my eyes away. Instead, I smile.

She smiles back, offering a little wave as she goes past.

It's a small thing, but it's something. And a tiny something is better than all these past months of nothing.

The wind kicks up and I pull my scarf tighter around my neck. The warning bell rings and I squint my eyes through the sprinkles of white. I'm about to give up when I see her. Her peacoat is bright and happy, her hair is long and loose under a cream-colored knit hat. She's with Haley, their shoulders bumping against one another as they hurry through the parking lot. They're laughing as their booted feet stomp up the brick stairs.

Haley sees me first, a question settling between her brows. I'm clearly waiting for them, my eyes tracking Clover as she gets closer. She doesn't see me though. Her gaze is turned downward while she digs for something in her bag.

"Hi," I say.

Clover's head snaps up, but her eyes don't widen. She doesn't look surprised. I don't know why, but somehow, that makes me braver. Like she expected me to be standing right here, waiting for her. A smile spreads across her pretty mouth.

"Hey," she says.

"Hey," I say again.

"Hi."

"Um . . . okay," Haley says.

Clover and I both laugh.

Then I reach out and take her hand. Her gloved fingers lace between mine and just like that, I'm not alone. I miss my sister. I'm pissed at my dad and I ache for my mom and I don't always know where I fit.

But for now, my hand fits perfectly right here.

WHAT MAKES US HEROES

"Hero vs. Villain"

Julian Winters

IT'S OFFICIAL: I HATE MAROON 5.

Honestly, it's just one song. Some bittersweet, soft rock tune about an inevitable breakup when the sun comes up. It's on heavy rotation inside this coffee shop, The Last Bean.

I hate that this is the second time I've noticed it playing in the last three hours.

Okay, I really hate that I've spent three hours being the most pathetic, low-key stalkerish, ex-boyfriend ever. I haven't moved from the little round table near the front door. Not even to take a leak, which is imminent considering how much watered-down iced coffee I've consumed.

My left foot taps in rhythm with my anxious heartbeat.

I watch the door.

I wait for someone who doesn't know I'm here.

"Double iced café mocha with light whip!"

Corny, vintage breakup music aside, The Last Bean is one of my favorite places. The interior is all aged wood and brick. Large storefront windows are framed by iron. Naked light bulbs are suspended from the ceiling by black cords, dancing their gold beams across dark oak tables. The sweet aroma of ground espresso hangs heavy in the air.

A bell on the door chimes whenever someone walks in. I startle each time, nearly knocking over my drink.

It's never him, though.

Two tables over, a curvy girl watches ASMR YouTube videos on a MacBook plastered in anime stickers. She has almost reddish-brown skin, her hair streaked pastel blues, pinks, and greens like cotton candy.

We're the only people here other than April, the barista behind the bar, and some old white dude who keeps grumbling at a crossword puzzle. Figures. The Last Bean is too unpretentious and small to hang out at on a Friday night.

My phone buzzes twice on the table. Then it lights up, blaring a *Steven Universe* song I swear I deleted from my music app a year ago.

"Is she *serious* right now?" I mutter.

I snatch up my phone to silence it as Cotton Candy Girl giggles, slipping on her headphones. There are ten new notifications, all from Mom. Six texts, two missed calls, and, finally, a video on PeekAView, the video messenger app she created.

Having a technopath for a mother means that even if you turn your phone on *vibrate* and delete everything but the basic apps, she can still find a way to reach you.

I hunch over the table, lowering the phone's volume to watch the message.

"Shai, baby, this is Mom . . ."

Clearly.

"I wanted to make sure you got to the coffee shop okay? Is he there yet? I didn't call his mom like you begged me not to . . ."

Ohmygod.

"It's not as if that woman would answer my calls, anyway. She really thinks she's something, doesn't she? Her son was lucky to have you, do you hear me? LUCKY!"

That's not how it feels.

"Anyway, you're gonna fix that tonight, right? You were cute together. I'm not just saying that because dating someone like him would really make a difference in our world . . . I mean *your* world, baby. Yours. You were great for each other . . ."

Were we?

I shake my head. It doesn't matter. I'm here now.

"Are you wearing a Yolanda Spencer–approved outfit? I noticed you left the gray cardigan *I* chose for you on your bed. I'm not mad about that . . ."

Yeah, you are.

I pause the video to check my outfit. It's acceptable. A navy-and-white pinstriped collared shirt under a bloodred "EST. 2005" sweatshirt. The colors complement my rich, dark-brown skin. My black skinny jeans match my black boots.

I'm a soft eight if I'm being generous.

I press play.

"Did you fix your hair?" She sighs. "I can't have my baby out there looking a hot mess when he's trying to win back the love of his life . . ."

At that, I lock my phone, carelessly dropping it on the table. The screen is already cracked down the left side. Not from superhero activities; just my basic clumsiness. I tug at the stray ends of my thick black hair. On top, it sticks up at all angles, partly from my curl sponge, but the sides are shadow faded.

Dad wants me to cut it low, or be bald like him.

"I'm tired of the clean, sexy bald head being credited to all the criminals and masterminds. Black superheroes invented this look. I'm reclaiming it," he constantly reminds me.

I agree with him, but my hairstyle fits me. Besides, Logan used to love to pull his fingers through my hair when we kissed.

"*Ohmygod*, Shai," I whisper to myself, disappointed. One, I didn't know how to tell Logan I wasn't a fan of his bony fingers messing with my hair. Two, I'm not maintaining this look for some boy. I have way more chill than that. Literally.

I stare down at my iced coffee. Well, coffee-water; the ice has melted. I curl my fingers around the plastic cup and close my eyes. Deep inhale, slow exhale. Something tingles in my veins, racing up my chest and limbs like vapor. It tickles my nose, stings my cheeks, but I feel it.

Behind my fingers, the condensation solidifies and the cup chills.

Letgoletgoletgo.

This is the hardest part—shutting my power off once I tap into it. It's one thing to decrease the temperature until the ice re-forms. It's another to lose control and turn The Last Bean into The Frozen Bean.

Slowly, the chill retreats from my fingertips, slithering deep into my muscles until it's balled up in my chest.

The bell above the door chimes, but I'm too focused on recalibrating my breaths to open my eyes.

"Hey. That's cheating."

I shiver, but not from the lingering effects of my powers. I *know* that voice.

I blink one eye open, then the other. Standing over my table is a boy, in a white Henley and black joggers, who I'm too familiar with. And not in the kisses-like-Logan way.

"What up, No Chill," he says with the slickest grin.

The coolness inside my chest expands again. My breath exits through my gritted teeth in a white fog. "Why are you here, Lev—"

"Whoa, whoa, whoa." He holds surrendering hands out in front of himself. "No need for that. Just Kyan, okay?"

"Kyan," I snap back, trying to reel in the ice already hardening around my knuckles.

"We don't have to do the usual dance," he says, still smiling. "No costumes. No parents. No cameras around for you to show off your Crest-toothpaste-worthy smile for."

He's right. No one's paying attention to us, though I'm never too sure when Mom might tap into my phone with her powers.

When my shoulders relax, Kyan snorts. "There you go, No Chill."

"It's *Shai.*"

There are definitely directives involved with superhero life. Or, in my case, a HITW—a hero-in-training-wheels. Obviously, informing anyone of your real name breaks the most cardinal of rules.

Thing is, I've known Kyan since we were five years old. Before Arctic and Levin became our public identities. Before people—mainly my parents—decided Kyan's family's ways of achieving their goals made them villains. We were just two kids kicking a ball around during recess.

Kyan's much taller now, nearly six-foot. His warm, golden complexion contrasts with his almost black eyes. There's faint scruff under his chin, across his upper lip. But his cheeks are still soft-looking, the skin around his eyes boyish.

I guess we both have that going for us—the too-young-to-save-or-destroy-the-world look. Except, I lack Kyan's neat eyebrows—mine are bushy. I'm also kind of scrawny where Kyan's athletically built.

Plus, his smile is almost beaut—

Hold up!

A flare of heat forces the coldness out of my cheeks.

"Why are you here?" I ask.

Kyan leans over my table, his brow furrowed. "To rob this place." Thin streaks of green lightning circle his irises like veins. The air's charged. Sparks sizzle off his fingers, almost shocking me.

Ice surges down my arms.

Then, he laughs, straightening his body. "Bruh, you should see your *face.* You really think I'd do that?"

I do. Well, I *don't*, but it's not like it isn't something his parents have done, so . . .

"I just wanted to get away from my mom for a bit," he says, licking his lips. "Recharge."

My phone buzzes, then lights up. We both glance at it.

"Is that still a . . ." Kyan motions toward my lock screen. "Thing?"

It's a photo of Logan and me, arms around each other, a lit Ferris wheel illuminating our smiles in the night.

One of our last dates.

"Yes." The lie tastes gross on my tongue. "Not really." My left leg begins to shake under the table. I watch my phone screen go dark, ignoring another message from Mom.

Tonight's all her idea. For weeks, she *suggested* I try to talk to Logan. Rekindle whatever we had. As if I'm the one who broke up with him and not the other way around. As if I don't recognize that us being together—Magz, a level-one superhero and me, a level-two HITW—is great publicity for my family.

QUEER TEEN HEROES IN LOVE—WHY THE FUTURE IS IN GOOD HANDS!

Truth is, some days, I miss Logan. That's expected from a first boyfriend, right? But I don't think he's The One my mom hopes he is.

Also, I'm only sixteen. What the hell do I look like calling the first boy I made out with "The One"?

"Where is Mr. Magnificent?" Kyan asks, looking around.

"It's Magz." I cringe.

Yup, I'm dating—*dated*—someone who thinks shortening his hero identity to Magz is a vibe.

Breaking news: it's not.

"He's . . ." When Kyan's eyes meet mine, curious and wide, I look down, shutting up. I swirl the re-formed ice in my cup, drinking a third of my coffee—heavily diluted by cream and raw sugar, the only way I'll consume it—before exhaling another frosty breath. "He's not here."

Above me, Kyan's quiet through the end of a Troye Sivan song. Then, with a smile in his voice, he says, "So, he's ghosting you."

My head snaps up, frustration wrinkling my brow. "*No.* I'm just waiting."

I don't include the "I'm stalking his favorite coffee shop, the one we used to come to on weekends, the one he stops by on Fridays before doing the hero thing with his parents for the late-night news, hoping he'll give us a second chance."

Kyan doesn't need those details.

"Sounds . . . desperate."

"F off," I growl.

Kyan barks a laugh that startles Cotton Candy Girl. She sighs annoyedly, shifting until her back is to us.

"Come on, Shai." He drags out the chair I've been saving for Logan, then sits across from me despite my irritated expression. "You can cuss around me. Swear I won't tell Super-Mommy."

"Bite me."

He nods, smirking. "That's better. Do you only use the R-rated shit in the bedroom?" He drums his fingers on the table, tiny green lightning streaks flickering around them. They're so faint, only I notice.

The fact is, I don't like discussing what happened between Logan and me, sexually. I wish I hadn't rushed into that part of our relationship. Months later, I don't really think it's what I wanted for myself. I didn't want it to be simplified to "a fun time," as Logan called it before he ended things.

"Yo. Shai?"

I flinch out of my thoughts.

"Look, that's my bad." He pauses, watching me with a blank expression. "I don't know what . . ." He wiggles a finger between me and my phone. ". . . went down between you and Mr. Generic Netflix White Boy. No offense about the sex thing."

I snort, barely maintaining a scowl. "Since when do villains apologize?"

He *pffts*. "I'm not a villain. You know that."

"Heroes certainly don't rob banks."

"No, they just cheese it up for the cameras and handle community situations diplomatically, right?"

"Your methods—"

"*My* methods?" He grins. "That was all Mom's plan. She needed to fund the neighborhood's greenhouse and youth environmental outreach program the mayor's team is shutting down."

"Yeah, well . . ." The words cool on my tongue. "There are better ways to accomplish that goal."

Kyan rolls his eyes. "Did Super-Mommy write that speech for you?"

"Whatever."

"Listen, my mom has a thing for orchids and smiling, underprivileged kids, okay?"

I sigh. "Fine, but that doesn't excuse your dad being in prison."

"You don't even know why he's there, do you?"

"For being a criminal," I reply dryly.

"No, for fighting the system." Kyan tugs his fingers through his brown hair.

We have almost identical hairstyles except his is a little longer on top. He has two studs in his ears while I only have my right cartilage pierced. Getting Mom to agree to that was hell.

"He was *peacefully* protesting when all that shit went down at Wonder Heights," explains Kyan. "You remember that?"

I nod.

Wonder Heights is a train ride away from where I live. My parents used to guard it along with our neighborhood before more and more heroes started populating the city. A year ago, three freshmen Black girls were harassed by members of Wonder Heights High's football team. Of course, because the boys were economically blessed and white, the police and school's administration replied with soft consequences. There were daily protests outside the school until at least three of the boys were investigated, then expelled.

I wanted to attend the protests, but Mom thought it'd be safer to protect our area instead.

She said, "Your voice can still be heard by ensuring this doesn't happen here, too. We're the faces that give our community hope."

I didn't agree. Just being a *face* doesn't feel like enough. I'm more than a mouth-piece from a distance. But what adult listens to a sixteen-year-old in matters like that?

"Wait," I say. "If he was only arrested for protesting, why's he still locked up?"

"Pops likes it there. Says he's getting to motivate and educate younger, incarcerated guys." Kyan chuckles weakly. "Anyway, he gets free meals. Stays in shape. Doesn't have Mom nagging him."

I slouch in my chair, biting on my straw. "I didn't know that. The news made it seem—"

"Like my dad resisted arrest? Put his hands on a cop?"

"Yeah."

"He probably did." Again, Kyan laughs. "But he's doing what he has to to create a change."

"Robbing banks and assaulting people don't sound like it'll make a change."

I wince. Damn, I really do sound like my parents.

"If the system is set up to always work against us . . ." Kyan waves a finger between us. ". . . while continuously letting others . . ." This time, he points at my phone. He means Logan. ". . . benefit from their privilege, then it's a broken system. You can't fault the people it oppresses for taking what they need to feel human."

"Okay, Malcolm X," I tease.

Kyan smiles, warm and bright and like our childhood.

Before our parents' words got in our heads.

Before we stood on opposite sides of the same playground.

"You do that a lot," he says. "Space out."

Another rush of heat settles into my cheeks. I'm so grateful for that extra melanin in my skin, so Kyan can't see the blush. But I spot his when I catch him watching my mouth.

Why is he doing that?

"I never noticed that before." He up-nods toward my face. "The dimple in your left cheek."

It's not a dimple. It's a scar—my first battle wound from attempting a solo mission a few months after my powers initially manifested. Turns out most fourteen-year-olds are sidekicks for a reason. I held my own against the three arsonists until the police arrived, though.

My parents grounded me for two weeks. No phone, TV, or internet. It was worth it.

It's also how I met Logan.

Mom arranged one-hour training sessions with him during that period. "His parents are hero royalty," she said. "He'll be a great influence on you. Much better than . . ."

She never said his name. It didn't matter. Our family had long stopped interacting with Kyan's.

Logan was a great influence on my out-of-control hormones every time he'd practice flying shirtless in our backyard. A fantastic distraction, who was so slick with his flirting, I missed it the first few times. Eventually, he crawled into my chest, warmed my heart, then recklessly gnawed out a chunk of it, spitting it on the ground, and soaring away.

"Shai."

Hot fingers brush the back of my hand, green lightning retreating up Kyan's wrist when I snatch it away.

"What?" I say roughly.

An affronted expression flashes across his face. "Yo, I'm gonna grab a drink," he says in a cool, even tone. "You want a refill?"

"No," I nearly snarl. I don't know why I'm acting as if my parents are standing over me, disapproving of my interaction with a boy who was once a friend.

"Aight. Sure." Kyan shakes his head. "Whatever." He edges around the table to get to the counter behind me.

Again, I exhale a breath of freezing air. I don't care if Cotton Candy Girl or Crossword Puzzle Guy or anyone notices. I need the ice out of my lungs before I lose it.

The bell above the door chimes loudly.

"Shai?"

This time, it's Logan . . . holding hands with another girl.

Right. Ex-boyfriend, remember? There's absolutely no reason for my heart to feel so shredded, limply climbing outside of its already shattered cage.

"Sup, Logan?" I choke out.

He pushes his free hand through his gilded-brown hair. I love when he does that. It opens a clear view of his hazel eyes, his pale gold skin no longer rich from summer sun, that charming smile he flashes in selfies before posting on his verified, superhero Instagram account.

#MagzIsHot.

His fitted denim jacket hides most of the stretched, plain white T-shirt underneath. Even though Logan hasn't fully come into his powers, he's still a level-one hero—flight, superstrength, and Olympic-level physique included. One day, he'll develop the same superspeed and invulnerability his parents have.

The tiers of superhumans are unnecessary. They separate us rather than unite us. As an elemental, I'll never be above level two. It's considered an average power. But I can stop a falling building with my ice the same way Logan can with his strength.

"Didn't expect you to be here," I say when I realize I've been quietly ogling Logan for far too long.

Yup, real smooth Shai Spencer.

"I didn't—" Logan falters. He rarely does that. His parents have trained him to be picture-perfect with responses. "I didn't expect you to be here either."

He glances at the girl next to him. She's much shorter than his six feet—level-one status is a real flex when it comes to height—with light brown eyes, shiny, crow-black hair, and a round nose. She has a nice fawn skin tone, dressed in a pale yellow sweater and ripped jeans.

"Just chilling," I say, struggling to breathe again.

Logan snickers. I miss that noise.

I miss the bobble of his Adam's apple.

Those long fingers that tighten around the girl's fingers.

"Is this Maroon 5?" she asks.

"Uh." Logan shrugs. "I think?"

"I love them."

Ohmygod, even with her magnetic smile and the way she shrugs off Logan's offended look like she's refused to change her opinion because some boy doesn't respect it, I'm still slightly frustrated with her. But only about the music thing.

She leans against Logan like she belongs there.

And I don't anymore.

Every sharp, cold needle that shifts under my skin hurts. I'm not sure if it's my powers or the disappointment. The latter, probably.

"Gabi and I are here for . . ." Logan motions toward the counter, then something weird morphs his expression.

The heels of the chair next to me scrape against the ground, then a smiley Kyan sits.

"Sorry it took so long, babe." Kyan angles his head until his face is turned away from Logan and Gabi, his lips nearer to my hair than ear. He whispers, "This okay? I can back off. Not trying to disrespect your personal space or anything."

My eyes lock on Logan, who's glaring in Kyan's direction.

"I just thought, you know. If this guy doesn't have a problem showing up with a date, then let's give him a show, right?"

Kyan fakes a chuckle. The skin around Logan's eyes tightens.

Oh!

I recline awkwardly until I'm pressed against Kyan. His arm rests around my shoulders. His hand covers mine on the table. I spread my fingers until his fit between them. Lightning curling around ice.

"It's okay," I finally say, forcing confidence into my tone. "Did you get your . . ." My words die as I glance down at the drink next to my empty cup on the table. I cock my head back to look at him, wide-eyed. "Berry Blast?"

Kyan rolls his eyes. "I like the green tea extract in it. Plus, too much caffeine makes me nauseous, remember?"

I don't. Another side effect of our parents' beef. I try to wrap my brain around the fact that Kyan drinks fruity Berry Blasts. Chunky blackberries and ice float in a sea of translucent lavender.

I expected villains to chug iced Americanos before plotting world domination.

Then again, that's Logan's favorite drink.

My brain circles back to Kyan's earlier words:

I'm not a villain. You know that.

The nerves fade from my fingers the more they rest between Kyan's. His hair tickles my cheek when he whispers, "Damn, does he always get that red?" in my ear.

I smile. The only time I've seen Logan's face this shade is when he's pissed.

He frowns. "So, this is—"

"Kyan," says Kyan, up-nodding at Logan. "It means *King*."

I almost lose it at the smugness in Kyan's tone. Logan appears to be on the verge of exploding in a different way.

"Nice," he says tensely. His eyes drift to mine. "This new?"

"It's—"

"You could call it that," Kyan interrupts me, pressing his temple to mine. His breath smells sugary.

Would his kiss taste the same?

Yo, what the hell Shai Spencer?

"But I was hoping it would've happened a lot sooner," Kyan continues, turning his head until we're staring at each other. The emerald lightning circling his irises glows intensely. "Growing up with this goon, it's kind of hard to avoid falling for him."

"*Excuse me,*" Logan says louder than I can think it.

This is an act, right? Kyan's simply putting on a show . . . very convincingly when he licks his lips, eyeing my mouth, then turning toward Logan.

"If our parents hadn't gotten in the way, things might've escalated before . . . his last relationship." Kyan sizes Logan up. "I'm just saying, bruh."

"I'm definitely not your—"

"Uh, this has gotten really awkward," Gabi announces, taking back her hand. "I just want an iced coffee." She shifts around the table, headed in the direction of April and the front counter.

"Wait, sweetheart—"

"Oh no, I don't do pet names. It's *Gabriela* or *Gabi*. Damn the patriarchy," Gabi shouts back.

Logan sags, shaking his head. Then he examines me. The corners of his mouth lift. Something awful crawls up the back of my neck.

"Nice outfit." He pushes his hair back and, suddenly, it's not so attractive anymore when he says, "Almost like the one you wore on our first date. The ArcMagz would approve."

I *really* hate that ship name.

I hate that, even though we still follow each other on social media, Logan has untagged me from all his pictures. Every one of his new posts includes at least one person commenting, "Are u & Arctic still together??? 😩"

Kyan clears his throat. My hand almost flinches away when a shock of electricity pricks my knuckles. "Is that shade, All-American Boy?"

Logan sucks air through his teeth. "Just pointing out that Shai's upgraded style came from us—"

"We're gonna go," I cut in, pushing out of my chair before Logan can finish. I'm done letting him claim any aspect of who I am—past, present, or future. I tug at the sleeve of Kyan's Henley. Already, the temperature's chillier in the coffee shop. Behind my teeth, everything's frosty. "Our movie starts soon."

"It does?" Kyan asks, head cocked.

"Yes, *babe*."

Kyan lifts his hands, palms out again. "Cool, cool. Let's bounce."

I nudge by Logan, pretending the scent of him—a heavy layer of body spray hiding the acute, clean smell of fresh air from flying high in the clouds—doesn't tug at my lungs. Or the way he whispers my name, "Shai," like he did when no one else was around to comment on our relationship, doesn't ache under my skin.

I can hear Kyan's high-tops squeaking on the floor as he follows me out the door.

We're barely around a corner before I double over, nearly heaving up my iced coffee.

"You okay?"

There's a heat hovering over my lower back, as if Kyan's tentative to touch me. As if he's asking for permission first.

I nod twice, simultaneously answering his question and giving my consent.

Electric pulses chase the chill up my spine.

"If I overstepped my—"

I straighten up, shaking my head. Kyan's soft face drinks up the silver light from the moon and streetlamps. He blinks rapidly, an anxious habit I remember from when we were younger.

"You called me babe," I say, accusingly.

Instantly, pink floods his cheeks. *Light-skinned-boy problems.*

"You *liked* it." Cockiness drips off his words.

"I *didn't*. Like Gabi, I'm not into all that 'claim what's mine,' hyper-masculine bullsh—" I cut myself off, but Kyan's already grinning.

"That's not very hero-like."

"Whatever." I twist away from him. "Thanks . . . for doing that."

He shuffles next to me. "No biggie." His elbow brushes mine. "You seriously wanted to get back with *that*?"

I shrug. I'm too embarrassed to tell him my mom wanted this. That, yes, I miss Logan's touch and laugh and stupid hair, but not enough to use it to elevate my family's reputation in the hero headlines. Not enough to forget the pain of being tossed aside for . . . being me.

"I just don't see us working in the long run" were Logan's last words.

He was right. I can't see it either.

"Pissing off that Archie Andrews rip-off felt damn good," Kyan whispers, smugly.

"Did you mean it?" I ask.

"What?"

"The thing about it being hard to avoid falling . . ."

I don't want to finish. Kyan Coles, also known as Levin, also known as my supposed rival, can't possibly have any kind of feelings for me other than irritation.

He says, "Nah."

Exactly. That's not how this whole thing works . . .

"I didn't avoid it," he finishes.

My head snaps in his direction. He takes a slow sip of his drink, watching me with hooded eyes. Something quite the opposite of freezing swirls in my belly.

"You never said anything."

Kyan tips his head back, laughing at the starless sky. "Because of our parents!" His nostrils flare, his jaw tightening. "It's high-key frustrating that they want the same things from this world, including for us to thrive in it, but they just can't see it."

I blink at him.

"Just like you can't see you're better than that," whispers Kyan, again waving toward The Last Bean. "Aren't you tired of going through the motions? Tired of pretending we hate each other for their sake?"

I am. I'm *exhausted*. But I never thought Kyan would be the one to help me wake up.

We stand quietly, the November air frigid even without my body emitting so many arctic waves. There are deep wrinkles in Kyan's brow as he stares at his sneakers. My boots feel heavier. This stupid sweatshirt and collared shirt are too snug.

My phone buzzes in my back pocket. It's probably Mom, who got a call from Logan's mom, who has probably already notified the media that the Spencer family is nothing but an average, Black family of superheroes undeserving to share the same spotlight as level-one heroes like Magz and company.

She's probably already shouted about how Arctic, basic-ass elemental hero, fraternizes with villains like Levin.

She's right. I'd rather hang with Kyan, because I want to, rather than Logan, because I have to, any day of the week.

"Hey," I say, my mouth already curling into a smile when Kyan's eyebrows raise. "We're gonna be late for that movie."

"Huh?"

"The movie," I repeat, stretching my hand out, fingers wiggling in the nippy air.

Cautiously, his fingers meet mine.

"Aight, *babe*," he says, smirking when I groan. "But I have a curfew, so we might have to ditch before the end credits."

"Wait, *you* have a curfew?"

"Yes, Shai," he sighs. "Politically incorrect nocturnal activities aside, my mom will beat my ass if I stay out past eleven p.m., even on weekends."

I guffaw. My curfew's ten p.m., but Mom owes me for this whole reunite-with-Logan stunt.

I'll try my luck with ten thirty.

Kyan stops us midway to the theater. The tip of his nose is pink, matching his cheeks. He's got that whole wide-eyed, anxious look again. "I'm honestly all about respecting boundaries, so don't laugh when I ask this."

I almost snort.

"Can I kiss you?"

And . . . *oh!*

I nod.

"Sorry, I meant *verbal* consent." He squeezes my hand. "I don't want to misread any signals or risk—"

I shut him up with my mouth on his. His lips are soft and warm. He's a couple of inches taller than me, so I push up on my toes. I like the way his hand cups the back of my neck rather than sinking into my hair. I like it a lot.

His kiss tastes like sugar and berries.

It also tastes like a redefinition of what a hero is to me.

AND

"Love Triangle"

Hannah Moskowitz

IT STARTS AT A HORRIBLY BORING PARTY.

It's the beginning-of-the-school-year cocktail party for rising seniors to mingle with their teachers—a Redwood Academy tradition. They chat with you like you're an adult for one night and then they act like it never happened and go back to treating you like a fourteen-year-old during the year; unless, of course, you get in trouble, and then it's *you should know better, you're almost an adult.*

None of this has happened to you yet, but standing there in your silk-poly dress, your hair up in a chignon your mother had to help you with, you sense it the way you know when it's going to storm.

You're supposed to know better, but better than *what,* exactly? You're not so sure about that. Yet.

There are a few new students here, transfers in for senior year. Billy's talking to one of them now, listening in that intense way he does, like every word you're saying is so important. He's badly in need of a haircut, and his curls are poking out from behind his ears. His suit is a little too small—he had a growth spurt last summer—and between that and his standard dishevelment and nervousness he looks very out of place. It's incredibly charming. He doesn't look at you, but he stretches out his arm to invite you over, like he somehow just knew you were there.

He slips his arm around your waist when you get close. "This is my girlfriend," he says to the new student.

You turn your eyes away from Billy and see the new student for the first time. He's shorter, with golden skin and dark eyes, and the kind of easy smile you've tried to practice in the mirror. He isn't wearing a full suit, just a shirt, pants, and vest that fit him perfectly, and he's still laughing a little at whatever Billy, your Billy, said before he introduced you.

"Hi," he says. "I'm Enzo." He shakes your hand and glances down at the space between your thumb and your wrist. "Are you an artist?"

There's a splotch of paint there that you forgot to try to get off before you came. You and Billy, you don't see the paint anymore. "Some days I like to pretend I am," you say.

"I'm like that but with just, generally being a human," Enzo says.

His eyes have this sparkle you can't explain.

You love Billy deeply, intensely, permanently.

But you did not love him instantly, and right now, his arm around you, your eyes on someone else, you feel yourself starting to sweat.

You run into Enzo again at the tail end of the first week of school. You're in the library during your free period, eating an almond butter and honey sandwich and drinking an iced chai, reading Eliot for AP English, when whatever class he's in comes in as a group and splits up to scour the shelves. Enzo ends up near you and makes his eyes sparkle and says, "Hey, you."

You're surprised he remembers you. "Looking for something?"

"Philosophy. We have to pick a writer for a semester-long project."

You point. "Philosophy's over there."

But instead he sits down at your table, across from you, not too close. "What are you reading?" he says.

You show him. "Prufrock."

He sighs. "I used to love that, but a teacher at my old school totally ruined it for me."

"Ew, how?"

"I'm not going to ruin it for you!"

"No, now you have to."

"She said the whole thing was about some guy who can't get it up anymore," Enzo says. "She said most literature is about that and Prufrock is a prime example."

You stare down at the book, at a poem you no longer want to read. "So, it's all just a metaphor for that?"

"According to her, at least."

I groan. "I hate men. I hate men's insistence that we hear about their dicks. Have them, whatever, let them hang out, just don't drag me into it."

"I still don't know why she told us that," Enzo says. "Let us believe it's about what we want it to be about. Who's that hurting?"

"You're in philosophy?"

"Yeah. We didn't have it at my old school. Any recommendations?"

"Avoid the existentialists. They're depressing."

He laughs. "What do they believe?"

"That nothing you do has any inherent value. Nothing means anything, so doing something bad is the same as doing something good, on like, a cosmic scale. All value is what we attach to it."

No one has ever looked at you so closely when you speak.

"That *is* depressing," he says.

"I told you."

"Or," he says. "I guess it could be freeing, right?"

You feel the tips of your fingers tingle.

"I mean," he says, "if nothing means anything, we don't ever have to read about impotent men again. We'll decide what the great books are."

"I saw that boy from the party again," you tell Billy that night, after you've polished off omelets made with whatever you could find in his fridge. You're lounging on his bed while he reorganizes his closet. Billy is one of seven kids, smack dab in the middle of three brothers and three sisters, which means his parents have their hands too full to be concerned with things like whether or not their seventeen-year-old is having sex with his steady girlfriend. Your mom took you to the doctor to get on birth control. Everyone knows you two are real.

"Which one?" he says, from within the shirts.

"Enzo."

"Oh, yeah." Billy pulls out a hanger. "He's in my government class. Do you hate this? Nana got it for me."

"It's a sweater."

"So?"

"You're not supposed to hang sweaters."

"Oh." He takes it off the hanger immediately, and you feel a tenderness towards him that makes it hard to stay still. You've been with Billy for almost three years. There have been rough patches, but this isn't one of them.

"I don't hate it," you say, and he smiles at you. It's so easy with him, so comfortable, and he makes you laugh in the car and makes you scream in bed and wraps his arms all the way around you when you're cold. You've thought since you were fifteen that you'll probably marry him, and when school or your family or life gets too hectic, you cling to that thought like a life preserver. There is a future here.

"I like him," Billy says abruptly.

"Enzo?"

"Yeah. He did some kind of big grandstanding thing in government class that totally threw Mr. Purino off his game. I think he's a socialist. Enzo, not Mr. Purino."

"I like him too," you say.

Billy and Enzo become friends. Not best friends, maybe not even close friends, but Enzo easily folds into Billy's friend group. You're only peripherally a part of it—it's mostly guys, and aside from Billy you generally prefer the company of girls, so you're closer with your tennis friends and some of the girls from drama club—but on the days you sit with Billy's friends at lunch, Enzo is there, passionately enraged about someone else's problems, covering his face with his hands and laughing at himself when he gets too intense and then telling hysterical jokes without cracking a smile. Billy watches him with reverence. All the boys do.

You do too.

Billy's birthday is at the beginning of November, and you're at the mall shopping for him and a little for you when you run into Enzo at the Smoothie King.

"Getting my mom a present for her birthday," he says, showing you a silver bracelet and a few charms.

"When's her birthday?"

"Next week. The fourth."

That's Billy's birthday. It feels so inexplicably strange, that you're tied to him in this innocuous way. Or that Billy is. But it feels like you.

"Can you help me find something for Billy?" you ask.

He remembers a video game Billy had mentioned, and you go to the store together and spend a while leafing through the one-dollar games, trying to find the one that looks the worst. Enzo wins with a game about dressing multicolor kittens. You get Billy his present and you're ready to go home, but it's started pouring rain outside and the bus stop is a block away.

"Let me drive you," Enzo says, *let me* like you'd be doing him a favor.

You think about Billy on the drive, his dimples and his curls and the way he never stands up straight, and about the year that you went to Six Flags for his birthday and got the roller coaster picture you still have on your nightstand.

"I'm not really into birthdays," Enzo says, out of nowhere.

"You just got your mother this gorgeous piece of jewelry."

"Yeah, I like my mother. I don't like birthdays."

"Who doesn't like birthdays?"

He shrugs, flicking on his turn signal. "They're a bullshit holiday."

"They're . . . literally the one holiday that wasn't made up by the greeting card industry," you say. "They're the holiday that you're born into. You bring it to the world instead of having it foisted on you. How is that bullshit?"

"It's also the only holiday that's just about one person," Enzo says. He slows down to meet traffic ahead. "What's going on here?"

You crane your head to see around the side view mirror. "Looks like an accident."

"Damn. I should have gone the other way."

You cross your legs and take a deep breath. You can smell his cologne, something with pepper and wood. You try not to look at the perfect curve of his ear and the spray of stubble across his cheek. By chance you know he's younger than Billy, younger than you, but he looks more grown up than either of you.

"Birthdays aren't just about one person," you say.

"I guess you could say they're about the mom too, but no one ever gives her any credit. So yeah, it's not like a real holiday where everyone's happy and coming together, it's like . . . woohoo, this day is exciting for exactly one person, congrats. That's not a holiday."

"Okay, but what if it's not one person?" you say. "Billy and your mom have the same birthday. Maybe it's like . . . celebrating the cosmic connection between everyone who happened to be born on that same day."

"You believe in that stuff? Cosmic connections?"

"I don't know. I think some people are drawn together for reasons they can't explain."

"I do too," he says. "People usually think I'm crazy."

He's not looking at the road anymore. There's no need to; the traffic isn't moving.

"To be fair," you say, "you do say some crazy shit sometimes."

"It's not what I say," he says. "It's just the way I say it."

"No. You catch people off-guard."

"I just say what they're thinking," he says, and you can see it right on the rim of his perfect, barely chapped lips. The urge he has to say exactly what you're thinking.

But he doesn't move towards you, and he doesn't say anything, and you reach for the door handle.

"What are you doing?" he says.

"If I don't get home soon my mom will worry."

"So text her, tell her we're behind—"

"I'm just going to walk to the bus stop."

"It's pouring."

You get out anyway. The rain's coming down in sheets, and within a few steps you're soaked to the bone. The paper bag holding Billy's present comes apart in pieces in your hands. You get to the bus stop, and the first bus that comes is heading towards Billy's place instead of yours, and you will take this cosmic sign pulling you towards the person you have always, always known was *yours*. You get on and shiver in your seat and think about Enzo's lips.

♡

The first thing Billy says to you is "What's wrong?" but you shut him up with your mouth against his, and before he can ask why you're drenched, why you're shaking, he has you up into his arms and up to his room. He peels your wet clothes off so carefully, like he's afraid it will hurt, and he covers your body with his and holds you with his hands in your hair.

You start crying when you're done. Because Billy is beside you and inside you and Enzo is still not gone.

The words come out before you can stop them. *So sorry. Didn't mean to. Nothing's happened. I can't stop thinking.* In a movie you know the girl would never, ever tell her boyfriend these things, but you've never kept anything from Billy and this really doesn't seem like the time to start, when you're overwhelmed and scared and you need the person you trust most in the world to tell you what you are supposed to do.

He watches you with sad eyes, but he doesn't get angry. He isn't surprised.

"I have to know," he says. "If you had to choose, who would you choose?"

"You," you say, immediately, truthfully. "But I don't . . . I don't want to choose."

He takes a deep breath and says, "I don't want to be with you if you're not happy."

Everything is falling apart on top of you. "You're saying you don't want to be with me?"

"No," he says gently. Firmly. "I'm saying I want you to be happy."

And maybe that's where it really all begins.

Enzo sits across from you at a table at the pizza parlor. "So how does this work exactly?" he says.

"I'm sort of making it up as I go along."

"So, you and I are . . ."

"Dating."

"And you and Billy are dating."

"Of course."

"And Billy and I are . . . ?"

You know that Enzo dates guys and girls. Billy's only ever been with you.

"You and Billy is between you and Billy," you say.

"I don't think it works that way. I think we're all interconnected now."

You're not sure you're supposed to like the sound of that, but you do. "Is that okay with you?"

He gives this small smile and a shrug with one shoulder. "I like Billy. I like you."

"I like you too."

"And you're positive he's on board with this? I don't want to . . . you know."

"He wants me to be happy."

"Right, but what about him?"

You've been asking Billy, and yourself, the same question for the past two days. You still haven't landed on an answer.

"I think he's going to get something out of it," you say. "He can date whoever he wants too. Maybe he'll meet some great girl he never would have looked at before, or something like that."

"You think?"

"I have to believe that what's good for me is what's good for him too," you say. "I have to believe we're part of each other."

So you date two boys. They whisper about it in the halls. Your parents give you sideways glances. Enzo continues dating other girls and boys and Billy looks at girls but never touches and holds you extra tightly at the end of the night.

The best times, of course, are when you're with both of them. At lunch at school, or at basketball games, or at the movie theater, the popcorn on your lap, three hands tangled together when you all reach in at the same time.

If there's a problem, it's you. Billy gets sick of you asking him if he's okay with it. Enzo gets sick of you checking in with Billy mid-date to make sure he's still okay with it. You look at these two, these beautiful, hilarious, sensitive guys, and you don't know why they think you deserve to have both of them.

You're at Billy's house for dinner one night and afterwards you have some stupid fight, the kind that starts out being over a French project and ends up being about his lack of responsibility and your need for control.

"You're just trying to pick a fight with me," you say.

"Why the hell would I want to do that?"

"You know why!"

His hands go into his hair. "Everything cannot be about that!"

"But it *is!*"

"I am sick of talking about it!" he says. "You're not going to be happy until you make me regret it and you can say you were right all along."

"So you regret it."

"That is not what I—"

"I know." You will not be horrible for the sake of being horrible. "I just don't understand why you don't."

"Yeah, well," he says. "Right now I don't either."

You leave before you manage to say anything else you'll regret and end up at Enzo's house. You watch an episode of some crime drama and eat peanuts and finally decompress enough to tell him what's going on. His reaction surprises you.

"You can't use me to escape from Billy," he says.

You sort of thought that was the point.

"It's not fair to either of us," he says.

"You're right. God. You're right."

"I'll bring you back to his place," he says. "You guys will work it out. You're tough."

"Why do you want us to work it out?"

He laughs. "I can't do this on my own."

The next day at school, you're at your locker when you see them walking down the hall. Enzo laughs at something Billy says and gives him a shove, and Billy slings an arm around Enzo's neck.

One night, Enzo calls you from a strange number. "Everything's fine," he says, in a way that tells you immediately that everything is not fine.

"Tell me what's going on." You thought he was at a friend's house with Billy, playing video games. You thought everything was fine.

"I got in an accident," he says. "On my way home."

"Oh my God."

"I'm okay."

You hear voices in the background, movement. "You're at the hospital."

"Yeah."

"Is your mom there?"

"She's on her way." He takes in a shaky breath, and the small whimper with it makes your throat hurt.

"How bad is it?" you say.

"My leg's broken. And they think there might be internal bleeding, I think? They did an MRI."

"Oh my God."

"They said I might need surgery. They're looking at the MRI now. I don't know. They said I could call you."

Your heart feels like it's in your ears. "Okay, I'm coming now."

"I don't think they'll let you see me. They said just family."

"Oh . . ."

"But I wanted to call you, I'm sorry—"

"No, no, shh." You close your eyes. "You're okay. It's going to be fine. I love you."

He promises his mom will call with news, and she does, three hours of staring blankly at Netflix later. No internal bleeding. He had to have surgery on his leg and he's out now. He's okay, he's okay, *he's okay.*

You call Billy to fill him in, and he goes from panicked to relieved to furious when he finds out how long you knew without telling him.

"I didn't want to lean on you because something was wrong with him," you say. "That's not fair."

"You wouldn't be leaning on me, we would be fucking leaning on . . . how could you not tell me? God, he's really okay?"

"He's okay."

"You should have called me right away. I mean, Christ, honey, he's my . . ."

"Okay. I'm sorry. Okay."

Billy flicks Enzo's ear. "Don't get up, idiot."

"I'm fiiiiine."

Enzo, obviously, is not fine. He has a splint going all the way up his leg and it'll still be another three months before he can put weight on that side. He's sprawled out on your couch right now, your head on his chest, Billy behind you both, a movie on your TV that nobody's watching.

He's not fine, but it's hard to remember that right this second.

"I'm getting up anyway," Billy says. "What do you need?"

Enzo looks at him plaintively. "A snack."

Billy sighs. "Peanuts?"

"Yes."

"Okay," Billy says, and just before he gets up, he leans over and gives Enzo, for the very first time, a small, beautiful kiss.

MY BEST FRIEND'S GIRL

"Best Friend's Girlfriend"

Sara Farizan

"DO YOU THINK SHE'S MAD AT ME?" HAL ASKS AS I OPEN MY LOCKER.

When your best friend has a jawline that looks as though it was perfectly chiseled out of marble, and he can breathe fire, it's hard to imagine that he has problems like the rest of us.

"I think you'd have to ask Clara that," I say, pulling the books out that I need for the weekend and stuffing them into my backpack.

Hal's problems are legitimate. I'll give him that. I want to help him because he helps everyone else around Gateway City on what is now a daily basis. Only there's something about my being one hundred percent there for him that, with all of his burgeoning superpowers, which include telescopic vision, I'm surprised he hasn't been able to see it yet.

"Have you talked to your girlfriend recently?" I ask him even though I know he hasn't because I always have to cover for him.

When there's an emergency that he feels he can take on like a bank robbery or a flood, I am his constant alibi. When Clara can't find Hal, she comes looking for me to ask if I know where he is. In order for Hal to save the day, I have to lie to her. I think all I *ever* do is lie to Clara. It's something Hal and I, unfortunately, have in common.

I started writing down excuses I've used to cover for Hal in a notebook so I can keep track of all the white lies and not repeat myself. It took me two months to finally come up with an excuse that I figured people wouldn't want to ask questions about after seeing a pharmaceutical ad on the side of a bus. When Hal saved a family from a car wreck three weeks ago, I told our homeroom teacher, Mrs. Siegel, that Hal had IBS. Of course, Hal wasn't thrilled with this excuse, especially when Mrs. Siegel pulled him aside after class and suggested a medication she was taking for her own IBS.

"No, Clara's been giving me the cold shoulder," Hal let out with a sigh.

He grips the strap of the backpack that has his costume in it. I don't think it's the safest way to carry his secret identity around, but Hal's parents don't have the means to build him a secret lair. They know he's special, but they *definitely* aren't aware that he's the vigilante known as Heatwave.

We both wished we could have come up with a better name before the press bestowed it upon him, but at the time Hal was figuring this whole superhero stuff out on the fly. (No pun intended. Hal doesn't have the ability to fly.) We didn't know whom to contact in terms of public relations for the caped crusader set, so the name stuck.

"I can understand why," I say as I close my locker.

He stares at me in utter confusion, the same way he did when we first met in pre-K and I asked him if he wanted to play. None of the other kids had. Maybe they were intimidated by his height, but I thought his being almost as tall as a third grader wasn't that big of a deal. We both loved playing with Matchbox cars and the rest was history. "She's been waiting for you to ask her to the dance."

"What dance?" Hal asks, towering over me while we walk down the hall together. I point at the posters on the wall for the stupid Flying of the Ships Dance. It's the thirty-fifth anniversary of when the first supers from outer space arrived on Earth after a small group of nonsupers from the Legion of Peace figured out a way to contact them to help prevent nuclear war.

"Shoot, I forgot," Hal says, running his fingers through his wavy black hair. When he is in his real form, his actual hair color is light purple and his skin is turquoise, but his biological parents from the planet Zyxbrog knew he'd have an easier time with life on Earth in North America if he had black hair, white skin, and male presentation, which was the set of features they set for him before he was sent to Gateway City.

"She's not angry, but she's getting there," I say as we exit school and walk down the sidewalk.

It's a nice day. There's no villain holding the city ransom, no meteor crashes, no landslides or tsunamis. It looks like we'll be able to get some rest. Or *he'll* be able to rest and I can finally study. My grades have dipped a little since starting to help out Hal's alter ego, but he can read with literal lightning speed as his species uses thirty percent of their brains, or so his biological parents told his adopted parents in a holographic message.

"What should I do? I feel like I keep messing up," Hal says, about to kick a rock, then stopping his foot midway, remembering he'd crush it and someone might notice. He's not as strong as Galaxy Woman, but he's stronger than The Pummeler, or at least, that's what I've gauged from my rudimentary research.

"You buy her some flowers," I say. "Preferably lilies," I say. I know they are Clara's favorite because she said so on our fifth-grade field trip to the botanical gardens. Of course, that was when it was a place you could visit and not central headquarters for Nightshade, a villain obsessed with saving plants from human beings. "Then you go over to her house around six thirty," I continue. That's when Clara will be showered and dressed after field hockey practice. "Then do your whole bashful, 'aw shucks you're so pretty' bit and ask her to the dance."

"Lilies. Right. Thanks, Alia," he says, clutching his backpack strap even tighter. "I can't believe she's . . . well, that she's finally mine, you know?"

"Remember, women aren't what?"

"Possessions, yeah, I didn't mean—"

"—I know. You're excited she's your girlfriend," I say with a small smile.

Hal had been enamored with Clara since we were all in third grade together. He thought she was sweet and beautiful and he was always incredibly shy around her. For as long as I've known her, she's been the most beloved and popular girl in school. Back in elementary school, I mostly saw her as the kid who read quietly and never wanted to play with the rest of us at recess.

"I think I might be taking on more than I can handle," Hal says, lowering his voice in case any passersby might be listening. "I want to keep helping people. But I can't lose her. She's . . . well she's everything I want."

"You don't *have* to do, you know, um, your after-school activity," I say. "It's okay to scale back. I mean junior year is hard enough without, um . . ."

"Chess club," Hal says with a smile. The son of a gun even has dimples.

"Right. *Chess* club," I say. "I think what you can do is awesome and chess club is so lucky to have you, but you can't help everyone all the time. Otherwise you might burn out, or sacrifice parts of your life and then—"

"Checkmate," he says. The smile is still on his face, but his pupils start to dilate as he stares past me. That's how I know he's using his telescopic vision.

"Trouble?" I ask.

"The news report on the TV in the old woman's apartment on Shuster Ave," Hal says. Shuster Ave is seven miles from where we stand. "Dr. Radium's goons are in a scuffle with Galaxy Girl at the museum of antiquities."

We quickly duck into an alley and he zips open his backpack while I keep watch.

"What were you saying about taking on more than you can handle?" I ask over my shoulder as I scan for any nosy neighbors, my back turned to him as he changes into his green spandex suit and purple eye mask. We bought it from a Halloween store with cash and made some alterations, but it's not the kind of costume that's made to withstand lasers or bullets.

"I can't let her take on seven guys by herself," Hal says as he taps my shoulder to let me know he's dressed.

I turn around and shake my head. "You look—"

"Ridiculous? Goofy?"

"Stupidly brave," I say. I try not to show him how worried I get because it's not helpful. Every time he goes out there, I get lightheaded, nauseous, and I can't focus on anything, like, for example, all the homework I haven't turned in.

"I'm only going to assist until the big timers get there," he says, trying to reassure me, his skin now his true hue.

When we were younger, I was the one who was assuring him. We were eleven when he decided to show me his real form. He was so nervous I wouldn't want to be friends with him anymore. His powers were new, and he was scared, but he didn't feel like he could tell anybody—not even his Earth parents. I told him that no matter what, there was nobody I'd rather look for frogs and turtles with near the lake, nobody I'd rather talk to about crappy horror movies with, and nobody else whom I trusted to have my back.

That was the same year Joey Hooper maybe had a crush on me and would call me names. Hal made sure Joey cut that out right away by challenging Joey to an arm-wrestling match. Hal didn't snap Joey's arm in two, but I swore I could hear the bone about to crack. It was the only time I was ever a little afraid of what Hal can do. I told him so the following day. He cried, then I cried, and we promised each other that we'd never do anything to hurt one another.

"Let me know when you get home," I say.

Hal winks at me, then closes his eyes, furrows his brow, and teleports out of the alley to where he needs to be.

"Be careful," I whisper to the kicked-up dust he's left behind. I take a deep breath before I take out my phone and look up which flower shops are open and have reasonably priced lilies.

♡

"Hey, Alia!" Hal shouts at me down the hallway outside of the school library. His arm is draped over Clara's shoulder. I guess the flowers worked.

"Hi, you two," I say as they walk toward me, giving Clara a brief nod.

She does the same, but holds on to Hal's dangling fingers on her shoulder, probably so she can make sure he can't run off anywhere.

"What are you up to?" Hal asks, beaming at me with the purest smile. I don't blame him. He's with the love of his life. We should all be so lucky.

"I was going to try and do this thing called studying," I say, my gaze fixed on Hal and the unabashed happiness on his face.

"Clara and I were going to hang out at the pier if you wanted to join?" Hal asks.

I notice Clara squirm a little out of the corner of my eye.

"I think you two should enjoy a romantic sunset on your own," I say.

Hal's smile crumbles a little.

"It has been a while since we've been alone," Clara reminds him.

"Oh," Hal says, looking down at her with adoration and concern. It makes me queasy.

"The three of us can hang out some other time," I tell him with a gentle smile, but I don't actually want to be their third wheel.

"Yes! Like at the dance!" Clara exclaims, taking hold of my arm.

I want to rip myself away from her, but I don't dare move a muscle. Hal would be able to detect my discomfort with even the slightest gesture. I don't want him to know that—well there's no point so I don't tell him. I'm forced to look at her gorgeous full lips, her always smooth, honey-tinted skin, her dark hair that always manages to have bounce and volume no matter the weather. It's one of *her* superpowers.

"I don't really do dances," I say. Up until now, Hal and I didn't really go for the school's social activities, unless it was mandatory. I suppose that's not the case anymore now that he's with one of Gateway West High's social butterflies.

"I promise you'll have a good time," Clara says, genuinely believing this is possible.

I glance at Hal. All he does is shrug with that same "aw shucks" energy that most find endearing, but lately I find to be extremely irritating and I don't know why. I feel her grip lower to my wrist. That's when I notice she's not holding Hal's fingers anymore. She's about to hold mine.

"You don't have to decide now, and there's no pressure, but think about it."

She lets go of my wrist but continues to inspect me. I've seen her look at Hal this way. It's usually when he's giving her an excuse about why he missed her game or why he had to leave a pep rally unexpectedly.

"I'll consider it," I say softly.

"I'm excited! I mean, I never know what to do with my legs when dancing," Hal says, tapping his feet haphazardly. Clara giggles and I can feel my organs shrivel inside of me, while I maintain a calm and affable exterior.

"I better hit the books," I say, taking half a step back from the couple.

"Okay. I'll talk to you later," Hal says.

"Yup," I say over my shoulder as I walk away.

"Bye," I hear her say faintly.

I'm probably imagining it, but it sounded a little melancholy. I didn't think she *did* melancholy.

I can hear the sirens outside my bedroom window. Three spotlights in the sky are summoning the big three of Gateway City: Galaxy Woman, Cosmic Crusader, and The Reckoning. The average citizen can see one of their logos blaze at least twice a month, but it's very rare that all three are called upon at once. Something's going down tonight. I pick up my phone and call Hal, but he doesn't answer. I really don't want him to get involved. If the big three are in demand, it's got to be serious.

I look up the Gateway Patch website on my computer to see what's being reported. Dr. Radium seems to be involved but it looks like there aren't any casualties . . . yet. I try Hal again. No answer.

"Alia?"

I let out a yelp. Then breathe a sigh of relief when I see Clara standing in my doorway, waiting to be invited in like a vampire.

"What are you doing here?" I ask, annoyed at myself that I'm so easily startled. The thought of losing Hal and the anxiety that engulfs me every time he risks his life to save others keeps me on edge.

"Your mom let me in," Clara says with a worried look. "I'm sorry, I didn't mean to scare you."

"You didn't scare me," I say, perhaps a little more icily than I should. She hasn't done anything wrong. I have to keep reminding myself of that: none of this is her fault. I get up off my bed and pull out my desk chair for her. "Have a seat," I say. It's too late to tidy up the clutter on my desk, but I wasn't expecting any guests. Come to think of it, I usually don't have any guests aside from Hal.

"I hope I'm not intruding," she says, sitting down a few feet away from me while I sit on the edge of my bed. "I would have called beforehand, but I don't have your number." She looks around my room, occasionally smiling at something she sees. "Don't you think it's strange that we've known each other for so long and we don't have each other's numbers?"

"Should we?" I ask with genuine curiosity.

"Yes," she responds, her gaze now fixed on me instead of the posters and books in my room. She fishes her phone out of her pocket and hands it to me.

I make sure not to touch her hand when I take the phone in mine.

"It's a good idea, I guess," I mumble as I type. "This way you can text me if you need to get a hold of Hal."

"We don't always have to talk about Hal," she says.

I blink and then save the number in her phone before I hand it to her. I'm careful not to make eye contact with her when I do so.

"Can I get you anything? Water? Juice?" I ask, keeping my tone neutral as I brace myself to look at her again.

"No, thank you. Your parents already offered. They're so sweet," she says. "I can see why Hal loves being here. Why he loves hanging out with you."

"What can I say? Hal has great taste in best friends," I say with a fake chuckle.

"That he does," she says quietly, looking at me with curiosity before she looks away. "I take it you don't think he has the best taste in girlfriends?"

"What?" I ask, my voice suddenly an octave higher than I'd like. I take a moment to clear my throat. I want her to get out of here. She's not supposed to be in *my* room, she's supposed to be in *his*.

"I know you don't like me," she says, focused on me again and holding her hands up to keep me from protesting. "And it's okay, you don't have to."

"I don't—"

"I want you to feel like you can be yourself around me when the three of us are hanging out. And I don't want to get in the way of your friendship with Hal. He talks about you all the time."

"Funny," I say with a real chuckle. "With me he talks about *you* all the time."

"No wonder I get on your nerves," Clara says. "I'm not all that interesting."

"That's not true."

The words spill out of me, but I shut up right after, sucking in my lips, hoping she didn't hear that. I swallow, trying to compose myself, and I notice that she is looking at me the way she does when she is trying to figure Hal out. I want to tell her that I think she's *too* interesting. That I think about her more than I should.

She looks past me and out my window at the emblems in the sky.

"All three of them tonight," she says shaking her head. "It's all so out of control."

"Dr. Radium is on the loose again," I say grimly.

"Heroes, villains, I wish both of them would go away and leave the rest of us alone," she says. "Do you ever wonder what life would be like if they never came? If we were forced to solve our own problems?"

"I can't imagine it," I say, but really, it's because I can't imagine my life without Hal. "You aren't an anti-masker, are you?"

"No!" she exclaims. "I have no qualms with heroes being here." Clara rubs her arm like she's warming herself up after being in the rain. "It just seems like they are going to have to rescue us forever. When does it end?"

"But the heroes sacrifice so much for us," I say. It sounds like I'm reminding her, but I wonder if I'm trying to remind myself. I see how much Hal sacrifices for the city: his body, his time, his feelings. He is always looking out to help strangers even when we both know he shouldn't have to.

Clara sighs and diverts her attention from the logos in the sky back to me.

"I'm not saying they haven't. But doesn't it seem like the villains only showed up in response to the heroes?" She gives me a look and then sighs again. "Anyway, I didn't come here to have a 'which came first the chicken or the superhero' with you."

"So why did you come?" I ask softly.

"Three reasons," she says. "One, I'm worried about Hal. He's always tired and he always flakes on me. I'm not asking you to tell me what's going on with him, but could you just nod or something to let me know he's okay?"

For a moment, all I can do is look at her. Honestly, I don't know if he is okay or not. I have no idea if he's in trouble right now, so I can't promise her that. She deserves a great many promises and declarations. But for now, I can't promise her much of anything.

"If we're there for him, he's going to be okay," I say.

This answer doesn't please her as she puckers her lips in disappointment. I forget myself and stare at her lips again. My God, what lip gloss does she use?

"That leads to the second reason," she says, crossing her arms across her chest. "I don't know if I can be in a romantic relationship with him. I think he's wonderful, but I don't think he's honest with me the same way he is with you. I hope he still wants to be friends, because he's so important to me, but if you want him, he's yours."

She stares at me in shock when I laugh. "I'm sorry," I say, wiping the corner of my eye but I can't stop smiling. "I'm not laughing at you. Hal and I—I love him but I will never be *in* love with him."

"Okay," she says, her 'trying to figure me out' expression back in place.

"Hal adores you, he always has," I say. "You don't have any competitors. Whatever you decide to do about whether you date him or not, that's between the two of you."

"You have a great laugh," she says, her smile mirroring mine.

There's a warmth in the way she says it that almost makes me forget I'm not supposed to like it. Almost.

"Hal has a great laugh, too."

Her smile fades and then she says, "That he does."

Neither of us says a word, but she keeps looking at me in a way that makes me nervous. I clear my throat and move in my chair. She uncrosses her arms and stands up. It's for the best, I tell myself even though I want to stop her as she turns to leave.

"What was the third reason?" I ask, unable to help myself.

She stands in my doorway, her hand on the wall, then looks over her shoulder and decimates me with her smirk.

"I wanted to thank you for the flowers," she says.

My mouth drops for a moment until I remember I'm not actually invisible. That's Mister Miraculous's power. Hal and I think he's kind of a drip in the super world, but we'd never admit that, as he's very beloved around these parts.

"Hal had no idea what I was talking about when I thanked him for my special delivery, so I figured he had some help," Clara explains. "How did you know I love lilies?"

My jaw tightens. I want to tell her I know because I pay attention. I listen. I remember when Clara said they were her mom's favorite flower. That when she sees one, she knows her mother is looking out for her from wherever she is. I remember when Clara came to school the day after her mother's funeral because she didn't want to miss a big game against Harbor Have and let her field hockey team down. That was the same year we were in English lit together. We were the only two people who read *Their Eyes Were Watching God* for summer reading while everyone else in the class decided to read *Of Mice and Men*.

At school we talked about books, we talked about our favorite authors, then Hal asked me if the three of us could hang out. He told me he couldn't believe the girl of his dreams was someone he could finally get close to because of me. He said I was the ultimate wingwoman. We joked about it, but I didn't find it funny. It was only later that it occurred to me that I didn't laugh because maybe she was the girl of *my* dreams. Only I hadn't allowed myself to dream about her because of Hal. I eventually bowed out of our group hangs because I couldn't compete with a super-man. The hero always gets the girl, right? I'm not even a sidekick—I'm the expository moral support.

"I don't know what you mean," I lie.

"Don't you?" she asks a little sharply. "He's a big boy, Alia. He doesn't need you to fly in and save the day all the time—especially when it comes to me."

"I don't think you're a damsel in distress," I say, trying to avoid her gaze, but we both know the truth: I did send those flowers for Hal. But I won't do it again, I tell myself. It's not my place.

"I hope to see you at the dance," she says with what looks like a hint of a grin before she walks down the hallway.

I wake up at 2 a.m. when I hear a buzz.

It's a text from Hal. He's okay, but he helped out the Cosmic Crusader and can't wait to tell me all about it.

I don't text him back because I feel guilty.

I had hoped the text would have been from her.

"You sure you don't want to come?" Hal asks as I tie his bow tie for him in his room. It still looks a little crooked, but I think he could wear an adult-size onesie and look like a billion dollars. Though I guess when he wears his Heatwave costume, he sort of is wearing an adult-size onesie.

I reach up to brush off a piece of lint and then put my hands on his shoulders.

"It's not my scene. Besides I am looking forward to hearing the play-by-play later," I say, backing away from him.

He twirls for me with his arms outstretched. "Not too shabby," he says with a wink.

"You're going to be the belle of the ball," I say with a smile.

"Clara is going to love it, right?"

I continue to smile, but he gives me a confused expression. I must have blinked or twitched or done something his telescopic vision picked up.

"Who wouldn't love you?" I ask.

He relaxes and blushes a little. He has a deep insecurity about being a burden to his parents, wanting to earn his keep on Earth, wishing he wasn't the only one of his kind here. I'm always mindful of letting him know how wonderful he is and how lucky we are to be around him.

Hal has a corsage in a plastic box that he's going to place on Clara's wrist. He got a lily on his own this time, but I don't think he thought to ask what color Clara's dress would be, so who knows if it will match. I didn't remind him to ask her.

Then the gas-up music on Hal's radio is interrupted by a wheezy, high-pitched, sinister voice.

"Good evening, citizens of Gateway City," the voice screeches through the speaker. "Don't be alarmed, it's just good old Dr. Radium wishing you good tidings. That is, until eight o'clock tonight."

"That's what he sounds like?" I ask, surprised. I always thought he'd have a deeper voice underneath that helmet of his.

Hal shushes me, listening far too intently for my liking.

"I have taken your beloved Galaxy Girl," Dr. Radium continues. "She's fine for the time being, so long as my experiments this evening go undisturbed. If the Legion of Dopes or the authorities do interfere, however, I'm afraid Galaxy Girl won't be a part of our galaxy any longer."

Hal rushes past me to the window and stares outside.

"Don't you *dare*, Hal," I say, knowing he's using his telescopic vision to try and find where Dr. Radium is hiding her.

"He's not going to be expecting me," Hal says. "I'm not in the Legion of Hope."

"You are sixteen," I yell. "You are not equipped to go up against a deranged supervillain by yourself."

"Yes, I am," he says matter-of-factly. "You know I am." He turns away from the window and begins to undo the bow tie.

"You can't stand her up," I say, exasperated.

"I won't," he says, motioning for me to hand him his backpack, but I don't. He gives me a look like I'm the one being unreasonable as he walks past me to retrieve it. "You can pick her up, tell her I'll meet you two there, then I'll teleport back in time before the dance even starts."

"*I* can pick her up?" I say, my anger getting the better of me. "She doesn't want to go to the dance with me. She wants to go with *you*!"

"I know," he says slowly as he starts taking off his suit jacket. "But I can't let Galaxy Girl die."

"I don't want *you* to die, you idiot," I plead. I'm trembling, but he doesn't seem to notice. Instead, he shoves the corsage box and his dad's car keys into my hands.

"It's one night. Gateway City needs you. I need you."

I look into his eyes and see the twinkle that appears when he gets all inspirational. And I fall for it every stupid time.

"You better show up at that dance or she's going to end it."

"I'll be there. I promise," Hal says.

♡

Clara's aunt opens the door about two seconds after I push the doorbell.

"Oh! Hello," she says, looking past me and trying to find Hal.

"Hello, Ms. Huang," I say, wearing a dress that's a little tight because I haven't worn it since my cousin's wedding last summer. My hair is in a high bun because I didn't have time to do anything fancier with it. "I'm Alia Shadid. Hal had a family emergency, so he's running a little late, but he's going to meet us at the dance," I say at superspeed.

"I know you, Alia," she says with a smile. "You've been going to school with Clara since forever. She's always talking about how smart you are."

"Really?" I ask, then internally freak out because I shouldn't have said that out loud.

"Would you like to come in?" Clara's aunt asks as she opens the door wider.

I follow her inside only to have my heart almost stop when I see Clara walk down the stairs. She is wearing a black dress that I could imagine Nightshade might wear if she wanted to seduce a super before turning them into mulch.

"Of course, it's you," Clara says a little breathlessly.

"Sorry," I say once I regain the ability to speak. "Hal has a family emergency, but he's going to meet us there."

"Don't apologize," she says. "Is everything with his family okay?"

"I hope so," I say honestly. "Oh um, he got you this." Then I hand corsage box.

"Should I pin the boutonniere I got him on you?" she asks, one eyebrow quirked up.

"You can pin it on him when we get to the dance," I say, hoping that will assure her that Hal is going to be there.

"If you say so. Though, I think it might look better on you," she says, sashaying to stand beside me.

I feel my face get hot as she gets closer.

"Since Hal isn't here, you have to fill in for the photo."

I smile politely even though I am doing my best not to think about how this feels like a date.

I'm not her date.

I'm not her *anything*!

Ms. Huang gets her camera ready and points it at us.

"Okay you two beauties," Ms. Huang says. "Smile!"

Clara puts her arm around my waist and I try my best not to react to her touch.

"Perfect! You both look so beautiful."

"We do," Clara says, turning to me, "don't we?"

I can feel her breath on my cheek and her lips are so close to mine that I feel like I might scream.

"Hal will make sure Clara is back by 11:30," I say to Ms. Huang.

She has a perplexed smile on her face, but then it fades as she kisses her niece on the cheek and tells her to have a great time. Clara says she will, and I sincerely hope that's true.

I just hope Hal gets to the dance in time.

Clara is talking with her friends under the streamers and balloons shaped like space-ships. I'm surprised to find they are all pretty cool and I guess I never gave them much of a chance before. Until now, I always figured they wanted to talk to Hal and were only being polite to me. I smile and try to subtly check the clock above the gym doorway. It's 9 already. I'm scared that Hal might be hurt, that Dr. Radium is causing havoc, or that Galaxy Girl is dead, or all of the above.

"Hey," Clara says as she bumps her hip with mine. "Having fun?"

"Dances aren't the worst," I say with a smile. "Hal should be here any minute."

The DJ plays a slow song and suddenly couples start leading each other to the dance floor.

"Do you want to dance?" Clara asks me.

"It's a slow song," I say, but she doesn't seem to understand. "Slow songs are, you know, for like, dates and stuff."

She takes my hand and squeezes it. "I'd like to dance with you."

Before my brain gets in the way, I squeeze her hand back. Friends can slow-dance, I guess.

I hold my arms out like I'm a ballroom dancer and also so there is plenty of space between the two of us.

"Do I lead?" I ask. I'm not really sure what to do, but she just laughs and leans into me.

"Let's not overthink it," she says as her cheek touches mine. She puts her hands on my back and, eventually, I relax and put my arms around her shoulders. "See? You're a natural."

"All we're doing is turning around in circles," I say. Clara laughs again, but I can't help but think that Hal would probably know when to dip her or how to sweep her off her feet. "Hal is going to want to cut in any second now."

She takes a step back, the warmth of her cheek leaving mine. She looks me in the eye and whispers words I never thought I'd hear.

"I don't want him to," she says.

Without her gaze leaving mine, she slowly starts to lean in to kiss me.

But before she's able to close the distance I murmur, "I can't. I want to, but I can't."

Her lips never touch mine, but she licks hers as though they have.

"But you do want to," she whispers. "If . . . I mean if—"

"—My best friend wasn't in love with you?" I ask sadly.

"Doesn't it matter if I'm in love with him?" she asks with a slight annoyance in her voice. "That's the great thing about *dating*. You're not betrothed to someone for eternity."

I was about to object, but she's right. She's a person with agency, not a candy bar that Hal can call dibs on.

"So, I guess I wasn't so great at hiding how I felt?"

"You were until I mentioned the lilies," Clara says. "How long have you felt . . . about me?"

"A while. But not as long as Hal," I say, trying to avert my eyes from her, but I can't. I feel like I'm suddenly under Dr. Radium's Hypnoto-Ray. "I'm not . . . I mean Hal is really something." He's powerful, but he's also practically perfect. While on the other hand, I'm flawed in more ways I could possibly count. There's no way anyone would pick me over him.

"So are you," Clara says. "And, for what it's worth, I think you and I could really be something, too."

"Oh," I say, taking in every inch of her face. I want to tell her that's worth more than she knows.

After a brief silence, she asks, "Is that a good 'oh' or a bad 'oh'?" Though her smile indicates she already knows the answer.

"Goo—" I start to say when the gym doors to my left slam open. I turn to see what is going on and then mutter, "Uh-oh."

"A good 'uh-oh'?" Clara laughs until she follows my eye line.

Hal has burst into the room still looking sharp in his tux even though he isn't wearing his bow tie. I let go of Clara, but I can feel her eyes on me.

"I am so sorry I'm late," Hal says as he approaches us. He has a smudge of dirt underneath his chin, a little sweat on his brow, but he's safe, and that's all that matters.

"Is everything okay?" I ask.

He turns to me, looking disappointed.

"Family emergency is taken care of," he says. "Everything okay here?" I notice that his jaw is clenched and his pupils are dilated. Then it hits me, he was watching us. My tears start to well in my eyes as I realize that he's finally seen what I've been trying to hide this whole time.

"Fine," I say, trying to keep my composure in front of both of them. I search for his dad's car keys in my purse while Hal tells his girlfriend she looks beautiful. Clara half-heartedly thanks him as I hand him the keys, still unable to look at either of them. "You two have a good time." Then I quickly stride toward the exit before either of them can see me cry.

I'm in my pajamas a few hours later when Hal texts to see if he can come over. I text back yes, and he teleports into my room, still wearing his tux. The papers on my desk flutter up in the air when he appears and slowly fall as we look at each other. I've wiped my face clean of makeup and tears, but I don't have to wear a mask of my own making anymore—he knows the truth.

"How was the rest of the dance?" I ask as I sit cross-legged on my bed.

"Okay," he says. "Clara broke up with me."

"Do you want to talk about it?"

"Do *you* want to talk about it?" he asks calmly.

I look down at my comforter, trying to figure out how to answer him. I hate this. We've never had any trouble saying what's on our mind to one another before.

"I'd never betray you," I say, finally.

"I know," he nods. "Maybe if I was honest with her, things would be different." He comes and sits at the edge of my bed and I scoot up and join him. His feet are planted firmly on the floor while mine dangle a little. "Dr. Radium got away, but I saved Galaxy Girl. I've been invited to join the Legion."

"Woah," I say, genuinely impressed, "really?"

"Galaxy Woman said I am ready to be sworn in at the Temple of Peace. Haven't decided if I'll take them up on it yet," he says. "But, if I do, I figure they'll at least give me a better suit. I don't mind the name Heatwave so much anymore, though—it's kind of grown on me."

"Wow," I mumble. Once he has the backing of the Legion, he won't have much use for me anymore. He'll have a whole new crew of superpeers and buds to watch out for him.

"Yeah. It's the big time," Hal says. "I don't really believe it."

"I do. You've always been big time to me," I say truthfully.

He smiles a little and we sit in a semi-comfortable silence for a few moments. "Are we going to be okay?" I ask.

"Eventually," he says. I start to feel horrible until he saves the day yet again. "Like in a day or two."

"I didn't mean to—"

"—I know," he says. "I'm sorry that you felt like you couldn't tell me. I don't know that I've been a good friend lately, but you're the only person I tell all my secrets to. I figured you'd do the same."

"I couldn't talk about her," I say softly. "I know you love her."

"I get it. But I love you the most."

The silence engulfs us again, but it feels less heavy than before.

"I didn't need telescopic vision to see that she was really worried about you after you left tonight."

"Nothing's going to happen," I say.

"If it does, it's okay," he says. "I mean, maybe not at first, but eventually."

"Like in a day or two?" I joke.

"More like a month or two," he says. We both chuckle at that. "Or at least until I get to know Galaxy Girl a little better."

I raise my eyebrows at him in surprise.

"You do have a lot in common," I say. "She should be so lucky."

"Not as lucky as Clara. You're the best, Alia."

Before I can say anything, he smiles at me, and flashes out of my room.

"Do you think if I ask her to prom she'll come?" Hal asks me. I don't know Galaxy Girl's secret identity, but if she does come to the dance, she would be revealing herself to me. He gobbles up his ice cream cone in no time while we walk along the pier.

"Doesn't hurt to try. Have you two talked about who should be let into the inner circle?" I ask.

"She wants to meet you," Hal says. "If you can keep who she is a secret."

"I think I can handle it," I say.

The Legion's given Heatwave some pretty cool resources so I don't have to keep lying for him. It's also been good to set some boundaries with what I can help Hal with and what I can't.

The night sky lights up. Hal's Heatwave logo is in the air above us and I still haven't got used to it. I don't think Hal has either.

"I better go," he says, eyeing the public bathroom.

"Text me when you get home," I say, even though I know he has a whole team of supers who are supporting him, too.

"You know it," he says cockily as he jogs to the restroom. "Have fun tonight."

Clara comes out of the ice cream shop, two cones in her hands. She passes me my coffee cone and holds on to her mint chocolate chip.

"Thank you," I say and kiss her cheek.

"You're welcome," she says as we link arms.

"Hal had to take off."

"He's okay?" she asks, taking a big swipe at her ice cream with her tongue.

"Yeah. He's okay," I say honestly.

"Good. Should we head over to mini golf? Or is that a date night cliché?"

"I think mini golf sounds great."

She doesn't tighten her hold on me as we stroll down the pier. She knows I'm not going anywhere.

(FAIRY)LIKE ATTRACTS LIKE

"Mutual Pining"

Claire Kann

"DOES THIS MAKE ME LOOK FAT?" MARTIKA ASKED, LOOKING AT herself from every possible angle in the mirror. Her costume fairy dress shimmered with molten gold jewels and evergreen leaves in the bright vanity lights.

At Fairydust Sleepaway Camp, the magic of makeup turned humans into fairies.

Nia, who had been fanning her newly attached pointed fairy ear tips to help them dry faster, paused for a beat and asked, "What?"

Martika whined. "Don't look at me like that. James said I gained a couple of pounds. It still fits right?"

". . . What?"

"Why are you always like this?"

"Like what?"

"Please *stop* saying 'what.'"

Nia turned back to her mirror, mischievous grin out in full force. Specificity was *everything* when you didn't have the ability to lie. Her curse, as she liked to call it, came in threefold. One: Absolutely no lying. Two: She *had* to answer direct questions. And three: she saw sparks shoot out of someone's mouth when *they* lied.

She'd given Martika's ill-phrased questions an honest loophole of an annoying answer because she could. Because it was funny. Because her very thin friend was fishing for compliments from the wrong fat girl.

"I'm being serious. Tell me the truth," Martika pressed, but still hadn't specified that "this" and "it" meant *the dress*.

After a dramatic, and relenting, sigh, Nia decided on mercy. She looked her friend in the eyes. "Stop being ridiculous. You look as beautiful as ever."

"Really?" Martika smiled too, slow and dazzling as if with each passing second, she believed the compliment that much more.

"Really." Nia used a little foundation to darken her pointed ears. The latex, a soft tan, was nowhere near a match for her dark-brown skin tone. The company didn't, or wouldn't, make them any darker. "And you should dump your boyfriend."

"One! Two! Three! Eyes on me!" a loud voice said.

Nia turned in her seat just in time to watch Craig, the camp's manager, stride into the dressing room. She stood up and walked with Martika, trailing just behind the other fourteen fairies who had already gathered around him.

Craig had stopped directly in the center of everything wearing his usual getup—yellow shirt, black gym shorts, and a whistle around his neck—because that made *so much* sense. They worked at Fairydust Sleepaway Camp, not Camp Crystal Lake. "All right, group assignments," he said, clapping his hands. "Group One, Cabin Tinkerbell, will be Edward and Silvia. Group Two, Cabin Titania, will be Nia and Glory."

"You always get the best cabin," Martika whispered with a pout.

"Because I *am* the best," Nia said calmly. Meanwhile her brain had started shrieking *Glory? GLORY??*

Across the fairy circle, Glory's amber eyes shone with her usual wicked look as she stared at Nia—part deviant mastermind, part FBI agent, ready to conquer anything standing in her way.

A familiar and exhilarating shiver rippled down Nia's spine. They'd met at camp during orientation three months ago. Almost immediately, she'd felt drawn to Glory like a twitterpated moth to a blazing fire, enthralled and transfixed without a speck of common sense left to save her. That feeling still hadn't faded.

Nia spun around, retreating to her vanity to finish getting ready. Sitting, she took three deep breaths in and out, closing her eyes to focus and find her calm. Her ability, as her parents liked to call it, had to be kept a secret at *all* costs.

Nia was adopted—and neither of her parents had an ability nor any clue where hers came from. They didn't know how to guide her, but they could teach her how to keep herself safe. She'd never forget the terrified look in her dad's eyes when he'd said, "The government experiments on us when they think we don't have superpowers because they've always gotten away with it."

They told her about The Tuskeegee Study, horrifying cases of organ donors being left to die in hospitals and implied consent, monsters like J. Marion Sims, who still very much existed in doctors like those who believed Black people didn't feel pain, and so much more. "We won't let them have you," they'd promised her.

Because of that she kept her friends at a distance and perfected the art of deflection. The responsibility to keep it secret, keep it safe, not just for herself, but for her parents, too. No one could ever find out the truth. When someone suspected anything off about Nia, a simple "Lying's not my thing. I don't see the point of it," usually pacified them and kept her secrets safe for another day.

But that *never* worked on Glory, the only person she'd never been able to fool completely. No, *she* was always watching Nia, always testing her. And even though she knew she shouldn't, Nia let it become a thrilling game between them—who could outwit the other—and it stopped being fun the exact moment Nia realized she had one more secret she wanted to keep from Glory.

Hands steady, Nia strategically sprayed a light mist of extra-hold hairspray on her face and sprinkled glitter across her nose and cheeks. She'd done her hair at home—pulling her braids up into a high ponytail—but added in colorful flowers and bangles to complete her look.

"Nia?" Glory said.

"That is my name, yes," she said sounding colder than intended. *Cool,* she told her brain. *Be cool. Not glacial.* And then, she looked up. *Jesus, help me.* Her heart seized, stopped, and stuttered back to life.

The last time they'd been paired up to work together, Nia almost died.

Okay, no, not really.

Nia couldn't tell lies, could barely even think them, but that had absolutely nothing to do with being overdramatic and hyperbolic. Her heart *could* actually explode. Maybe not from being overwhelmed with feelings she never asked for, but it didn't know that.

Glory must have changed out of her clothes quickly. She lounged against the side of Nia's vanity in her cornflower-blue and silver teardrop dress. Her skin sparkled, warm and golden, as did her mane of honey-colored curly hair, left wild with thin strips of tinsel wound around select curls. Every fairy had been given liberty to pick one extra thing to make their costumes their own. Glory had chosen a pair of short fangs to attach to her canines—a pointed smile for the trickster fairy.

"It's been a while, hasn't it?" Glory always spoke with a measured confidence, making everything she said and asked feel like the challenge it was. "How have you been?"

Nia winced from the force of being asked a direct question she couldn't maneuver around. "Fine," she said with a bright smile.

"Just fine?"

"*Amazing,* actually," Nia said, pairing it with a sarcastic look.

Glory's eyes narrowed ever so slightly. "Amazing how?"

Some days, Nia was positive Glory had figured out all three parts of her curse. "I love my job, my friends are the best, and I've been on like a bazillion small summer getaways with my parents," she said, in one cathartic breath. "Thanks *so much* for asking."

Glory then took it upon herself to sit down next to Nia on the small bench, her back to the mirror. Her perfume, sweet and floral, immediately sent a shock of *oh no, oh god* straight to Nia's senses.

"I've been thinking about you." Glory kept her voice low, like her words were only for Nia.

Around them the dressing room bustled with chaos—clothes being tossed, make-up being traded, wings and glitter galore. No one noticed them or looked their way. No one could hear Nia's heart jackhammering in her chest or see her suddenly clumsy hands shake as she applied her lipstick—a deep burgundy color. "It seems like every time I've tried to talk to you lately, you run away so I'd been hoping Craig would pair us together again."

"Why?" Nia asked before she realized what an epically bad idea that was, and Glory, oh she smiled like a cat who had just caught the canary.

"Why not?" she asked.

Shit. Nia clamped her mouth shut, turning away, and trying to command her body to relax. Open-ended questions like that could be countered if she were careful, but Glory's confession had knocked her off balance. The truth felt too dominant, too ready to fly out of her mouth.

Because I'm different. Because I'm scared you know my secrets. Because I like you.

Because Nia *had* been running away, trying to protect her secrets and her heart. The last thing she wanted was to be forced to confess her feelings because Glory asked the right question.

In seconds, the burn of compulsion began to set in, roasting her throat and shooting fireworks behind her eyes until a small headache began to form. She had to give an answer.

"Nia?" Glory asked, leaning back, eyes on her.

I won't be beaten. Not like this.

Nia willed the fire to shift to her belly, propelling her will forward. She turned back to Glory, game on. "I haven't seen you perform in a while," she said, focusing her intention. "I'm one of the best fairies here. Most of you can't keep up with me so I prefer to be paired with someone up to my standards."

Glory blinked in surprise. "You think you're better than *me*?"

"I said *most*. I'm better than most."

A spike of burn hit Nia quick like a sucker punch and faded. She had answered the question in context to her own—her body didn't always appreciate her creativity, especially when she skidded straight past deflection and veered too close to deception. The punishment for trying to lie outright felt like every inch, every organ, every muscle, every nerve in her body had been set on fire. She'd only experienced the agony of being burned alive from the inside out once in her life, when she was seven, and swore to never put herself through that again.

Once was more than enough for an entire lifetime.

"Are you willing to bet on that?" Glory asked.

"On what?"

"Who's the better fairy?"

"If I think I'm the best, and you think you're the best, it's an arbitrary tie."

"Then we'll use the kids to decide," she said. "At Sunrise Breakfast whoever has more younglings on their side of the table wins."

"Wins what? Clout?"

"And glory." She grinned at her wordplay with a daring look in her eyes. "If I win, you'll owe me one wish. In the unlikelihood that I lose, I'll give you the same."

"That's too vague of a prize," Nia said. "What would stop you from wishing for something I don't want to do?" *Or confess to*, she thought.

"You'd have the same freedom with me."

"I trust myself to be a good person."

"Give me some credit here," Glory said with a laugh. "A secret, then."

"No."

"A promise?"

"Same difference."

"A promise is way less severe than a wish." Something shifted in Glory's eyes— and Nia knew exactly what it was. "What do you want?"

Right on cue, the truth popped into Nia's brain: *I want to get to know you, honestly and without being afraid, and I want you to know me, too,* but she said, "Right now, I want some water." She picked up her eyeliner to give her eyes wings and she'd layer it with two sets of lashes later. "Tell me what you'd wish for. What kind of secret? What sort of promise?"

For the first time since she'd sat down, Glory averted her gaze. "I don't know yet." Pale sparks of light shot out of her mouth fading into the air.

Nia froze as a jolt of realization flitted through her stomach. Glory knew *exactly* what she wanted and had lied about it. This wasn't a spur-of-the-moment bet—it was a setup. She'd been *preparing* for this moment.

"How about this," Glory began. "We perform our fairy hearts out and after our younglings go to sleep, we'll finalize the details. That way we'll both have an idea of how much we're willing to put on the line before sunrise."

"And if we don't agree?"

"That's the rule. We have to choose something. No backing out. Nothing vague. So, are you in?"

Nia looked in the mirror, focusing on Glory next to her. Whatever she asked for she had to be prepared to lose in return. Kids could be fickle—they could love her best, but still sit with Glory because she was beautiful. Nia wouldn't blame them. She'd do the same, probably.

The game they played had always been an unspoken thing, but now, Glory was clearly after something. Nia knew she should say no. She knew she should try to keep things how they had always been between them.

But she wanted to know. She had to. And she wanted to *win*.

"I hope you enjoy losing. I hear that kind of thing can be hard to deal with."

Fairydust Sleepaway Camp had a second set of talent: humans who'd been cast and tasked with keeping the fairies in line. Behind the scenes, they made sure everything ran smoothly—a crucial magic ingredient to making sure each event was a success. And on the auditorium stage, they told an elaborate story: a tale of whimsy and danger, reenacting how they'd painstakingly captured every fairy by learning their True Name and "convincing" them to work at the camp so they could meet all the wonderful kids in the audience.

The crowd loved it—gasping and laughing, clapping their hands, and shouting *I believe in fairies!* when asked.

Nia stood in line next to Glory, waiting in the theater wings for their turn to be introduced. They were the same height—the warmth from Glory's shoulder almost touching hers made her ball her hands into fists. *Too close, too close, too close.* She concentrated on her breathing. In and out. In and out.

Glory turned her head slightly, watching Nia. The gentle slope of her nose crinkled as she smiled. "You can't possibly be nervous." Her voice had a dark teasing edge to it, but she'd kept her questions to herself, so Nia kept silent, eyes to the front. "Although I wouldn't blame you if you were. You talked a big game, but we both know I'm the best."

"Who is *we*? And why are they lying to you?"

"Ah, there you are," she whispered in that soft tone, same as before in the dressing room.

Finally, their turn. The host introduced Cabin Titania: Nia, a musical fairy who would sing them to sleep at night (or anytime they said the magic word), and Glory, the trickster fairy tasked with keeping them on their toes with riddles, so they could earn special prizes. They walked onstage together, waving and blowing kisses to the crowd.

Seeing all those shining eyes and gap-toothed smiles light up with the purest joy never failed to send Nia floating straight to the moon. Covertly, she clicked the button on her bracelet that made her wings flap every few seconds. A little girl in the front gasped in delight and pointed when she saw them move—Nia winked at her. She smiled at the adult next to the girl for good measure as she took her place in line.

The adult, however, didn't return her smile, choosing instead to stare at Nia's legs. It was a hard look to miss and unfortunately, she'd gotten used to it.

All the fairy staff wore the same costume, dresses and tunics designed and cut from the same rainbow cloth. Nia just happened to be the only fat fairy on staff, so naturally the uniform fit her differently. Her lovely, perfect, ten out of ten, seafoam-green dress dotted with mini pastel pink water lilies barely reached mid-thigh and the spaghetti straps had been designed for someone who never experienced the unbearable weight of boobiness a day in their life. But it did fit better than the dress she'd worn on her last shift. She'd stepped on the stage and could practically feel the complaints being composed by concerned parents about indecency.

Nia tugged at the sides of her dress, trying to pull it down. She didn't feel shame about her size often, had even gotten past her frustration from dealing with her friend's complaints about their size in front of her, like Martika had earlier. But sometimes, it was as unavoidable as not being able to lie. Embarrassment felt just as hot and almost as horrible.

Glory gave her a curious look. "That dress looks really good on you," she whispered, holding Nia at the wrist to make her stop—but it didn't last. All at once, she seemed to realize what she'd done and pulled her hand away, swallowing hard as she turned her attention back to the crowd.

What just happened? Nia thought, careful to not let the confusion brewing inside show on her face. She touched her wrist where Glory's hand had been, marveling at the feeling stunning her from head to toe. Her heart, her lungs, her *everything* reacted in chaos—*This is not a drill! We have made first contact!* The fairies were encouraged to be playful and physically affectionate with each other, but she'd *never* done that with Glory.

They didn't see each other outside of camp, didn't text or call. All they'd ever had was stolen moments during their shifts and long conversations after hours that Nia practically lived for. She remembered each one, especially the last when she'd felt the unmistakable desire to kiss Glory. The urgency of it surprised her—and made her run away. God, if Glory touching her wrist for five seconds made her react like this, kissing her might truly send her to the Great Beyond after all.

"Game on," Glory whispered as they left the stage. She walked in front of Nia and had balled her hands into fists at her sides.

The kids had already been presorted into their groups, making it easier for them to file out of the auditorium together. First, they stopped by Cabin Titania to put their things away, claim their beds, and have proper introductions. Each kid, now transformed into a fairy youngling, got a chance to choose a new fairy name for themselves while Glory recorded it in the fairy guest book. The very second they finished Nia allowed herself to fall completely into character.

Every time a youngling shyly whispered the magic word to her, she broke into song, belting out stolen choruses from 1980s synth power ballads. During arts and crafts, she shared her best makeup tips and encouraged the younglings to decorate their brand-new wings with their hearts and not their minds. Next, they took a walk around the camp and rode some of the carnival-like rides. She sat with the kids too scared to go on by themselves and took selfies with them on the carousel. For dinner, they hosted an elaborate picnic in a "secluded" area of the camp right beside the fairy mound the younglings were absolutely not allowed to enter under any circumstances, lest they be whisked away forever. She taught them the best way to eat decadent fairy cakes, drizzled with honey with a dollop of cream.

At sunset, they brought all the younglings back together for a fairy revel that lasted until sunrise—commonly known as a dance party that lasted until 10 p.m. Nia made it her mission to search for the wallflowers with zeal, inviting them to join her group, and before she knew it, she'd been surrounded by little ones. A lot of them really hadn't figured out what rhythm was yet, bless their little hearts, but jumped and moved around with their whole soul anyway.

Nia's shifts simply never, ever felt like *work*. She'd done her job, same as always, and all the while, she knew Glory had been watching her. Glory didn't bait her with direct questions, didn't try to distract her at all, didn't try to steal the youngling's attention. She had played her role, played with the kids, and *watched* Nia.

It wasn't that Nia didn't care because of course she did. She'd practically developed a second curse: the ability to sense the precise moment Glory's eyes were on her. A silky feeling skimming across her skin. A welcome jolt restarting her already beating heart.

Even now as they walked back to Cabin Titania, Glory hadn't stopped. A youngling stumbled over his feet, so sleepy he could barely walk. Nia scooped him up without a word, balancing him on her hip while he rubbed his sleepy face on her shoulder. They made eye contact over his head—another shock, another current of longing.

Their assigned human handlers met them at the cabin to help put the kids to bed. The whole process (quick showers, brushing their teeth, pajamas, tucking them in) took about an hour. As promised Nia sang the "Goodnight Younglings" song—an original composition, this time. They said goodbye to their kids with promises to see them in the morning for breakfast.

Once they were outside Glory asked, "You're still a cabin kind of girl, right?"

"Right."

Some staff, like Glory, lived close enough to go home when they clocked out or had a car to drive themselves. Nia preferred the staff cabins—much easier than asking her mom to come pick her up at midnight when her first shift ended and bring her back to start her next one at 7 a.m.

"I'll walk with you."

"Oh, you don't have to. It's not far."

"I want to," Glory said, already leading the way.

Strings of connected lights had been set up along the cement paths and threaded through the bushes. They blinked in patterns, meant to resemble fireflies, and were pretty, but not exactly helpful in the visibility department. According to Craig, fairies using flashlights would ruin the illusion and aesthetic. Luckily, they had the full moon shining overhead on their side.

Glory kept her gaze on her feet as she walked, uncharacteristically quiet, which was a bit unnerving. The scarce bit of light fighting against the darkness made her look impossibly softer. So deep in thought, she looked almost sad—was Nia reading her wrong?

"You okay?" she dared to ask. Nia wasn't sure what she'd been expecting. Maybe Glory gloating? Being so confident about winning it would be borderline obnoxious? They still had to finalize their bet, but if Glory didn't bring it up, neither would she.

"You're going to win," Glory said. A breathy laugh of surprise escaped her. "I watched you all afternoon. You really are a cut above the rest of us."

"Oh. Well. I tried to tell you." Nia shrugged. She had done her best, not to win the bet, but because that's just what she did. An opportunity to make youngling dreams come true wasn't something she took lightly. Even if it were only for two precious days, magic could be real for the ten and under crowd. Besides, the camp wasn't exactly cheap—she knew some families saved up specifically so they could send their kids for their birthday or as a special treat. "But you were pretty good too."

"Not good enough to win, unfortunately," Glory said with a wry grin that didn't last. "Have you decided what you want for the bet?"

"I haven't thought about it, actually," she said and then remembered that Glory had lied earlier. She could ask for that. "I want to know what you would've asked for with your wish. If I win, that's what I want."

"Now, that's ironic—you wanting secrets from me."

"What's that supposed to mean?"

Glory *tsked*, releasing an epic side-eye. "I'm not stupid, Nia." If anything, she was too smart, too observant.

"I know that," Nia said carefully. Being forced to tell the truth was the bane of her existence. Was it wrong to ask someone else to do the same because they lost a bet? She added, "And I never said you were."

"So, do you actually want me to say it out loud?" Glory stopped walking, turning to face her. "Are we really going to bare our souls right here and right now?"

"No," Nia whispered, unsure of what else to say. Whatever she'd stepped in, she wanted to step right back out of it. Fear made her wary, jumpy as a rabbit. With the right question, Glory could trap her.

"Just wish for whatever you want. We don't even have to wait until sunrise. I lost. I know that," Glory said. "Whatever it is, if it's within my power, I'll give it to you."

I want to get to know you, honestly and without being afraid, and I want you to know me too.

Nia didn't know Glory well enough to trust her, but *god* did she want to. Maybe that's why she'd always been so willing to play the biggest secret of her life like a game with Glory. If she found out, then Nia could be herself. What *if* Glory knew? Would it really be the end of the world as she knew it?

There would *always* be a power imbalance between them, for sure, but she couldn't be afraid forever, could she?

Closing her eyes, she took a deep breath to steel herself, ignoring her anxious heart, screaming at her to reconsider. When she opened her eyes, she said softly, "That really was it. I honestly wish to know what you wanted for winning our bet."

Glory flinched back, in surprise as if Nia had slapped her. Her face had begun to flush upward, like a thermometer in boiling water. Not even the dark could hide it. She balled her hands into fists, biting her lip and looking away. "I wanted— to ask—" She swallowed as if she were fighting against herself, trying to stop herself from speaking.

Nia recognized that resistance, something she knew intimately and better than anyone else.

Oh my god.

Oh. My. God.

Glory was fighting against *compulsion.* Her eyes widened and tiny beads of sweat appeared on her forehead. "Willyougoonadatewithme?" She exhaled, sighing in relief as her eyes fluttered close for a moment.

But now it was Nia's turn because Glory's answer had been a direct question. The compulsion slammed into her and she whispered "Yes" at the same time Glory said, "I'm sorry."

Glory bowed her head and continued, "I didn't want to ask because I knew you'd have to answer, and I didn't *actually* want to know, but I also did because I thought maybe you liked me.

"You've just been avoiding me so much lately that I wasn't sure anymore. And then you barely talked to me while we were working today so I was going to ask for something completely different if I won."

Nia froze in place, stupefied by her own stupidity. That precious feeling of liking someone, warm and surreal and slightly nerve-wracking, had always felt like it was hers and hers alone. She couldn't imagine someone like Glory ever being flustered enough to feel it too, let alone feel it for her. But there she was, red as a tomato, earnest and upset.

Glory looked up, eyes searching Nia's face. "You weren't supposed to ask me what *I* wanted. I wanted to grant *your* wish. I wanted to show you we're the same."

"Well, you definitely did that," Nia said, too shocked to even smile. Everything was happening too fast. The night was still around them, but she could practically feel herself hurtling through space on a giant rock. Glory *liked* her. And they were the *same*? "Did you know about me? This whole time?"

"I had a feeling," Glory said, that intimate, soft tone of hers making a comeback at the perfect time. She stepped closer to Nia, leaving hardly any space between them. "When I first saw you, I just knew, you know? There was something irresistible and familiar about you, but I realized it wasn't wishes. I figured out it was related to questions somehow." She shrugged. "That's as far as I got."

"Wishes?"

"Yeah. It's my magic word. If anyone says '*I wish*' I have to try and do whatever they say. They can't force me to hurt myself or do something impossible like making money appear out of thin air, but other than that if I can't do it—" She trailed off. "Let's just say it's very unpleasant afterwards. How does it work for you?"

Nia told her the three rules and then asked, "Are you adopted too?"

"Yeah." She nodded. "My family doesn't know about it. Yours?"

"My parents do and they're super protective," Nia said and added conversationally, "so, we're both cursed."

"Is that what you call it?" Glory laughed, crinkling her nose. "And," she continued softly, "we like each other?"

"I think so."

"Okay. Good." Glory exhaled, shaking the nerves out of her hands with another gentle laugh—such a shy, vulnerable side of her that Nia had never seen. She couldn't help but wonder what other sides Glory had been hiding and if she'd get to see them—because she wanted to.

Nia reached out, taking Glory's hand. "Come on," she said, gently tugging her to follow. They still had to clock out at the cabins. But then after . . .

"I don't think it's a curse," Glory said, eyes on hers. "And I don't think the FBI will come for us."

"How did you—"

"Every time someone makes a wish, I learn one of their worst fears in return. That's why I was sorry. I didn't realize how afraid of our power you were."

Our power. Those two words made her feel lighter than air, filling her up with dizzying happiness. They really were the same. "Do you know where it comes from?"

"No, but maybe we can try to find out together." Glory squeezed her hand, anchoring her to reality and that moment. "Maybe we really are fairies. That'd be really funny."

THESE STRINGS

"Sibling's Hot Best Friend"

Lilliam Rivera

THE MOST TRAGIC STORY EVER TOLD IS THE TALE OF PINOCCHIO.
If you've never heard of the story, it is about a talking block of wood carved into a puppet by Geppetto, a poor wood-carver. The wood-carver insisted he only wanted to show Pinocchio love, but the puppet wanted to become a real boy. Pinocchio longed for human adventures and he tried but his wild escapades always ended in disaster, which somehow proved Geppetto's point that he was right in being strict. Maybe you would put the blame on Pinocchio for not staying put, but I don't. I know what it's like to be stuck, to be pulled in only one direction. Like Pinocchio I am forced to heed rules that keep me quiet when all I want is a tiny bit of adventure.

I gaze at Oscar who uses delicate hands to manipulate the strings of an old puppet taken from our archives. The puppet is hunched over and sitting at the very edge of a stage, as if it is weeping. Oscar is so good at what he does you believe in this puppet's sadness. I know I do. I also can't stop staring at Oscar.

"That looks really great," I say. "Maybe lift the puppet's head a little bit."

"No one asked your opinion. Will you get out of the way?"

The person saying this is not Oscar. No, that voice belongs to my older brother Julián and he once again proves my point about Pinocchio. Some families have taco trucks or invest in portable bookmobiles—not us. The Marin family owns the city's only Latinx traveling puppet show, Marin's Magical Teatro of Puppetry. Puppets have been part of my whole life. My father is a puppeteer. So was my grandfather, my great-grandfather, and so on. We are a family that builds and restores puppets. It is what we do best. We bring joy to many, young and old.

But there's one hitch. Although I'm a Marin, I only do the administrative and puppeteering part of the business. I've never been able to be on the creative front like my brother Julián, to share my ideas about new shows and be a showrunner. Whenever I try to, I'm shut down. Men have always been the voice of Marin's Magical Teatro of Puppetry and I'm so sick of it.

"I want to hear what Lili thinks," Oscar says. Unlike my brother and the rest of my family, Oscar is the only one interested in what I have to say. He's really tall with bushy hair and his smile is like when you see a butterfly appear out of nowhere. It is a sweet surprise, a sunbeam hitting a calm river, the first hint of rain, a rainbow, a . . .

Yeah, another problem of mine. I got it *bad* for Oscar.

"You just need the right type of music to go with it," I say. "The audience will be filled with sentimientos."

Julián bristles.

"Stop wasting Oscar's time," he says.

"She's not," Oscar says. "She's right. I should hold the puppet's head up. See?" He does the scene again with the new iteration. It looks so much better, so soulful and real.

"I'm the one in charge here, not Lili," Julián says before turning to me. "Don't you have ticket sales to check?"

Julián's latest idea is to create a YouTube Channel. I offered to come up with puppet show episodes for the channel. The scowl Julián gave me then is the same one he flashes right now. I leave them both in the children's outdoor theater, otherwise known as our backyard but embellished with a tiny stage.

I should be used to Julián shutting me down but it still hurts, especially when Oscar is around. Julián and Oscar have been inseparable since kindergarten, and Dad quickly took young Oscar under his wing. He's one of our best puppeteers now. Funny, I always thought Oscar was just my brother's annoying best friend growing up, but ever since he returned from a summer spent in Costa Rica things changed. I couldn't help notice how he let his hair grow out and his long lean muscles—anyone with eyes can see that.

But it was our recent conversations that sealed the deal for me. When he came back from Costa Rica, he no longer spoke to me like I was the bratty younger sister. We talk about everything: our love for puppets, about traveling and seeing more of the world. Oscar never laughs at any of my ideas. Instead he keeps encouraging me to tell Julián and my father how I feel. He sees me in a way no one else does and I think he feels the same way for me that I do for him. I mean, I hope he does.

I enter our house and head to the kitchen where I last left my laptop. Every Saturday morning, Marin's Magical Teatro of Puppetry hosts a show for kids in our backyard. The admittance is only five bucks, but we usually just let the neighborhood kids watch it for free. There was a time when my father owned his own theater downtown. I have fuzzy memories of running around backstage with puppets hanging from the ceilings, but rents became too high and he had to close it down.

"Good morning my petite Lili," Mom says as she sips her morning coffee.

I was named after the movie *Lili* starring the dancer slash actress Leslie Caron. It is a 1950s classic that no one ever heard of except for my mom and me. If you look at pictures of me when I was a kid I sported the same cute French bob like Leslie did in the movie. I still have a cute bob, but it's more like an homage to the French new-wave actress Anna Karina now. I also have freckles and they're sprinkled across my nose and fair skin like pepper.

"Good morning," I say as I check the online sales, which aren't many.

Our Saturday shows are mainly a tradition Dad would never end. Although he works full-time at the Jim Henson Creature Shop as a mechanic and animatronics specialist, he allocates as much time as he can to running the traveling puppet show. After the theater closed down, he invested in a large van and converted it with a tiny stage. The traveling show visited countless schools and festivals. Now summers are our busiest months, but commercials and contract work is where the real money is—we are hired to do music videos, ads, even puppet film cameos. Julián thought if we did these videos, we could drum up more business. As a showrunner, he gets to direct and order the puppeteers around. Which is great for him, but I know I can do it too.

"How does it look out there?"

"Okay, I guess. Oscar seems to know what he's doing," I say, trying to sound all nonchalant.

Mom's eyebrows go up in response. She's fully aware of my pining although I've never technically mentioned how I feel about Oscar. I refuse to call it a crush because the word makes it sound as if it's destined to fizzle out.

Dad enters from the workshop, a converted garage that houses all of our archives. I try my luck once more.

"Hey Dad, I thought maybe today I can be the showrunner and Julián work backstage?" I say. "It would be good practice for me."

Dad gives me a warm smile and then he lightly brushes a strand of hair away from my eyes.

"Not yet petite Lili," he says. He pours himself a cup of coffee and heads to his private workstation. His answer is always the same.

"Soon," Mom adds, and the discussion ends as quickly as it began.

I stare at my computer's keyboard. If I were anyone else I would slam the laptop closed. That's just not in my nature. Instead, I sigh and do as I'm told because, if anything, I am a dutiful daughter who listens and obeys. I'm almost sixteen years old, only two years younger than Julián, but I will always be petite Lili to my parents. Oscar doesn't treat me like a child. Why can't they?

Eventually I help set up chairs in the backyard underneath a big tent, so the sun won't toast any of the tiny heads in the audience. It's only a half-hour show and we've done it so many times. We should try new things. Incorporate current songs that are popular like a BTS puppet dance or a TikTok challenge with the puppets. I have so many ideas to punch things up. Too bad my list is just that, a list on my laptop that keeps growing and growing.

When the kids are finally settled, I join Oscar and Julián backstage. The stage is a small wooden structure with large curtains concealing what happens. Out front, the children only see the stage and the puppets entering and emerging from behind curtains. Backstage, we stand on small step ladders to be able to maneuver the marionettes. It's a tight squeeze but we manage. Unlike the previous somber show Oscar was trying to create this morning, this show is way livelier with old songs most of the neighborhood kids know by heart.

"They're ready," I say and place myself beside Oscar. Julián presses the button on the sound system and the first song begins. He soon leaves us alone so we can work. I try not to think of the amount of times Oscar presses against me—it's too many to count. Instead I try to concentrate on delivering joy onto the stage through the different puppets—the singing sunflowers, the chirping birds, the comical mariachis.

Towards the end of the show, there is a scene about a young girl who longs to be with the moon and how the moon serenades her until she falls asleep. This is the finale and it's a way of calming the children from the excitement that happened moments before. Oscar plays the moon and I the little girl while Julián hands out tiny puppet moons on sticks to the kids.

"I only want to be with you," I say as the little girl. "Why can't I stay with you?"

"If you look up to the sky, you will see me again," Oscar says as the moon. "I will always return. Look up."

"What if the clouds deceive me? What if the twinkling of the stars confuses me?"

"I am the moon and I will always return. Now be still. Close your eyes and dream."

Oscar inches closer. This part I love more than anything and, although I've performed this scene countless times, I still look forward to it with all my heart.

"I will close my eyes and will dream only of the moon," I say, turning to Oscar who stares back at me. He must feel this between us. He must. "I will dream of you and wait for your return."

Then the lullaby plays that serenades the little girl until she falls asleep.

"I have an idea for the show," Oscar whispers as the song plays. "I think you'll like it."

"Does Julián know?" I ask, nervous for both of us but especially for me.

Oscar shakes his head. "He's too busy with his camera. We can work on it tomorrow."

"He won't be happy if he finds out," I say.

"We're not doing anything wrong. Just working." And I wonder if what I'm feeling is really all in my head. That this is really about work and nothing more.

"Okay, sure," I say and Oscar's beautiful smile makes me think otherwise.

I allow the kids' screaming and applauding to cover the butterflies fluttering inside me.

It's Sunday and Julián is having a discussion with Dad. From the kitchen window I can see Oscar hard at work mending the puppets from the archives. After the weekend shows, Sunday evenings are for taking care of the old puppets, making sure the delicate toys from previous years are preserved. We each take a project or two. It's been a tradition ever since I can remember, except Julián has broken our custom again, and Dad isn't pleased.

"The deposit is due this week," Julián says. He holds out a copy of an application for a film institute.

"How is this going to help us?" Dad has a tiny hammer, nailing a new crossbar. "If you are attending this film course, who will be the showrunner?"

"I can handle both," Julián says. "Will you please let me do this? It will add to the business. We need to be on camera more. We can't keep doing the same thing."

"The same thing has been working for us for generations," Mom says.

"I, ummm—" I try to interrupt, to volunteer.

"Not now, Lili," Mom says.

There's no point. I grab my stuff and walk to the workshop.

When I open the door, I find Oscar hunched over the table, headphones on, engrossed in the task before him. I settle at the other end of the table. His brown curls practically cover his eyes. I press down on my bangs.

"Are things heating up out there? Can't tell with these things on," he says, pulling off his headphones.

"Yeah. They'll sign him up for the film course, but it's going to cost Julián a whole lot of sentences," I say.

"Not sure Julián has enough words to ever convince Mr. Marin."

It's hard to ignore how much my father wishes Julián was more interested in the puppets. He just never has been, even as a little kid. He's always wanted to do film, but as the only boy in the family it only makes sense Julián will eventually take over the family business.

"So, Lili, when are you going to talk to your dad?" Oscar asks as if he's reading my thoughts. This has been our pattern in recent interactions. Oscar nudging me to confront Dad.

"I keep trying but no change. I guess they're used to me being behind the stage, not in front like Julián."

Oscar stops what he's doing. "They are wrong."

Of course, it's easy for Oscar to say this. As much as he's been around us all of our lives, he's still not family. He can make these observations without the brunt of actions yielding devastating results. Case in point: There's a family rumor about my great-grandmother Amelia and how one day as a ten-year-old kid she decided to lead puppet shows all on her own. She did this during her lunch break at school for free. When word got out about her lunchtime performances, her parents swiftly ended them and Amelia never once picked up a puppet, crushing her creativity for good.

"I just feel you deserve more. You are really talented," he says, and I'm left scrambling to find the right words to respond to his kindness.

"Do you want to try out the new thing you were talking about?" I shyly ask and walk over to his side of the table. He takes out the old man puppet Julián was videotaping yesterday. Then Oscar searches the archives. One wall is dedicated to music, albums and tapes of various songs used in shows stored in alphabetical order. Another nook has marionette prototypes. A box of puppet heads. Another of clothes. Oscar stands in front of the large bookcase where we store old puppets labeled with the year they were created and their names. He carefully pulls out a beautiful puppet of a young woman with long brown hair. She's wearing a red dress with flowers. The puppet is from the 1950s and hasn't seen much life. It needs a paint job and the dress is dull. He hands the puppet to me.

"Poor Francesca," I say, using a towel to wipe her face. "She's seen better days."

"I was thinking, maybe he is sad because he's thinking of his love for Francesca. Maybe she appears to him. What do you think? Too corny?"

"No! She appears to him to share this memory of dancing together," I say. "To remind him of the beautiful moments they had."

Oscar manipulates the old man to express his sadness and loneliness. "Why don't you try this?" I say and show Oscar how the sad puppet will look like when he sees Francesca again.

"You're really good at getting at the heart of a performance," he says as he tries out what I show him.

"I like finessing the idea," I say of directing.

"Don't you think they would want you to do the thing you love?" he says, stopping.

"They keep seeing me as the little kid, the one that used to follow you and Julián around. They don't see me the way I am now. Grown."

"I see you."

My heart beats so fast. Can he hear it too?

"Really?" I ask.

"Yeah, I do. Ever since I got back, I don't know, I feel really comfortable around you," he says. "Julián is my bro, but he can't chill, not like you. It's like you and I speak the same language, you know what I mean?"

Strange how suddenly time stands still as he tells me this. He looks at me deeply, longingly, with dark-brown eyes and I can't help but wonder, Is this really happening?

Suspirar, it's what I do. As the sigh leaves my lips, Oscar leans forward. His lips are as soft as his fingers now resting over my hand. We kiss for the first time ever and it feels right. Everything feels *right*.

Then, suddenly, Oscar pulls away.

"Damn. I'm sorry, Lili. I shouldn't have done that."

Huh?

"I . . . what?" My face is burning up, catching on fire.

"It's not that I don't want to. It's just, you know. It's not cool. Your brother would kill me if he found out."

My brother. How did Julián enter this stage only meant for two? I don't look up. I can still feel his lips on mine and I also feel really foolish.

"I'm sorry," he says again.

"Hmm," I mutter. I put down Francesca and walk out.

I hear him apologize again, but I don't want his words to reach me so I walk as fast as I can.

It's hard to avoid someone when you work closely with them, but I do my best. Whenever Oscar enters a room, I excuse myself and walk out. This goes on for a few days and it's working for me but it is so painful. And, unfortunately, today is Saturday, which means we will be working backstage together again. I'm dreading it.

"They're ready," I say. I don't look at Oscar, but I know he's looking at me.

"Lili, we haven't spoken about what happened," he says.

I can't even bring myself to stand by him although it's my job. I guess I didn't think this through, how to work with Oscar without having to be near him. It's an impossibility.

"I don't want to talk about it," I say finally. "Let's just forget it."

Julián stomps backstage. He is in a bad mood. Things with Dad must not be panning out. I shake my head at Oscar who continues to talk. Now is not the time. Actually, the time for this talk is *never*.

"Lili, hear me out," Oscar says.

"What the hell is going on with you two?" Julián asks.

"Nothing," I say. "We're ready to go."

It feels like everyone backstage is weathering their own storm and we're all going to get hit with lightning.

"Stop talking and concentrate," Julián says.

But Oscar won't stop. "Lili, I didn't mean to hurt you," he says. "The kiss wasn't a mistake—what I did afterwards was."

140

Oh no.

"What the hell did you say?" Julián says, quickly in a rage. "What did you *do* to Lili?"

Oscar stands, his hands raised, trying to placate Julián, but my brother only heard the words he needed to hear.

"I would never hurt Lili, bro," Oscar says. "Let me explain."

"You did what? You kissed Lili?"

Julián pushes Oscar so hard he falls back, toppling the stage.

The kids scream. I scream.

"Julián, stop!"

Julián forms a fist while Oscar tries again to explain the situation, all the while kids are freaking out along with me. Oscar and Julián had fights before, wrestling matches, those kinds of things, but not this. This is *real*.

My father and mother race out from inside the house towards the stage. Before Dad can pull Julián off Oscar, Julián is able to throw the one punch that lands squarely on Oscar's face.

Today's performance is definitely over.

For a full week I avoid everyone and stay in my bedroom. It's easier to take cover especially when the house feels so crowded with emotions. It also gives me time to process everything.

After Dad broke up the fight and Mom quickly ushered the kids out of the backyard, I led Oscar to the kitchen to tend to his eye. He sat slumped in a chair and I'd never seen him so sad. How could things go so wrong in such a short amount of time?

"Press this against your eye," I said, handing him ice wrapped in a towel.

I was about to leave when Oscar took hold of my hand.

"I'm sorry for not owning up to my feelings," he said. "I like you and I should've told you how I felt."

I wanted to scream with joy.

"I was being a coward. Scared of what Julián would think," Oscar said with a sigh. "Well, now I know what he thinks."

I chuckled at this, then squeezed his hand back. "You better ice that."

Afterwards, things got progressively worse, but not between me and Oscar. I send him a text hello. He responds by wishing me good luck. There's a family meeting today to air out our feelings of frustration. We are all meant to share and so I guess the time is now to make myself be heard.

My parents are seated on the living room couch while Julián is on the armchair. I sit on a simple wooden chair that used to belong to my great-grandmother Amelia. There are pictures of Amelia watching the puppet performances seated in this exact chair—she never missed one. Relegated to watch but not to star. Will I succumb to the same fate as Amelia?

"You are not listening to me," Julián says. The discussion already began without me. "I want to work in film."

"The Marin business is a *family* business," Dad says. "Videos are great but it's not what we do."

They continue like this for like a half hour. Julián pleading for his dream while Dad offers his points, then Julián responds. There is a moment when I'm not even sure why they asked me to be here. I mean, Julián isn't the only family member with dreams. As I listen to them, I can't help but grow more frustrated, they've been ignoring me for so long. I can't take it anymore and I shouldn't have to.

"Can I say something?" I finally say.

Here's my chance. They are looking at me. This family I love.

"I will be the showrunner. I'm more than ready," I say. "It's time I do more for the business than tickets."

"I don't know," Mom says.

"I'm sixteen years old." I stand up from the chair. I speak loudly and clearly but I don't shout. I take my time. "Let me show you what I can do before you say no. It's all I'm asking. The Marin business is my business. Stop pushing me out."

Everyone looks at me—and I mean really looks at me—for what feels like an eternity. I press down on my bangs and hold my head high.

It is Sunday and it's a beautiful clear day. I find Oscar in the workshop tending to the puppets that were damaged in the fight a week ago. His black eye is fading, but you can still see a faint trace of it.

After the family meeting, Julián made amends to Oscar. I don't know what was said, but things seem to be fine between them although not exactly the same. It must be hard to grow up with someone and expect them to act a certain way and then they change. All three of us are taking things very slowly.

Everyone knows how Pinocchio ends up becoming a real boy with the help of a fairy. Although he goes on to live a life as a human, his puppet does not and it lies lifeless on the bed. How tragic that must be, to abandon what was once a part of you. I cry every time I think about it. I would have never abandoned my past life because it is what shapes me. Growing up can be painful, but the journey can also be full of surprises and wonder.

"How is Francesca doing?" I ask.

"I'll have her looking brand new in no time," Oscar says. "Just a tiny stitch here. New strings there. She'll be dancing soon."

I join Oscar at the workstation. We both work on mending the broken puppets together. Oscar doesn't have his headphones on and he quietly hums a tune. Sometimes he sneaks a glance over to me and sometimes I meet his glance with mine.

I think I'm going to like this new Sunday tradition.

THE PASSOVER DATE

"Fake Dating"

Laura Silverman

MY GRANDPARENTS SET THE TABLES A WEEK IN ADVANCE. WHITE
tablecloths first: the one with the rose embroidery on the adult table, plain white
cloths over the rest. Then the china, the set they were given on their wedding day
fifty years ago, white, navy blue, the thinnest trim of gold lacquer. Silverware after,
just the regular stuff, not the real silver, not after my cousin Alana's date stole three
spoons and a butter knife. Then glasses, two each, one for water and one for wine
(or grape juice at the little kids' table).

Finally, the Seder plate, proud and center of it all.

The cooking also starts a week in advance. We all help. My grandparents make
the main dishes, brisket and matzo ball soup. My family makes charoset, grinding up
nuts and apples and spices. And we boil the eggs, *gross*. Aunt Barbra and Uncle Larry
buy the gefilte fish and the wine, *so* much wine. Aunt Judith and Aunt Cheryl make
the kosher for pesach desserts, flourless cake and fruit salad. And my eldest cousins
make matzo from scratch—and also bring more wine.

It's a family affair. A family *tradition*.

Unfortunately, it's also a family tradition to bring a date to Seder. This has been
a storm cloud of annoyance over my head since I turned thirteen. My grandparents
love to share our Seder and the story of Passover far and wide, with Jews and non-
Jews alike. From the time of our b'nai mitzvah, we're highly encouraged to bring a
date. And if we don't, the questions will never stop:

What? You don't like anyone?

You're too shy?

It doesn't have to be a boy, you know! Bring a girl, a nonbinary person, we love everyone!

Sometimes, the questions are more pointed:

What? So, you're going to be alone forever?

Impressively, my great-aunt Esther said that last one without a hint of irony when I was only fifteen.

My siblings and cousins all got with the routine immediately. My older brother Josh brought a date to the Seder right after his bar mitzvah. Alyssa was on debate team with him. She had silver braces and a dappling of freckles across her nose. My grandparents loved her. They also love the dates my older sister, Audrey, brings, a different boy every year, each one more impressive than the last.

My older cousins are either married or bring dates. And even my younger cousin Marty brought a date last year, a soft-spoken boy named Tyler with red hair.

He wore a *tie*. It was *adorable*. Everyone swooned.

And then—

And then everyone looked at me and asked where *my* date was.

I'm eighteen years old and about to come up on my sixth year of failure. Of course, I've told my parents how outmoded it is to force their children into romantic relationships. Romance isn't *for* everyone. Some people don't want a romantic relationship.

And some people, well, some people are eighteen and would maybe possibly definitely kind of want a romantic relationship, if only they could figure out how to string together two sentences in front of a cute boy.

I'm not a total shy hermit. I talk to my family and my friends. I answer questions in class. I make people laugh, occasionally. But stick me in front of an attractive boy, and I clam up with beet-red skin.

It's embarrassing. Archaic. Absurd.

Boys are not special. There is no reason to feel less confident around them. Boys are just humans. It's not a big deal. I could talk to a boy if I wanted to.

And I do want to. Because I can't handle it anymore. I can't handle one more Passover Seder being asked, *And where is your date, Rachel? Oy vey, I hope they didn't get sick!*

Passive-aggressive Aunt Cheryl.

No, thank you. It's not happening.

This year I'll bring someone to Seder just like everyone else. That'll show them. And then next year I'll go off to college, and maybe I won't even come home for Seder.

Maybe I'll stay at school and eat chips and hummus on my dorm room floor like a freaking adult.

Yeah, that'll show them.

Now, just one problem: I need a date.

Matthew Pearlman plays tennis, is on the model UN team, and wears a polo shirt to school every day. He is the epitome of preppy. Not exactly my taste.

But he also has soft hair, intense brown eyes, and a jawline you could write poetry about. He's also single, a requirement for this venture. And we used to be friends in middle school, so I have an in.

Matthew and I always sat together in the back row of Ms. Baumstein's sixth-grade Hebrew school class. We would do anything but pay attention. Matthew enjoyed making paper footballs and flicking them at various goals. I enjoyed decorating his paper footballs with a variety of flowery designs. We held an ongoing, increasingly competitive streak of hangman, and Matthew would mutter a little red-cheeked curse under his breath every time I stumped him.

It probably goes without saying that Ms. Baumstein *hated* us.

I, however, loved us. I looked forward to every Tuesday and Thursday afternoon because it meant spending ninety minutes in the back of a classroom with Matthew, our knees tucked under a desk far too small for growing preteens, snorting and laughing as we received glares from our peers. I was always happy next to Matthew. It was my favorite part of the week, the beginnings of a crush blooming inside me. And the best part was that it felt like I had all the time in the world to let that crush grow. There was no rush, no care, no worry.

But something happened over that long stretch of summer between sixth and seventh grade. Matthew changed. Became a guy's guy who didn't want cute doodles on his paper footballs. Became a guy who stood in the hallway with a pack of other guys, laughing as loudly and as obnoxiously as possible whenever anyone passed by. Became a guy who didn't want to sit in the back of a classroom and play hangman with me.

And, I guess I changed that summer too. Became quieter, less sure of myself. Became aware that people didn't look at me in the way they looked at my older sister, Audrey, with her thick hair, long legs, and a quick-witted response for any comment.

Became aware that the world wasn't made for me to thrive in, that it was my job to find some way to navigate myself to a piece of happiness.

Matthew and I never talked much after that summer. Sometimes, in regular school, we'd ask if the other had last night's homework. Or give a quick head nod as we passed in the halls. But soon even that connection disappeared and, by the time we made it to high school, my friendship with Matthew Pearlman was a faded memory, fragile and worn at the edges, like the flower I pressed into my notebook from the day of my bat mitzvah.

The last time we spoke was a year ago. Matthew surprised me by pulling me aside in the hallway. I was startled to come face-to-face with him after so much time apart. At first I expected the rosy-cheeked sixth-grader I once knew, but the Matthew of today has lost the roundness in his cheeks. In the hallway, with students crowded around us, moving from one class to the next before the bell rang, Matthew asked me if Audrey had a prom date yet. My heart, which I hadn't even realized had taken off with a flutter, dropped to my stomach.

Yes, she has a date, I told him. *Of course,* she had a date. Audrey Ableman basically had her senior year prom date lined up when she was still in utero, and if that somehow fell through, there was a line of eager young men happy to take his place. Matthew was interested in Audrey, just like everyone else in the world. I've got to get to class, I told him, then disappeared into the crowd.

That was the last time we spoke.

Matthew doesn't like me, probably doesn't even think about me. And despite that ridiculous case of heart flutters last year, I don't like him either. That was nothing but surprised adrenaline. Sure, Matthew has grown more attractive over the years. But I'm not attracted *to* him. He's the kind of guy who's going to join the Jewish frat in college and binge drink his college education away, then land a nice cushy job because his brain is good with numbers, while I'm going to toil away with my visual arts degree and barely eke out twenty thousand a year selling handmade jewelry and pottery.

Yes, I know I could major in something else—or, not go to college at all. But that's not an option in my family. At least in the arts, I can do something with my hands. I can make something.

I do not like Matthew Pearlman.

Matthew Pearlman does not like me.

But Matthew Pearlman is my best shot at a Passover date.

I watch him throughout the entire lunch period. He sits in a pack of other boys who wear polo shirts. They talk and laugh loudly and take up a lot of room. They shoot their empty drinks and food wrappers into the trash can like basketballs. They miss half the time and never bother to pick the trash up. They are—annoying.

My best friend, Cassandra, sits next to me. She nudges me in the side every thirty seconds. Her short blond hair is bobbed around her shoulders. "Are you going to do it yet?" she asks. "Time's almost up."

Time is almost up—time for lunch, and time to find a date. Seder is tomorrow night. Like so many other things in my life, I've waited until the last possible second, and now I get to deal with the wonderful anxiety-ridden aftermath.

"Okay, okay." I lean back from the table but don't stand. Have I forgotten how to stand?

No, it's not that. I just don't know how to get to Matthew in that group of boys. Interrupting that much noise seems like an insurmountable task.

But then, luck seems to be on my side. Matthew throws his carton of chocolate milk in the trash and misses the shot. But unlike the rest of his friends, he stands up to walk over and pick it up. This is my chance.

I rush out of my seat so fast I bang my knees on the table. "Ouch! Damn!" I shout, muffling my voice with a hand over my mouth. I can feel Cassandra wince behind me.

I recover and run up to the trash can just as Matthew is throwing away his milk carton. "Hey, there, Pearlman," I say breathlessly.

Pearlman? *What?* I do not call people by their last names. I am not a "bro."

Matthew turns to me, then looks down, which is where I'm located. *Pearlman* is approximately one foot taller than me these days. Guess it's from drinking all of that milk.

"Hey, Rachel," he says, a bit of surprise on his face. "What's up?"

"Um."

I didn't really think this through. I didn't think about *how* to ask him. I only fantasized about the looks on my family's faces when I walk in with a date on my arm.

"Rachel?" he asks. His voice sounds soft around my name, pleasant.

"Um," I repeat. Then rush out the next words. "I need a date to my Passover Seder. Second night. Everyone in my family brings dates. And I've never brought one before. For reasons. And I thought I could bring you this year. Obviously not as a real date. Just to like shut up my family. And yeah my sister will be there, so maybe you can talk to her. And it's tomorrow night. Do you want to go?"

I'm practically panting by the time I'm done with my spiel.

And I almost faint when he shrugs and says, "Sure." There's even a slight smile on his face, probably thanks to the mention of Audrey. "Sounds fun."

"Oh." I'm in shock. "Well, great. Thank you."

He tucks his thumb into his khaki shorts. "No problem."

"And it's *not* a date," I repeat. "It's just, you know, to keep my family from being annoying."

He nods. "Right. Cool. Your family make brisket for Passover?"

I smile, relief trickling through me. "Always."

"Nice." He holds up a hand for me to high-five, then realizes that's much too high for me to reach and lowers it. I slap his hand only a little awkwardly.

As he walks away, I exhale. I can't believe I just did that.

Passover date secured.

Matthew: Can I bring anything?
Me: Nope! All covered!
Matthew: Cool

~five minutes later~

Matthew: My mom says I have to bring something
Me: Haha, okay, whatever you want!
Matthew: Matzo?
Matthew: Wait, no. You'll already have that.
Matthew: Fruit?
Me: We have fruit but could always have more!
Matthew: Nah, I'll think of something. See ya soon

My dress doesn't fit, which is a problem of being the youngest sister who also doesn't like shopping. It's too long on me, too big. Audrey is shaped like a pin-up girl, all softness and curves. I'm shaped like a pin. A really tiny one that falls between the cushions. It's fine. I like my body. I like myself. But this dress most definitely doesn't work on it.

"Mom!" I call, walking over to her bedroom. I find her blow-drying her hair. I scream so she can hear me over it. "Can I borrow a dress?"

She waves her hand toward her closet. "Whatever you want, sweetheart."

Mom is closer to my stature. But also thirty-five years older than me. I raid her closet until I find a plain, sleeveless blue silk dress. It's a little Ann Taylor–looking for my taste, if I had taste, but it fits like an article of clothing should and makes my pale skin look soft instead of sickly. I'll call that a win.

"You look lovely!" she says as I walk out the door.

She's probably trying to butter me up. She probably feels bad for me. Rachel, single as always. I've decided the sweetest revenge will be making it a surprise. Let them all think they know what's going to happen until the last possible second, and then boom—

Rachel will have a date.

When we arrive at my grandparents, the house is chaotic, as usual. Ten different people yelling at once in way too small of a space, little cousins running around in circles, chasing my grandparents' labradoodle, the sounds of cooking and serving and setting all crashing through the kitchen and dining room. I say hello to cousins and aunts and uncles and meet all of their dates—some who have been here before and some who are wide-eyed and seemingly alarmed by all of the noise.

My brother, Josh, is already here with his girlfriend, Cara. They're both seniors in college and planning on becoming dentists, which is great, I guess. Dentistry is a good job. It's important to keep your teeth healthy. But I'd be lying if I said I didn't judge them the tiniest bit for such a boring occupation. And kind of a weird one. Who elects to poke around people's mouths for the rest of their lives? I'm not saying they have some kind of kink, but I'm not *not* saying that.

But yeah, Cara is nice and all. She always gives me a big hug when she sees me and asks how my art is going, and when she goes to get herself a drink, she asks if anyone else needs anything. I like considerate people.

We settle in on the three-seater couch. Josh knocks into my shoulder and says, "Flying solo again, huh? You're a brave one, Rachel."

See? Even my brother makes a thing out of it.

Why does my family care whether or not I have a date?

Why . . . why am I not enough on my own?

I choose not to answer him and instead scroll through photos of a dog Cara is thinking about fostering, even though she doesn't have time to foster a dog, but look how cute he is and it'd only be for a month or two.

A few minutes later, the door opens again. I hear a chorus of "hellos" and "oohs," and I know it must be my sister. I watch as people gravitate from the kitchen toward the entryway to say hello to her, the shining center of every party. I wonder who she brought this year. It's a different man every time, a rotating display of delights, each seemingly more impressive to my family than the last. And this year, she had college boys to choose from.

Approximately ten minutes of greetings later, Audrey enters the kitchen with her date in tow. He must be six-foot-three, and he has light-brown skin and perfectly manicured facial hair. He's dressed nicely, put together but not too formal, slacks and a cotton button-up. His smile flashes across the room, and I can practically hear my entire family swoon.

"Rachel!" Audrey spots me and rushes over into the living room, leaving her date hapless, surrounded by a knot of aunts and uncles.

My attitude melts away a little at her bright smile and the genuine excitement in her voice. I stand up just in time for her to pommel into me with a hug. "Ooph," I say, hugging her back. She smells the same as always. In the ninth grade, Mom gave her a mini bottle of Clinique perfume as one of her Hanukkah gifts, and she still wears the same scent to this day. Even though Audrey is only sixteen months older than me, the age gap feels far larger. She seems mature and worldly in a way I'll never be. At nineteen, she feels like a full-grown adult, so different than even her freshman-year cohorts.

"Missed you," she says, ruffling my short curls. "Three months is three too long."

Even though Audrey's college is only a ninety-minute drive away, she rarely comes home. And I missed her last visit because Cassandra and I went to a late-night *Rocky Horror Picture* show and then crashed at her house after until two in the afternoon.

She hugs me one more time. "It's so good to see you. I'm glad I'll have you to myself to catch up!"

Great, another no-date dig.

And it's at that moment that the doorbell rings.

"Who is that?"

"Who rings the bell?"

"Who's there?"

A chorus of questions fill the house, and I rocket out of my seat to save Matthew from a full-front attack. Suddenly my pulse is racing, hard. I wipe damp hands on Mom's silk dress, probably leaving a mark there for the rest of the night. I shove through the kitchen, then up to the door, just as my aunt is opening it.

And there he is, Matthew Pearlman, standing on my front stoop and holding, of all the things in the world, a giant wheel of cheese, bigger than his head.

"Hi." He smiles at me and then gestures to the cheese. "I panicked. Happy Passover?"

I expected victory. I expected sweet, sweet victory. Rachel brought a date to dinner. Everyone will bow down to my power.

Instead, there's mostly confusion.

"Who's this?"

"Annie, is this one of yours?"

"Why so much cheese?"

It is *a lot* of cheese. I grab Matthew's arm and pull him into the house. Clearing my throat, I say, "Everyone, this is my date, Matthew Pearlman."

His cheeks are tinged red as the questions continue and I give his arm a quick squeeze of comfort. Poor guy. Didn't know what he was getting into, all to sit next to my sister through a three-hour Seder. There are questions and more questions followed by more questions, as is the Jewish way. My grandma shuffles through, brisket baster in hand, and says, loud enough for the whole neighborhood to hear, "Rachel brought a date! I never thought I'd see the day! Come here, young gentleman, what's your name?"

"Uh, Matthew," he says.

"So lovely to meet you, Matthew. Isaac! Come meet Matthew."

Once Matthew has met my entire extended family, all while still stuck in the entry-way, guilt eating at me that I got him into this, a smoke alarm goes off in the kitchen, and everyone maneuvers that way to ensure the house isn't burning down (it's not).

And, very suddenly, we're alone.

I look up at him. His cheeks are red, just like they used to be in the back of that sixth-grade classroom.

"I'm sorry," I say. "You can back out. I'll understand."

He laughs. "Nah, they're not that bad."

"I don't believe you in the least."

He shrugs, then glances down. "Sorry about the cheese." His face pales. "Oh crap. There's brisket for dinner. I brought cheese to a Passover dinner. This is so not kosher. I'm sorry, I'll—"

"—Matthew." I instinctively grab his arm with my hand, as if to quell his panic. I then quickly drop it, hoping he somehow won't notice. "Don't worry about it. We don't keep kosher. But I am curious, how *did* you land on a wheel of cheese?"

"My mom insisted I bring something, but fruit was covered, flowers felt cliché, and you can't bring any good dessert on Passover. So I stopped by a farmers' market on the way over, started browsing, and uh, this was the result." He grimaces. "Embarrassing, I know."

Bashful is kind of a cute look on Matthew. Young, sweet. When he's surrounded by all of his friends, he gives off douche vibes, like, the least douche of the douche group but still.

He's wearing his usual fare, an outfit appropriate for the golf course, pressed khaki shorts, a polo shirt, and an Apple watch. Between his outfit and my silk dress, I feel like we're a match made in suburban heaven. Except, of course, we're not a match. This isn't a *real* date. This is a one-time favor to get my family off my back.

"Don't be embarrassed," I say. "What kind of cheese is it?"

"Um."

He actually has to check the tag, which makes me laugh. "You're telling me you bought a lifetime supply of cheese, and you don't even know what type it is?"

When he smiles at me, I feel this strange little tingle of warmth down my spine. "I *told* you. I panicked. And it's . . . aged cheddar."

"Well, I like cheddar cheese."

"Me too."

"How long do you think it would take us to eat that whole thing?" I ask.

"Hmm." He assesses the wheel. I wonder if his arms are getting tired from holding it. They do look like rather strong arms. "I guess that depends on how much time you want to spend in the bathroom afterward. If your family is as lactose intolerant as mine . . ."

I wrinkle my nose. "Ew. Gross."

He winces. "I know. My bad. Sorry I hang out with guys too often. It's warped my brain. Too many bodily function jokes."

"Rachel! Get in here—I want to meet your date!" my mom suddenly calls from the living room.

"You already know him!" I shout back.

This, of course, only arouses more interest, and she calls for me again. "Sorry." I wince. "Do you mind?"

"That's what I'm here for," Matthew responds.

Something about that answer makes my stomach hurt a little, like I ate too much cheddar cheese. When we were talking just now, it almost felt normal. Like we were hanging out just to hang out, like we used to. Like we were spending time together because we enjoy it and not because I need to con my family.

"Here, um, let's put that down somewhere so you don't have to carry it around all night."

"How funny would that be, though?" Matthew asks. "For the rest of your life, your family will be like, 'Remember that guy who held on to a wheel of cheese for the entire Seder?'"

I laugh. "That would be pretty funny, but I'm not sure it's quite worth committing to the bit." I scan the entryway, pick a decorative vase off a table and put it carefully in the corner. "The cheese can go here. To greet our guests."

"Perfect," he says.

We then make our way down into the living room where my parents, siblings, and their dates are all sitting together. I take a quick breath. Crap. They're going to know. They're going to know I'm faking it and that Matthew isn't a *real* date. The thought of that embarrassment makes my shoulders tense, and I almost consider turning myself in just to get it over with, when, out of nowhere, Matthew grabs my hand.

His grip is warm, soft. Our fingers lace together with ease. It's so—natural.

My cheeks heat. I look at my feet and softly mumble, "Thank you."

He gives my hand a light squeeze in response as we walk into the room. Everyone's eyes go to our laced hands, and with renewed confidence, I lead Matthew to the open set of chairs. We sit down, hands still clasped together. *God*, I hope my palm isn't sweating.

"Everyone," I say. "This is Matthew. You, uh, know him from synagogue probably."

Matthew says hello to everyone, and my parents give him the routine questions, asking about senior year and where he's hoping to go to college. You would think parents would pick up on the fact that we hate talking about this stuff, but it's always the first topic of conversation.

I'm surprised when Matthew says he's planning on majoring in architecture at Georgia Tech. "My dad wanted me to go into economics," he says. "Better money, more stable. But I don't know, I guess I like the idea of building something."

I glance at him, heart suddenly thrumming faster in my chest, and say, "Me too. I like creating something I can physically see. Something I can, uh, touch."

My cheeks flame red on that last word, and I swear Matthew gives my hand the tiniest of squeezes, which makes my pulse leap.

Fake. This is fake. He is not a real date. This is just for show. He's probably just paying attention to me so as not to give away his giant crush on Audrey. Playing it cool.

I clear my throat and turn to Audrey's date. "I'm sorry," I say. "I don't think I ever got your name."

"Ah, yes, I think Audrey forgot to share it." My mouth drops open. The boy has a freaking *English accent*. And dazzling white teeth. Audrey has outdone herself once again. "I'm Sahil. Nice to meet you."

He holds out his hand, and I drop Matthew's to shake it. "Nice to meet you too. How'd you and Audrey start dating?"

"Are we dating now?" Sahil asks, leaning back and throwing an arm around Audrey. "I'm flattered."

Audrey clears her throat. Her voice comes out bright, peppy. "We're in the same history class. This is technically our first date. But, you know, college, time gets away from you."

"The truth is she turned me down the first two times I asked," Sahil shares, "and so when she came running up last week with this invitation, I was surprised but happy to accept. Thank you for having me."

Typical Audrey. She probably gets asked out a hundred times a week. I glance over at Matthew, who's watching Audrey as well. A knot of jealousy tugs at me.

I fidget with the hem of my dress as conversation continues. It was silly, trying to look nice. There really was no point to it at all.

♡

The food smells *amazing*. Unfortunately, we have to get through about ninety minutes of Seder before we can eat any of it.

"Is your family celebrating tonight?" I ask Matthew. He's sitting on my left. Audrey and Sahil are across from us. Josh and Cara have graduated to the "young adult" table, the older cousins and my youngest aunt and uncle. At least I'm no longer at the kids' table. They kept sticking me with the little ones. They said it was because there wasn't room anywhere else, but part of me felt like if I had a date, I would have made it to the older kids' table. And look, here I finally am.

"We only observe the first night," he says.

I nod. "Yeah, that's why we throw this big Seder on night two. More guests are able to come. My grandparents love to make a showing of it."

Matthew smiles. "Our family is really small. It's nice there are so many of you."

I laugh. "It's chaotic."

"But nice," he insists, eyes catching mine. There's that little swoop again.

I look around the table at all of my family, grandparents and parents and siblings and aunts and uncles and cousins and dates. There are so many of us. A whole tribe just in and of itself. And every year we gather around this table to celebrate Passover—through sickness and bad weather and more alluring plans, we show up and sit down together and read the story of our people and eat. We do *a lot* of eating.

"Yeah." I turn to him and smile. "Pretty nice."

"So." He scoots his chair closer to mine and throws an arm around my shoulder. I feel every inch of my body heat as I lean in. I've never done this before, been close to a boy like this. He smells good. How does he smell so good? Do I smell okay? "Favorite Passover food, go."

It takes all of my concentration for my voice to come out normally. He's looking at me, but I can barely take some side glances at him. I actually wish he'd go back to looking at my sister. The concentration is a lot to handle. He's really committing to the job.

"Matzo pizza," I answer. "Hands down. Crispy. Savory. Delicious."

"Cheesy," Matthew adds.

I laugh and turn to him now. His brown eyes are bright and smiling. *Fake date, fake date, fake date.* "Very cheesy," I say. "I bet that cheddar would go well on it."

"Enough cheese to last us in the desert for forty years."

"You brought a good gift after all! It's Passover-themed. What about you? Favorite Passover food?"

His smile falls. "I can't tell you."

I narrow my eyes. "Why not?"

"Because it's a . . ." He puts up air quotes. "'Controversial opinion.'"

"Now you *have* to tell me."

He scoots even closer, turning so our knees bump together. He really is putting in the effort to convince my family this is real. "Fine," he says. "But you're not allowed to say anything in response. Deal?"

I nod. "Deal."

"I really like gefilte fish."

I gasp and lean back. "Gross! Ew! Nooooooo!"

"You promised!" he shouts.

We're both laughing so hard my sides hurt. It reminds me of being back in Ms. Baumstein's class again.

"Excuse me, children?" I hear my grandfather ask. "I'm sure your discussion is very entertaining, but if you'd like to put it on hold, the rabbis have something important to share."

Matthew and I exchange a conspiratorial look, then clear our throats, turn back to the table, and pick up our Passover Haggadahs. As my grandfather begins to read, I glance over at my sister. She has the strangest expression on her face. She almost seems . . . well, sad.

We break for dinner after the first part of the Seder. Half the family shuffles into the kitchen to serve, and the other half stays in the dining room so we don't break fire code limits in the kitchen. There are the usual arguments about everyone wanting to help. Eventually the most dominant personalities win. Surprisingly, or maybe not so, Matthew is one of them, insisting on helping even though he's a guest.

Once he's left the room, Mom gives me a raised eyebrow of approval. I give a small smile but then again feel the guilty tug. Mom approves of the boy I'm dating. But I'm not dating Matthew. I'm not even *on a* date with Matthew. None of this is real.

"Hey," Audrey nudges my foot under the table. Sahil has gone to the bathroom, and I can hear that he's gotten into a very long conversation with one of my uncles about his gluten intolerance. Poor Sahil.

"Hey," I say back.

She angles her head to the left. "Wanna go outside for a minute? Too busy in here."

I shrug. "Sure."

Serving dinner is always a whole ordeal that takes three times as long as it should. It'll be another ten minutes before food is on the table. Our brother and Cara are nowhere to be found, and it crosses my mind that they might have snuck off to the guest bedroom like they did three years ago. Now *that* was a story that will never be forgotten by our family. I really didn't need to know that my brother owns Pikachu boxers. Strange and *gross*.

Audrey and I walk out onto the tiny front porch. I smile to myself as we pass the wheel of cheese on the way. Weirdest gift ever.

As soon as we step outside, Audrey lets out a giant exhale.

"Yeah." I nod. "It's loud in there."

She sighs again. "It's not just that."

"What?" I ask.

"It's exhausting." She lifts her arms. Her green eyes look tired. "The whole thing. Bring a date. Impress the family. It's ridiculous. Why can't we just ever enjoy each other? Why isn't that enough?"

I freeze. Her question so closely echoes the one I just had. I didn't realize she felt that way too.

"Yeah," I say. "I agree. At least it's easy for you, though. Guys are always falling over themselves to be with you. You've always had a date."

Audrey gives me a weird look. "Seriously, Rachel?"

"What?"

"Guys aren't falling over themselves for me. Maybe they're tripping over themselves to get away from me. Yeah, I've always had a date but a different one. I can't get a guy to stay with me to save my life, and then I'm always scrambling last minute to find a date for this stupid thing so I don't get pestered for the rest of the year."

"Wait, what?" My brain rushes to catch up.

"Guys don't actually *like* me," Audrey says. "They see my breasts and hair and legs, and they *think* they like me, but then they spend time with me and poof they're gone. I'm not like you. I'm not interesting. I've never had a guy look at me like Matthew's been looking at you all night."

I freeze, then ask, "What are you *talking* about?"

"Matthew. He's obviously super into you."

"Uh, no he's not."

"Yes, he is."

"No, he's not!"

"Yes—"

"He's not even a real date!" I shout.

Audrey leans back, surprised by my volume. "Wait, what?"

"He's not even a real date. I just asked him to save me from the migraine of going single to another one of these things. He only agreed because you would be here. I think he has a crush on you or whatever."

Audrey shakes her head. "No way. I promise you're the girl that boy has a crush on."

I want to believe her. I'd like to believe her. But there's no way that's true. Matthew doesn't like me. Maybe—maybe in sixth grade there was something there. But we were just kids, silly, little kids. And now we're nothing, classmates, peers at best.

I shake my head and mumble, "Whatever." Then, everything else Audrey says hits me, everything about herself. My heart lurches. I step forward and take her hand and link our pinkies together, like we used to do when we were little girls. "*I* think you're interesting. You're cool and funny and smart. If boys don't want to be with you, it's because they're not worthy of you."

Audrey rolls her eyes. "Sure. Thank you."

"I mean it." I nudge her foot with mine. "You're awesome, Audrey. Don't let shallow boys make you think otherwise. Promise?"

She smiles, small and soft, and I can tell she believes me. "Okay, promise." Audrey glances back at the door. "This whole thing is stupid. This whole bring a date thing."

"It's *tradition*," I say. "Our family's evergreen excuse for this outmoded rule."

"Well, when we're in charge, we'll have a new rule, bring anyone you want or no one at all. Just show up and be ready to eat."

"That sounds nice," I say. Audrey throws her arm around my shoulder. The sun is setting, pink horizon sky. "That sounds really nice."

I'm awkward throughout dinner and the second half of Seder. Matthew Pearlman couldn't *like* me. Certainly not. He's here as a favor. And because Audrey is the prettiest human on the face of the planet. And for a good Jewish meal.

Audrey only thinks he likes me because we've been playing the ruse so well. We really pulled one over on her and the rest of the family.

After dinner, everyone separates to mingle and eat dessert. I load up a plate with fruit and flourless brownies, and that's when someone asks, "Wait, didn't Matthew bring some cheese?"

Matthew and I exchange a glance and burst into a fit of laughter. *Some* cheese is an understatement, to say the least. I pull up a heralding trumpet sound on my phone and play it as Matthew walks the cheese into the kitchen. Everyone laughs and claps. We put it on the table, and Dad goes to work cutting some of it up. I poke toothpicks into a few pieces, add them to my plate, then shuffle through the crowd to find Matthew.

He's nowhere in the house, and for a moment, I worry he left. Which would be totally fine. His job was done. He was my date. He doesn't owe me anything.

But then I find him out on the porch, in the dark, cool night air. Relief sweeps through me that he's still here. He smiles when he sees me, then gestures to his phone. "Mom called, just wanted to know when I'd be home."

"Sorry," I say. "We're keeping you late."

"Nah." He shakes his head. "It's fun. Besides, I've got to see which kid finds the afikomen."

Most families place the afikomen in a reasonably easy hiding spot. My family? Of course not. Every year my grandparents think of the trickiest place possible, and the little kids spend hours making a mess of the house in search of it. Utterly wonderful chaos, just like the rest of the night. One year they hid it at the bottom of the dog food bag, like *under* the kibbles. The dog had a field day with that one.

"Um." I clear my throat. "I brought some of the cheese for us to try. Want a piece?"

Matthew grins. "Most definitely."

I walk forward and pass him one of the toothpicks. It's nice out here. Quiet, cool. For once, I don't feel awkward around a boy. I feel comfortable. Like this is normal.

We pick up our toothpicks and clink them together like champagne flutes. "L'chaim," Matthew says.

"L'chaim," I reply.

We bite into the cheese and chew. It tastes good. It tastes—

Matthew nods. "Mmm, cheesy."

I laugh. "My assessment exactly." We finish off my dessert plate, while fantasizing about all the yeasty carbs we'll eat when Passover is over. When there's a short lull of silence, I say, "Thanks for doing all of this. I think we really pulled it off. You're a good actor."

There's silence again after that. I'm not sure what I said wrong, but Matthew is giving me a funny look, one that makes my skin feel all warm and tight. I wait until I can't stand it anymore and ask, "What?"

Matthew shakes his head a little, glances at his phone, then takes a breath and looks back at me. His eyes make my stomach flip. "Rachel, I'm not a good actor." He pauses. Shrugs. "I just like you."

"You what?" the words come out fast and without thought.

Matthew smiles. Hard. And suddenly my heart is beating so intensely I can feel it in my throat. "I *like* you," he repeats. "I thought that was obvious."

My brain is running a mile a minute. This isn't right—this can't be right. "No." I shake my head. "You can't like me. You like Audrey. You wanted to ask her to prom."

"What?" he asks, confused.

"Last year," I say. "In the hallway, you—"

It seems to dawn on him. His cheeks go red. "Um, no, oy this is embarrassing. I was trying to figure out what your prom plans were, but we hadn't talked in so long, I didn't know what to say. So I was nervous and awkward, and I panicked."

I nod. "You panicked."

Matthew smiles. "I panic sometimes. Hence the cheese."

I nod again. "Hence the cheese." Silence beats between us once more. "So you like me."

"Yes."

"Like, *like* me, like me?"

"Yes."

"*Why?*"

Matthew laughs, which at first doesn't seem like the best sign. But then he says, "Well, I've always liked you, I guess. But I thought you were out of my league. Wouldn't want to be with a guy who had a bunch of meathead friends. I thought it was never going to happen, but then you asked me to this Seder, and I thought maybe . . . maybe there was a chance."

"Wow," I say.

He laughs again, but fidgets too, fingers tucking into his pocket.

It occurs to me that he's *nervous.*

I tilt my head. "So, you like me as in you want to kiss me and stuff?"

There's surprise in his eyes, sweet, eager surprise. "If you'd be okay with that, yes."

More silence as I compute. I really wasn't expecting this. I don't know what to do with this information. Matthew Pearlman *likes* me. And I—oy vey—I guess I like him too.

I take a deep breath. "Okay then."

"Okay, what?"

"You can kiss me."

I smile, and so does he.

The kiss is soft and gentle, and well, a little bit cheesy.

BLOOM

"Love Transcends Space-Time"

Rebecca Barrow

ENGLAND, 2005

You can use the garden all you want, Mera's mother used to tell her, *but you mustn't ever touch the orange blossoms. All the other flora? You know what to do with those. I trust you. But those orange blossoms hold time in them, Mera. We mustn't play with time. We only care for those ones. We don't use them. Do you understand? Do you promise me?*

Mera hears her mother's words as she holds the orange blossom to her lips. *Yes, yes, I understand,* she thinks, *but you're not here anymore and what am I supposed to do? How am I supposed to obey, when the one thing you always told me not to trouble is the only way I can get back to you?*

They hold time. The pink spiked leaves, they are for closing wounds; and the purple ferns, they work best for emotional anguish, and on and on—Mera knows the garden better than her own body, by this point. Her father works out at sea and she stays here, in this house her parents built, and she cares for the garden her mother coaxed to life before her own life was ripped from her.

Mera closes her eyes and tips her face up to the cloudless sky, the sun searing shadows on the insides of her eyelids. "Do you know what it's like?" she whispers to the air. "I'm all alone. Because of one man, because of this world we live in where he took you from me and got no punishment for it."

Her lips rustle the petals as she talks. Eleven years, her mother's been gone. Eleven years, Mera has been waiting, gathering courage. Reading the scribbled notes in her mother's journals, over and over. Helping the ground heal and be reborn and tenderly coaxing the orange blossoms to life, over and over.

But now she is ready. Now it's time.

It's time, it's time, she thinks, and before she can frighten herself out of it she presses the bloom into her mouth and grinds it between her teeth and—

No. 1

There is no way to control the orange blossom; it is the wildest and unwieldiest of all flora. It gives you what you need. It takes you where it is that you need to be, when you need to be.

Do not fight the orange blossom. It is powerful beyond anything you can comprehend.

Handle rarely and with extreme caution.

For a long time Mera feels underwater. A peaceful kind of oblivion, the weight of water in her lungs.

Caught in a slipstream.

And then Mera feels something like a hand reach inside her and dig its nails into her lungs and she comes to with a sudden, wrenching gasp.

She lies there for a while, feeling the pulse of something living inside her—the blossom maybe, is that it, is that what's beating in a place entirely separate from her heart?—and it's only when the pain becomes more dull than flame that she realizes she doesn't know where she is lying.

She doesn't know *when*.

Mera finds herself in a field, the grass around her yellowing and brittle, the kind that comes from a long dry summer without a hope of rain.

When she stands, she sees she is at the crest of a hill, and down in the cradle below her is her town. Somewhere down there is her home that doesn't exist yet—at least, not if she has returned to the right time.

She turns, to the open land behind her. And down there, out in the farmlands: the man she has come to kill.

Mera stretches her back, her neck, a gentle check of her body to be sure she is okay and complete. There is so little study of the orange blossom that even arriving whole wasn't a guarantee. Neither was her belongings journeying with her, but there they are—her leather backpack stuffed with a change of clothes, her careful pouches of the flora, a paper map.

She slings the bag over her shoulders and then stares, considering her path.

Somewhere, in town, her mother is probably alive. Working in a bar and falling in love with Mera's father and tending to a balcony of curling-tendrilled plants. There's a sharp ache in Mera's heart and she thinks, *I could go to her. I could find her and see her and I would smile at her, a stranger in a bar, and she'd smile back at me and some part of her would recognize something within me and she'd ask, "Have we met before?" and I would shake my head, but it'd be okay because I'd be seeing her.*

It would be so easy, but Mera feels the blossom kick at her lungs. No. That is not what she came here to do. She doesn't know how long the orange blossom's effects last, she doesn't know how long she'll be in this time. And the goal is to get her mother back permanently. That means finding the man who killed her and ending his life, before he ever gets the chance to end her mother's.

"You can't waste this time," Mera whispers to herself. "It's all you have."

So she turns away from the familiar shape of her hometown and begins her long walk, to the east, to her goal.

To kill.

No. 14
The flora are living, sentient beings.
Do not presume to know more than the power that makes them
    breathe. We are responsible for their care and creation but we
    do not know all there is about them.
Work quietly, but with pure intention.

She aches, sweat in the small of her back by the time she arrives.

It's a rambling farmhouse, set away from anything or anyone else, with chimes hanging off the railing of the deck and a golden weathervane way up high on the roof. It's still; there's no wind. Mera has planned this journey so many times in her mind and it took her longer than she thought to cover the distance, but she's here now. Outside the house of the man who killed her mother and now she's ready for the next part of the plan.

She sees a curtain move as she crosses the field leading up to the house, the yellowing grass snapping beneath her feet.

She imagines how she looks, to the man inside. Like a rabbit wandering into his trap. That's how anyone else would see her, and she knows what people would say—*Get away, girl, it's not safe* or *Look at the state of you, what do you expect to happen?* or *Is it a death wish you have, then? Surely must be, for you to be acting as stupid as this.*

Mera tightens her hold on her backpack straps and blows an escaped curl out of her face before it can stick to her sweat. Yes, she has a death wish. She wishes for a death. But most people, they don't have the means, or the guts.

Mera has all the means she could need, and there is steel inside her, somewhere beside the blossom. So it's not a wish anymore.

It's a destiny.

"I am ready," she breathes, lips barely moving as she repeats it to herself, climbing the steps to the front door. "I am ready, I am ready, I am—"

And then the door wrenches open before Mera can even reach the top step. "Who the fuck are you?" the girl in the doorway bites out. "And what are you doing here?"

She's lit from behind, this girl.

Honey-bleached hair and gleaming copper skin marked all over with freckles, constellations across her nose and forehead and high cheekbones, and further down, over her round shoulders and along her chest, dipping below the neck of her cotton dress.

For a moment Mera has the impression of leaves filling the space behind the girl, a familiar earthy-floral scent, and a sharp sense of déjà vu.

A girl, and a garden, and a prickly memory . . .

The girl is staring at her, and it's her eyes that truly capture Mera's attention. Not the wideness of them or the clarity, the length of her lashes or the rough makeup scrawled around them, no.

It's the hollowness in them. An odd thing to notice, maybe, but it's hard to miss when you're so used to seeing it staring back at you from a cracked bathroom mirror every single day. There's a special kind of empty, of weary, and there's no way to hide it. Even when you're beautiful, as this girl is. You can dress it up but still, it's there, always.

Inside her chest the orange blossom unfurls and loops around her organs, tightens so that her breath comes shallow, a slight rasp.

It's saying something to her, Mera knows, but she doesn't know what. What she does know: This girl is not supposed to be here.

This was not part of the plan.

"Do I know you?"

The girl is still staring at Mera but she looks a little less hostile now, less like she's ready to rip Mera's throat out. "What?"

"I said, do I know you?" Mera repeats. "You look—" *Forget how she looks,* her mind whispers. *You are on a mission. Whoever this girl is, she's not a part of it.*

Mera straightens, remembers the steel in her. Come *on*, fucking focus. "I'm looking for Richard Wells," she says.

And the girl in the doorway, her shoulders drop and she lets out a single bite of laughter. "Of course, you are," she says. "Well, sorry, stranger. You're a little too late."

Late?

Mera steps up, unconsciously, closer to this girl. "What do you mean?"

She shakes her head. "I mean Richard Wells is dead. So whatever he did to you, whatever he owes you, you won't—hey, wait, shit—okay, okay, just sit there—"

He cannot be dead.

No, no, he can't be dead because I came here to kill him, I came all the way back to a time when he would still be alive so that I could be the one to take him out, to stop him in his tracks, and then he would never have the chance to lay a hand on my mother and she'd get to live the life she was supposed to and he would be dead, dead, dead by my hand but if he's already gone then I'm too late, am I too late, when am I? When the fuck am I?

When Mera comes back to herself—a moment or a few minutes later, she isn't sure exactly—she is inside the farmhouse. Sitting at a long raw wood table and her bag is on the floor in the corner and for a moment she thinks *I am trapped*. Then she thinks about bolting, leaving her bag and whatever part of her just died in this place and time, and get far from here. Get home, get back to her time.

But then the beautiful girl appears and she's looking at Mera with such tenderness that Mera feels salt tears pool along her lashes.

Inside her the blossom pulses, loud.

She was stupid, she realizes now, to think she could end up in the time she needed. Isn't that what all those warnings were about, isn't that exactly why her mother taught her that the orange blossom was the most dangerous of all their notions?

With one hand she rubs at her ribs, as if she can soothe the bellows beneath them that way, as if she can pass a message to the flora inside her. *I get it, I understand. Please, let me breathe.*

"Okay?" The girl sits beside Mera, facing her. "You were really out of it for a second there. Sorry."

"For what?" Mera says.

"I forget, sometimes," the girl says, "that you can't just announce somebody is dead. Even when that somebody was a waste of space who deserves no mourning."

Mera shakes her head. "Oh, no," she says, and opens her mouth to say the girl's name but, of course, she doesn't know it. "I'm sorry. What's your name?"

The girl half-smiles, like it's normal for her to have a stranger in her home—well, Mera assumes this is her home, from the ferocity with which she answered the door, from the comfortable way she moves through the kitchen. "Delphine," she says. "Yours?"

Delphine. An echo in the corners of her mind, a voice in an old garden . . . "Mera," she says.

"Mera." Then Delphine tips her head to the side. "So why are you here, Mera?"

What is she supposed to say? *I came from another time, to kill the man who lived here, to reset a cycle and get my mother back.*

And I have failed.

All that work, all that effort, the buildup to finally taking the leap through time and making the kill—how many years did it take to gather the courage to do it? To know she would take a life? Because that's not what the flora is for; her mother had always taught her that alongside each individual flower's properties, they were *for protection, only. If someone is going to harm you, or somebody else, that's okay. But not for our own petty grievances, revenge. The energy you give out comes back on you, too, Mera. Never forget that.*

But Mera had justified it to herself because the man she was coming to kill was going to put her mother in danger and so it was protection, wasn't it?

Not that it matters, now. She came back too late. If Richard Wells is dead in this time, then her mother is already long gone. Instead of landing far enough back that Wells hadn't yet even locked eyes on her mother, let alone killed her, she has landed in a world where he got away with that crime and who knows how many others. A world where her mother is still dead, a world, she realizes now, where some younger version of her exists already in mourning. Suddenly she aches to run to her younger self and comfort her, but that is a risk too far. She's already fucked things up enough.

She blinks a few times and finds Delphine still watching her, expectant, awaiting an answer to the question Mera almost forgot she'd even asked. *Why are you here?* "Wells," Mera says after a moment. "How did you know him?"

Delphine rakes a hand through her hair, and Mera watches how it falls back in front of her face, slow waves shielding Delphine from the world. "He was my father."

Fuck.

Mera closes her hands into fists and flinches. When she uncurls her left fist, there's a mark in the middle of her palm.

"A splinter?" Delphine says. "Wait one second."

She gets up and breezes across the room, Mera watching as she tries to understand. This girl, this Delphine, she belongs to the man who killed Mera's mother. *I am so close*, Mera thinks, *but still so, so fucking far.*

Delphine returns with a pair of tweezers and sits, reaches out and, before Mera can process it, takes Mera's splintered hand in her own. "I'll be quick," Delphine says, and bows her head.

Delphine has a gentle touch. Her fingertips skate over Mera's palm, tracing the lines on her skin. Thumb on the underside of Mera's hand, rubbing over her knuckles. Her hands are warm and soft, the opposite of Mera's, weathered from all those hours digging in the dirt and plucking thorns and roots. Delphine makes small noises as she works, like an off-key lullaby that sends pins and needles pricking across the back of Mera's neck. It is familiar enough that she wonders where she's heard it before—in the birds that nest outside her bedroom window? The wind singing through the trees on a hot summer day?

Inside her the blossom grows warm, like a small sun inside her chest. And when it beats now, it is in time with her heart: here. here. here.

Delphine looks up, a slight smile across her lips. "Done."

Done?

Mera lifts her hand and stares at the tiny pinprick hole in the center of her palm. She didn't even feel Delphine working the sliver of wood from her skin. "Oh," she says, barely even a sigh, because she can't think of what else to say. "Oh."

"You look tired." The way Delphine says it is not unkind, and the moment she does Mera feels the exhaustion turning her bones heavy, slow.

She *is* tired: all the planning, for nothing. All the anticipation, the wonder of being able to see her mother again, seeing something beyond the handful of old pictures that flatten her. She looks at Delphine. "You asked before," she says. "How I knew him. Your father."

Delphine rubs at her neck. "I know he did something bad to you," she says. "He did something bad to every single person who was unlucky enough to get in his way."

Her fingers leave a red mark on her neck and Mera knows, suddenly and completely, that she is a victim here, too. "He did something bad, but not to me," Mera manages to say. "To—my mother."

"Oh." Delphine nods. "So it's retribution you wanted. Well. That's something we have in common, then, isn't it?"

Mera wants to know what else they have in common: Does Delphine know what it's like to be so lonely it becomes a physical pain? Does she like the feel of the sun on the back of her neck? Is there a memory, a familiarity, twisting just beneath the surface of her mind, just like Mera's?

There's a long moment of silence, and Mera doesn't know what to do, where to go next. She thinks about going to the place where her mother is buried, lying down on the grass there and waiting however long it takes for her to snap back to her own time. *When I'm back I can start over*, she thinks, but the idea exhausts her and the guilt that follows that exhaustion is hot. What is she going to do, never see her mother again? She can't give up, can't—

"This is going to sound strange," Delphine says, her gaze skipping over and past Mera as she speaks, chin in her hands. "Being that I'm the daughter of the man who did something bad to your mother, but you look so tired and my mum taught me my manners, so I think I should ask you anyway. To stay, for dinner." She laughs, and it's a sound like the chimes on the porch. "I never get to cook for anybody but myself. And you're the first person I've seen in weeks, you know? I've been here, packing up this house and wondering what the fuck I do next and then here, you turn up, and I think you're as tired as I am and I would like to cook for you. And I hope that doesn't sound so strange you'll want to run away right now."

Mera looks up and Delphine is smiling. "Okay," Mera says. "Okay."

Delphine shows her upstairs, to a small room with green wallpaper, and she tells Mera to make herself at home. Rest or shower or whatever else she feels like. "Do you eat meat?" she asks. "I could roast a chicken."

Her mother used to roast a chicken once a month, dressed up with herbs from the other side of the garden and wild potatoes. It's the memory Mera has held on to through this whole process, imagining succeeding in her task: her mother would be alive again, dancing in the kitchen, filling their home with the smell of the herbs and the sizzling of the chicken. "Yes, I'd like that."

When she's alone she strips out of her clothes, steps into the shower, and washes the sweat off, then dresses while she's still damp. Sits on the edge of the bed to stare in the round mirror on the wall, wondering how it is she came to be here.

She shouldn't feel okay here. It is strange to feel even a little bit comfortable in the home of this man, his daughter. But then again, it doesn't feel like *his* home. Not in the kitchen with the warm table and the pastel rainbow of plates on display. Not in this room, with the mirror carefully placed at the right height for a girl just like Mera.

She looks at herself and brushes her fingers over the dark circles beneath her eyes, almost purple. The rest of her face is soft brown, burnished by the sun from all her flora-tending, and she's not wearing any makeup, which suddenly feels wrong. She wants to look pretty, for Delphine.

You are beautiful either way. Her mother's voice rings clear in her mind.

Mera smiles as she turns away from her reflection.

"Let's eat outside," Delphine says.

They sit at a small round table in the garden, although it is hard to know where the garden ends and the farmland begins. Delphine's house faces out over fields that stretch as far as she can see, all empty and faded by the sun. "Is this all yours?" Mera asks when her plate is empty. She was hungry enough to eat without feeling self-conscious, the way she usually does, always aware of people looking at her body and her plate and all the other shit that comes with being seventeen.

"All this land?" Delphine leans back and stretches her arms above her head. "No. Well—maybe? I'm not sure."

"Are there other farms, then?"

"No, I mean—" Delphine sighs. "It does belong to us. Me. The farm, the house. This is my land but I don't know if I'm going to keep it."

Mera leans her elbows on the table. "Was it just the two of you here?"

"Oh, no, no, I haven't lived here for the past couple years," Delphine says. "I was with my mum. We left, me and her." She closes her eyes. "Left in the middle of the night because it was the only way we could get out, you know?"

Mera understands.

It's the emptiness, the washed-out hollow she saw in Delphine's eyes earlier. She hasn't ever seen it so clearly in anybody else before.

"Where is she now?"

Delphine smiles without any mirth. "She died. Can you believe it? She got sick and died, and then a month later I get a letter from my father's solicitor telling me he's dead, too, and that I am now responsible for all of his affairs." She shakes her head. "It's my own fault for turning eighteen. If I could have stopped time and stayed seventeen, I wouldn't be here. But the clock never stops, so here I am."

"I'm so sorry," Mera says. She would be embarrassed at the sincerity in her voice if she didn't know what it means to hear that. "I'm so sorry that happened to you." Mera reaches across the table and touches her fingers to Delphine's wrist.

Delphine's pulse is rapid and she looks at Mera, her lips parted.

And then Mera is filled with a sensation like she's falling, like the air in her lungs has been snatched away by a gale-force wind, like she's looking down on this scorched patchwork of earth from somewhere high, high above. And she doesn't know if it's the blossom or herself, and she doesn't know how long she has left—

That's the uncertain thing, isn't it? How long before she is pulled back to her present, until the flora metabolizes its way out of her system and she has to leave this time?

Leave Delphine.

What if you didn't have to leave her? a voice in the depths of her mind whispers. *What if this is exactly where you are supposed to be, my love?*

"What is it?"

"Hmm?" Mera blinks, then shakes her head as if that will force out her mother's voice. "Oh, nothing."

Delphine looks like she might cry, and she rubs at her temples. "Sorry," she says. "Jesus, I don't know what's wrong with me. I just haven't seen anyone in so long and then you come along and you should hate me but you . . . don't. You just don't."

Mera picks up her sweating glass and takes a long sip of the pale lilac drink Delphine made, sweet and sharp. "You aren't responsible for the things he did," she says. "Besides, you and me, it feels like—" *Like we have almost too much in common,* is how that sentence should end, but the words on her tongue are really *Like there is some reason I came to this time and met you, like there are parts of me that already know you.*

Delphine is staring and shakes her head again, says so softly it's almost inaudible, "You're really beautiful." Then winces. "Jesus, sorry. That was weird."

Mera feels heat in her cheeks, then before she loses the nerve says, "Thank you."

In the long quiet that follows, only the evening birds in the background for noise, Mera watches as Delphine turns her hand, palm upward so Mera's hand rests in hers now. She has no blemish in the center of her skin, just the lines of a life and pale veins beating beneath.

"I am so sick of being all alone," Delphine says softly. "I almost forgot what it felt like to not be so fucking lonely."

I've never met anybody who understands that feeling before, Mera wants to say.

I think the orange blossom brought me to this time because of you, so I could find you, so I could meet you, she wants to say.

I think I could fall in love with you, she wants to say.

She says none of it.

Mera says nothing at all, only takes Delphine's hand with the same gentle touch as Delphine used on her earlier.

And then Mera abandons the gentleness as she pulls Delphine towards her and their bodies come together, their arms wrap tight around each other and it is all Mera can do not to cry into Delphine's amber-perfumed skin.

"This might sound strange," Mera says, "but I think I've known you. I feel like I could know you forever."

Delphine's words fall right into Mera's ear, her breath a hot glide against Mera's skin that sends the blossom into a frenzy, a thousand small bursts inside her skin. "So why don't you stay?" Delphine asks. "For tonight. Where else do you have to be?"

There is only one problem with that. What can she say—*I want to be here, I want to stay, but I ate a flower in the future and sometime soon it's going to wear off and I'll have to leave?*

Yes, a part of her says. *That's exactly what you have to tell her.*

Mera tightens her arms around Delphine, to better feel the weight of her, the substance of her body, the full realness of her. *We are worlds apart but for now we're here, together*, she thinks. *I will tell her. But not now.*

And out loud: "I want to know everything about you."

"I'm not that interesting—"

"I don't care," Mera says. "I want to know it all."

"—blue. The color the sky is on a perfect spring day, those little flecks of cloud. And in the morning, when it's a little hazy still—"

"—I was really small, but I remember. She taught me how to garden, how to cook, how to fix things. Anything she could do with her hands. I was never good at school, that's why I stopped going, but I was good at all the things she taught me—"

"—always knew, you know? You grow up and there's things about your family you're not supposed to talk about—"

"—caramels. The really sticky kind that glue your teeth together—"

"I don't think I've talked to another person this much since . . ." Mera exhales. "Fuck, I don't even know."

"Me neither. Or I talk but none of it's real, none of it means anything, it's like I'm just playing—"

"The perfect part, right? What everyone wants you to say."

"This is the first time I've said anything real out loud in so long and it's like . . ." Delphine takes Mera's hand and places it on her chest, to feel the rapid-fire beating beneath. "I feel alive."

Mera keeps her hand on Delphine's heart and feels the pulse echo inside her own rib cage, where the blossom beats.

I *feel* alive.

Delphine falls asleep first, stretched out in the pile of blankets they made in the middle of the garden. It's almost morning already, the sky shifting from darkness to that yellowing predawn light, and Mera wants to sleep too, but once she closes her eyes it'll be over. It'll be the next day, and she'll have to tell Delphine the truth.

So instead she drinks more of the concoction Delphine made them and sits beside her sleeping form and wonders what to do next. When the blossom wears off, she'll be transported back to her own time. But that doesn't mean she has to stay there. *All I have to do is harvest the last of the orange blossoms, and then—*

Mera inhales the honeysuckle air. Then what? Try to save her mother again, and almost certainly fail again? Or try to come back to Delphine, a girl she barely knows, except that it feels as if she does. Like Delphine holds something *more* for her. Delphine is the future, where her mother is the past. Maybe that's what the blossom is trying to tell her. *Or maybe I need to make my own decisions and stop giving these things so much power*, she thinks. *The blossom, my mum's voice.*

Next to her, Delphine stirs, her freckled face turning towards the light and her lips parting for a sigh to slip out.

Mera watches and suddenly she knows this is the first time Delphine will wake up beside her, and she doesn't want it to be the last.

So I'll go back, get the blossoms, and come back to now, she decides. *It brought me here the first time, it'll do it again.*

And her mother—

Mera closes her eyes, remembering. Hands in the dirt, whispering the right words into the soil.

She would understand, Mera tells herself. *She knew love, and loneliness. She would still love me if I took care of my own loneliness.* And Mera lets herself lie down now, next to Delphine, and watches until she falls asleep, too.

She is woken, quietly and gently, by Delphine's hand on her ankle. "Hey," she says softly. "I don't want you to burn. The sun comes in too hot here in the morning."

And it's the sweetest thing, but it makes Mera want to cry because now it is morning, and now she has to shatter this moment. She sits up and rubs at her eyes before opening them wide to take all of Delphine in. Morning hair and the remnants of yesterday's rushed makeup, pink cheeks and a thumb in her mouth as she chews her nail.

Mera goes inside herself, for a moment, searching for the blossom, and she finds it still wrapped around her organs, but nowhere near as bright as yesterday, nowhere near as strong.

"Delphine," she says, full of sorrow. "I have to tell you something. I need you to listen carefully, okay? Listen."

Delphine is staring at Mera, her head shaking slow and then fast. "Again," she says, "tell me again, I don't understand, how did you get here, how did you find me, what—"

But Mera has already told her about the orange blossom three times, and she knows Delphine understands, it's just that she can't comprehend. And who can blame her? Accepting that time travel is theoretically possible is one thing but staring the result of it in the face is another. "I know it's a lot, but—"

She jolts because there's a feeling like a hand grabbing hold of her spine and yanking—

This is it, isn't it?

Time to go, the blossom warns.

Mera puts her hand on Delphine's knee. "I wish I could explain the rest, I wish I could make it clearer to you but it's okay, it's going to be okay, because I'm going to come right back. I swear, I'll be back here before you know it and I can explain everything, my mum, your dad—"

Delphine looks at Mera's hand on her leg and then up at Mera, nodding. "Okay," she says. "I believe you. But how does it work—how long do you have left, when will you—"

The first thing Mera sees when she comes to is clear blue sky.

"Shit." She groans as she sits up and her entire body aches, but that's not what she feels the most. No, it's the absence of anything inside her.

I'm back, then, she thinks.

And then she thinks of Delphine, left behind, and her heart squeezes. She gets to her feet. It's okay. All she has to do is go home, get back to her garden, and then she can go back.

Mera opens her left hand to look at her palm, the mark in the middle. A physical reminder that she was there and of what—who—she left.

And she sets off, towards home.

The walk is easy, downhill most of the way. She finds her bag halfway down the hill, dropped as if it was an afterthought, and she carries the weight of it comfortably the rest of the way. She is thinking of Delphine the whole time, holding that first snapshot of her behind her eyelids, as she rounds the corner to where—

Mera stops short, standing still with shock.

"*No.*"

Where her house should be there is nothing but a burnt-out husk.

No. 33
Time is:
strings on a harp
current of the coldest sea
contortionist on a tightrope.
The slightest movement and things go off key,
    off path, off balance.
Make sure that whatever the blossom gives you is
    worth what time will take in return.

The fire inspector talks her through it. An electrical fault, he says, and with an old structure like this—

Mera nods like she understands, but she knows it wasn't some faulty wire that razed her home to the ground. It was her actions, her playing with time. *You get back what you put out,* her mother had told her so many times. She went back for vengeance, used the blossom for ill purposes, and so this is what she reaps.

"Lucky you don't have close neighbors," the inspector says. "All those trees out the back? Could have been much worse."

When the inspector leaves, Mera walks around the shell of her home to the space behind it and sinks to her knees in the dirt of the scorched garden. In the place where the flora she and her mother had tended should be.

There's nothing now. All of their work, gone. Her connection to her mother, gone.

Her only means of getting back to Delphine—*gone.*

Mera makes a call to her father, put through to him out at sea because these are special circumstances and besides, everyone he works with knows about their sad life.

"Mera?" he says, and it's the first time she's heard his voice in months. "What's wrong?"

"Dad," she says. "It's gone. It's all gone."

They don't talk long, never do, even in an emergency like this. He tells her he'll come back as soon as he can, that she should go to a hotel for the night, put it on the credit card.

As soon as I can means at least a month, Mera knows.

So she goes to a hotel, the cheap kind with faded prints on the wall and something sticky on the bathroom floor. Then she curls up on the bed, beneath the window letting in moonlight, and weeps. It is rage, it is grief, it is the sense that her entire life means nothing because she has nothing except for hurt. The blossom brought her back to Delphine's time because that was when she needed to be, but what was the point? To show her a girl who she never thought could really exist, someone who feels so familiar, who understands the sadness of the world and what it is to be so hollow and then rip her back, take away any chance she'll ever see Delphine again?

She cries, the smell of smoke still clinging on her skin, a weight that keeps her pinned to the bed. Delphine is back then, back at the farmhouse, and she's waiting for Mera to come back because that's what Mera promised. And what will she do? What will she think when Mera breaks that promise?

I have abandoned her, Mera thinks faintly, *I have lost her and I left her—*

♡

Mera pushes herself off the bed, sharply awake under the moon now.

Wait.

She is at the farmhouse. She exists here, in this time. She will be older, but not so much and Mera can go to her and explain why she didn't return, and it'll be okay because Delphine still exists and isn't that the beauty of time?

♡

Mera spends another day and night in the hotel room, because although she wants to leave now now now, her time-traveling body needs rest. On the third morning, she packs all her possessions, wondering only briefly what might be left in the house's burnt remains, and then leaves.

The walk feels longer this time—her anticipation, her nerves. What if Delphine doesn't remember her, or care, or want her at all? What if it's too late, in this time?

Stop, she tells herself. *Just keep moving and you'll get there.*

♡

When the farmhouse comes into sight, Mera's heart soars. *She is so close, so close.*

As she approaches she takes in the grass, still yellow, and the fields surrounding, still empty, and the house—

She slows as she gets closer. Something about it looks wrong. She was only there for a day, but she remembers it as if it were a hundred days and the house before her does not match that memory. It feels—

"Empty," Mera breathes.

She drops her bag and takes the steps two at a time so she can press her face to the pane in the front door. She tries the handle; it opens. She doesn't bother calling out.

It's clear, from the layer of dust on the floorboards, the pile of post built up behind the door, the way the sun filters through the stale air.

There's nobody here.

She left, is all Mera can think. *Delphine must have left here, sometime between yesterday— no, then, the past, her present, my future, now.* It settles over her, another layer on the blanket of exhaustion making her body feel so heavy. The only person she's ever met who saw her and it feels like whatever might have existed between them has ended before it could have even begun.

She sucks in air between her teeth and presses the heels of her hands to her temples. It's confusing, time. All of the other flora are clear and decisive: you know what they each do, how they work, what to use, and when to use it. But the orange blossom—

Even without it inside her, Mera feels it. An aftereffect, one that drifts with her as she finally moves further into the house. Walks through the hall and into the kitchen, where Delphine plucked the splinter from her palm with such ease.

And then she sees the envelope on the table.

She holds her breath as she moves closer, but she lets out a soft, sad sigh when she sees how her name written on the front has twisted and feathered. The ink bleeding like it was underwater.

Water. Mera touches her hand to the table, dragging her fingertips lightly. Yes, there it is: it's warped. A burst pipe, maybe, or rain coming through the cracked ceiling. Maybe kids, who broke in, accidently spilling their stolen cider across a stranger's belongings. Could have been anything, really, because years must have passed since Mera left. Who knows what happened in between, where Delphine went. If she even really existed at all.

That's what Mera thinks as she opens the letter, already knowing what she's going to see but going through the motions anyway. The paper that slips out is already disintegrating, leaving pulpy feathers on Mera's fingers as she takes in the faint blur that maybe once was Delphine's writing. She chews her bottom lip as she tries to find any readable fragments, to convince herself that what Delphine wrote was *I miss you,*

I'm sorry, if you see this come find me and not *You abandoned me, was it all a lie, are you even real? Don't try to find me.*

The only thing she can make out for sure, though, is the end of the scribbled date in the top left corner: August 17th, 1996.

Nine years ago, Mera thinks. *So I went back at least nine years.*

Only a few years short of what she needed in order to save her mother, dead in 1992.

But it's too late for all that, she knows. Her mother is gone, and now so is Delphine. Long, long gone.

Mera lets out a sad, soft *oh* and shreds the letter. Then she begins to pace, circling the kitchen, face turned to the ceiling.

So what now? Back to the smoldering husk of her home? Out to sea, where her father has hidden away for so long now?

Everyone in her orbit is gone now. And she herself—

Might as well be gone, she thinks, and then she trips on something, falling hard. The impact on the tile floor jars her knee and her wrists and the empty house echoes with her swearing.

"Shit," she says again, rolling on to her side. Her bag is in the middle of the floor, contents spilled, and she groans as she gets to her hands and knees to crawl over to it.

She only cares about the vials, and she gathers them and lays them in a neat line across the floor, running her fingers over the glass. No cracks. Lucky. Wherever she goes next, she'll need them.

Maybe I could propagate them, she thinks, although she hasn't tried before—there was no need. But now she could have her own garden, keep the rituals going, keep tending the flora the only way she knows how.

Mera picks up the vial of thorns and shakes it, watching the spikes tumble into each other. "Don't worry," she tells them. "I'm going to get you back in the ground where . . ."

And then she forgets what she is saying. In amongst the purple thorns, there's a tiny spark of something else. A color somewhere between coral and rust, the shape of it delicate and small. She holds her breath as she unscrews the vial and tips the contents into her palm, shakes the thorns away and there it is, sitting next to and almost as small as the scar in the middle of her palm.

A seed.

That night she dreams of Delphine.

Mera is in the bedroom Delphine showed her to last time, in that same bed. And the dream feels as real as if Delphine's there, in the flesh, standing at the foot of the bed and putting her warm hand on Mera's ankle and shaking her gently awake. "I don't want you to burn," dream-Delphine says and Mera sits up, somewhere between awake and the dream, as Delphine sits on the edge of the bed.

"You left," Mera says, eyes wide open but not seeing. "I told you I would come back. And I can, now. I just have to grow the blossom, and then I'll come back."

Delphine reaches over and tucks a curl behind Mera's ear. "But if you come back for me, how is it that I never saw you again?" she asks. "Shouldn't this have already happened for me? Do you even understand how this all works?"

Her words swim around Mera's head, float into her mouth where she swallows them so she won't choke and then she blinks, and she's awake, and Delphine is gone again.

Mera doesn't want to go back to that cheap hotel. Besides, it's quiet out here. Private.

To her surprise the water still runs and the lights still flicker on. *Someone somewhere must be paying for this*, she thinks, but then she forgets about it.

It's not her home, and she feels a small amount of guilt for claiming this place with all its ghosts, but what else does she have? So she finds the nearest phone box and calls her dad again, leaves a message with his superiors, that she's staying with a friend. *Don't worry about me. I'm safe. The house can wait until you get back.*

Like she told Delphine, she is good with her hands. She walks around the farmhouse and makes a list of small repairs she can handle: the peeling wallpaper above the stairs, the broken banister, the clouded windows. And then there is the garden.

Mera marks out the plot of land that will be home for her flora. A neat rectangle, right by the spot she and Delphine slept, where the plants can get plenty of both sun and shade. She unreels a green hosepipe, digs little divots, small sleeping beds for her remnants to lie in: a row of the purple-thorned wildflower, a line of green leaves, a scattering of the one that unfurls deep navy petals and can make a person sleep for weeks. And the tiny slice that is a seed, she plants in a corner all by itself. It has deep roots, needs space to flourish.

When she's done, Mera sits back on her heels and wipes two dirt streaks over her sweaty face.

"Live," she whispers. "I need you."

It takes time for a garden to grow.

Mera wonders if anyone has noticed that she hasn't come home.

The weeks, months pass, and the farmhouse begins to feel like her home. She strips the wallpaper above the stairs and paints the walls a soft ocean green, mends the banister so it no longer leans away from the stairs like it's about to climb free. She turns on the radio at night and sends a letter to her dad when she learns he won't be returning for another six months. *It's okay, my friend is happy for me to stay, I'm helping around the house, it's all good.*

It should make her sad, she knows, how they barely even orbit each other, but he has never been the same since her mother was killed, and ever since she was old enough to take care of herself, he has been out at sea. It's what works best for them. Or it's what they can handle, at least.

In the evenings, Mera measures the flora's growth by taking a leaf on each plant between her fingers and rubbing gently, understanding with that movement what each of them needs—more water, less light, a different kind of incantation. She performs her duties and she tries not to think about the things Delphine says in her dreams. Poking holes in her plan, the loop of time they're twisting around each other in.

Almost every night she dreams of Delphine.

It gets colder and Mera protects the plants, covering them in a soft layer of compost. She learns how to build a fire in the fireplace and takes long baths in the pitch-black evenings, and watches far-off fireworks from the front porch on New Year's Eve. Then when the weather turns, February becoming March becoming April, the mornings getting lighter earlier and the afternoons warmer, she runs the length of the garden and back naked, because she can.

I am happier, she thinks, one afternoon deep into spring, sitting on the edge of the deck and staring at her garden. *Maybe I am . . . happy, here.*

But.

She stands and walks over to the flora, bending over the orange blossom. Well. There's nothing orange about it yet, only the deep green of the stems and long leaves. Soon, though. She has worked her fingers bloody coaxing it from that single seed, and that is all well and good, but it all depends on the bloom. If she said the wrong words or fed it the wrong intentions at any point—

Mera stops herself and blows gently on the leaf nearest to her, smiling as it rolls in on itself.

I'm still coming for you, Delphine. Just wait for the bloom.

It happens on a Thursday.

Mera is carrying a pile of washing outside to hang on the line and there it is. The brightest, shiniest, proudest orange sphere, edges ruffled and crinkled, blooming for all to wonder at. Mera drops her clean underwear right there and holds her fingertips to her mouth.

She is careful, when she cuts the stem. There is only one flower right now, and she whispers a thank-you to the remains as she does it, so the other unopened bulbs will know they are still wanted, respected.

Upstairs she sits on the edge of the bed she thinks of as hers, now, and for a moment she tries to focus, think of when she wants to go to. Then she remembers that the blossom is in control. Doesn't matter if she screams and cries for it to drop her back in the right place; it'll take her where it wills. Mera holds the blossom to her lips, her breath rustling the petals. It has to work. Doesn't it?

She bites before she can think too much more and the taste seems to ignite something locked inside her body, a memory of a strong, beating floral heart—

It is the same as before: the underwater feeling, the oblivion, the weight in her lungs. Then the searing pain, and then—

She is awake.

It takes a moment to orient herself and when she does, she's lying on her side with the sun searing into her eyes. Mera stretches her fingers, feeling the grass beneath her. Just like before, she has landed in an open field, and she exhales.

A good sign, she tells herself. *It is working like the last time.*

When she sits up, though, she sees she is not so far from the farmhouse; it shimmers in the near distance, and her heart pounds at the sight of it. Or maybe it's the blossom, back to its insistent pulse.

If it worked, if I got it right, then I'll know as soon I step inside that house. If it worked, Delphine will be right there.

So Mera runs.

Through the fields, long grass tangling around her bare ankles, a stitch in her side.

And all she can think as she runs, hot morning air in her blossom-wrapped lungs, is that she's been alone for so long. That until she met Delphine, she hadn't even considered the idea that another person in the world could see her, feel like her, even want to know her. And giving up on the idea of getting her mother back was painful but worth it, if it meant having someone like Delphine. Someone to look forward to, someone to bask in the glow of.

Mera runs, her mind flashing through the images she has of Delphine: asleep in the garden, head bowed with tweezers in hand, openmouthed smiling over dinner, standing so fiercely cautious on the front steps of the house. For years Mera had been untethered, the only thing even close to keeping her on earth that plan of hers, that drive to kill. Now, these months spent looking ahead instead of back—she believes in herself again, has a hope for her own life, of growing roots into this place.

Mera runs, her lungs aching and her feet burning on the hot ground, but the house grows larger and then she is off the ground, on the weathered front steps, and she slams her palms flat against the glass as she calls out, "Delphine!"

She's breathless but calls as loud as she can. "Delphine, it's me, it's Mera, I came back."

But she can hear it, in the way her voice slides through the door and dissipates. In the way the house seems to shimmer and breathe, like it is just waking up.

There it is. The all-too-familiar emptiness.

And a part of her is already accepting what lies beyond the front door, but another part, spurred on by the twist inside her ribs, tells her to keep going. *Come on, step inside, maybe it did work, maybe you're not a complete fuckup of a failure.*

She swallows and tries the handle, and the door swings open. "Hello?"

Mera walks in and the last of her misguided hope burns out, leaving a smoke of disappointment bitter and thick. Because the inside of the house is not as she saw it ten months—years?—ago, but what she has turned it into. The walls she painted, the banister sanded down and refinished, her own shoes in the hall.

Delphine is still gone, and Mera is still stuck in her own dead-end time.

It seems like an hour passes while Mera stands in the hall, but she doesn't know how time works anymore, so maybe it's only a minute or maybe it's an entire day.

She feels the blossom inside her, which is the part that makes no sense. It's there, she grew it, she raised it, she ate it. She's not some novice; this has been her whole life, the most important education her mother gave her.

So how is it that I failed?

In the end, she walks through the house and out into the garden, where everything looks just how she left it. On the table is the battery-powered radio she listens to while she feeds the flora, and now she sits on the edge of the deck, turns it on to the news. The presenter announces the date in her soft Irish accent and Mera closes her eyes.

One day.

I have gone back in time one whole fucking day.

And she begins to laugh. Eyes closed, face turned up to the burning sun, she laughs so hard her body hurts because what else is there to do? All that effort, all those plans and that time and here she is, one day earlier. If she doesn't laugh, she'll fall apart, so it's all she can do, laugh and laugh and throw the radio so hard it splinters against the back door and in the absence of its chatter it is just Mera's laughter and the hush of the garden and the snap of a branch—

Mera's eyes fly open.

She has spent so much of her life surrounded by plants, trees, green, that she knows their sounds intimately and she knows when a branch snapping is an animal or an approaching human. Like she hears now.

She stands and thinks about calling out but doesn't. Instead she moves, quickly and quietly, through the garden toward the noise, which comes again as she closes in.

Mera crouches and grabs the small shears lying by the wisteria, holds them in front of her chest and stills. And it's like the earth stills with her, a moment where nothing moves, the entire world in one held breath.

Then a figure steps out from the trees and Mera drops the shears. "What—"

"It's okay," Delphine says. "It's okay—"

"It's okay," says the girl in the white dress. "I'm not going to hurt you."

Mera looks up at her. She is seven and small and this girl—who is older, like the McNally girls down the street, almost a grown-up really—this girl who wandered into her garden smiles down at her, like they are friends. But Mera has no friends, only her father.

Mera shakes her head as Delphine steps forward. "Wait," she says. "This isn't real. You can't—" *You can't be here but there, too*, is what she's trying to say. But her brain is working faster that she can keep up with, piecing together Delphine and the blossoms and that feeling Mera had the first moment she saw her, of somehow knowing Delphine already—

And Delphine comes towards her now, like she's really here, like Mera isn't making her up, even though she looks exactly the same as the last time. It's not decade-older Delphine, but sleeping-under-the-night-sky Delphine, in a white dress and battered boots, a backpack slung over her shoulder.

"Mera," she says, up close now, so her breath ghosts over Mera's face. "It's me. I swear."

She lifts her hands and places them on either side of Delphine's face and she is so warm, *so real*—

"Oh my god," she says, finally getting it. "You're really here. I found you."

Delphine shakes her head, Mera's hands still holding her. "No," she says with a smile. "*I* found *you*."

Delphine tells Mera how she waited, once Mera was gone—one moment solid and then just an empty space.

Waited for her to return, like Mera had said she would. Then waited, thinking she had imagined it all, and waited, an anger growing at this maybe-imagined girl who'd abandoned her, and waited, for the feelings to pass, and waited as the longing never went away but only grew.

Delphine tells Mera how she lay awake at night remembering what Mera had told her about the orange blossom, still not quite able to believe it. And so one night she thought that she could find out, for herself, if any of it was real.

"There had to be a version of you where I was," she says. "So I went looking."

"It's okay," says the girl in the white dress. "I'm not going to hurt you."

Mera looks up at her. She is seven and small and this girl, who has wandered into her garden, smiles down at her, like they are friends. But Mera has no friends, only her father.

She looks at the house, wondering if she should call to him, but then the strange girl kneels. "Mera," she says, "I promise it's okay."

Mera snaps back around, stares at the girl. "How do you know my name?"

"Because I know you," the girl says. "You said you would teach me about your flowers. Will you do that?"

"You were there," Mera breathes. "In the garden, years ago. That's why I felt like I knew you. Oh my god. I had forgotten all about it but you were *there*."

Delphine nods, her eyes shining. "I was there," she said. "I found out where you lived, and I went there to see if you were real, and—do you remember the rest?"

Mera does now, this girl in her garden who she had proudly shown the flora to—but carefully, not giving their real names, not giving a hint of their properties. *We protect that*, her mother had taught her, and even seven-year-old Mera had respected that.

"But it didn't matter that I never told you what they really were," she says, watching Delphine. "I'd already told you, hadn't I?"

"I thought if you couldn't make it back to me there must be a reason," Delphine says. "I convinced myself, anyway. So I decided I could be the one to come to you."

Then she swings the backpack off her shoulder. Opens it.

Inside glows bright as the sun with so many orange blossoms that Mera can't even begin to count them all. "So I took some," Delphine says. "And I did like you said, I ate it, and now—"

Mera laughs, but it's real this time, an astonished pleasure because she had thought this was all for nothing and she was never going to see Delphine again. But the blossom—brought her forward. Right when she needed her to be. "Here you are," Mera says. "Now."

Delphine looks beyond Mera. "You've been here the whole time?"

"I was trying to get back," Mera says, and then, "I missed you. I missed you so much, so so much."

Delphine laughs and contained in it is all the birdsong Mera has heard in the early mornings, the *hush-hush-hush* of grass waving in the breeze, the stream in her favorite field tumbling over smooth stones.

"I missed you too, even when I was mad at you." Delphine leans her forehead against Mera's. "I wanted to forget all of this, but I couldn't forget how I felt when I was with you."

Mera reaches down to pluck a blossom from Delphine's stash, rolling it between her fingers. "Now we have time," she says. "Look. We have so much time."

She throws her arms around Delphine and they hold each other so tight, desperate, a relief in their breathless laughter.

Inside her the blossom beats on, persistent, undimmed.

No. 1 (note: revised)
You should use the garden all you want. You should
    touch the orange blossoms, for they hold time,
    but more than that; they hold you.
They will always hold you.

TEED UP

"Oblivious to Lovers"

Gloria Chao

THWACK. PRACTICE SHOT #368. ONE HUNDRED THIRTY-TWO MORE to go for this pre-tournament driving range session. I'm trying to focus, but it's even harder than normal today.

From behind me, I hear snickering. "That's her," someone whispers.

"Obviously, you idiot," another voice responds. "See anyone else on their period here?"

"Maybe—bleeding out your ass again, man?"

Hilaaarrious, aren't they? I don't know who they are, but I picture them as the next few balls. *Thwack.* Pure contact. It soars high and beautiful, traveling three hundred yards. I actually don't like golf very much, but I sure do like shutting up pompous jackasses who define me by my genitals.

Golf was exciting at first. I still remember my first swings in the backyard, feeling like if I gained enough momentum, I could fly into the sky. My parents had never watched or played golf before, but when they read about Yani Tseng—a star golfer from their homeland of Taiwan—they bought me a set of toddler clubs. Ten years ago, when Yani nabbed the coveted title of number one female golfer in the world, my parents had asked me, "Don't you want to be just like Yani?" Because I was over the moon about seeing a girl who looked like me on television, seven-year-old me yelled "Yes!" without fully knowing what I was agreeing to. Since then, my life has been teed up for me.

The older I got, the harder the practice grew—swinging five hundred times a day, sometimes even without a golf ball. But it paid off. At age nine, I became the youngest player ever to qualify for the US Girls' Junior Championship. At thirteen, I was driving the ball the same distance as the men, two hundred eighty yards. The notoriety was intoxicating, addicting. I was on the map, a household name to those who followed golf and even some who didn't.

But once I was old enough to see all the sacrifices my parents made in the name of my golf career, the fun turned into pressure. My father left his office job so his schedule would be flexible enough for him to take me to tournaments. Then, my mother lost her job as a nanny because the family worried my growing fame would impact their kids. As we eat through our savings, the need to provide for them, pay back all they've given up, has grown to the point where it feels like our future depends on this tournament, this round, this putt.

It doesn't make me a hoot to be around. Which may be why the only people around me are just watching, waiting for me to fail.

Another group of snickering boys walks by me on the range. I don't catch their words, but I'm sure they're about me. I'm used to being in the public eye, but this tournament is a whole new level.

After winning the US Girls' Junior Championship two years in a row, my parents signed me up for the US Junior Amateur, a historically male-only event. We had to confirm that females were even allowed to apply since it hasn't been done before. My parents thought that if I could make a splash in the most prestigious boys' tournament, it would launch my professional career, which will start as soon as I turn eighteen in a few months. "Sponsors will be knocking down our door! You could make as much as Yani!" My parents paint a pretty picture.

When the United States Golf Association (USGA) received my application, they reached out to see if I wouldn't be better off competing with my peers in the girls' event, which was happening at the same time. This only ignited my need to kick some ass in the US Junior Amateur—which might be what I told the USGA on the phone. I played in the Arizona qualifier and earned my spot fair and square. Tomorrow, the championship starts. If I play well, I could have a long, grueling week ahead. After two days of stroke play, the lowest sixty-four scores make it to match play, in which players battle head-to-head until there is one (wo)man standing. Somehow, I'm more alone than ever and there's *even more* pressure than before. This week feels like I'm playing for girls everywhere, like I'm combating the men-only golf clubs and everyone who has ever said that women's sports don't matter as much.

And the environment only reinforces this pressure. The snickering jerks are my fellow competitors, the ones who can't stand that I might be better than them in a sport that traditionally gives men a leading edge.

I try to focus on my practice, but then I hear:

"How do those things not get in the way?"

"Or do you mean, how does she not spend all day looking at them in the mirror?"

Sometimes I wonder if my parents put me in golf to surround me with the worst boys so I wouldn't want anything to do with them. They didn't have to explicitly tell me not to date when I turned thirteen because I was already on the same page. Though, of course, making it forbidden until I win my first LPGA (read: professional, with big prize money) tournament was what started to change my mind. Then, probably, the hormones. The one relationship I did have was short, secret, and doomed from the start.

I pound range balls harder, pushing one to the right uncharacteristically. Giving them something to *actually* laugh at. I tell myself that they probably didn't notice, but I know I'm wrong; someone is always watching.

"You okay?" a voice calls out, proving me right (unfortunately). "You're hitting those balls like they hurt your family."

"Don't worry about it," I say, returning to my practice and striking just as hard as before.

"Well, I'm rooting for you," the voice says. "I've been a fan of yours since you started dominating the girls' events years ago, and I think it's so cool you qualified for this."

At that, I look up. He's already turning away, a sheepish I-can't-believe-I-just-said-that cringe on his admittedly pretty cute face.

He's getting in your head, I hear my parents say. Other people have an angel and a devil, I have two angels that sound exactly like my mom and dad. Maybe all the players here banded together and elected that guy to faux flirt with me since he's the best-looking. I wouldn't put it past them, going to great lengths to make sure they didn't lose to a girl. And it wouldn't be the first time a fellow competitor tried to sabotage me (psyching me out, making noise during my putts, intentionally putting down the wrong score for me—I've seen it all).

I let him walk away, and I refocus. This tournament is going to be mine.

"Mama, can we please just eat somewhere close by?" I beg later that night. "Karen's Dumpling Shop is an hour away, and the name doesn't sound promising." Not to mention I'm bone tired and my tee time for the first day of the tournament tomorrow is eight in the morning.

"You'd rather have fast food than Chinese food?" my mother scolds.

My real wish is to eat in the clubhouse like the other players, but I know better than to suggest that. I grew up around golf and in country clubs, which means I also intimately know the discrimination my parents are running from. To be fair, we would hunt down Chinese food wherever we went, but even in the implausible scenario in which the clubhouse was serving authentic soup dumplings, we wouldn't have stayed. The quiet looks lingering a second too long, the slower service, the refusal to call us by name even when we have nametags—a person could only deal with that for so long before they stay away, even when it's less convenient. I try to convince myself it's for the best that I won't be subjecting myself to more whispering tonight.

After shamefully (shamelessly?) using my early tee time as an excuse, we settle on getting Mexican food from a nearby restaurant with four stars on Yelp.

Over a smorgasbord of enchiladas, tacos, and flautas—we always eat family-style, even when it's not Chinese food—my mother makes a toast:

"You've been practicing your whole life for this weekend, Sunny. Your baba and I are so proud of you." My father nods, raising his glass too. "Your grandparents would be so proud if they were here."

My grandparents died before I was born, but they still loom large in my life. I think my parents feel guilty for leaving Taiwan, for not being around when my grandparents fell ill, and for living a better life now than they left behind. Which (unfortunately) means, on top of everything else, I'm also shouldering the pressures they handed down; my success would justify the sacrifices everyone made.

After we clink glasses and sip our drinks—Jarritos for them, just water for me since I'm in tournament mode—my mother folds her hands in front of her. "I saw you look at that boy during practice."

Like I said, perpetually watched.

"Which one?" I say with a straight face.

"You know the one. The only one you looked at." I shrug. She continues, "He's trying to get to you."

"I know, Mama."

"You know how dangerous that is. You know they say whatever they need to so you'll think they like you, so you'll be distracted, so you'll mess up. Don't forget about Dylan."

His name punches me in the gut. And heart.

"I would never let Dylan happen again," I say sincerely. Sometimes I want to remind her that I was the one who'd been most affected, that part of the horribleness had been their reaction, but that would only lead to more yelling.

Unaware of my inner storm (or ignoring it), my mother nods and we dig into our food.

The next morning, since time is of the essence, I convince my parents to let me eat the clubhouse breakfast buffet for tournament players. They don't join, which is for the best. I need to focus.

I'm lost in my thoughts at an empty table, a full plate in front of me, when a now-familiar voice asks, "This seat taken?"

He's persistent, I'll give him that.

I'm trying to mentally prepare for the round, I'm about to say, but then I notice that the rest of the seats in the dining room are already full.

"You don't have to ask, it's a communal space," I say while burying my face in my eggs. Eating before tournaments is always for sustenance; finding that balance of getting enough nutrients to be able to perform without making yourself want to throw up from the mix of nerves and bacon grease.

He slips into the upholstered chair beside me, his plate piled so high with bacon, sausage, and potatoes that I gag just looking at it.

"How can you do that before a tournament round?" I ask sincerely, also noticing that his aura is emanating with excitement, not anxiety.

"I've been waiting my whole life for this," he says as he shovels food into his mouth in a pattern: one bite per food item so he has a smorgasbord in his mouth. My little Taiwanese heart sees you, buddy.

He's eating so ravenously I must be staring, because he blushes. "I want to make sure I finish in time to digest and warm up, you know?" he explains. "Er, well, what's your routine? This is my first time qualifying for a national event so I guess I could use any tips you've got."

Not exactly what I predicted, but close enough: he wants my help. And maybe he wants to get in my head, too.

"Hit the ball, find it, repeat," I say, which, all kidding aside, really is my best advice. It's all I think about when I play—no thoughts about my score, what anyone might be saying, or how my parents are wringing their hands underneath their sun umbrellas in the gallery.

He laughs. "No, really, what goes on in your head when you're kicking ass?"

I shrug. "That's really what goes on in my head: hit the ball, find, repeat."

"Huh, no kidding. Maybe I need to stop thinking so much about my grip, my swing path, my release, or how I missed the last shot." He grins. "I know, I know, you're wondering how I qualified. Maybe it was my lack of nerves since I didn't think I had a shot?" He shrugs. "All I have going for me is my love of the game, which doesn't get me far. But one day in the future, when I'm golfing on the weekend, recovering from my office job, I'll tell my playing partner that I got to eat breakfast and play in the Junior Am with Sunny Chang, now the number one player on the LPGA Tour." He scarfs down his last couple bites of food, winks at me, then stands.

I barely hear his "See ya out there," because his last words are haunting me.

"And now on the first tee, from Scottsdale, Arizona, Sunny Chang!" the announcer yells.

Okay.

One. Ignore everyone, especially my parents, who look like they're about to shit themselves (Jesus, guys, it's the first shot of the first day).

Two. Test the wind by throwing some grass in the air—okay, about a one-club wind in my face.

Three. Take the driver from Sean, my swing coach and caddy (who can sometimes be harder on me than my parents, believe it or not).

Four. Tee the ball, then let the muscle memory take over.

The world fades away and it's just me, my club, and my Titleist Pro V1 ball with a heart drawn on it. Because I might as well flaunt my gender everywhere for girl pride, for spite, and maybe also to get in their heads too.

I hit the ball flush, the pure sound dancing in my ears. I have to hold back my smile as I retrieve my tee and move to the side of the tee box.

♡

Nine holes in, I experience something that has never happened in my decade of playing tournament golf.

The two other guys in my threesome drop out. (And for the record, "threesome" is a dirty word only to nongolfers, okay?) I've seen players drop out before, of course, but not in a USGA championship, and not *both* players in my group. But I guess I shouldn't be too surprising given their current scores. They've been missing fairways and short putts all day.

Me, on the other hand? I've been having a consistent round, as usual. So far, there were only a couple of squirrely shots to brush off and I've been able to ignore everyone, even Sean berating me. My superpower. But Jimminy Bob and WhatsHisFace dropping out affects me. Mainly because I need to be re-paired with someone so we can keep each other's scores, but also because of yet another unexpected thing: Jimminy or WhatsHis's dad flips his shit on me.

"It's that girl's fault!" he yells. "She distracted Jeremy!"

Okay, fine, *Jeremy*. Close enough.

"This is a boys' event!"

No one, not a single soul, not the officials or Sean or even my parents, come to my defense. Once again, I have to channel my superpower. I say nothing as the officials scramble to calm Jimminy Senior down and find me a new playing partner.

I'm not religious, but in that moment, I say a prayer. It's a small one, with a bar so low I doubt anyone could limbo beneath it. *Please give me someone who shuts his mouth and just hits the ball, finds it, and hits it again.*

"Sunny Chang," calls out the official running toward me. "You're now paired with Liam Russo. Please exchange scorecards and continue."

I freeze. The tall, lanky boy approaching me has a cheek-to-cheek smile on his (very) cute face.

Someone heard my prayer. And apparently I am such a jerk I didn't even ask for his name earlier.

"Oh man, did my day just get better," Liam says as he shakes my hand.

Okay, now I'm convinced. He's trying to get to me. No one talks like that unless they're trying to (poorly) hide sinister motives, like charming me into looking at his tousled hair instead of reading my putt. Speaking of which, how did he get it to stick up just right from his slightly askew visor?

Liam introduces his caddy as his father, who looks like he's never caddied a day in his life. What if it's an act so I'll let my guard down?

Dang it, he's already in my head.

"Nice to meet you," I say curtly. Then I finish all the obligatory changing score-cards and blah-de-blah before getting my head back in the game as quickly as I can. I try to make myself ignore Liam Senior, who is letting Liam's clubs whack against each other, no headcovers on.

Liam picks up on my not-so-subtle hints and steers clear of me for the next three holes, save for a fist bump on the eleventh green after I sink a thirty-foot putt.

On the thirteenth tee, I briefly wonder if I should share some of my secret snacks. Sean and my parents only let me eat wheatgrass and whey nutrition bricks during rounds, so I have to sneak my preferred fuel in. Will he be grossed out by my seaweed packets and White Rabbit candies? But since he's not minding me, I should do the same. I've never been one to open up to other people, especially not first.

After I decide not to open up, the skies open up. The Universe is having a grand ol' time with me today, huh? I grab my rain gear and prepare to continue playing, but then the horn blows. There must be lightning on the radar.

I follow Sean to the nearest rain shelter. Lucky for us, it's a snack shack and not one of those dinky roofs propped up on four pillars. This one has bathrooms and drinks and free snacks.

Sean and Liam Senior prop the golf bags under cover, and Sean immediately grabs paper towels from the bathroom to clean off my clubs. Liam Senior bumbles a bit, then parrots Sean's every move without subtlety.

"You're distracted today," Sean says as I walk by. "Take this time to pull it together."

I give him a half-assed nod, ironically because I'm distracted—by how earnestly Liam Senior is fussing and scrubbing.

Inside the snack shack, without thinking, I say to Liam, "It's really sweet that your dad cares so much." Even if he doesn't know what he's doing. *Especially* since he doesn't know what he's doing.

"Pops is awesome. Doesn't get the game but wants to be a part of it for me."

It's funny how straightforward that sounds, yet my parents "being a part of the game for me" means something completely different.

Despite the red flags from before and my usual risk-averse behavior, I ask him, "Why do you like golf?"

He blinks at me a few times, then laughs. "Is that a joke?"

I wish. I continue to look at him, face serious. I need to know. Because if he can give me that answer, then my problems will be solved. I can find the joy in this, please my parents, and march down my predetermined path with resolve and, fingers crossed, happiness. I often feel like a walking oxymoron, a girl named Sunny with no sunshine or happiness on her horizon.

Realizing I'm serious, Liam turns his laugh into a throat clearing. "Um, I don't know. I like that it's outside, it's a good workout, no two shots are ever the same, I'm always thinking about strategy and obstacles and wind. And it's you against yourself. What other sport has that? You have your own personal goals, and when you achieve them? It just feels—"

"So you don't care if you win? If you can make it professionally? If you make money?" I blurt out.

He laughs. "I will *not* make it professionally. And that's okay." He smiles. "But you will."

He's trying to make me feel good—or maybe butter me up—but it accomplishes the opposite.

"So, tell me," Liam says, leaning forward. "What does Sunny Chang like about golf?"

That I can make money and support my parents. That society tells me I'm good at it. At least, that's why this has become my life plan, because what kind of ungrateful fool would turn down the opportunity of a lifetime for something as ridiculous as happiness? And perhaps I won't be happy doing anything. Maybe it's not in my DNA.

Except when I think about getting a regular job, working with other people, I'm flooded with relief. Because that doesn't involve playing tournament rounds back to back to back with no time to recover, with my parents breathing down my neck, with my nerves strung so taut they're going to snap any day, any putt now.

I'm just exhausted. Traveling, never sleeping in my own bed, not having any friends . . . One weekend, I would love to be able to read a magazine, get an ice cream cone, make a joke to someone and hear them laugh. To *not* feel like if I miss this next shot, I will be a failure, and I will be letting my parents down.

I haven't said anything to Liam for too long. Which in and of itself tells him the answer to his question. Still, I hope he doesn't put it together. But he's already two steps ahead of me.

"Is it the pressure?" he asks.

I tell myself not to admit anything, but my head nods once as if it has a mind of its own.

Then he asks, "Do you think you'd enjoy golf if you weren't competing?"

I ask myself that All. The. Time. But I've never voiced it out loud. And I'm not about to now, in the middle of a tournament, to a fellow competitor I just met.

I manage to give him a small shrug.

"Sorry about the comments I made earlier, about the LPGA tour," he says sheepishly.

I start shaking my head before he finishes his sentence. "No, not at all. You were very kind."

"Well, I'm sure it didn't help."

And just like that, he knows my deepest darkest secret. The one I've never told anyone before. That I *couldn't* tell anyone, for fear of it getting back to my parents. Anxiety shoots through me like my nerves are on fire—the same way I feel on the last few shots when I'm in contention to win a tournament. But this is much more serious.

"I was just joking," I say unconvincingly.

Just in time, because my parents walk in, sopping wet. They usually take a break after nine holes to get a snack and calm their nerves (you know, because this is the most stressful thing *for them*) before rejoining me around thirteen or fourteen.

My mother's voice slices through the air. "Sunny!" She glares at Liam, then comes and pulls me to another table.

"He didn't get in your head, did he?" she asks.

"No," I lie.

♡

When play resumes twenty minutes later, it's still raining but there is no longer a risk of lightning. I walk outside to see Sean panicking.

"Sunny, I'm sorry," he blurts out. "I didn't have your side pocket zipped all the way and both your towels are wet!"

Rain + no dry towel = wet grips = quite the disaster.

Part of me doesn't even care. It's almost an excuse for me to try to enjoy this round. Only almost. Because my mom is losing it. She hasn't said anything, but from the scrunched-up look on her face, I know it's taking all her energy not to explode.

I think of what she and my father have given up. I think of all the female athletes out there I'm playing for. And I try to find a way to solve my problem and calm my mother down and, and, and . . .

"Here," a voice says from behind me.

Sean, my mother, and I turn to see Liam holding out a dry, fluffy golf towel.

"Why?" flies out of my mother's mouth, to which Liam's eyebrows shoot up.

"Thank you," I say quickly before my mother can ask him what he's up to.

The rest of the round passes in relative quiet. I suspect it's because my parents are following me closer than normal, daggers shooting out in all directions but mainly at Liam. They affect my game more than Liam ever could, but I refrain from telling them that.

I don't let myself look at the score until the end of the round, and I exhale in relief when I see that I'm even par, which is well within the cut line. If I hold it together tomorrow, I'll make it to match play.

Liam and I take our hats off on the eighteenth green and shake hands. He holds on a second longer than normal, then pulls me slightly closer as he whispers, "Hope I see you at dinner."

I suddenly feel an overwhelming need to escape my parents and be at the clubhouse dinner despite the alarm bells in my head, despite my mother's warnings, despite my worries that the other players won't welcome me.

Maybe you want to go because you're *trying to get in* his *head*, I lie to myself. But obviously that's wrong. I've never done that before, and I'm not about to start now.

Really, I feel pulled to Liam.

♡

I lie to my parents. I tell them the clubhouse dinner is mandatory, knowing they won't bother checking with a USGA official, knowing they won't want to join me. I feel as guilty as I do awkward when I walk into the dining room that night.

I spot Liam and make a beeline for him.

"Exactly the person I was hoping to see," he greets me.

"Why are you nice to me?" blurts out of my mouth as I sit down.

"What do you mean?" he says with a laugh.

"No one's ever done that without wanting something," I admit, talking fast. "Do you want advice? Or an in with Sean?" He's one of the best swing coaches around and only takes referrals. "Or are you trying to get in my head? Maybe you don't want to lose to a girl."

Liam's usually sunny (ha) demeanor vanishes, and for the first time (since *yesterday—you've only known him* one *day*, I chastise myself), a storm crosses his face. He seems to deal in extremes with his emotions based on how fast and how far he falls, and weirdly, I'm jealous he's able to do that, and so openly.

"Seriously?" he says, and shame washes through me.

"I'm sorry, but you don't know what it's like to be me." And strangely—or not so strangely since I'm apparently someone else with Liam, someone with loose lips—I tell him about Dylan. About how we'd met on my high school golf team, about how I had believed him when he said he liked me, about how I snuck out of my house to date him, only to discover that he was using me for my fame.

"He even talked to the press about us!" I finish, leaving it at that because I don't want Liam to know the rest of the details. Like how Dylan did it with full knowledge that it would destroy my relationship with my parents. And how it started out laughable, with Dylan claiming he'd "brought my game to a whole new level," but then, when I dumped his sorry ass, he retaliated by telling the press how I used to sneak off with him during golf practice and that I "kiss like a dead catfish." My parents had already been suspicious due to my recent string of losses, and when they saw the article, they didn't want to hear what I had to say—not that I had much. Not only did they not support me, leaving me to deal with my public embarrassment alone, but they made my world even smaller with more restrictions. I went from attending public school to homeschooling, my training schedule intensified, and they began monitoring my emails.

Liam's face softens. "I'm sorry you had to go through that. For the record, I would never leak anything to the press about you, not that they would care what you had for breakfast . . ." He chuckles, then hesitates. "Though, maybe I did have an ulterior motive when I first talked to you."

I knew it. I absolutely knew it. Why had I shared so much? This will be another painful lesson, just like Dylan. Maybe my mother was smarter than I gave her credit for.

Liam's mouth quirks up. "I may have had a small crush on you." He covers his eyes. "I've been following your career for a while."

I laugh. That can't be it. He's joking. But he keeps his hands over his eyes and says nothing else. After a minute of silence, he brings his right hand away and peeks at me with one squinted eye.

Is he for real? Who puts their feelings out there like this? And it only proves he's just like my parents and Dylan and everyone else—he only sees me for my golf abilities. He liked me before he even knew me.

"You're not going to say *anything*?" he jokes. But I'm not in a joking mood. He brings his hands down. "I will admit that the previous crush was superficial and maybe more about, you know. I mean, I just—but now, well . . ." He drifts off. Then he clears his throat, embarrassed. "Never mind. Um, you played really well today."

"Thanks."

"I . . . could have done better," he says with a laugh.

"Did the rain shake you up a bit?" I ask. His scores after our snack shack break had been all over the place.

"Um, yeah, maybe," he mumbles. Then, louder—too loud—he says, "When do you think the food's going to come?"

I'm about to apologize for embarrassing him when his dad joins us.

"Hey Sunny!" he greets me. "If you're done with the towel, do you mind returning it? It's our only one."

And I put it together. Liam didn't lend me a spare towel; it was his *only* towel and he played like crap in the rain because of it.

"Why did you do that?" I ask, when obviously I should have said thank you, but *why would he do that?*

Liam smiles. "I'm rooting for you. I want you to make even more history than you already have." Beside him, his dad is beaming too.

I don't know what to say. After staring at Liam for way too long, I manage two words: "Thank you."

"My pleasure."

Dinner passes in a delightful blur. Others join our table, but Liam, his father, and I keep to ourselves. They share stories about their chaotic, loving family—Liam has young twin sisters who wreak a lot of (cute) havoc, and it's because of them that his mother can't be here today—and I find it hard to share anything because I just want their stories to fill up my heart. I also can't bear to share any of my memories following their happy ones. But Liam seems to already know what's going on in my head and carries the conversation.

I'm glad my parents aren't there . . . until I bid Liam and his father goodnight. Once I'm alone, the guilt consumes me, especially when I return to our room and see that my parents have saved some crab Rangoons and dumplings for me—my favorites.

"We missed you, Sunny," my mother says.

"Me too," I lie.

Last day of stroke play. I just have to have a decent round and I should be in the top sixty-four that advance to match play. Liam has to have a great round, but he's still in the running.

Usually, this day of the tournament is when ice flows in my veins. When I somehow find that balance between staying calm and also feeling every nerve ending in my body.

But today, I'm the opposite of icy. I feel . . . sunny. I'm chatting with Liam, relaxed, and playing some of the best golf of my life. For the first time, I feel the breeze in my hair, hear the birds chirping, and notice how high a hawk is being carried by the wind. My mother, on the other hand, looks like she's popping a hemorrhoid. But she says nothing since I'm making birdies.

"Is this what golf is like for you all the time?" I ask Liam as we walk down the fairway together, our caddies a few steps behind.

"Not when I'm playing like crap," he jokes, but he laughs and I hear the answer of *yes* in his chuckles.

"So what's your plan for the future?" I ask, genuinely curious. He said yesterday that he wasn't going pro, but he's not bad and could at least give it a try.

"The dream is to get a college degree while also playing on a golf team. But if I have to choose, education comes first."

I haven't even thought about college. For as long as I can remember, the goal had been to go pro as soon as possible, i.e., earn money as soon as possible.

"Do you have a college you're most excited about?" I ask.

"Stanford. Top-notch golf, top-notch education in practically everything."

Stanford. Wow. I like the sound of that. Not too shabby, right? Tiger went there. And . . . I suddenly realize that college would delay going pro, but it wouldn't preclude it. I stop walking abruptly.

Liam halts beside me. "Sunny . . ." I look at him. "What do you want?"

No one's asked me that in a very long time, including myself.

I don't know, I think honestly. "I don't know," I say out loud.

"Well, that's progress already right there." With a wink, he turns to the left and jogs to his ball. The one that's marked with a green four-leaf clover for luck. Which is fitting. Because he *is* luck, the personification of it, for me.

For the first time in my life, I enjoy my round of golf, I enjoy the company of my playing partner—maybe a little too much, and my nerves aren't strung so taut I'm on the edge of snapping. I shoot four under, and I not only qualify for match play, I'm the stroke-play medalist with the lowest score over the first two rounds.

Liam looks happier for me than my parents, despite not qualifying for match play himself. He may even be happier than I am, no matter how hard I try to muster up my enthusiasm.

Liam's leaving tomorrow. I'll probably never see him again. I try to ignore the hole expanding inside my chest. I barely know the guy.

And he's only attracted to your golf skills, my mother scolds in my head.

My parents aren't there when I'm awarded my stroke-play medal because it happens inside the clubhouse before dinner. They did say they were proud of me before they left to eat elsewhere, but it feels strange to be celebrating a win without the people I'm winning for. As the USGA official places the heavy bronze medal around my neck, my eyes go to Liam, the only person there rooting for me. I focus on him so I don't have to look at the other disappointed faces in the room.

When I take my seat beside him, Liam fist-bumps me. "I can't wait to see you win this whole thing."

"Are you going to stick around?" I ask with way too much enthusiasm. I try to tone it back.

"We're staying with my uncle and flying out after the tournament's over, so I was thinking about coming to watch the rest of it, especially now that I'm friends with the leading contender." Liam nudges me, then grows thoughtful. "You know, it's too bad you already have Sean, or else I'd offer to caddy for you."

I would take anyone over you're-distracted-today Sean, not just very cute boys who make me feel good. "You'd do that?"

"Yeah, of course!"

I take a sip of water. "Just because—" *of your celebrity crush*, I want to say, but calling myself a celebrity is pretty gross and an exaggeration. But I don't know how else to word it. I anxiously rub my feet back and forth on the carpet as I ask, "Are you offering just because of a childhood crush or whatever?"

He flushes as pink as the radishes on our salad plates. "No, I mean, yes. I mean, well, yeah, I talked to you that first day because of . . . that . . . but, as I tried— and failed—to tell you yesterday . . . I like you now. After getting to know you. I like you. Like, *like* like." His blush deepens.

Ignoring how adorable his bumbling nervousness is, I ask the first question that pops into my mind: "Why?"

His eyebrows shoot up. "Why? Because you're a badass and you're smart and talented and honest and hardworking and strong and it's really cute when you swing at those range balls like they're the jerks who say all those awful—"

I kiss him. Before, when I kissed Dylan, it felt like a chore. But this? Oh man, this was rainbows and butterflies and sparks—literally, ha, from static electricity.

Everyone in the clubhouse goes silent. And for once, I don't care. I don't need to go hit range balls. When I pull back from the kiss, it's just us in the room. Even when some of the surrounding animals start hooting and hollering, I just see Liam.

"Will you caddy for me?" I ask.

♡

I consider waiting until tomorrow morning on the tee box to tell my mother about Liam caddying—she would be more restrained in public, especially country club public—but I don't want to do that to her.

Or so I thought. When I tell her that night, she makes me regret that decision by storming around our hotel room cursing in Mandarin. Then, she turns to me and exclaims, "He's going to tank this for you!"

"Ma, he's not even in the tournament anymore. How can he have another motive?" *And he likes me!* I want to squeal but obviously don't.

"He can't stand that you're in this and leading. He's just like everyone else! He wants the girl to lose!"

I tell her about the towel, and how it was his only one.

She shakes her head. "That could be setting up his final plan—giving you a treat so you'll let your guard down and then, bam! He swoops in for the kill!"

"I promise that's not it. I got to know him," I say evenly through my teeth.

"It's been two days! You can't know someone after two days!" she argues.

Fair. But it's not even about that anymore. I just want to enjoy the rest of the week and have more golf days like today. "Mama, can't you trust me?"

"It's not about *trust*."

"I play better with him," I say quietly, my last shot. "That's why I did so well today."

"Sunny, we've been preparing for this your whole life. You need to take it seriously. We can't be changing things up last minute." It's the same speech she always gives for every event, every shot. Each swing I take is the most important, a make-or-break situation. No wonder my nerves are fried. "This is it, the big finish to launch your career! Isn't this your dream?" she asks. "I'm just trying to help you achieve your dream."

"It's *your* dream," I say before I can stop myself. But I can't hold it in any longer. "I'm doing all this for you."

"Why wouldn't you want to be famous, successful, rich? Of course you're doing it for you."

"How would you know when you haven't asked me what I want since I was seven?"

My mother falls into a stunned silence.

I seize the opportunity and continue. "I know you've sacrificed a lot for my golf, but so have I. I've never had the chance to be a kid or laugh with friends or—"

"Because you're too good for that. With talent comes responsibility."

"What if I want to know what college is like? What if I want to take classes and make friends and go on dates?" *What if I want to take a step back so I can remember what I like about golf?*

My mother is barely listening to my questions before her answer tumbles out. "Those are nice thoughts, but you'd have to give up money and fame and your prime golf years to do it."

"Isn't that for me to decide? If I want to give those things up, shouldn't I be able to?"

My mother doesn't respond.

"I'm not saying I want to. I don't know what I want, not yet. I just . . . want to feel like I have room to breathe. That I'm allowed to choose where I eat dinner and who caddies for me and—"

"Okay." My mother's voice is so quiet I almost don't hear her, but those two syllables are too huge not to hear. "Okay, that boy can caddy for you. But we'll talk about everything else later."

It's a small step forward, but I sleep soundly that night.

ONE YEAR LATER

Thwack. Pure contact. It soars high and beautiful, landing on the green. I walk up to the ball and hole the putt for a birdie.

"That's the lowest score anyone has posted out here all season," Liam yells, running up to me.

I wasn't even keeping score.

"Oh man, Coach is going to lose his mind when he hears about this," Liam laughs. "He's going to be at your door tonight begging on his knees."

"Next year," I say with a shrug. I take a look around the Stanford Golf Course. "But if I lose this feeling, I'm out again."

I haven't played a competitive round since the Junior Amateur. My parents and I are still working through the aftermath of that tournament, of me attending

Stanford and not playing on the golf team my first year. We're still waist-deep in rubble, but that's a torso better than being neck-deep like we were six months ago.

I tell Liam, "I might still have a dream of winning the US Amateur since I didn't win the Junior." Made it to the top eight, with Liam caddying for me all three days I was in match play.

"I don't care what anyone says, you won that week," Liam says. "You made history."

"I won because I got you."

He takes my putter and lays it on the green. "I think it's pretty obvious I'm the lucky one here." He slips his four-leaf clover golf ball into my pocket. The seaweed wrappers stuffed in there crinkle. I slip my heart (golf ball) into his pocket, which crinkles with White Rabbit candy wrappers. I wrap my arms around his neck. He scoops me up in his arms, and we kiss.

He tastes like sunshine.

BOYS NOISE

"Only One Bed at the Inn"

Mason Deaver

"NEW YORK." I STARE AT FELIX FROM MY SEAT IN FRONT OF THE PIANO.
"You want to spend the weekend in New York?"

He'd walked into the music room with this wide smile on his face and a pep in his step. Truth be told the moment I saw him, I knew he had a secret, he's so bad at hiding them.

"It's technically a day," he says. "A couple of hours really."

"Oh fun." I place my hands on the keys again. "What's this for?"

"Your birthday, Lev. What else?"

"My birthday isn't for two more weeks."

"I know, that's what makes this the surprise." Felix sits down on the bench with me, pulling the sleeves of his sweater down to cover his hands. "So . . ."

He stares at me intently.

I can't help but blush at the way he looks at me, and panic at the way my nerves fill my heart when he sits this close, our knees touching.

"We're going to get in trouble," I tell him.

"Better to ask for forgiveness than permission."

"That logic is so flawed."

"But that's not a *no*."

"Who's going?"

"Just the two of us."

I wait a bit, weighing the options in my head. Right now, the last place I should be is alone with Felix Young, on the opposite side of the country, away from our bandmates who'd save me from any awkward fumbling or terrible choices. But when Felix looks at me, his warm brown eyes big like a puppy dog's, the answer is obvious.

"Fine."

"Excellent!" He pulls down the key cover, barely giving me enough time to move away my hands before my fingers get crushed.

"I was playing!"

"You need to pack; we leave in the morning!" He's already halfway out the door.

"Fine."

"So why New York?" I ask him as we walk through LAX.

Normally we'd have a ring of security that surrounds us, but today there's nothing to protect us from any fans that might notice, except for the sunglasses, hoodies, and masks that hide the lower halves of our faces.

I'd be lying if I said my heart isn't thudding in my chest.

Anyone could see us.

"I thought it'd be nice, visit your old stomping grounds," Felix says, his backpack slung over his shoulders. We'd both packed light, what would we need for just a few hours in New York anyway?

"'Stomping grounds'? Who has ever said that?"

"People! I heard it on TV once!"

"Pfft, okay." I shake my head. "Who else knows we're going?"

"I told Mickey, just in case the label put an APB out on us."

"We're going to be in so much trouble when we get back . . ."

"Hey!" Felix wraps an arm around my shoulder, which is tough because I'm a solid foot taller than him. "You let me worry about that."

Felix has always been seen and marketed as the baby of the group—even though he's six months older than me—he's the baby, I'm the cold, stoic, shy one, Mickey is the big brother, Drew is the handsome pretty boy, and Corey the hot "nerd" who wears fake glasses. All things that none of us are really like in real life, but we accept the roles we're given.

Not that we have a choice. We do what the label wants us to.

Eventually, Felix's arm falls back to his side since it'd be incredibly awkward for us to walk around with his feet nearly dragging off the floor, but I want him to stay so badly. I want to feel closer to him. I want his arm around me, I want his hand in mine, I want . . .

I want *more*, and I know I *shouldn't*.

Things would just get messy.

Hell, I don't even know if Felix is queer. None of us are allowed to present as anything other than cis and straight, it's *actually* in our contracts. We need to be marketable to our "straight female audience." Never mind that the fans wouldn't care. We're shipped with each other constantly: fan fiction, art, videos, edited pictures and posts, all made to look like we're dating or hooking up with each other. I'm tagged in no less than a hundred posts every single day where I'm paired with Felix. Or, when the label gets involved, tells me to look at Felix during a certain part of a slow love song, or tells Drew to grab Corey and dance with him onstage. We've read some of it out loud backstage, laughed at the things the label makes us do, put the edited pictures or fan fiction links in the group chat.

I never care when it's Mickey or Drew or Corey laughing.

But when it's Felix . . .

When we sit down at our terminal, I pull out my phone, willing our managers to call and end this entire trip. But it doesn't do me any good.

"Gimmie." Felix holds out his hand.

"What?"

"Your phone," he says. "No distractions."

"I'm not distracted," I say.

"Yes, you are!" He snatches the phone right out of my hand, and I don't fight him as he turns it off and slips it into his backpack. "You can have this back when we're home again."

"Okay."

"It's *your* birthday trip. I'm not going to let anyone ruin it."

"Fine." I tuck my hands into my pockets. "Where are we going anyway?"

"To New York," he says with a smug grin.

"You know what I mean."

"You'll see."

"You can't tell me now?"

"Well, young Levi. That would spoil the surprise."

I feel a surge of nervousness as he uses my name. We've already risked so much just going through the TSA precheck, but either the attendants didn't know us or they just didn't care.

"If you keep my phone that means we have to share AirPods on the flight."

"Fine by me." Felix pulls out the earbuds, handing one to me and keeping the other for himself. While we listen, we wait, Felix's head resting on my shoulders, and I barely dare to breathe for fear of disturbing him.

Felix takes sleeping meds once we're on the plane so he can pass out and not have to deal with flying anxiety, which leaves me with my thoughts for five whole hours. I try to read this book Mickey lent me, to listen to music, to watch a movie, but nothing catches my attention because my mind won't stop racing. There's the fear of being caught, which could happen at any time; from our fans *or* our managers.

And the way Felix is bundled up against me certainly isn't calming my heart either.

When we began training for our debut four years ago, I knew instantly that I liked him.

But it was just a tangential crush then. I was thirteen, just discovering that boys are *very* cute, I looked at him and realized that I thought that he was attractive, that was it.

That was all it was.

Falling in love with him has been one long accident, and I don't know how much longer I can do it. The way he says my name, even when it's just the two of us talking, the way he smiles when he sees me, the way *I* feel when I see him.

The skip my heart does, the flutter in my stomach. It's the small things, the comfortable intimacy that we share with each other, the kind that comes from spending the last thousand odd days together, from feeling that we're the two that fit the best together. It's moments like this that I can't stand, because I don't know where it leaves me with Felix. I don't know if he wants more, or if this is just what friendship is to him. The way we gravitate towards each other, the way that he's the one I go to first when I have a problem or news to share, the way we drape ourselves over each other when we're relaxing backstage, share the bed some nights when I can't sleep.

Even now, we're listening to Felix's playlist on *my* Spotify account because he doesn't want to pay for his own; and I don't even care.

I want him so much more than he'll ever realize, and I wonder if I'll ever have the courage to ask him for more.

♡

"Lev?" I feel a pushing on my shoulder. "Lev?"

"Hmmm?"

"We landed."

"What?"

"Like five minutes ago. We're headed towards the gate."

"What?" I repeat, my mouth gross and eyes crusty. Sure enough, the plane is slowly driving along the tarmac. "Landed?"

"Yes," Felix sings. "Can't believe you slept through that."

"I contain multitudes." I smile at him. "So, what's our first stop?"

"The hotel," he says.

"I'm starving."

"Well lunch can be a part of the equation."

"Goodie."

We sit back, Felix situating the black bucket hat back on his head, matting his bleached blond hair, and he pulls his face mask back up. The things we have to do just to walk around a city.

Honestly, sometimes I wonder when it's going to be enough, when we'll finally be done with music. Not that I ever want to be done, but after years in the spotlight, being on the covers of magazines, performing at awards shows, signing thousands of autographs, being crowded by fans wherever I walk; I'm craving a place where I can work behind the scenes like recording, mixing, producing.

Those are the kinds of things I expected to do when I first explored the music scene online, but one *really* good audition later—and then several follow-up auditions, a year and a half of training—and I was plugged as the lead guitarist in a boy band that would storm the world in just a few short months. I never could've known how much my life would change.

But it did, for better or worse.

It takes us half an hour, but eventually we're off the plane and in a Lyft heading into Manhattan. Felix falls back into his seat, fishing his phone out of his pocket. I can read the text over his shoulder.

MICK: Managers are officially pissed. They've got security ready to drive all over LA. Expect a call ☹

Like clockwork, the text vanishes, and our head manager Stephen's name pops up.

"Let me," I say.

Felix hands the phone to me and I shut it off, putting in my jacket pocket.

"If I can't have my phone, neither can you."

He smiles. "Fair enough."

I brighten at that smile, thinking about all the times he's shared it with me. If I ever asked to pinpoint my favorite thing about Felix, I think it'd be impossible. There's his smile, his always messy hair, his booming laughter, his love of musical theater that he tries to hide, the way he performs, his dedication.

There's a lot to love about Felix Young.

"What?" He looks at me.

I didn't even realize I was staring. "Nothing."

"Weirdo," he says, the grin still on his face. "Food or hotel first?"

"Hmmm . . . would you hate me if I said I was craving McDonald's?"

"It's your birthday." Felix sighs. "So, I suppose I can't really hate you, can I?"

"I suppose not," I tell him with a smile on my lips.

Food comes first.

We didn't even get weird looks from anyone inside the McDonald's because we certainly weren't the strangest-looking people on the street. At the hotel, we checked in quickly, picking fries out of the bag as we rode up to our floor.

I miss food that's bad for me.

Every day is filled with such a rigorous workout and diet plan so that we all stay conventionally attractive, so fries are usually out of the question, and McDonald's is *always* off the table.

"Maybe it's just because I haven't had it in years, but McDonald's is hitting different," Felix says, putting the keycard to the door.

"It's not just you," I say while I chew.

Felix booked us in one of these pod-style hotels, with sleek white walls and neon-blue lights anywhere they could afford to put them.

"Wait," Felix says when he steps inside.

A spike of panic hits me, and I prepare for the worst. But no, when I step in behind him, he's standing in front of the bed.

The *single* bed.

"I'm sorry," he says. "I swore I booked a two-bed room."

"Do they even have those here?" I ask. I wouldn't think there'd be enough room. It doesn't even look like a bed, it's more like a couch that I'm hoping will convert.

"Sorry."

"It's okay," I shrug, tossing my backpack onto the floor. "Won't be the first time we've shared a bed."

Though that absolutely never gets any easier for me. And that's not even the worst part.

Looking around, I realize that the entire room is just that, one singular room. The bathroom is tucked away in the corner, with only a frosted glass wall between the shower and the place where the bed sits.

This is *fine*.

Felix and I have seen each other almost naked before, it's happened dozens of times in the dorm we all stay in, it's happened backstage.

It's fine.

I'm fine.

"You okay?" Felix asks. "Your ears are getting red."

I duck my head to hide my embarrassment. "Yeah, of course. Let's just eat."

"I want to shower first, you go ahead." Felix sighs, slipping out of the top half of his disguise in record time.

It's not a big deal. It *won't* be a big deal.

Though the jump in my pulse says otherwise.

"Oh Lev, look at the view."

The window is just a thin pane of glass, a small gateway into this city that I'd grown up in, that I'd left behind so many years ago. We're still close enough to the ground floor that we can see people walking around, the pool on the roof of the YMCA across the street, the bricks and steel that make up the buildings that sweep the skyline in front of us.

"I miss this city."

"Your parents still live here? We could see them."

"No, they moved upstate when I left," I say. "Think they wanted a change of pace."

"When's the last time you saw them?"

"Last Christmas," I say. If I'd known that when we signed our contracts, we'd essentially entered into an agreement that the most we'd see our parents is over

FaceTime, I don't think I would've signed it. Dad thought about fighting it, he thought the language about parents being a distraction was bullshit, and he has the legal training, but he didn't want to ruin this opportunity for me.

"You ever think about leaving?" Felix asks.

"Sometimes," I say.

"Hmmm," he says and walks away, closing the sliding door to the bathroom behind him. A second later, I hear the water start to pour from the shower head.

The question surprises me, coming from him.

Though, after years of this, I'm sure we're all tired in our own ways. Drew and I have talked about this before, about leaving, breaking the contracts, the huge legal fees we'd have to pay. It just doesn't seem worth it. We're only obligated for two more years, and then . . . who knows.

Then there's everything with Felix, and what would happen if I actually had the gall to tell him how I feel. If he'd accept me, if we'd be able to be together, even if it were just in secret.

Or if he'd hate me.

I don't know which is worse.

At least, if he hated me, I'd know where we stand. Sure, things would be awkward, having to spend so much time together. But maybe that could be my way out? I could make a big statement coming out as gay, finally be open about being trans, too, the label would have a fit and maybe break my contract—then I could go home.

I could be *free*.

But then I wouldn't have Felix, not unless he came with me.

And who knows where we'd be if we weren't in the band together. Maybe he'd find his own friends, his own hobbies, possibly go back to live with his parents far away from me. Maybe leaving wouldn't solve anything.

I hate this.

Why did I have to fall for him? I could've just minded my business, stared at the porn on my phone, daydreamed about having a boyfriend or partner one day that I could sleep with in bed, wake up next to, hold their hand, watch movies with, take for long drives where we wind up getting lost.

But no, instead I fell for one of my best friends.

One of the four people on this planet I'm contractually obligated not to fall in love with.

"So, there *is* a super special final stop on this trip," Felix says as we walk down the sidewalk, edging by people, the horns of the cars blaring on the street next to us, the roar of the subway underneath our feet, the wind blowing through the buildings.

I missed this city so much.

"But we have a few hours until then, so what do *you* want to do?"

"My choice?"

"This is your birthday trip, dummy," Felix says, bumping into me with his shoulder.

"What's this super special final stop?" I ask.

I can tell he's frowning, even underneath his face mask. "You're just hell-bent on ruining the surprise, aren't you?"

"I was just asking."

"I plan this whole thing!" Felix throws his arms out dramatically. "And you want to ruin your entire day!"

"Shut up." I laugh at him, trying to grab at his hand, but he pulls away from me. "Fine, you don't have to tell me."

"Good, I don't want to ruin it," he says. "Now, where are we going?"

"Hmm . . . I don't know." Now that he's expecting something, the pressure is on.

"Oh come on, there's not *one* place you want to go?"

I think, and I think, and now there are too many options. Too many restaurants I've missed, too many stores I want to spend hours wandering, too many places I want to see. Then I notice that we're getting closer to 7th Ave.

Duh, of course.

"Planet Record," I say.

"What's that?"

"This record store I grew up going to. It's amazing, we *have* to go."

Felix presents me with his arm, and I happily hook our elbows together. "Lead the way."

Except we don't quite make it to Planet Record, not without a pit stop first. We're walking by the Gucci store and Felix stops in his tracks.

One thing that will *always* catch Felix's eye: fashion.

"Did you bring something nice to wear tonight?" he asks.

"Um." I brought one change of clothes, and it's really just a fresh shirt and underwear to wear tomorrow. "Define *nice*."

"Okay, come on. The record store will still be there," he says, taking me by the hand and dragging me inside. We take in the stark white walls, the four racks of clothing available, filled with all-black outfits that each cost probably double the rent of the apartment my family used to live in.

"Does the place you're taking me have a dress code?" I ask, flipping through a few of the jackets.

"Stop trying to spoil the surprise!" Felix says.

Then a saleswoman walks up to us. I think she is trying to make sure we can afford to shop here just as much as she's trying to help us find something to purchase. Felix takes several leather jackets off the rack and demands that I try each of them on.

I'll admit, I look hot in each of them. I stare at myself in the mirror with each new jacket, and I actually feel good about myself.

Growing up, I rarely ever felt confident in my body. And those feelings only doubled down when I realized I'm trans. Going through puberty in a body that didn't feel like it was my own was hell, staring at myself in the mirror each morning, binding my chest, wishing desperately for hair to sprout from my chin like I was the Big Bad Wolf.

You'd think that working in an industry that wanted me to hide being trans would've made things worse, but it actually helped in a way. Having to lean into being so aggressively masculine, so that none of our fans suspected; actually being able to afford to go on testosterone; and having my voice masked by Auto-Tune to make it sound deeper until it adjusted—it helped me figure out that part of me. I guess, if nothing else, I'll always be grateful to the label for that.

Twenty minutes and three thousand dollars later, we walk out of the Gucci store with a brand-new leather jacket complementing my outfit.

"Can't believe you talked me into buying that," I say to Felix as we keep walking towards the record store.

"Please, you love it," he says. "And you look really good in it."

"Yeah?" I feel hot again, the temperature kind, not the attractive kind.

"Come on, let's go to your precious record store."

Planet Record is my favorite music store in the world, bar none. The only stores to come close were a vintage store in London and this really cool store in Japan that carried *everything*. Planet Record is the best, though. Not because it carries more, or its prices are better, but because this was the store I grew up with, spending my saved-up lunch money so that I could buy new records and CDs, even in the age of streaming.

This was the place I spent the most time when I was younger, always begging Mom to bring me here during the weekends. It was the first place I saw someone playing a guitar, and the woman let me try it out and gave me the most basic lesson, which made me fall in love with the feeling of playing, the rush, the stretch of my fingers, the feeling of the calluses.

"Oh wow," Felix says as he stares at the tall ceilings, the tables filled with records, CDs, cassette tapes, old and new music from all over the world. "This is so cool."

It's important to me that he likes this place.

"I love this store," I tell him, going right for the new music. I can already see the *Igor* vinyl that I've been dying to add to my collection.

"Do you think they have our albums?" Felix asks quietly.

"Probably." I look around, it's changed a lot in the time since I was here last. "There, go check the Pop-Punk section, that's probably where we are."

There are a few other albums I've been meaning to get, and by the time I'm up to the register, I've had to buy another bag because my backpack is too small.

"You've got a lot of good picks here." The cashier shuffles through them, his smile warm. Tyler the Creator, Brittany Howard, Charli XCX, Billie Eilish, Björk, Sufjan.

"Thanks." I laugh nervously, and then Felix finds me.

"Hey Lev, they've got two left of the new album!" He shows me the records, as if we don't already both own too many copies of our own music.

"Adding those?" the cashier asks.

"Nah, we already have them," I joke, but he doesn't catch on, thankfully.

"Those are our last two I think," he says. "They always sell out fast, so I'm surprised they're even still here. Our stock usually doesn't last a week."

"Really?" I don't know why that's so surprising. Sometimes it really does hit me out of nowhere that we're one of the most popular bands in the world right now, selling out entire stadium world tours, performing on television for millions of people.

I guess I just don't like to think about it that much. I'd rather save that energy for the stage. I take my bag and keep walking around with Felix. I want to spend as much time here as possible because who knows when I'll be back again?

I glance over at Felix and our eyes meet, and as if on cue, one of our songs starts to play.

"You're joking," I whisper.

Felix just grins at me; he's totally eating this up. "'Oh, keep going on, going on, making that noise!'" He sings quietly, strumming along to an invisible guitar. "'I'll just be over here making friends with your boys!'"

It's unbelievably adorable, watching him play along, banging his head back and forth. Our first song was titled "Boys Noise" by the band Boys Noise, from the debut album, wait for it . . . *Boys Noise*. It's one that quickly rose through the charts and dominated the radio, it's still played even three years later. In all honesty, I get tired of playing it live, but seeing Felix enjoying himself, it makes me like the song a little more. I love watching him sing, his lips moving quietly, the energy behind his eyes even though we're just in some local music store he'd never heard of an hour ago.

He catches me staring. "What?"

That's twice today. Why am I so obvious?

"Nothing. Should we head out? Explore some more?"

"Yeah, totally—"

A tap on the shoulder interrupts him—a girl appearing out of nowhere.

"Hi, sorry. But are you Felix from Boys Noise?"

"Oh, um . . ."

"I heard you singing," the girl says. Then her eyes light up and her voice takes on a different tone. "Oh my God, it *is* you!"

I don't even know how she knows because eighty-five percent of Felix's face is still covered, but I guess if you're a huge fan then you'd know your idols even under the worst circumstances.

"Can you please sign this album, I carry it with me everywhere, it's my good luck charm, please—"

"I ah—" Felix glances back at me as he takes a few steps back.

"OMG, it's Lev!" a boy screeches, I didn't even realize that we had drawn so much attention already. It takes all of five seconds for a crowd of people to surround us, mostly younger kids and teens, all holding out albums and CDs and records and shirts and Sharpies for us to take.

One person screams at me to have their babies.

Another person pulls on Felix, nearly bringing him to the ground.

"Lev!" he cries.

He's quickly vanishing into the crowd.

"Okay everyone! Calm down!" the cashier shouts, but no one cares.

We're trapped in a store with fans who keep filtering in off the street somehow, as if they were all here waiting for us, ready to ambush, and all without an ounce of security.

"Felix." I grab on to his hand, yanking him up. "Sorry, we've got somewhere to be," I yell to the people around us. "Sorry."

"Lev! Felix! Can I have a picture!"

"Please sign my arm, I want it tattooed!"

"Sign my album please!"

"Please look at this drawing, I have it on my phone!"

"Can I send you the link to my fic?"

"Felix." I pull him closer to me. Somewhere in the struggle he lost his hat and sunglasses, so I can see the fear in his eyes as he waits for me to say something. "Run!"

We bolt through the crowd, as quickly as possible, my hand never letting go of his. We finally break through, pushing through the glass doors, and we sprint as fast as we can down the sidewalk. I don't know if anyone is following us, and I don't dare to look back and see. All I know is that Felix is there beside me and that's what matters. I don't know how far we run, but we keep going and going and going until Felix is begging me to stop.

"Lev, Lev! Please."

Our stride slows, chests heaving in unison as we both double over.

"That was hell."

"I'm so sorry," Felix says. "I'm so sorry, Lev."

"Why are you apologizing?"

"I should've been more careful," he says, his voice still sounding shaky.

We both stand there, catching our breath, and I try to deny the way my hands shake, the surge of adrenaline I feel. I stare at Felix and he stares back. Then we both start to laugh. I don't know if it's at each other or at the way we're so out of breath or at the way that stampede of fans seemed to come out of nowhere, or if it's simply because we don't have the energy to do anything else.

"That was—" Felix starts to say.

"—Yeah," I finish. "Yeah."

"Do you think we lost them?"

I look down the street and, while the sidewalks are crowded, I don't see a group of teenagers rushing towards us, so maybe we're safe—I think? "I don't know."

"Should we go back to the hotel?" he asks.

Felix looks like he's been through it. His hair is sticking up in all directions and his eyes are wild with either adrenaline or fear, or both. "Do you want to?"

"You still haven't taken me to this last place," I say.

"Do you still want to go?"

"Of course."

He smiles at me, still a little out of breath. "I need my phone. I need to look up directions."

Thankfully, it's still in my pocket and not in the hands of our fans. "You could just ask me. I probably know where it is."

"You definitely know," he says. "That's why I'm keeping it a secret."

"Whatever, Young."

"Hey, don't sass your elders," he says, pointing a finger at me. "We're like twenty blocks away."

"Oof."

"Yeah."

"What time is it?" I ask, looking up at the sky. It's been nice not having to worry about my phone all day, but I don't like not knowing what time it is.

"Only four."

"We could walk it," I say. "It's nice out."

"Yeah?" Felix smiles at me. "Well come on, it's this way."

"You know, I'm starting to see why you like this city so much," Felix says a few blocks later. He'd been quiet, but it was that nice kind of quiet, the kind where we were simply enjoying each other's company without the pressure of filling the space between us with small talk.

"Oh yeah?"

"I mean, it's really pretty, even if it is messy sometimes," he says. "I could do without the pigeons, the traffic, the smells, and it feels like my hands are going to get sticky if I *look* at something the wrong way."

"Hey, that's *my* city you're talking about—"

"—But," Felix quickly interjects. "It's also very pretty, and lively, and the people seem . . . I don't know, happier isn't the word. Richer? I guess. Things feel different here."

"As opposed to Kansas?"

"Well, you certainly can't buy a hot dog in the middle of the street where I'm from."

Felix doesn't talk a lot about his upbringing. All he's really shared with me is that his parents own a farm and he has a younger sister who's a big fan of the band. She came to one of our concerts when we performed in Wichita. Other than that, Felix doesn't talk about his home life, the schools he went to, his old friends.

"Do you miss it?" I ask him.

"Kansas? Not really, it was boring, and a kid like me doesn't belong there."

"A kid like you?"

"You know, short, effeminate, someone who appreciates a good musical." Felix laughs, but just as quickly, his smile fades. "I do miss my family."

"Yeah, me too," I say. "Your folks seemed nice when we met them."

"They're okay, they try. That's all you can ask from parents sometimes."

"That I understand."

I remember when I first came out to my parents, trying to explain to them that it wasn't as if I was born in the wrong body, it's just that the body I had didn't reflect who I saw myself as. There was nothing wrong with the body I was born with, it just never felt like *mine*. I can't remember how many times I explained it and even now it doesn't quite make sense to me either. Maybe I was tired of the stereotype that every trans person has to feel like everything about their body is wrong. My body was fine, there were parts that I liked—there are parts that I still like and don't plan to ever change. It's that it wasn't *me*. My brain and my body weren't working together, they were fighting against each other.

And that was scary.

"You ever think you'll want to publicly come out?" Felix asks, but then he quickly doubles back. "Sorry! I just—I didn't mean it that way. I'll—let me just shut up."

"No." I laugh. "It's fine, I promise."

"You don't have to talk about it if you don't want to," he tells me.

"Who says I don't want to talk about it?"

Felix shrugs. "I don't know, the managers never like it when we do."

I pull him in close, wrapping my arm around his shoulders. "Last time I checked our managers aren't here."

The smile lights up Felix's face again. "Very true."

"I don't know," I start to say, "I like to think that I would, that it'd matter to our trans fans, but—"

I pause.

"But?"

"But . . . I don't know. It feels like my business and sometimes I want to keep it that way."

"I feel that. If any of us came out to the public at large, everyone and their mom would have an opinion about it."

"Yeah, I just don't think I'm ready to be the topic of discourse and think pieces yet."

It already bothers me knowing that people online just talk about me and Felix and the other boys like we aren't people: in conversations that we aren't a part of, dissecting our every move to prove who we're in love with, which relationships are fake, who secretly hates who. "I think I want a few more years of being with myself."

"I can respect that," Felix says and gives me a nod, but then he steps in front of me. "Okay, close your eyes."

"What? Why?"

"Because we're two minutes away," he says, glancing at his phone. "And I want to keep the surprise."

"Pfft, okay." I cover my eyes with my left hand. "You'll make sure I don't walk into traffic, right?"

"I gotchu," Felix says, and then I feel his hand around my free one.

Okay Lev, don't freak out. This is fine, you've held hands before. Not that it ever gets any easier, like at all. I'm sure he can feel the way my heart beats in my chest, the heat that fills my hand and the way it makes my palms sweaty.

"Okay, let's go!"

Felix starts running, pulling me along with him. I keep my eyes covered the whole time, but there's no mistaking the familiarity of the neighborhood, even before Felix had me close my eyes I knew where we were heading.

I *know* this city.

The two minutes turn into what feels like just a few seconds as we run, taking a turn down a street, and it's when the smell hits my nose that I know for sure where we are.

"Okay, stop!"

"You brought me to Ari's?" I say without even looking.

"What?" Felix stops so abruptly that I slam into him, nearly knocking him over. "How did you know?"

I finally take my hand away from my face, looking at the silver building that occupies the corner of 7th Ave and 12th Street, the bright-red neon and the glowing light that radiates from the windows, the dirty chrome exterior that makes it seem like the diner was pulled right out of history.

"Please, I'd know this place anywhere." I should at least, I spent almost every single day after middle school coming here with my friends, doing our homework, studying for tests, talking. It was *our* place.

Suddenly, I'm sad thinking about how I left all those people behind. Friends I haven't seen in years, people I stopped talking to.

"How'd you know to bring me here?"

"You talk about it all the time," Felix says. "I remember, you always ask if we can stop by here when we come to the city."

And the managers would tell me that we were too busy, that our schedules were too packed with too many interviews and performances and bookings.

"Felix." I look down at him, unsure of what to even say.

It may not seem like much, but this was the best present he could've given me.

"Come on, let's eat," Felix says with a smile. "I'm starving."

"So, what do I order?" Felix asks, eyeing the menu.

My hands are already sticky and that coffee smell . . . slightly burnt, mixed with the smell of bacon. It feels like I'm actually home again for the first time in a long time.

"You're making a mistake if you don't get the pancakes."

"Pancakes?" Felix sticks his tongue out. "Disgusting."

"Don't be a baby."

I glance at him over the menu, but we're both smiling, and the longer we look at each other, the harder we find it not to laugh. Felix breaks first, almost throwing down his menu as he rears his head back, the sounds of his warm laugh filling my ears. I feel so lucky.

"Thank you, for this," I tell him.

"Of course."

"No," I start to say, "really, this entire trip. Even though we were chased all the way to 26th Avenue, it's been amazing."

"I'm glad you feel that way." He smiles at me and I melt. "When was the last time you were here?"

I don't even have to think about it. That day was totally normal, there was nothing out of the ordinary about it but, because it was my last day here, it's become ingrained in my memory. "Eighth grade, a few days before we moved on to high school.

"My friends and I sat in the booth at the end of the restaurant, right on the corner, and we talked about what high school was going to be like while I tried to look cool in front of Mark Aster by drinking black coffee, and then Jessica Martin and I talked about the boys we had a crush on.

"Then, I never saw any of them again.

"It was already so much harder to see your friends in the summer, even when you just lived down the block from each other, but the next day my mom and I saw the ad for the band audition. Then, one week later I was performing in an empty room with a bunch of old dudes in suits staring at me, and three weeks after that I moved out to Los Angeles alone. I didn't even get a chance to say a proper goodbye, moving across the country, my schedule immediately packed with vocal and guitar practice, choreography lessons, being trained on how to answer interview questions, how to behave in public, taking the perfect picture with fans, there was a lot more that went into being in a boy band than I knew. In the rare moments I had to myself, I barely had time to sleep. I remember going on Twitter one time, before the label made me delete the account so they could set up my official one, the one they actually run, and seeing my old friends say I'd gotten too good for them, that I was ignoring their calls and texts, that I was famous now and didn't have time for them.

"I hadn't talked to any of them since."

"That's sad," Felix says, listening carefully.

"Yeah, well." I shrug. "What can you do?"

"Have you ever thought about finding any of them?"

"Yeah." But then we fell into the months of practice where we were only allowed to make phone calls to our parents, and even those were rare. We just lost each other—and we'll probably never find our way back.

Even though I'm filled with this bitterness, and this longing for my friends again, if I hadn't left them behind, I wouldn't have joined the band. I wouldn't have found Mickey or Drew or Corey—I wouldn't have Felix.

Maybe that's just the give and take.

I had to give up my old life to get the new one. Even if it is hard ninety-nine percent of the time and there are days when I wish I could go back and nights when I can't sleep because of how stressful everything has become, days I don't want to wake up because I know the hours ahead are just going to exhaust me. Every day I get to spend with Felix, makes it all feel worth it.

Maybe that's what love is? Romantic or platonic. *A give and take.*

"This is where you surprise me by bringing out all my friends," I tell Felix.

"Sorry, I'm magical," he says with a sadness weighing on his voice. "But not that magical."

"It's okay," I say and smile. This was the perfect birthday, being in my city again, the food, the shopping, spending the entire day alone with Felix. Even if we're going to be in so much trouble when we get home, probably put on some kind of probation and locked in the apartment for the next month. Whatever our punishment is, these few precious hours will have been worth it.

"I guess we have to go back to the hotel now, huh?" I ask Felix, checking the time on a clock hanging on a nearby building.

We sat in the diner for five hours just eating and talking and eating and laughing and eating and more eating.

So much food.

Our trainer is going to be pissed when we come back and tell her everything we ate. But it's so worth it.

"Our flight is at noon," Felix says, "figured we could sleep in a bit."

"I like that plan."

"The hotel is a long walk; do you want to get a Lyft?" he asks.

I look around at the somewhat empty streets, the sun long gone so the night had become a little chilly. Suddenly, I'm very glad for this leather jacket.

"Let's walk, we need to burn off the calories," I say, plus the more time I get with Felix, the better.

He gives me a smile and we start walking.

I think I miss New York at night the most. The way that the lights make the sky glow, the neon colors and music playing, the warmth of the restaurants, stores, and clubs filled with people. The sidewalks are mostly empty if you take the right streets, which means no more hiding behind a mask.

"Thank you," I say, breaking a long stretch of silence. It wasn't even awkward; it rarely ever is with Felix, but I wanted to say that to him. "For today, it was amazing."

"I wish we could've stayed longer," he says. "It would've been cool to see more of the city."

"You mean more than Madison Square Garden? Or the green room of *Good Morning USA*?"

Felix laughs. "Not that those places aren't *stunning*! But I've liked seeing your New York a lot better."

Why does he have to go and say things like that? Is he trying to kill me?

That's when Felix loops his arm through mine, so I guess that's my answer.

We continue to walk and walk and walk until we finally make our way back to the hotel, going through the strange entrance where a futuristic robot claw will take your luggage, to the elevator that takes us to the *proper* lobby a few floors up.

"Hey . . . the bar's still open," I say, glancing at the spot behind the front desk that opens up to a long patio area outside, complete with booths and tables decorated with the same neon lights as our room. There are only two people out there, and they both look so distracted with each other.

Felix gives an exaggerated gasp. "Are you suggesting that we consume alcohol whilst under the age of twenty-one? What a rebel!"

I cover my mouth, so he doesn't think I'm laughing at him. "Did you just say 'whilst'?"

"What did I say about respecting your elders, Lev?"

"Please." I rub the top of his head, his hair slipping easily between my fingers. It's such a simple feeling, but I never want to stop touching him. Running my hands through his hair, holding his hand—I want so much more than that, too.

"New York at night is so quiet," Felix says, playing with the sleeve of his jacket.

"You really think so?" I ask, listening to the honking horns, the subway, the people shouting.

"Like not quiet but . . . ." Felix seems to think for a moment. "*Quiet*, you know?"

"I—" He catches my stare and I stammer, quickly turning away. "No . . . I don't know. This city has never been quiet."

"Forget it."

I want to find his hand again, because it feels like something is about to happen. Something monumental, something life-changing, something right out of a movie, but I don't. Instead, I drape my arms over the railing of the balcony. That'd be an easy escape I suppose, just leap over the edge to escape my feelings for Felix. Sure, I might end up with a few shattered bones and be out of commission for months, but wouldn't that be better than a broken heart?

"Thank you again, this was an amazing birthday." It's so hard for me to find my words all of a sudden.

"Just amazing?" Felix asks. "Not perfect? Spectacular? Mind-blowing?"

"Well my parents rented a pony for my eighth birthday, so it'd be pretty hard to top that."

"Oh, well. Sorry I'm not as good as a horse that isn't even fully grown!"

"No, no! I'm kidding!" I wrap him in close and he plays like he's trying to get away. Felix loves my hugs too much to really fight them. "It was perfect, it really was. It feels like it's been so long since I got to celebrate my birthday, or since it felt like it was worth celebrating."

I breathe in his smell.

"Thank you."

"I'm glad." Felix twists in my arms, so that he's facing me.

I think it's hitting us both just how close we really are. Just inches away, our mouths barely open. This close, I can count the freckles and pockmarks that are usually hidden by layers of makeup, the near-invisible blond hairs that decorate his upper lip because he didn't shave this morning, the brown hairs between his eyebrows because no one has plucked them for a few days. Every imperfection on Felix's face is just making me love him more and more.

And I can't stand it.

"I think I'm about to ruin your birthday," Felix says.

"How?"

"Because I'm about to kiss you."

I stare at him, my heart threatening to burst out of my chest and leap off the balcony just so it can die before anything ruins this moment.

"Then do it," I tell him.

He leans up and our lips meet. It feels like it takes hours for my brain to register what is happening, and for it to send the signals to my lips, so that I will kiss him back. He tastes so good, and his body feels so right in my arms.

I never want to let him go.

I want to die kissing Felix Young.

If I did, I'd die happy, that much I know for sure. He still tastes like the hot chocolate he drank instead of the coffee, mixed with honey from his favorite brand of lip balm, the one that he keeps stockpiled in every room of our dorm. Just in case.

I love kissing him.

"Happy birthday," he says.

"I've wanted that for so long," I tell him, daring to part our lips but pressing our foreheads together.

"You have?" Felix asks.

I nod slowly.

"I have too," he says. "I just didn't want to ruin things."

"I felt the same way," I tell him, going in for another kiss. This one is just as magical, just as electric.

"Looks like we were both wrong," he says and I laugh.

"Does that mean . . . you want something more out of this, right?"

"I do."

"I do, too."

"The managers are going to hate me. I drag you to the other side of the country, there's a mob that chases us, *and* we're coming back as boyfriends?" Felix laughs.

The word "boyfriend" makes me pause, but it feels so natural. Because that's what I want to be to him. At least for now, hopefully I'll become something else, a different title.

One day.

"It'll be fine," I say, smiling against his forehead.

"I bet money that we're all signing NDAs on Monday."

"Well that's their problem," I say before I kiss him one more time. This one is chaste, shorter compared to the others, but I don't mind. I'm looking forward to discovering all the ways I can kiss Felix Young.

"Come on." He pulls away, still taking my hand. "I'm tired."

"Let's go to bed then." I kiss him again.

That night, we fall asleep wrapped in each other's arms for what has to be the hundredth time, except now, it's different. The warmth of his body radiating beside me as I listen to his soft snores, as I stare at the shape of his eyes and his lips, the slope of his nose and the mole on his right cheek, the sparse hairs between his brows that can't technically be called a unibrow, the empty piercing holes in his ears.

With him around, he's all I want to focus on. I don't think about how much trouble we'll be in tomorrow when we land in LA, how both of our phones are probably filled with calls and texts from the others, the managers, the label, and bodyguards. I don't think about how we were probably trending on Twitter for at least a few hours because we were wandering around New York and got caught. I don't think about how I don't want to go back to work, how I'm scared to be myself, how I'm worried that people will find out my secrets and out me.

The uncertainty worries me, of course it does. Sometimes it feels like my entire life is full of nothing but uncertainty.

But with Felix, that uncertainty feels a little less scary, a little easier to manage.

Because when the morning comes and the sun shines through our window, as I listen to the sounds of the cars on the street beneath us, the people shouting for their taxis, handing out flyers to anyone that will take them, carrying their trays of coffee back to the office, the birds that fly by, the far-off sound of a boat somewhere, the bell of a nearby church, I can at least be certain of two things:

That Felix Young is here with me in this bed.

And that I never want to leave him.

GIRLS JUST WANT TO HAVE FUN

"Secret Royalty"

Malinda Lo

PRINCESS QĪNGHÉ ARRIVES AT ISAMAR STATION

By Lee Kelly, Imperial Correspondent

After a whirlwind visit to the Five Golden Planets system, Princess Qīnghé, youngest daughter of the Radiant Empress Zhǎngsūn and the Glorious Emperor Tàizōng, arrived at Isamar Station, gateway to the planet Isamaria, on her imperial-class ship, *Splendid Phoenix*. This marks the twenty-third stop of the princess's eighteenth-birthday tour, wherein she will visit fifty of the Zhonghua Empire's key cities, stations, and planets. Princess Qīnghé is scheduled to remain at Isamar Station for five days for some much-needed rest before disembarking for Isamaria, where she will tour the planet's famed tea plantations and diamond mines. Tonight, she will attend a banquet hosted by Isamar Station Chief Executive Rohan Bir. Stay tuned for live updates.

IT'S PRINCESS TIME!

[Posted to Isamar Station socialnet by Malika Joss]

Get ready, Isas! For the next week this feed will be All Princess All the Time as Princess Qīnghé, Zhonghua's Sweetheart, the Dimpled Delight, visits our exceptional corner of the galaxy. If you spot the princess in your corridor, snap a pic and tag me! And if you meet her, tell me if she's the sweetheart she seems to be! Even her brother Tai, known for his charming yet vicious quips, has nothing but love for his meimei. Let's give her a warm Isa welcome!

♡

It was five minutes till closing time on Friday night, and Fei Cheng couldn't wait to leave. The Fix Is In, her parents' Downstation repair shop ("If it's broken, we can fix it!"), was empty except for her, and there hadn't been a customer for over an hour. She was tempted to close early, but the last time she did that she missed out on a last-minute repair that went to their rival across the corridor (The Repair Lair), causing her to lose a hundred-yuan commission that could've gone directly into her college fund. So now she puttered around the tiny shop, putting things away while she waited out the last few minutes.

The Fix Is In looked like an overstocked walk-in closet, but everything had its place. Fei knew where every spare part went, and she took pride in helping her parents keep the shop neatly organized. There was just enough room for a customer to come inside and stand in front of the counter, which was outfitted with every tool known to humanity. Fei couldn't fix everything yet (her mom tackled the really difficult jobs), but she was a genius with comm devices, which brought in most of the money anyway. People were always dropping those things or accidentally infecting them with socialnet viruses.

Fei's comm chimed and she pulled it out of her pocket to check the message. It was from her best friend, Malika Joss:

> **Photo shoot running late but I'm gonna try my hardest to meet you at Hot Noodles! Order me my usual and keep your eyes peeled in case the princess shows!**

Fei groaned. Malika was ranked number nine on the Station's socialnet chart, and she was convinced that landing an exclusive interview with Princess Qīnghé would push her up the chart and make her a ton of yuan too. While Malika had a healthy handful of sponsors who'd love to pay for a princess exclusive, Fei doubted that Malika could get anywhere near the princess, much less an interview. Those were tightly controlled by Imperial Public Relations, and Malika didn't have the connections. ("Yet," Malika would counter.)

Fei replied to Malika's message:

> **Don't be too late, I'm hungry.**

The shop door whooshed open and a girl rushed in, glancing behind her as if to make sure she wasn't being followed. She was wearing a ship's crew dark gray jumpsuit that was a bit too big for her.

"Can I help you?" Fei asked. "We're about to close."

"I need to fix something," the girl said. She had very short black hair that curved like a soft cap over her head and big brown eyes, and Fei thought she looked a little nervous.

"We can fix anything," Fei said. "What's broken?"

The girl reached into her pocket to pull out a battered comm. "I accidentally locked it," she said. "Can you open it?"

Fei took the comm and noted that it was at least four or five years old. When she raised it, the screen glowed to life and a hologram of a white puppy wearing a pink bow floated up and barked.

The girl looked a little embarrassed. "It's my old comm. I just—I need to get some stuff on it and for some reason it doesn't remember what I look like and—can you unlock it?"

Fei glanced at the time. Two minutes till closing. "Yeah, I can unlock it. Seventy-five yuan is the base rate and it goes up depending on the comm's security protocols."

The girl wasn't fazed. "That's fine. But can you be quick?"

Fei was surprised—and a little suspicious. Usually people tried to negotiate the fees. Plus, there was something about the girl's face that made her wonder if she'd seen her before—those big brown eyes seemed kind of familiar—but Fei couldn't seem to place her.

"It'll take about ten minutes," Fei said. "As long as there isn't any unusual security on it."

"That's fine!" The girl sounded relieved. "I'll just—" She glanced around the tiny shop and realized there was nowhere for her to go. "I'll just wait here?"

"Sure." Fei opened one of the drawers beneath the counter to take out a scanner to unlock the comm. As she got to work, the girl carefully leaned back against a wall of shelves and looked around. She had a delicate, slightly pointed chin, a cute snub nose, and dark pink lips. Fei realized she was staring at the girl and hurriedly dropped her gaze to the comm, but not before she saw the girl giving her a curious look in return. There was something about it—a quirk of her eyebrows, a sharpening of her gaze—that made Fei wonder if the girl was checking her out, too.

As she tried to focus on the puppy comm, she hastily took mental stock of her own appearance. Dark blue jacket with multiple pockets for her tools, faded but clean gray The Fix Is In T-shirt, old-school but newly trendy jeans, comfortable boots. ("Geek chic," Malika had said once, describing her look.) Fei's mostly short black hair had fading red tips that needed to be trimmed, and now flopped over her forehead. That morning Fei had thought she was having a good hair day, but she hadn't looked in the mirror in a while.

She surreptitiously eyed the girl, who quickly looked away and acted as if she was super interested in the box of nanotech couplers on the shelf beside her. Fei grinned to herself and checked the scanner. It was running now, and she could see it wouldn't be a difficult hack. It looked like the comm had never had real security on it.

She did her best to ignore the girl as she started a decrypt script, but she was hyper conscious of every sound in the small shop—the girl's breathing, the sound of fabric as she shifted in place, the little *ping* as the script finished its first cycle.

"Does that mean it worked?" the girl asked, leaning over the counter to look.

Fei smelled something sweet, as if the girl had brought frosted cupcakes with her. "Uh, almost," Fei said. "I do have to run a second decrypt because the comm is old. But it shouldn't take much longer."

"Thank you," the girl said, flashing her a dimpled smile. "I really appreciate your time."

Fei felt a tiny flush on her face. "Uh, sure."

Finally, the puppy that had been whirling above the screen poofed, allowing access.

"All set," Fei said, sliding the comm across the counter.

"Wonderful," the girl said, giving her that sunny smile again. "How much do I owe you?"

Fei did some quick mental calculations. "One hundred twenty yuan."

The girl sent the credit through her unlocked comm, and Fei saw the shop's central comm beneath the counter light up in receipt. She squinted down at the display. That was weird—the name attached to the credit was blank.

"Did it go through?" the girl asked.

She checked, and the credit was in the store's account. "Yeah," Fei said. It probably didn't matter that there was no name. Yuan was yuan.

"Excellent!" The girl pocketed her comm and was about to leave when she asked, "Oh, can you tell me how to get to the Downstation night market? I'm afraid I'm new to the area and I got a little lost on my way here."

"Take a right out the door," Fei said, "then follow the blue corridor on your left just after the transport tubes."

"Thank you!"

"You're welcome."

Fei started to shut down the shop for the night, but the girl paused at the door and turned back.

"May I ask," she said, "what's your name?"

"Fei Cheng."

"I'm Jing," the girl said, and extended her hand.

A rusty knowledge of Upstation etiquette learned from serial dramas came to her, and Fei reached out and shook it. Well, it was more like she squeezed it awkwardly. Jing gave her that dimpled smile again. "Charmed," she said, and then left.

Fei thought the girl's formality was odd, but she was definitely cute. Too bad she seemed to work on a ship. She probably wouldn't be on Station for much longer.

Isamar Station was one of the most popular tourist destinations in the galaxy. It had something for everyone, from ship crew looking for a fun weekend break to wealthy socialites hoping to brush shoulders with Imperial elite at a glamorous Upstation resort.

Nearly all the trade that flowed from the planet Isamaria out to the Empire went through Isamar Station, which meant the Station had become a hub for merchants hoping to cash in on the planet's luxury goods. Those merchants and their families had to be fed and housed and entertained, which had brought acclaimed chefs and designers and artists and musicians to the Station, creating a class of tastemakers who depended on the hardworking Isas—native-born Station residents—to keep the Station running smoothly. And because Isas worked for the merchants and rarely had the yuan to enjoy the artist class's entertainment, they built their own wonderland in their own section of the Station: the Downstation night market, which soon became a tourist attraction in their own right.

Fei had been born on Isamar Station and grew up Downstation. The night market, which was located in a warren of halls and corridors around the Station's HVAC and water reclamation facilities, had long been familiar to her. She had her favorite food stands (including Xi'An Hot Noodles) and arcades, and she knew many of the vendors who sold everything from tourist souvenirs to knockoff Isamar designer fashions. As Fei made her way from The Fix Is In to meet Malika at Xi'An, she wondered what stands Jing might visit.

Maybe because the girl was on her mind, Fei thought she kept seeing her out of the corner of her eye. But every time she turned to look, she wasn't there. She told herself to forget about it and checked her comm for an update from Malika, but there were no new messages. Fei hoped Malika wouldn't be too late. She was starving, and she couldn't wait to inhale a warm bowl of hand-pulled chili noodles.

Xi'An Hot Noodles was one of the most famous noodle stands in the night market; people often lined up for hours to taste a new flavor combination. When Fei arrived it was still relatively early, so the line was about fifteen people long and had only begun to wind around the seating area next to the Wishing Wall. Fei got in line and glanced around, taking in the glowing paper lanterns hanging from the Station's HVAC system overhead, the Isas dressed up for a Friday night with newly colored hair (this month's trend was a violent shade of teal), the vendors hawking sale items commemorating Princess Qīnghé's visit, and . . .

"Hi," Jing said, stepping into line right behind her.

Fei blinked. Jing was still there. "Hi," Fei said, surprised.

"I saw you over here and I wanted to try the hot noodles," Jing said. "Is this a good one? I don't know which one to try."

"Yeah, this is a good one."

"I've never had the Xi'an noodles before. I read all about them on socialnet and they sound *so* good. Do you have any recommendations for which one to get?"

Jing looked at her expectantly, almost like an eager puppy, and Fei was reminded of the hologram she had hacked through on the girl's comm.

"I like the wide hand-pulled noodles," Fei said.

Jing looked very serious as she read the menu screen above the noodle stand. "Yes. Maybe I'll get those. Do you think I should get extra chili oil?"

"If you want to burn your tongue off, yes."

Jing laughed. "You're funny."

Fei didn't think she'd said anything funny, but she liked the idea that Jing thought so. The line moved up beside the Wishing Wall, and Fei watched Jing take in the hundreds of notes posted on the curving metal wall.

"What are all these messages for?" Jing asked.

"Isas—Station residents—post their wishes here after they come true," Fei said.

"Why?"

"It started a long time ago, in the early years of the Zhonghua Empire." Fei felt a little like a tour guide, but Jing was listening attentively, so she continued. "Isamar Station was attacked by the Federation, and this section of the Station was breached, but because all the Isas worked together to plug the breach and keep each other safe, nobody died and the Federation soldiers were captured when the Army moved in. Ever since then people have left their wishes here in remembrance of that time."

"That's so inspiring! Look—this one says 'I wished to fall in love and now I've met the person of my dreams.'" Jing smiled at the handwritten note, then looked at Fei. "What would your wish be?"

Normally, Fei would be self-conscious about revealing her wish, but there was something so open and accepting about Jing that she didn't hesitate to answer. "I want to go to engineering college," Fei said. "I want to fix more than broken comm devices and HVAC units."

"What do you want to fix?"

"Starships. I've already been accepted to Isamar Station Engineering College, but I don't have the credits for tuition yet. I'm hoping to save up and go in a few years. What's your wish?"

Jing's expression seemed to fold closed, and she looked away from Fei and back at the Wishing Wall. "I . . . I just want to have some fun. On my own terms—like this."

It made Fei wonder what kind of terms Jing was normally under. She was about to ask what kind of ship she served on when her comm chimed. She pulled it out to see an excited message from Malika.

> **PRINCESS IS MISSING!!!!** Huge uproar all over imperial
> social channels. She was supposed to go to the Chief
> Exec's banquet tonight but she never showed! Keep an
> eye out, here's her latest look.

The message included a video of Princess Qīnghé dressed in an elaborate pink-and-gold silk gown, wearing a headdress that consisted of a long purple wig topped with glittering diamond-and-ruby halos that actually rotated.

Jing was looking over her shoulder and asked, "What happened?"

"The princess is missing."

Jing's face seemed to go pale, and there was something about her frozen expression that oddly resembled that of the princess in the video. Qīnghé looked like she'd rather be anywhere other than trapped in that rotating headdress.

Another message from Malika came through:

> **Can you IMAGINE how many yuan I'd rake in if I found her? My sponsors would LOVE ME FOREVER.**

As the line inched forward, Fei surreptitiously studied Jing's face. Those eyes definitely resembled the princess's. And her lips—they were just like those of Zhonghua's Sweetheart. Weren't they?

Jing caught her looking and gave her a tentative, nervous smile.

Those dimples.

Fei's heart began to race. She responded to Malika:

> **When are you getting here?? I'm at Xi'an.**

Fei wasn't sure if her sudden (and admittedly, a little wacky) suspicion was true, but Malika would know.

Malika responded:

> **Ten minutes tops. Order me my usual!**

"These are so *good*," Jing gushed. She had just taken her first bite of Xi'An Hot Noodle's Special #1, hand-pulled chili noodles. Now she took another big bite, shoveling the noodles into her mouth with chopsticks and closing her eyes to better taste them. "Mmmmm," she murmured.

Fei almost felt as if she should give Jing a moment alone with her noodles. She compromised by looking away while Jing chewed. Fei had her own bowl of Special #1, too, while Malika's bowl of hot-dry noodles (Special #4) was waiting nearby. Jing had insisted on paying for all of them with her puppy comm, which only made Fei more suspicious. Either her wacky theory was correct, or Jing was trying extra hard to impress her. Fei caught herself briefly wanting to believe the latter and flushed.

"Aren't you going to eat?" Jing asked.

"Um, yeah." Fei quickly pulled her bowl closer and started to eat her own noodles. Her stomach growled at her first taste of the chewy, slightly bouncy hand-pulled noodles. They were tossed in a savory, vinegary dressing, and the chili oil left a pleasant burning sensation in her mouth.

"There you are! Sorry I'm late!"

Malika suddenly appeared at their table and plopped down in front of Special #4. Fei's mouth was still full so she couldn't properly introduce Malika to Jing, but she saw Jing's eyes widen as she took in Malika's appearance. Her lavender-colored hair was twisted into tiny crystal bead–tipped braids, which were pulled up into a trendy topknot. Malika was wearing a sleeveless hot pink blouse with a draped neckline, and her bare brown shoulders were dusted with glitter. The glitter had also been applied to her eyelids and cheekbones, making her appear to shimmer as she moved.

"You're—you're Malika Joss," Jing said, shocked.

Malika smiled magnanimously as she acknowledged her fame. "Yes I am. Hello! Fei, you didn't tell me you brought a friend."

Jing smiled at her, and Malika's gaze instantly sharpened.

Fei choked down her noodles and said hastily, "Malika, this is Jing. Jing, Malika. Malika, can I talk to you for a sec?" Before Malika could object, Fei dragged her from the stool. "We'll be right back!" she called to Jing. "Just want to make sure I got her order right!"

Malika kept trying to look back as Fei pulled her behind a nearby HVAC support strut. "Fei, is that—that can't be—"

"Shhh!" Fei whispered. "Do you think it's the princess?"

Malika peeked around the support strut at Jing, who was still eating her noodles. "I have to cross-check my database—she's not dressed up—" Malika began cycling rapidly through the photos of Princess Qīnghé on her comm.

"Where did you find her?" Malika asked.

Jing told her the whole story, and then asked, "What do you think?"

"Let's go back and talk to her. See if she does anything princessy."

"Princessy?" Fei said skeptically.

Malika shot Fei an exasperated look before she left the shadow of the support strut. *Princessy*, she mouthed.

Back at the table, Malika sat down and extended her hand. "I'm so sorry we didn't have a proper introduction before Fei so rudely dragged me off."

Jing smiled her dimpled smile and delicately clasped Malika's hand. "Charmed."

Malika blinked, but her smile didn't falter. "Me too. *Charmed.*" She gave Fei a brief, meaningful look, then asked brightly, "What brings you to Downstation?"

"I've just heard so much about it," Jing said. "The noodles especially!"

"Mm hmm. Anything you want to do while you're in the neighborhood?" Malika asked. "Shopping? Dancing? There's some amazing art behind the transport tubes. So many famous artists got their start right here."

As Malika acted like an exceptionally focused tour guide, Fei heard the sound of approaching music and looked up to see lights flashing. Downstation was home to plenty of amateur musicians and deejays, and on a weekend night there were pop-up parties all around the night market. Soon the music was loud enough that Malika and Jing had to stop talking, and they all turned to watch as a sort of parade approached. It was led by an Isa with drone speakers floating overhead, blasting an addictive dance beat. Next came an Isa dressed in platform boots and a glittering purple bodysuit, her long silver hair cascading down her back as she strutted and sang over the music. Behind her came a throng of Isas and tourists, dancing and cheering and clapping.

Jing's face was lit up with excitement. "This is so amazing!" she shouted over the music. "I've only seen this on socialnet!"

Jing's feet were tapping and Malika's shoulders were grooving, and even Fei, who thought of herself as kind of a terrible dancer, couldn't help but nod her head in time.

"Let's dance!" Malika cried, grabbing both of their hands and pulling them to their feet.

Jing squealed and immediately jumped in, trying to copy the moves of the Isas at the front of the parade. They were doing some fancy footwork that Fei recognized, but had never been able to do herself. Malika got into it, though, and Fei laughed and watched them until, to her surprise, Jing stepped out of the throng and reached for Fei's hand.

"Come on!" Jing called.

Feeling a little self-conscious, Fei let Jing pull her into the crowd, where she began to lead Fei through the dance steps. The crowd pushed them closer together, the bass thrumming through their bodies. Fei could smell that sugary cupcake smell again as Jing shimmied to the music, and the joy on Jing's face was so infectious that Fei began to relax. Fei saw Malika behind Jing, raising her comm to take some photos as she mouthed, *Get closer!* The singer had launched into a classic song about wanting to dance with someone who loves you, and the entire night market was singing along, including Jing. She lifted one of Fei's hands overhead to expertly spin her around and then directly into her arms, as if they were in a ballroom instead of the seating area outside Xi'An Hot Noodles.

Jing laughed. "Your expression! It's priceless! Don't you ever dance?"

"Not very often," Fei admitted.

She felt a little dizzy, partly from the spinning but mostly, she knew, from Jing's closeness. She had long dark eyelashes and a scattering of barely visible freckles across her cheeks. Princess Qīnghé didn't have freckles, but she also never appeared in public without a filter, and Fei wondered if she was seeing the princess as she truly was. In any other situation, the thought would have paralyzed her with nerves, but everyone in the night market was singing along to the chorus (including Jing), and Fei was giddy enough to sing along too.

Soon she forgot about whether she was dancing with a princess. She forgot about Malika snapping photos nearby. She forgot about the people around them and was only buoyed by the joy and excitement that seemed to lift up their feet as they danced. Jing was smiling that smile, and they were dancing very close together now, and a warm buzz went through Fei's body. The beat of the music was hypnotic. She saw Jing's mouth moving as she sang the lyrics to the song, her lips pink and plush beneath the warm golden night market lights.

It took a moment for Fei to realize that the wave of motion passing through the crowd wasn't another dance move. Malika grabbed Fei's arm and yelled in her ear, "Stop staring at her! Look behind you!"

Several people in uniform were barreling through the night market, separating the pop-up partyers as they came toward Xi'An Hot Noodles. Fei and Jing both spun around to see half a dozen more people outfitted in Imperial Security uniforms approaching. Jing's face went white.

"Your Highness!" the man in front called.

Everyone in the crowd began to look at them. The singer stopped singing, but it took another few moments for the deejay to stop the music.

"Your Highness, please come with us," the man repeated, his voice amplified through the night market.

Jing twisted away from Fei and fled.

It was pandemonium in front of Xi'An Hot Noodles. As the pop-up partyers realized the princess was in their midst, they tried to get closer to her while the IS agents tried to keep them away. Jing darted toward the noodle stand with Fei close behind her, while Malika and everyone else pointed their comms at her to stream the melee onto the socialnet.

One of the IS agents got close enough to grab Jing's arm, but Jing slipped out of his grasp and shoved a stool in his stomach. Another one ran toward her, yelling, "Your Highness, come back here!"

Seeing the panicked expression on Jing's face, Fei tripped the agent, who went flying to the ground.

"Thank you!" Jing said gratefully, dodging around a table.

"We can't stay here," Fei said.

"Where can I go?" Jing asked.

Fei grabbed her hand and said, "I know a way out."

She led Jing through the obstacle course of overturned stools and tables created by the crowd, which had noticed that the princess didn't want to go with the IS agents. One partyer tossed a half-empty bowl of noodles at an agent and yelled, "Run, Your Highness!"

Jing blew the partyer a kiss as the agent slipped on chili oil. "Thank you!" she called.

Fei pulled Jing around the Xi'An Hot Noodles counter and through the flapping door into the kitchen, rushing past the cooks who were gawking at their sudden appearance.

"Fei?" one of the cooks said, stepping away from her station. "What are you doing here?"

"Rana," Fei said in relief. She and Rana had gone to school together. "We need to hide. IS is after her. Where's the vent door?"

Back in the early days of the Empire, vent doors were often used as escape routes into the HVAC tunnels if the Station was attacked. It had been decades since then, but due to Isamar Station's status as a major trade hub, those tunnels were still used for smuggling—or sometimes for teenage pranks. Fei had grown up knowing her way around the HVAC tunnels, and she and her friends were well aware of how to sneak around unnoticed behind the main corridors.

Wordlessly, Rana led them to the back of the hot kitchen and reached beneath a counter to press a hidden button. A metal panel opened in the wall beside the trash bins. "You owe me an explanation," Rana said as Fei led Jing inside.

"I promise!" Fei said. The panel closed, leaving them in the dark, and Fei pulled out her comm to use as a light. They were in a rectangular metal duct that was just tall enough for them to walk through. It extended to either side, and Fei could feel the whisper of fresh air blowing across her face. She checked their position on her comm and gestured to the left. "This way."

"Where are we going? How did you know this was here? Are you a smuggler?" Jing laughed a little, as if the idea delighted her.

"I'm not a smuggler, I'm an Isa," Fei said. "These tunnels lead to the water reclamation facility. And we better get going. Rana won't let the agents through that vent door, but they'll probably just find a different entrance."

As they went quickly down the tunnel, a message from Malika popped up on Fei's comm:

Station-wide alert just went out! They're on the lookout.

"I'm not going to be able to hide forever," Jing said reluctantly.

Fei knew Jing was right, but she didn't want to accept it. She glanced over her shoulder at Jing; her face was downcast in the comm's glow. Fei had been planning to take Jing out by the level three HVAC corridor, where she could head around the corner to the transport tubes, but now a new idea popped into her head. "This is your first visit to Isamar Station, right?"

"Yes, why?"

"Do you want to see a place that only Isas know about? It's not on any tourist maps, but it's the most beautiful part of the Station."

Jing's disappointment turned to curiosity. "What is it?"

"You'll see. It's just a few minutes away."

"Then let's go." Jing smiled, and Fei thought the photos really didn't do her justice.

They exited the HVAC tunnel through another hidden panel and stepped into a dim corner of the Station. Across from where they stood, a single blue light glowed above an old-fashioned hatch in the wall, the kind that had been used during Station construction to seal off corridors in case of hull breaches. Fei went to the ancient keypad mounted beside the hatch and entered a code. It had been the same for as long as she could remember, but only Isas knew it. A moment later a hiss indicated the seal had been broken, and she spun the wheel to pull the hatch open. A pearly glow emanated from the space beyond the opening, and Fei said, "After you."

Fei heard Jing's gasp of wonder as she stepped through. Beyond the hatch was a small room, no larger than the kitchen of Xi'An Hot Noodles, but multiple stories in height. Lights embedded in the floor illuminated a wall of clear pipes filled with rushing water. It was like a giant waterfall, except the water rose *up* in some of the pipes, while it tumbled down in others.

"What is this place?" Jing whispered. Liquid shadows played over her face.

"We call it the Spring," Fei answered. "But it's really just a quirk of Station architecture. The room has no engineering purpose, but it's beautiful. I think every Isa artist has left something on the walls."

Fei shined her comm's light around, revealing pictures of transgalactic ships, human faces, planets, flowers, and all sorts of abstract shapes. They had been painted or drawn on the metal walls as far as the light could shine, and there was more beyond that. Fei watched Jing slowly turning around as she took in the Spring and the art, until their eyes met in the pearly, watery light.

"Thank you for showing me." Jing's eyes shone.

"You're welcome," Fei said. "Here—there's one more thing."

She sat down against the wall across from the water pipes and gestured for Jing to sit beside her. Then she felt for the switch that she knew had been installed at the base of the wall and pressed a button.

The soft white lights turned pale blue, and as they lit the liquid-filled pipes, the entire room seemed to ripple as if it was underwater.

Jing sighed. "It's so beautiful."

For one moment, Fei let herself wonder what it would be like if Jing could stay Downstation. A bubble of happiness rose up in her.

And then another message from Malika flashed on Fei's comm.

**IS says they're tracking her via an old comm.
Do you know what they mean?**

The bubble popped.

"What happened?" Jing asked.

Fei showed her the message, and Jing's face fell.

"They're going to find me soon," Jing said. "I should go before they get here. I don't want you to be penalized for helping me."

She got to her feet, and Fei scrambled up after her. "You're going now?"

"I have to. I shouldn't have used my old comm, but I needed some yuan and I thought it would give me a few hours. I guess it did." Jing gave Fei a wavering smile. "Thank you for showing me the night market. And the noodles! And this place—it's wonderful."

"Did you have fun?" Fei asked, trying to fend off her rising sadness. Jing was a princess. Of course she wasn't going to stay Downstation.

Jing smiled that dimpled smile again. "I had so much fun." Then she pulled Fei into a hug.

Fei could smell Jing's cupcake scent. It was beginning to make her weak in the knees.

"I'm sorry I have to go," Jing mumbled.

Fei felt Jing's breath on her cheek. She pulled back just slightly, just enough, and Jing's pink lips trembled, and then they were kissing—soft at first, tentative, as if they were asking if it was all right, and then it was *all right*, and Jing made a little sound in her throat and Fei tightened her arms around Jing in that too-large jumpsuit, fingers stroking the feathery softness of her short hair.

It ended much too soon, and Jing reluctantly stepped back. "Goodbye," she said.

Fei didn't know what to do. She couldn't ask Princess Qīnghé to stay, but she couldn't bring herself to say goodbye. She helplessly watched as Jing pushed open the hatch and stepped through, leaving her in the Spring.

Fei stood there in the watery blue light for several minutes, until Malika's message popped up on her comm.

**They found her down by the transport tubes.
Where are you??? I have photos!**

TWO DAYS LATER

On Sunday afternoon, The Fix Is In was quiet. Fei worked steadily through a backlog of repair jobs, trying to forget about what had happened the last time she'd worked the closing shift. Ever since Friday night, the socialnet had been all princess all the time, with numerous deep dives into how Qīnghé had evaded Imperial Security (she'd disguised herself as crew and slipped out in a delivery van), where she'd gone (Xi'An Hot Noodles was even more famous now), and who she'd escaped the night market with (no one knew). Fei had kept quiet about her part in the princess's escapade, although Malika kept trying to convince her to do an exclusive interview.

Fei's comm chimed and she wasn't surprised to see another message from Malika, but she was surprised to see what it said.

I won't post them if you don't want.

The message was accompanied by a bunch of photos. Fei couldn't resist—she opened them. There was Jing eating noodles, her eyes half-closed in ecstasy. There was Jing with a giant smile on her, surrounded by the pop-up party. And there was Jing dancing with Fei, their arms around each other as they gazed into each other's eyes. Fei's heart thudded. She briefly closed her eyes, then looked at the photo again.

It was real. This was evidence.

But it didn't change anything.

She sighed and closed the photos. She knew Malika was still angling for that tell-all interview, so she wrote back:

I'll think about it.

The door to the shop opened, and Fei glanced at her comm to note the time. "We're closing in a few—" she started, but then she saw who was there, and the words died on her lips.

Princess Qīnghé was standing in the doorway. Behind her, a retinue of IS agents and attendants peered into the shop around the princess's shoulders. She was wearing an intricately tailored jacket with multiple, layered collars in deepening shades of blue that reminded Fei of the Spring. Water drop–shaped diamonds dangled from her ears, but she wasn't wearing a wig as she normally did in public. Her short black hair was uncovered, the way it had been on Friday.

"Hi," the princess said, smiling. "Are you still open?"

"Y-yes, Your Highness," Fei stammered.

"Please, call me Jing," she said. "That's my personal name. I think we're on a personal level now, don't you?"

Fei's heart lifted. "Jing," she said. "How can I help you?"

Jing set a sleek new comm on the counter. "Take a look."

Fei picked it up and a message appeared:

This is for you so we can keep in touch privately.

Fei looked at Jing. "Really?"

Jing nodded. "Really. But also, I have some free time tonight. I was wondering if you want to go dancing? I heard on Malika Joss's socialnet that there might be a party in the night market."

Fei felt dizzy. "Really?"

Jing laughed, her brown eyes lighting up. "Don't tell me you hate dancing?"

The closing-time chime rang out from the shop's main comm, and Fei smiled. "No, I love to dance."

PRINCESS QĪNGHÉ FINDS LOVE DOWNSTATION
[Posted to Isamar Station socialnet by Malika Joss]

Isas, citizens of Zhonghua, I have an exclusive!!! Princess Qīnghé will be joining me right on this feed to share exclusive details about her Isamar Station holiday romp *and* the Downstation girl who melted her heart. You won't want to miss it!

DISASTER

"Second-Chance Romance"

Rebecca Podos

TWO DAYS LEFT

I am seventeen years and fifty-six days old when I realize I've been wrong about asteroids all my life.

When I thought of them—if ever I did—I pictured the grainy photos in last year's astronomy textbook. Smudged thumbprints of light, multicolored and coldly beautiful, blazing across the star-spattered backdrop of outer space. Turns out, those were comets. *Comets* are made of ice and dust, asteroids of metal and rock. Which shows you how little attention I paid to the textbook versus the latest copy of *MixxZine* that I'd tucked behind it. Sailor Moon > the regular moon. So images of the asteroid Callisto on the TV in our dorm's common room take me by surprise. Ugly and pockmarked, like a battered chunk of human bone hurtling through the black.

Hurtling toward Mom and Dad down in St. Petersburg, Florida, while they sip their coffee on our porch swing, watching the evening breeze sway the royal palms (I want to picture them that way, instead of glued to CNN like me). Toward JoJo, my five-year-old sister, streaking through the sun-crisped grass in her jellies before bedtime. Toward Bubbe and Papa picking avocados in their backyard in the coolest part of the day, the whole ocean unrolling beyond their fence.

And hurtling toward the Frost Preparatory School for Girls in Boston, where I sit on this prickly couch in my common room, totally alone.

Even before the big news broke yesterday—before falling rocks from space decapitated the Great Sphinx of Giza and cratered Lake Nakuru in Kenya, RIP flamingos—the Frost campus was all but empty. I got permission to stay on the gated grounds for the summer because of my internship at the Museum of Fine Arts (awesome for those college applications I, along with the rest of the class of 1999, may never fill out). So it was always going to be the hall mothers who live on campus year-round, a few international students with similar arrangements, the janitorial staff, and me.

And Jem, as often as she could come. She was supposed to be here . . .

No. I don't need to think about Jemma Bridgeham when there's an asteroid-not-comet headed toward Earth, three days from impact. According to the clock in the corner of the screen, that's 43 hours, 18 minutes, and 6 seconds.

5 seconds . . .

4 . . .

They've cut from a replay of last night's press conference with some NASA dude to the president, sweating behind the podium. He drawls, "My fellow Americans, we're being faced tonight with a dire challenge. The Bible's got a word for this—"

Across the common room, the phone rings. I stumble from the couch and sprint to reach it before it stops. "Hello?" Desperately, I cup the handset to my mouth like it's an oxygen mask.

"Adina?"

Because our dorms don't have phone lines, all calls come through the common room, one per hall. During the school year we have to sign up for a time slot in the call log. There are thirty girls in Tyler Hall, all fighting to call their friends back home or that boy they met at a mixed dance with Stamper Academy, our brother school. Serious calls—sick relatives or dead dogs, that stuff—came through the hall mothers' offices. But I saw Miss Potter, my own hall mother, leaving campus in the dead of last night. And Abrielle Boucher, a French student, tennis team captain, and the only other summertime resident of Tyler Hall, flew the coop this morning for her local boyfriend's summer house on Martha's Vineyard (I thought she might ask me to come with, but she didn't, which is fine). So there are no rules, and the only girl who could be getting calls is me.

"Hi, Daddy." I turn my back to the TV and press the plastic to my ear until I imagine I can hear the ocean. Not cold and gloomy blue, like the water that laps at the pilings in Boston Harbor, but jewel bright and Florida-warm.

"Sorry it's so late, honey."

"That's okay. Where's Mom? How's JoJo?"

"Mom's at Bubbe and Zayde's. We're moving them into the spare room, just until—just for a few days. Johanna doesn't really . . . we told her folks are getting ready for a really bad storm."

"That makes sense." JoJo knows about hurricanes by now.

"Listen, honey. I've been calling everyone I can think of since we talked last night. Airlines, every travel agency in the yellow pages, bus companies. I couldn't get through most of the time. Dial-up keeps going out, and folks aren't showing up for work since they heard the news. Plus planes aren't taking off with, you know, cause of the rocks flying around up there, so—"

"I can't come home," I finish for him, keeping my voice steady.

"I'd jump in the car this second if I could and pick you up. But all the channels are showing the highways parked up, saying interstate travel's almost impossible. I don't even think I'd get there before . . ." Again, he trails off, but this time I can't bring myself to end the thought. Dad clears his throat. "Who's with you, honey? Is the staff taking care of you?"

"Yeah, Daddy," I lie. What else can I do? Tell him that the grown-ups on campus have all fled or forgotten about me completely? My family can't do anything about it from over a thousand miles away, besides worry themselves into an earlier grave.

"Is your hall mother there?" Dad pushes. "I'd like to talk to her, make sure she'll look after you until—until we can get you home."

"She's in bed." And wherever she is, she might be. It's almost ten now, after lights out.

"Tomorrow morning, then."

"Sure," I say feebly. Maybe I'll come up with something by the time Dad tries again.

Honestly, I'm a little disappointed with myself—you'd think I'd have a better plan for the end of the world than cowering in my bedroom, alone. Jem and I even talked about it once. We rented *Independence Day* with her dad's Blockbuster card last winter, and Jem said she wouldn't have bothered trying to leave the city, even with an alien ship hovering overhead. Why go out on a highway? No, if she had one day left, she'd spend it doing something she really wanted, but was too scared to do in the before-times. Like breaking into the zoo to pet the giraffes. She's so soft for animals; she melts like butter in a microwave when she passes a dog on the street, or even sees a field mouse scuttling across the grounds of Frost. I snuggled into her, buried my face in the warm crook between her jaw and collarbone, and said I'd come too, because I'd only want to spend the last day with her—

Oh yeah. The Bridgehams.

"Actually, I'm going to Jem's house tomorrow. To stay with the Bridgehams. So it's okay, Dad. I'm gonna be safe."

You might guess that Mom and Dad weren't thrilled by the idea of their daughter spending a minimally supervised summer in what seems to them like The Big City, especially before my final year of high school. So I reminded them that my girlfriend and her parents live only fifteen minutes away in Jamaica Plain. Jem could easily be a day student, like half the girls at Frost, but her dad went to Stamper, and loved it, and wanted her to have the full boarder experience. Anyways, I told my parents her family would drive to campus once a week, and I could sign out to go to dinner with them, or to a movie at the Coolidge Corner Theatre in Brookline. The Bridgehams, I promised, would keep an eye on me.

And that *was* the plan at the time. Jem was gonna work it all out. She was gonna tell them, she promised to tell them. I found the guts to tell my parents I had a girlfriend—I came out to them in eighth grade when I was getting bullied at public school in St. Pete for supposedly peeping at Lisa Katz in the girls' locker room, which I did *not*—but I never talked about that night in early June. Our shouting match behind the tennis courts, and the Best Summer Ever that never was.

"That's really good, honey." Dad sounds so totally relieved that I don't regret the fib. Until he suggests, "Call us then, as soon as you're settled in. I want to thank her family."

Well, shit.

"It might be pretty late."

"That's okay. We'll be waiting."

"Sure," I mumble, stunned by the trap I set for myself and strolled right into.

"Then I'll talk to you real soon. We'll *see* you soon. The astronauts and the constr— the demolition experts, they're gonna take care of this. They know what they're doing. So you don't have to worry."

"I know, Daddy."

"We love you, Dina Bean-a."

I drop the phone onto the wall cradle before his pet name puts a wobble in my voice, then turn back to the Kennedy Space Center just in time for the launch countdown to reach zero. The *Hallelujah*, a huge shuttle stuffed with astronauts and like, construction workers ("demolition experts," the NASA dude insisted) lifts off. Of course, the government has known about Callisto for weeks, and this is the plan they came up with. The last hope of the planet rises into the night sky, flames roaring and smoke roiling, trailing bright white flame. I can't help but picture the people on board in hard hats instead of helmets.

The countdown-to-impact clock now reads: 43 hours, 9 minutes, and 15 seconds.

None of this is fair. This was supposed to be the Best Summer Ever. Jem was supposed to be around all the time. But it's August now, and we haven't talked once. And now, I have to get myself to her house by tomorrow night and sweet-talk her family into taking me in. That, or confess to my parents that I'm all alone. Then they might just pack JoJo, Bubbe, and Papa into the car and spend the next two days—maybe the last two days—inching toward Boston, arrival not guaranteed.

It's late, but I don't fall asleep for hours. I just lie on the common room couch with the TV turned down low, the final fight with Jem playing and rewinding and replaying behind my eyes.

ONE DAY LEFT

After accidentally sleeping through most of the morning, I waste another half an hour crying about it, unhelpfully. Lunch is cheese and peanut butter cracker sandwiches and a lone strawberry Smirnoff Ice I find in the mini fridge in Miss Potter's office. I drink it while catching up on the news. The astronauts and construction workers docked with the International Space Station in the early hours after I passed out. It split in half somehow, I guess—the Space Station, not the *Hallelujah*—but everyone's fine. When I can't put it off anymore, I step outdoors for the first time in two days, a little fuzzy headed and blinking in the midday sun.

According to the brochures the middle school guidance counselor in St. Pete gave my parents, the Frost campus is "20 beautiful acres of study gardens, soccer fields, tennis courts, and classrooms where your college-bound daughter and future leader can thrive." The brochures didn't lie. From where I stand on the white gravel path outside Tyler Hall, I can see the other halls, Hunt and Thorton, to the right. To the left, the library with its little koi pond and stone benches. Behind me is the visual arts building, my favorite part of campus and a huge part of why I'm here, and on scholarship. Frost's arts program feeds right into the BFA programs at RISD, Pratt, and The New School, with plenty of alumni to help a girl along. Whenever I wasn't in class, at the dining hall, or in Jem's dorm room, I was in one of the art studios.

Drawing was my main concentration, but I was happy in the painting studio, or sculpture, or ceramics, or photography; take your pick. Its stained glass windows glow candy-colored in the sunlight, calling to me now. I could bust one of them out, climb through, and curl up under a drafting table or in the dark room, like people must be doing in the pews of synagogues and churches right now.

Instead I pass it by and cut straight across the neat green grass, aiming for the staff and student parking lots beyond. I haven't changed out of the clothes I woke up in the morning before last—basketball shorts and a too-large Tweety Bird tee, now covered in cracker crumbs and a splash of Smirnoff—plus I forgot to put on shoes. So my socks are filthy by the time I reach the student lot. It's really just a senior lot because only seniors are allowed to have cars on campus. Except Jem got this shiny red Vespa scooter for her sixteenth birthday, and would park it on the sliver of weeds at the edge of the blacktop. We spent junior year zooming around Boston, the little two-seater rumbling through our bodies, me clinging to her like a barnacle.

The lot's empty now. Of course it is. What senior would waste their last summer before college at a girls' boarding school when they could be floating around their in-ground pools with suntanned boys? But I'd hoped to see a car in the staff lot, and that's empty, too. Bummer. I thought the groundskeeper was still on campus, at least.

I really am alone.

Slowly roaming the paths and lawns, I think through my options. I can't catch a ride to Jamaica Plain, fine. And if pilots and travel agents aren't showing up for work, why would taxi drivers? I could wander out onto the streets of Boston and bribe some-body with my laundry quarters to call my parents and pretend to be the Bridgehams . . . except Mom just bought that kind of caller ID that lists people's names, so she might wonder why Mr. Bridgeham is calling from a random payphone on Mass Ave.

Then I see it. A familiar blue Schwinn abandoned in the bike rack by the student union. It belongs to Abrielle Boucher. I guess she couldn't take it to Martha's Vineyard—they probably ride horses there, anyways. The bike isn't even chained up. Wandering over, I nudge the whitewall tires with one toe; they could use a little air, but they seem fine. Good enough to get me the five-ish miles to Jamaica Plain, probably. Let's be super clear: the very last person on planet Earth who I want to see is Jemma Bridgeham.

But here's the thing. Jem has been my best friend since the second day of freshman year, when we were paired up in the same twin kayak for Frost's teambuilding field trip on the Charles River. I mean, I have other friends here. There are totally girls I'm friendly with at Frost. It's just . . . I'd never met anyone like Jem, this Alicia Silverstone look-alike from a rich family who could've ruled our grade. She could've schemed with the other girls to get permission to study at the Boston Public Library, then spent an hour on her hair and makeup in case they found a cute boy in the encyclopedia section. She could've slipped into any clique and invited *them* to her house for the weekend.

But there I was, a scholarship kid from the south who hadn't gone to Frost in middle school like most of the students. One of the only girls who chose the uniform khakis over a skirt. Who spent her evenings in the visual arts building instead of the common room, had no clue how to use a straightening iron, and zero interest in the mixed school dances. Jem wanting to spend time together with me as much as I did with her was like this crazy miracle, even before we started spending time *together*. So I guess I didn't have much time for anyone else.

Maybe that's why Abrielle didn't think to invite me to come along. And why I can't remember the phone number of any of the day students, or think of a single home to go to beside the Bridgeham's.

Jem's family lives in a refurbished Victorian with central air-conditioning. Their guest bedroom has an attached bathroom with a claw-foot tub, tons of fluffy towels, and little soap cakes shaped like real cakes. They have two refrigerators, one just for snacks and bottles of water and Snapple.

The last time Jem took me home was just before the end of junior year. We were making up after a fight—we'd had more fights in the last month than I can count. Nothing big, just like, which movie to watch, who was doing our chemistry homework the right way, which study garden we should sit in, whether we wanted to go on the ski field trip or not. We were like pebbles in each other's shoes when we weren't falling all over each other, and I couldn't figure out why. But that weekend, we were so good. She sunned herself on a beach towel beside the basketball court, reading *Guns, Germs, and Steel* while I played five-in-a-row with Mr. Bridgeham. Mrs. Bridgeham laid out a build-your-own quesadilla bar for dinner—Jem's overflowed with jalapeños, while I put everything in mine but the plastic packaging the prosciutto came in. That night, we snuck out of our rooms. There's a ladder at the end of the third-floor hallway that leads to a trapdoor, up to a rooftop widow's walk. We lay on the quilt from Jem's bed, swatting away mosquitoes and staring up at the stars strong enough to pierce the light pollution. Then she leaned over to whisper the L-word in my ear for the first time.

A week later, in the woods behind the tennis courts, she took it back.

Jem's the one who called off the Best Summer Ever, not me. Why should *she* be surrounded by the people who love her and fancy soap and Snapple, while I sweat it out in an empty dorm room, with only CNN and a rotating fan for company?

So I decide to kill two birds. Three, actually:

Spend the apocalypse in comfort (or not—still have my fingers crossed for the interstellar construction workers)

Make my parents happy

Make Jem miserable at the maybe-end-of-the-world

It takes until evening to work up the guts to leave campus, because who knows what waits beyond the gates of Frost? I ditch my basketball shorts and putz around picking out the right outfit to wear to my ex-girlfriend's. It's hard—I've been lazy about laundry all summer, so I only have like three clean things at any moment. I find a pair of gently grass-stained shortalls, some fresh socks, and a Blue Öyster Cult T-shirt my parents bought me last Hanukkah instead of the Blink-182 tee I specifically asked for. Dad said the greatest gift they could give me was taste.

Finally I step into my Reeboks and pull my wavy brown hair into a low braid to tug on my favorite Miami Heat snapback. I stuff my backpack with my other clean T-shirt, a toothbrush, my teddy bear, and my mini photo album, careful not to bend the Polaroids of my family. Then it's time.

After days alone, the streets of Boston would probably seem wild anyways. But as I pedal up Boylston and onto Mass Ave, I pass what looks like an actual doomsday cult camped out in front of the Christian Science Library. Lots of white robes and signs with scripture that I, a Jew, have no hope of recognizing. A kid who looks a little like JoJo waves her poster board at me. I swallow the apple-sized lump in my throat and throw my back into it to speed away. I pass the Bread & Circus where I just bought snacks last week, and the glass windows are all smashed in. Folks really want their heirloom tomatoes and sunflower butter in the end times, I guess.

By Columbus Ave, I'm really sweating, even as the sky purples into evening. I swivel my hat backwards to feel the sticky August breeze on my forehead. The backpack thumps against my spine as I veer through Jackson Square, then onto Southwest Corridor Park. I don't know exactly how many miles between here and the Bridgeham's, but it's easy enough to retrace the route I've traveled so many times with Jem on her scooter, my hands fisted in her jean jacket. Of course I have it memorized. I wanted to remember every moment, the whistle of the wind around us, and the way the scenery streaked past.

On Washington, I pass the Midway Café, a rundown bar Jem snuck into to see Innerpink play when she was fifteen. It's so packed that grown men sit on the grimy sidewalk, drinking straight out of bottles under evening clouds that glow pinkish purple.

Jamaica Plain transforms from neighborhood to neighborhood, and I reach the Bridgeham's quiet, tree-lined road off Forest Hills Street a few minutes later. Hopping off, I walk my bike down the driveway and gaze up at the lilac-colored Victorian. I pause beside a massive hydrangea shrub, just now realizing this might've been a bad idea. Like, do I really want to spend my last days in misery, just to torture Jem? But as I'm thinking of pedaling right back to campus, a curtain on the ground floor shifts. A pale face peers out, and seconds later, the front door swings wide.

"Adina? Is that you?"

I drop my stolen bike beside the shrub and plod up the walkway to the wraparound porch. I've mostly caught my breath by the time I reach her, though I can't do anything about the sweat. "Hey, Mrs. Bridgeham. How are you?"

"Just fine, sweetie." And Jem's stepmom does look fine. *Weirdly* fine, for the circumstances. She looks the same as two months ago, her highlighted hair pinned into a neat French twist, wearing a fluttery sundress and café au lait lipstick, still immaculate even though it's closing in on her bedtime. "Jem, get down here!" she trills over her shoulder. "You've got company!"

I follow the sound of footsteps down one staircase, then another, until my exgirlfriend is standing right in front of me.

Jemma does not look fine.

No neat blond braids or beaded chokers, no mini dress or Sahara Sapphire nail polish, the only color she owns. Her hair is pulled into a greasy low ponytail, sleepless bruises below her hazel eyes. She smells like sweat instead of watermelon body spray. And her shirt . . . that's *my* shirt. My favorite painting shirt, splattered with a rainbow of oils and acrylics, just a few bits of mustard fabric still peeking through. I thought I lost it at the end of last semester, a victim of the laundry room chaos.

"You didn't tell us Adina was in the city for the summer!" Mrs. Bridgeham scolds her, but playfully, like I'm just a surprise dinner guest and not a windblown girl who turned up on their porch at the maybe-end-of-the-world. "Well, are you going to invite your friend in?"

My soul curls up like a dead shrimp inside my chest.

For two years, friends is all we were. Or at least, all we called ourselves while spending most every waking moment together. But we stopped being friends in October of junior year, when I got my wisdom teeth pulled. She swapped beds with my roommate for the week to serve me applesauce and pain pills as needed. She even hauled in her personal twelve-inch TV and VHS player (unlike me, Jemma Bridgeham is no scholarship student) so we could watch *Titanic* side by side, our hips and shoulders pressed together, while I held an ice pack to my face. When Rose and Jack kissed on the bow of the ship, she leaned in and kissed my shoulder instead of my lips so it wouldn't hurt. We had our first real kiss as soon as my gums healed up.

Except I guess that kiss wasn't real, not to Jem. I guess none of it was. She said as much when, just a week after she first dropped the L-word, she changed her mind.

I just don't think I'm like you.

Sure. I knew exactly what that meant. I watched that episode of *Ellen* last year, where Ellen freaked out about giving off gay vibrations, just like Jem freaked out about kissing and dry humping and spending every spare minute with another girl. Except I never got my airport moment, my "Susan I'm gay" moment.

All I got was dumped.

"Really, sweetie." Mrs. Bridgeham pulls me inside when Jem doesn't move. "If we'd known you were in town, we'd have had you over much sooner. Jemma, why didn't you tell us?"

"I—um . . . ," she stutters.

"It's not her fault," I interrupt. "Jem's invited me over, but I've been really busy, with the internship and stuff."

I'm not being nice. The lie is part of my plan: show up sweet as peaches and be welcomed inside, while Jem can't say a thing to stop it. How could she when she never told her parents about us in the first place?

"Well, you're here now," Mrs. Bridgeham soothes. "You can leave your sneakers there—you remember. Let Jem take your bag. Have you had dinner? Johnathan's working late, but he'll be along. Would you like some iced tea? I have a fresh pitcher in the snack fridge. How about some gazpacho? We've got plenty of leftovers. And I want to hear all about this internship!"

I'm escorted toward the kitchen while Jem floats after us with my backpack, pale and nauseous-looking, like a ghost regretting its last meal. We pass the empty family room with the big screen TV on, but muted. I catch the countdown clock at 21 hours, 34 minutes, and 12 seconds, plus a glimpse of the chyron below the flustered anchor—*Shuttle Hallelujah repaired, still on course for Callisto*—before I'm swept by. Mrs. Bridgeham doesn't even glance over at the screen.

We sit at the counter, Mrs. Bridgeham making small talk while I eat my gazpacho. She asks about the museum, my summer so far and, strangest of all, my plans after graduation. All the while, Jem stares down into her untouched glass of iced tea. It gets worse when Mr. Bridgeham comes home. Like his wife, he *looks* fine—his chinos ironed and his polo shirt with the pocket alligator tucked in, though it's after nine by now. Except he smells like the men outside Midway must. And when he calls my parents to confirm that I'll be staying with them for a few days, he slurs through an invitation to lunch at the Union Oyster House when they're in town.

At last we excuse ourselves, and Jem shows me to the second-floor guest room that Mrs. Bridgeham's made up, even though I know the way. I'm freaked enough that I forget that I hate her for a second, forget that because of this girl, my heart has felt cratered and cold as a comet all summer.

Sorry, an asteroid.

We lock eyes, and once we're out of earshot, she croaks, "They're just . . . it's just my family. Dad works, and Evelyn cooks, and nobody talks. Not about hard things."

She leaves me outside the bedroom without another word.

Of course I can't sleep, so I try to relax in the claw-foot tub of my en-suite bathroom. I dampen the pages of one of the paperback romance books I found on the nightstand—something called *Prisoner of My Desire*—but the print blurs away whenever I try to catch a sentence. Finally I give up, tossing it to the bathmat, and sink below the water. I still don't sleep afterward, but I don't sneak out of my room either. I lie awake the whole night, maybe my last night, with pillows piled over my head so I won't hear it if Jem knocks.

And so I won't hear it if she doesn't.

THE LAST DAY

"What do you girls have planned for today?" Mrs. Bridgeham asks, taking a careful bite to spare her immaculate lipstick (though this morning, sleepless bruises to match my own peek through her thick concealer).

I almost choke on my Belgian waffle.

Jem just sighs, no help at all. Mr. Bridgeham doesn't comment either. He sits at the counter instead of the breakfast table, I think so we won't smell whatever's wafting out of his coffee mug. At least he's wearing a fresh polo/chinos combo, while his daughter wears the same clothes she wore yesterday. The same shirt; *my* painting shirt. Nobody says anything about this, either, me included.

But when the scraping of our forks and the silence drags on, I pipe up, "Maybe . . . go to the park?" Franklin Park is just down the street, though we have absolutely no plans to go there. There's probably a doomsday cult camping out on the golf course.

"That will be nice," Mrs. Bridgeham says, satisfied. "It's supposed to be a sunny one. I think I saw that on the weather."

"Has . . . um, has anyone checked the news this morning?" I dare to ask. I snuck down three times in the night to watch. The last time, around 4 a.m., I learned that the *Hallelujah* had landed on Callisto. It lost one of its three main engines and broke an astronaut's leg in the process, so it's a good thing the demolition experts are doing the tough work. They dropped down off course, though, and had to hike to some crater valley with all of their nuclear space dynamite. I turned it off when the local weatherman started explaining mega-tsunamis, coming soon to a town near us.

Or not.

We'll find out today. At 4 a.m., the countdown clock read 14 hours, 45 minutes, and 4 seconds. Now, the oven clock across the kitchen reads 8:22, and while I'd never make the math team at Frost, I can do simple subtraction.

"Oh, I never watch the morning news," Mrs. Bridgeham says. "Nothing good comes from starting the day like that. What about you, darling?" She cranes around to talk to Mr. Bridgeham. "What are you up to today?"

He burps into his elbow. "Work."

"Wonderful. Well, off you all get. I want to do my deep cleaning today."

Is she serious? I ask Jem with my eyebrows.

Deathly, she answers with a wince.

Just because we hate each other doesn't mean we've forgotten how to speak without talking.

I don't really mean to follow through on this latest lie. But when I follow Jem out of the kitchen, hoping to catch my breath in my bedroom, I almost trip on her as she stoops down at the shoe rack. She ignores her glittery silver platform slip-ons and steps into her sturdy black Docs. "Come on, we can take my bike."

"We're not actually going to the park," I remind her.

"Why not? You want to hang around here while Evelyn deep cleans? You want your last day to smell like Pine-Sol?"

"It's not the last day," I protest weakly, though actually, I'm glad somebody in this big, beautiful house has at last acknowledged the possibility.

"Well, then it's the last day you have to spend with me," she shoots back.

I guess that's true. If the world doesn't end, I'll just bicycle back to campus and celebrate alone with the last Strawberry Smirnoff in Mrs. Potter's mini fridge, waiting for the adults to drift back. Waiting for the world to be normal again. And in the fall, we'll start school just like we would've. Except I'll probably sit at the emptiest table in the dining hall instead of with Jem and the Tyler girls. And I'll spend that much more time in the arts studios, alone.

I toe on my high-tops because what the hell. It's just one more day with Jem and my stupid, aching, asteroid heart either way. Not like it's gonna kill me.

Jem weaves the Vespa through abandoned cars in the street, dodging the people who wander occasionally into the road, staring up. I tip my head back too, holding tighter to Jem's waist, hands fisted in my own T-shirt so I don't blow off. There's nothing to see yet but bright, cloudless blue, as smooth as sea glass. There won't be until/unless Callisto breaks Earth's atmosphere, according to the NASA dude. And then it'll depend on where you are in the world. From Boston, they say we'll see a great white flash in the evening sky as the asteroid bursts through, a wide streak of flame like a shuttle roaring back to Earth, and then . . . mega-tsunami. Or we'll see a hundred pricks of light as the pieces burn harmlessly up and away.

It's anyone's guess right now.

I half expect Jem to veer off and take us to Midway to kill the morning, but to my surprise, we do head for the park. Not the woodsy hiking trails right off Forest Hills Street, but onto the road that cuts through to get to the parking lot of the Franklin Park Zoo.

I would laugh, but Jem might mistake it for crying.

We abandon our helmets by the bike, just leave them lying on the pavement. The lot is empty, the gate locked, and the ticket stand abandoned. So we hop the gate.

We don't talk, just walk the path together into the abandoned zoo—or nearly abandoned. We meet a lone gray-haired zookeeper in full khaki overalls coming out of one of the buildings, carrying plastic buckets full of grain and grass. I think we're about to get kicked out before we even make it to the Tropical Forest exhibit. But he sets his heavy-looking buckets down to catch his breath. "Some punks stole all our golf carts," he explains, hands on his fragile old knees.

Jem and I look at each other. For the first time since she gaped out at me on the porch, her eyes are alight.

I give her the tiniest nod.

"You want help?" she asks.

So we each haul a bucket to the Giraffe Savannah, where the zookeeper leads us into the barn attached to their grassy pen. We follow a raised walkway to the concrete enclosure and pour the feed into hanging buckets at giraffe-head height. The zookeeper shoves open the barn doors, and in the giraffes trot, a sweet-eyed pair of adults with a baby between them. We pet the muzzles of the parents, objectively one of the coolest things I've ever done, while the zookeeper explains that this isn't his usual job. The giraffe keeper is home with her family today, like the rest of his coworkers.

"But you came here?" I ask.

"Where else would I be?" He presses his sun-spotted forehead to the bristly spotted forehead of the male giraffe. "I've been working at the zoo for forty-two years. The animals are my family. This is my home."

Jem's cheeks are pink and tear-streaked when I glance over, and I quickly turn away.

For the rest of the morning, we follow the zookeeper, lugging prechopped fruits and veggies to the ring-tailed lemur pen and wheelbarrows full of hay and alfalfa to the zebras. The lions and tigers get whole dead rabbits and a bloody bone each—for a treat, the zookeeper tells us. It's hotter by the minute, and I'm sweating and exhausted when he calls for a lunch break. He lets us into the gifts and snacks shop with a borrowed set of keys so we can grab cold Cokes and snack cakes and little pretzel bags. Then he wanders back to the office to eat his bagged lunch. Jem and I find our way to the pavilion tent by the zebra exhibit and sit in the shade. We eat and drink and watch the breeze bat softly at the leaves, listening to the sounds of distant animals and each other's breathing.

"It's pretty gross out," she speaks at last. "You wanna go? I wouldn't blame you."

I shake my head, because the only place I want to be right now is here, with her, though I hate her. How messed up is that?

After lunch, it's back at it for the afternoon feeding and to clean the water fountains and bowls. We toss dead, dried insects into the trees at the flight cage and feed the finches by hand. When we've finally finished, the zookeeper releases us without ever telling us his name; he just thanks us, shakes our hands with his strong and wrinkled one, and trots back to the office to hang his keys up for maybe the last time.

Jem checks her pearly pink wristwatch. "We should start home. Evelyn wants to do a family dinner tonight. She's making another quesadilla bar just for you."

I feel the blood drain down to my toes. "Dinner? Is it that late?" It sounds crazy to say that the countdown clock slipped my mind.

Smiling so weakly her sun-blushed cheek doesn't even dimple, she says, "We should get a shower before dinner. And maybe you want to call home?"

I can't imagine what I'll say to my family while Mrs. Bridgeham bustles around, preparing dinner and pretending we'll all definitely be around to eat it. But she's just started to chop the fillings when Jem lures her away with a game of Go Fish, a favor I didn't see coming. Her stepmom is thrilled—I think she's been trying to tempt Jem out of her bedroom with a board game for days—and Jem's dad would probably agree to anything, as long as he can keep drinking from his mysterious coffee thermos. So I have the kitchen all to myself. I talk to everyone in turn, Dad and JoJo and Bubbe and Papa, keeping it quick. And it's, it's . . .

Yeah.

Finally, it's me and Mom, who does her mom thing by asking if I'm okay. And like, no, obviously I'm not, what with the apocalypse. But instead of saying that, I sniff into the speaker and confess, "Jem broke up with me."

"What?" Mom practically gasps. "*Today?*"

She sounds so scandalized that I have to laugh. "No, Mommy," I reassure her. Then I tell her everything, as if it still matters. What Jem and I whispered to each other on the widow's walk that night, and what we screamed at each other in the woods a week later. That I've spent the whole summer since walking from the MFA to my dorm room and back. How I'm only here tonight because I didn't want them to worry.

"Oh, Dina Bean-a." She sighs. I think she's about to tell me what a horrible bitch Jem is and how much better I am without her; everything I want to hear. Instead, she says, "Talk to her, baby. She's been your person for three years, hasn't she? Give her some grace, and give it to yourself. What else can we do, now?" Which is the exact opposite of everything I wanted to hear, and not very helpful.

I join the Bridgehams in the family room just in time to catch the end of the game. Mr. Bridgeham has about fifteen cards in his hand, with no pairs on the coffee table in front of him. He's staring with glazed, bloodshot eyes at the TV, still muted, not that it makes a difference. There's no anchor in the newsroom now. It's just an empty desk and endlessly scrolling chyrons, the latest reading: *Hallelujah detonations not yet underway, mission down to minutes.*

And it's true. The countdown clock says 17 minutes, 56 seconds.

"Adina, honey, take my spot?" Mrs. Bridgeham chirps. She's sitting with her back to the TV. "I've got to get to the cooking. Dinner around seven thirty, okay everybody?" She hurries out of the room without waiting for our answers.

"Want to play?" Jem asks, pale as bone.

"Actually, do you want to go up to the walk?"

She blinks at me. "Um . . . sure. We're just gonna go outside for a while, okay Dad?"

Mr. Bridgeham nods vaguely. Returning the favor, I leave so Jem can say maybe-goodbye to him in private.

Up on the widow's walk, the sky is purple-tinted running to deeper blue in the east, where I know the harbor waits.

"It's getting cooler," Jem comments, popping up out of the trap door behind me.

God, do I not want to talk about the weather.

The truth is, there's so much to talk about and nothing I want to talk about right now. Except the countdown clock must be down by another four, five minutes. And Mom is right. I have to say something.

"That's my shirt" is what I land on.

"Huh?" The breeze tosses greasy strands of hair across her sharpened cheekbones, and goddamn it, she's still beautiful, still the girl I can't believe I got to call mine for a while.

"You're wearing my shirt. My favorite painting shirt. You stole it," I accuse. "I loved that shirt."

Jem plucks at the paint-stained fabric, the shape of her jaw stubborn. "So what? You want it back now?"

"I want you to not have taken it away."

She doesn't dignify this with an answer, just gazes out over the rooftops of Jamaica Plain.

"And you didn't call," I keep going, angrier for her silence.

"When?"

"All summer. And the last few days. You knew I was in the dorms, and you had the common room number, and you never called me. Not even after . . ." I flap my hands at the sky.

Jem swipes her hair out of her face as she turns on me, suddenly just as mad as I am. "Maybe I didn't want you to hang up on me at the end of the world, *Adina*."

"I wouldn't have—"

"Yes you would've. I know you still hate me."

"Nooooo." I sound like JoJo at her most tired and least mature, but I don't care. "Why would I hate you, *Jemma*?"

She glares. "I don't know, maybe the same reason you broke up with me."

"I—what?" I splutter, stalled in my rage. "I didn't . . . you broke up with *me*!"

"No I didn't!" she shrieks, eyes wild. "All I said was I wasn't ready to tell my parents I was a . . . a lesbian."

"Yeah, I got that. You didn't want to tell them about me. Because you don't talk about *hard things* with your family."

"Because I couldn't talk about them with you!" she screams back.

I freeze. I swear, even the blood in my body freezes. "What does that mean?"

"I tried," she insists, wiping her nose sloppily on her forearm. "But you didn't want to listen to me."

"Um, I heard you. You said you liked boys, that you weren't like me."

"I said I didn't *think* I was a lesbian because I liked boys *too*. But you just freaked out!"

"Wait . . ." It's hard, what with the ever-darkening sky and a comet—fuck, sorry, an asteroid—on the brink of impact, and the girl I want to hate so close to me, but I try to wrestle my breath under control and think. To remember that night, the fight we had, the words we threw like punches. I insist, "You totally dumped me. And you know what, I should've seen it coming. You kept picking fights, you'd been doing it for weeks. You were looking for a reason to get out of this ever since I made that joke about renting a tux to take you to the next mixed dance."

"We were fighting because we were together literally all the time," she corrects, "and I liked you *so* much, but I couldn't . . . I didn't have any space to think. I knew everything about you, because you're always so sure about who you are and what you want, but all I wanted was a minute to figure something out about me. And what I *said* was that I shouldn't have told you I was a lesbian just because you said it first.

I like girls . . . I love girls, but I've liked a boy before. I had the biggest crush on this boy from Stamper in eighth grade. And then on this cruise I took with my mom in freshman year, I kissed someone who told me they didn't think they were a boy or a girl, and I liked them too. Do you get what I'm saying?"

"No." The countdown clock must be running pretty low right now, so I answer honestly.

Jem sighs and steps closer so she can drop her voice to a near whisper. "Did you know June 23 is Bisexual Pride Day? I didn't. Nobody ever told me. I didn't even know the word until this politician in Connecticut came out as bisexual, and I heard my mother talking about it with my stepmom. She didn't think it was a real thing, and Evelyn was like, 'Oh I think it is,' and then I went to the lab at Frost and looked it up with like, this whole big stack of books between me and the next computer so Melly Myers couldn't see my screen."

"Okay," I steal a precious second to process this. "So . . . I'm a lesbian. And you're bisexual," I sound it out.

Jem nods once.

"Okay. That's . . . that's okay. But . . . then why didn't you want me?"

She drops down to the rooftop, lightly freckled arms wrapped around her long legs and her face buried in her knees. "I did. I do want you." It comes out muffled, but I'm pretty sure I've heard her right. "I wasn't sure about me, is all, but I was always sure about you. I just needed a second . . . I didn't want this."

I sit beside her on the still-hot bricks of the widow's walk.

"And I know you don't want me anymore," she continues. "You just came to my house cause you didn't want to be alone."

"So what?" I say, when what I mean is *you're wrong*.

"Honestly, I don't even care." She lifts her head to scrub at her cheek. "Who cares? We only have—" She starts to check her watch.

I slap a hand over the glass face to stop her. "So you liked me, then?"

"I love you," Jem says easily, prying my hand from her wrist to fold her fingers through mine. Like it costs nothing to admit it, because she doesn't think she'll have to live with it.

"Okay." I take a breath. "Good. Cause I love you too, and I'm so sor—"

She slams her lips into mine before I can finish the apology, and we're kissing again, thank god. Not sweetly, but like all of the air left in the world is contained inside our bodies, and we won't stop breathing a second before we need to. Maybe this is pretend, but it doesn't feel that way. We feel like the only real thing. The last real thing.

Finally, she has to pull away for actual oxygen.

Sighing deeply, Jemma tips her head up, then whispers, "Dina," still breathless.

I follow the line of her throat that I've kissed up and down, her slender chin, her tear-streaked cheeks, and her big gold-green eyes, up and up and up.

There are fireflies in the sky.

No. There are pieces of asteroid, of metal and rock, hundreds of them, tiny points of light bursting into Earth's atmosphere, burning up and away to nothing.

Those fucking construction workers. They really did it.

With a shuddering sigh, Jem starts to pull her hands away to hide her face, I can feel it.

But I hold on tight. I wouldn't let go again if it was the end of the world.

THE NEXT DAY

ACKNOWLEDGMENTS

First and foremost, thank you to our contributors, who made this anthology possible, as well as a total delight to edit; we still can't believe we got to commission love stories from our favorite authors in the game, and we're so grateful to you all.

Thank you to Eric Smith for selling this anthology, and also for teaching us how to run an anthology.

Thank you so much to the team at Running Press Kids. To Britny Brooks, our dream editor. And to our production editor, Michael Clark; Valerie Howlett, our marketing and publicity lead; and our publicist, Nicole Banholzer.

One million thanks to our designer, Marissa Raybuck, and to illustrator Abbey Lossing for the cover of our hearts' desires.

Much love to you all!

AUTHOR BIOGRAPHIES

Rebecca Barrow writes stories about girls and all the wonders they can be. A lipstick obsessive with the ability to quote the entirety of *Mean Girls*, she lives in England, where it rains a considerable amount more than in the fictional worlds of her characters. She collects tattoos, cats, and more books than she could ever possibly read.

Ashley Herring Blake (she/her) is an author and literary agent. She holds a master's degree in teaching and loves coffee, arranging her books by color, and cold weather. She is the author of the young adult novels *Suffer Love*, *How to Make a Wish*, and *Girl Made of Stars*, the middle-grade novels *Ivy Aberdeen's Letter to the World*, *The Mighty Heart of Sunny St. James*, and *Hazel Bly and the Deep Blue Sea*, as well as the adult novel *Delilah Green Doesn't Care*. *Ivy Aberdeen's Letter to the World* was a Stonewall Honor Book, as well as a *Kirkus*, *School Library Journal*, NYPL, and NPR Best Book of 2018. Her YA novel *Girl Made of Stars* was a Lambda Literary Award finalist. You can find her on Twitter and Instagram at @ashleyhblake and on the web at ashleyherringblake.com. She lives in Georgia.

Gloria Chao is the critically acclaimed author of *American Panda*, *Our Wayward Fate*, and *Rent a Boyfriend*. After a brief detour as a dentist, she is now grateful to spend her days in fictional characters' heads instead of real people's mouths. Her award-winning books have been featured on the Indie Next List and the "Best of" lists of *Seventeen*, Bustle, Barnes & Noble, PopSugar, Paste Magazine, Chicago Public Library, and more. Visit her tea-and-book-filled world at GloriaChao.wordpress.com and find her on Twitter and Instagram at @GloriacChao.

Born and raised in a small North Carolina town, **Mason Deaver** is an award-winning, bestselling author and designer living in Charlotte, North Carolina. Besides writing, they're an active fan of horror movies and video games.

Sara Farizan is the critically acclaimed and award-winning author of the young adult novels *If You Could Be Mine*, *Tell Me Again How a Crush Should Feel*, and *Here to Stay*.

Her short stories have been featured in several anthologies including DC Comics' *Wonderful Women of History*, *Fresh Ink*, *All Out*, and *Come on In*. She watched too many episodes of *Smallville* and *The New Adventures of Lois & Clark* during her formative years and continues to read and write about superheroes as an adult. You can follow her on Instagram at @sara.farizan.

Claire Kann is the author of *Let's Talk About Love*, *If It Makes You Happy*, and *The Marvelous* and is an award-winning online storyteller. In her other life she works for a nonprofit you may have heard of where she daydreams like she's paid to do it. She loves cats and is obsessed with horror media (which makes the whole being known for writing contemporary love stories a little weird, tbh). Find more stories and random anecdotes on her website, clairekann.com.

Malinda Lo is the critically acclaimed author of several young adult novels, including *Last Night at the Telegraph Club*. Her debut novel, *Ash*, a lesbian retelling of Cinderella, was a finalist for the William C. Morris YA Debut Award, the Andre Norton Award for YA Science Fiction and Fantasy, the Mythopoeic Fantasy Award, and was a Kirkus Best Book for Children and Teens. She has been a three-time finalist for the Lambda Literary Award. Malinda's nonfiction has been published by *The New York Times Book Review*, NPR, The Huffington Post, The Toast, *The Horn Book*, and the anthologies *Here We Are*, *How I Resist*, and *Scratch*. She lives in Massachusetts with her partner and their dog.

Hannah Moskowitz is the author of over a dozen books for young adults, including *Break*, published when she was seventeen years old; *Teeth*; 2013 Stonewall Honor Book *Gone, Gone, Gone*; Sydney Taylor Honor Book *Sick Kids in Love*; and *The Love Song of Ivy K. Harlowe*. She lives in Silver Spring, Maryland.

Natasha Ngan is a writer and yoga teacher. She grew up between Malaysia, where the Chinese side of her family is from, and the United Kingdom. This multicultural upbringing continues to influence her writing, and she is passionate about bringing diverse stories to teens. Ngan studied geography at the University of Cambridge before working as a social media consultant and fashion blogger. She lives in France with her partner, where they recently moved from Paris to be closer to the sea. Her novel *Girls of Paper and Fire* was a *New York Times* bestseller.

Rebecca Podos is the author of young adult books with Balzer + Bray, including the Lambda Literary Award–winning *Like Water*; her next, *From Dust, a Flame*, will be published in early 2022. By day, she's an agent at the Rees Literary Agency in Boston. You can find her and her doodles at rebeccapodos.com, and on Twitter at @Rebeccapodos.

Lilliam Rivera is an award-winning writer and author of children's books, including her latest from Bloomsbury Publishing, *Never Look Back*, a retelling of the Greek myth of Orpheus and Eurydice set in New York. Her work has appeared in the *Washington Post*, the *New York Times*, and *Elle*, to name a few. Lilliam lives in Los Angeles.

Laura Silverman is an author and freelance editor and currently lives in Brooklyn, New York. She earned her MFA in Writing for Children at the New School. Her books include *Girl out of Water*, *You Asked for Perfect*, *It's a Whole Spiel*, *Recommended for You*, and the upcoming *Those Summer Nights*. *Girl out of Water* was a Junior Library Guild Selection, and *You Asked for Perfect* was named to best teen fiction lists by YALSA, Chicago Public Library, and the Georgia Center for the Book. You can contact Laura on Twitter at @LJSilverman1 or through her website, LauraSilvermanWrites.com.

Amy Spalding is the author of several novels, including the bestselling *We Used to Be Friends* and *The Summer of Jordi Perez (and the Best Burger in Los Angeles)*, which was named a best book of 2018 by NPR, the *Boston Globe*, *Kirkus*, and more. She lives in Los Angeles.

Rebecca Kim Wells is the author of fantastical books for young adults, including the acclaimed Shatter the Sky duology and *Briar Girls*. She has never been transmogrified into a mysterious purple blob.

Julian Winters is an award-winning author of contemporary young adult fiction. His novels *Running with Lions*, *How to Be Remy Cameron*, and *The Summer of Everything* (Duet Books) received accolades for their positive depictions of diverse, relatable characters. *Running with Lions* is the recipient of an IBPA Benjamin Franklin Gold Award. *How to Be Remy Cameron* and *The Summer of Everything* were named Junior Library Guild Gold Standard selections and received starred reviews. A self-proclaimed comic book geek, Julian currently lives outside Atlanta. His next novel, *Right Where I Left You*, will be published by Viking Children's Books in 2022.